Praise for the Dark Sword novels by
DONNA GRA

5! Top Pick! "An   eginning
to end, it's an   *Romance*

5 Hearts! "I d   *gerous Highlander,*
even to skeptics   nance – you just may fall
in love with the M   —*The Romance Reader*

5 Angels! Recommended Read! "*Forbidden Highlander*
blew me away." —*Fallen Angel Reviews*

5 Tombstones! "Another fantastic series that melds the paranormal with the historical life of the Scottish highlander in this arousing and exciting adventure. The men of MacLeod Castle are a delicious combination of devoted brother, loyal highlander, Lord and demonic god that ooze sex appeal and inspire some very erotic daydreams as they face their faults and accept their fate." —*Bitten by Books*

4 Stars! "Grant creates a vivid picture of Britain centuries after the Celts and Druids tried to expel the Romans, deftly merging magic and history. The result is a wonderfully dark, delightfully well-written tale. Readers will eagerly await the next Dark Sword book."
—*Romantic Times BOOKreviews*

4 Hoots! "These are some of the hottest brothers around in paranormal fiction." —*Nocturne Romance Reads*

The DARK WARRIOR series by
DONNA GRANT

MIDNIGHT'S TEMPTATION

DONNA GRANT

St. Martin's Paperbacks

This is a work of fiction. All of the characters, organizations, and events portrayed in this novel are either products of the author's imagination or are used fictitiously.

MIDNIGHT'S TEMPTATION

Copyright © 2013 by Donna Grant.

All rights reserved.

For information address St. Martin's Press, 175 Fifth Avenue, New York, NY 10010.

ISBN: 978-1-250-01728-4

Printed in the United States of America

St. Martin's Paperbacks edition / October 2013

St. Martin's Paperbacks are published by St. Martin's Press, 175 Fifth Avenue, New York, NY 10010.

10 9 8 7 6 5 4 3 2 1

To the members of my street team—
Donna's Dolls—all around the world!

Thank you for all that you are,
and all that you do.
This book is for y'all.

ACKNOWLEDGMENTS

As always my thanks goes first to my brilliant editor, Monique Patterson. I'm so very blessed to be working with such a wonderful person, and talented editor.

To everyone at St. Martin's who helped get this book ready, thank you.

To my extraordinary agent, Louise Fury. It's been an amazing ride so far!

A special note to my assistant, Melissa Bradley. Thanks for everything you all do. You make my life easier, and for that, I owe you so very much.

A special thanks to my family for the never ending support.

And to my husband, Steve, my real-life hero. You made me laugh the first time we met, and you're still making me laugh all these years later. Thank you for the love you've given me, for the laughter you brought into my life, our beautiful children, and the happily ever after life I always dreamed of. I love you, Sexy!

CHAPTER ONE

He tangled his fingers in her long, thick, ebony tresses, her sighs of pleasure making his blood singe his veins. Her feminine curves were a heady delight to a man starved for her.

Golden skin speaking of Spanish heritage and as smooth as satin called him to touch more of her. He lay on his side, her body pressed against him. His hand glided past the indent of her waist and over a gently flared hip down to her thigh.

Her legs parted instantly. His lungs seized when his fingers delved into the black curls, trimmed and partially shaved, hiding her sex.

"Please," she whispered.

Her voice, seductive and low, beckoned him, urged him. And he wasn't going to disappoint.

He groaned, his cock swelling even more, when her back arched and her nails dug into his shoulders. Her breathy sighs filled the room as he caressed the sensitive flesh of her sex.

It wasn't until she shook from need that he finally dipped a finger inside her. He ground his teeth together at the feel of her slick heat.

She was everything he wanted and more, so much more. To finally have her in his bed, to have his hands on her . . . it was almost too good to be true.

Her eyes opened, and he looked into dark pools of desire. She clung to him, her lips parted as her hips rocked against him.

He rolled her onto her back and settled between her legs. She grinned up at him, daring him to take her. His arousal grazed her sex, causing her to gasp at the sensation.

He fisted his hands in the pillow and brought his raging body back under control. He would have her, but he wanted her screaming in pleasure first. Only then would he fill her with his cock.

With a dip of his head, he bent and closed his mouth around a turgid nipple. His tongue circled the peak before he began to suckle.

She cried out and held his head between her hands. He moved to her other breast and teased that nipple until she was writhing beneath him.

Now, now he would kiss down her body until his lips were on her sex. He would bring her to the brink several times before he allowed her to climax.

Then he would plunge inside her, have her legs wrap around him as he brought them to ecstasy.

He kissed the valley between her breasts, but before he could place another kiss on her sweet skin, she rolled him onto his back and straddled him.

His heart missed a beat. She was a magnificent sight with her wealth of midnight hair falling around her shoulders to lay alongside her full, tempting breasts.

Her chest rose and fell rapidly. He was caught in her

fawn-colored gaze. For the first time in his life, he wasn't in control of the lovemaking. She was.

And it thrilled him far more than was comfortable.

Her full lips tilted up in the barest of smiles. A smile that said she knew exactly what she was doing to him. And she loved it.

He swallowed heavily, his rod jumping with anticipation. His balls tightened when she reached down and took him in hand. Somehow he kept his hands in the sheets, fisted tightly. Sweat broke out over his body as he fought to keep still for her.

Only for her. No other woman had ever commanded him in such a way, and he feared no other ever would.

She was on her knees, her entrance above his arousal while she ran her hands up and down his length. She was teasing him as he planned to tease her.

He'd never ached for a woman before. Not once had he hungered to have a certain woman in his arms. But *she* changed everything.

No longer could he hold off from touching her. He cupped her bountiful breasts and flicked his thumbs over her nipples. In response, she swirled her thumb over the head of his shaft.

He groaned and lifted his hips. His cock came in contact with the soft folds of her sex, and his control snapped.

As if she knew he had gone over the brink, she lowered herself onto him. He was mindless, feral with need. With a jerk, he pulled her down as he raised his hips until he was fully seated inside her. She groaned, her head thrown back and the ends of her hair brushing his thighs.

For a second, he couldn't move. Her tight, slick walls held him suspended between agony and pleasure, torment and release. He knew in that moment that she commanded his body.

His fear was that her reach would extend past his body to his heart, or worse—his soul.

With his heart hammering in his chest, she began to rock her hips. He closed his eyes to feel every delightful, perfect minute of her.

There was a slight thumping that intruded upon him, but he was determined to ignore it. He rolled over, taking her with him. He lost her in the blankets. Panic seized him as he searched, only to find himself clutching a pillow instead of her soft body.

Phelan opened his eyes to the pillow and flopped onto his back. He threw an arm over his eyes as his cock ached for relief.

"Fuck," he ground out in vexation.

The dreams he was having of Aisley intensified every night, leaving him aroused and unsatisfied no matter how many times he tried to pleasure himself afterward.

He had been on her trail for almost two months now. He still wasn't sure why he let her walk out of that nightclub after he first kissed her.

He hadn't expected her to run. Women didn't run from him.

But Aisley did.

That was part of why she intrigued him, but it went beyond that. She was different. That one kiss they shared had rocked him to his very core. No matter how he tried, he couldn't stop thinking about her. Or wanting her.

His mobile phone vibrated on the bedside table. Phelan pondered not answering it, but he knew they would only call again.

"What?" he demanded as he answered the call.

"What the hell is your problem?" Charon's voice asked with a note of irritation.

Phelan rubbed his eyes with his thumb and forefinger.

He hoped the call would cool his ardor, but if it didn't, another cold shower to start the day would. "It doesna matter. What's the reason for the call?"

The pause on the other end of the line had Phelan glancing over at the clock. The bright green lights staring back at him told him it was 2:33 in the morning.

"Charon," Phelan urged as the silence grew.

"We're getting desperate," Charon said tightly. "There's been no sign of Jason."

Jason Wallace. The very reason Phelan had to take extra time away from tracking Aisley. Jason was a *drough*, a Druid who gave part of his soul to the Devil in order to use black magic.

Phelan untangled his legs from the sheets and sat up. "I've seen nothing of him. Maybe Jason is dead as we've suspected all along."

"I need to know for certain."

Phelan drew in a deep breath, hating the weariness and worry he heard in his friend's voice. "Laura is safe. She's with you."

"Are any of us ever really safe with a *drough* about?" Charon asked. "My wife asks me to forget about Wallace, but I hear Laura on the phone with the other Druids talking about ways to use their magic to look for him."

Phelan scrubbed a hand down his face. How many times had the *mies* used the magic nature gave them to look for Wallace? The *mies* were the good Druids and luckily on their side.

Despite the Druids' magic and the powers within Warriors like Phelan, they had found nothing of Jason Wallace. The Druids had potent magic, but as a Highlander with a primeval god inside him, Phelan should have found Jason by now.

He had been alone for so long, and he thought it would

always be that way. Then he found Charon. An unlikely friendship had begun between them that brought them as close as brothers.

After one monster of a betrayal, Phelan found it difficult to trust. Charon had changed all of that. Phelan would do anything for the man he considered a brother.

However, it wasn't just for Charon that he searched for Wallace. It was for himself. He wanted to put the past behind him. He wanted to think of a future that included peace—or as much peace as a Warrior could ever achieve.

"I'm no' giving up," Phelan stated. "I'm tired of fighting *droughs*. First Deirdre, then Declan, and now Jason. It has to end sometime."

"Laura keeps reminding me there can no' be good without evil. There's a balance."

"Aye. This last time evil nearly won."

Phelan hated to think how close they had been to losing the last battle. Fortunately, Charon had made some powerful friends at Dreagan Distillery. Those "friends" ended up being dragon shifters.

The Dragon Kings had been around since the beginning of time. It was on their land the battle had been fought with the dragons in the skies and Warriors on the ground.

"It was too damn close," Charon agreed softly.

"Any word from Rhys or the others at Dreagan?"

Charon grunted. "Nothing. They have their hands full right now, but they're keeping an eye out for us."

"What of the selmyr?"

Just thinking of the hideous beasts made Phelan bite back a growl. The selmyr were ancient creatures that fed off magical entities. The Druids and Warriors were perfect meals. The only thing the selmyr feared were the Dragon Kings.

"Nothing," Charon said with a sigh. "The waiting is wearing on Laura."

"All will be well, my friend," Phelan vowed. "I can stop my search and help you keep watch over Laura."

Phelan would do it in a heartbeat after everything Charon had done for him, but he prayed he wouldn't have to give up searching for Aisley. He had to find her, to taste her sweet lips once more and know if the kiss had been a one-time thing, or if there was something between them.

"Nay. You and Malcolm are the only ones out looking for Wallace."

The first ghost of a grin pulled at Phelan's lips. "Ah, so the infamous MacLeod Druids couldna talk their men into allowing them out to look, aye?"

"Nay," Charon said, a smile in his voice. "Neither could the Warriors persuade the women to let them go."

"Oh, I can imagine the bickering going on at the castle now."

"Which is one reason we are no' there," Charon said. "Where are you anyway?"

Phelan rose from the bed and walked to the window to look out over the city. "Glasgow. I'll head west at dawn."

"Keep in touch."

"Same to you."

Phelan ended the call and tossed the mobile phone on the bed. He put his palms against the window and dropped his head. Without even trying to, Phelan could feel Aisley's magic.

It had always been so between Warriors and Druids. It began centuries ago when Rome invaded their land. The Celts stood against Rome, but that couldn't last forever.

That's where the Druids came in. The *mies* had no answer for the Celts, but the *droughs* did. They brought up gods long buried in Hell to inhabit the bodies of the strongest warriors from each family.

Those men became the first Warriors and soon defeated Rome. But the *droughs* hadn't been able to remove the gods from the men. It took the combined magic of *droughs* and *mies* to bind the gods.

The gods then moved through the bloodline to the strongest warrior of each generation. Until a power-hungry *drough* named Deirdre found the scroll detailing how to unbind the gods and which clan to start with—MacLeod.

It was the three MacLeod brothers who were matched in every way that were the first Warriors to have their god unbound. After that, it didn't take Deirdre long to find others.

Four hundred years ago the MacLeods, and the group of Warriors and Druids who sought sanctuary at their castle, nearly ended Deidre.

Unbeknownst to them, a *drough* in the twenty-first century had his sights on Deirdre. Declan used his magic to bring Deirdre forward in time.

While the Druids of MacLeod Castle combined their magic to send Warriors into the future to find Deirdre, Charon and Phelan had lived in the quiet glory of four centuries without *droughs* trying to take over the world.

It had been wonderful, and Phelan craved that same calm again.

But nothing could last forever. Deirdre and Declan had combined forces, but luck had been on the Warriors' side. It had been one of the greatest moments of Phelan's life watching Deirdre die.

It hadn't taken them long to kill Declan either. It should have ended there, but it didn't.

A year later a new evil took Declan's place—his cousin, Jason Wallace.

Phelan turned away from the window and walked into the bathroom to turn on the shower.

The Druids could overpower a Warrior. Phelan had not only seen it done, but had it done to him. Their only saving grace was the fact a Warrior could detect magic. A *mies* magic felt soothing and . . . right. While a *drough*'s magic was like something was trying to smother him.

Phelan stepped into the shower and closed his eyes as he took in Aisley's magic. Hot water pounded his shoulders, but everything he was centered on Aisley's magic. The feel of it wasn't just powerful and amazing. It was seductive, erotic, and altogether astonishing.

He wasn't sure where she was, but she was close. Close enough that he could feel her magic. It's how he was tracking her.

Somehow she knew when he got close, because she would run again.

But she couldn't run forever.

CHAPTER
TWO

Aisley Wallace sat on the roof of the building with her eyes closed. The thump of the music vibrated through the building's bricks and into her body, giving her the illusion that she was on the dance floor in the midst of a crowd of dancing bodies.

She didn't dare go into the nightclub since Phelan knew how much she loved the music and always showed up wherever she was. Though she couldn't go in the club, she could listen to the music.

Music always calmed her. It was a part of her soul. It moved her, touched her as nothing else could.

She opened her eyes and looked out over the city. It wasn't just Phelan she was running from, but Jason Wallace as well. She knew her cousin wasn't dead.

Jason was ruthless and brutal. He always thought of everything, which put him two steps ahead of everyone. There was no way he hadn't planned on dying and finding a way back to the living.

But Aisley wasn't sure if Jason was really dead. She hoped he was, she prayed he was, but she never had much luck in those sorts of things.

The sound of a motorbike had her sitting up straight. Was it Phelan? She jumped up and rushed to the edge of the building to peer over the side.

Her heart hammered wildly in her chest as she searched. As soon as she found the motorbike she knew it wasn't Phelan's. The thread of disappointment didn't go unnoticed by her, but she refused to acknowledge it.

She knew exactly who Phelan was. He and the other Warriors had hunted her and the other *droughs* with Jason. Which meant he should know who she was.

Yet he had kissed her. What a kiss it had been, too. Even two months later her lips still tingled when she thought about the masterful way he had seduced with one kiss.

What she didn't understand is why Phelan kissed her. He'd acted as though he liked it as well. How could that be when he had to have felt her *drough* magic? She was the enemy.

Was he teasing her before he killed her? Aisley turned around and sat on the edge of the building with a loud exhale.

For just a moment during their kiss, she had forgotten the person she was. For the briefest second in time, she had been just a woman kissing a gorgeous man in a darkened hallway of a nightclub.

Reality had come crashing down on her all too soon. She had been given a reprieve from Jason during the battle with the Warriors, a battle in which she had left Jason to his own defenses. If he was alive, he would never forgive her. Jason's retribution would be swift and horrible.

But neither was she about to find herself killed because she liked Phelan's kisses.

Two different men, two different reasons, but both had her on the run.

All she could think about was saving her own hide

when she should be delving into what she knew of Jason to make sure he was dead—and remained that way.

Aisley lifted her face as a gust of wind whipped through the buildings. Dark clouds, heavy with moisture had moved over the city a few hours earlier. They hid the moon from view, and it wouldn't be long before the rain came.

The seasons were shifting, and with it the daylight hours were growing shorter. Soon, there would be just a few hours of daylight.

Everything changed. Perhaps it was time Aisley had a change as well. At dawn she would leave Scotland and travel to England.

London was big enough for her to get lost in for a while. After that, maybe Paris. And then . . . who knew?

Being away from the place where so much disaster had befallen her could be just what she needed to free her from the past.

Aisley stood and walked to the door she'd left ajar that would take her into the four-story building, down back stairs, and to the door whose lock she had picked to get inside.

She rubbed her hands up and down her arms when she was on the streets once again. Her head was down, but she kept her eyes open as she hurried to her car, which she parked six blocks away.

No one bothered her, thankfully. After she was in her car, she leaned her head back against the seat and let her eyes drift shut. There was time for a few hours of sleep before dawn.

She should drive now, but she was too exhausted. All she needed was a little rest. That didn't involve dreams about Phelan kissing her, caressing her . . . making slow, sweet love to her.

Aisley could feel herself falling fast as sleep claimed

her. She welcomed it, only to find herself jerked awake when the rain began to pelt her window with fat drops loud enough to wake the dead.

"Damn," she murmured and blew out a frustrated breath.

Without sleep, she was cranky and her temper had a short fuse. Even when she found sleep, she woke with her body on fire, needy and aching for release from the desire that was drowning her thanks to that one damn kiss from Phelan.

She peered through the window as the rain poured in sheets too thick to see anything more than a few feet in front of her. Aisley reached for her iPod. With the earbuds secure in her ears, she selected a playlist, and then reached for the map.

Her route into England was set. She would take the M74 south out of Scotland. It was a pretty easy road, but there were others she could detour to if she needed it.

But just in case—and she learned how important a backup plan was thanks to Jason—Aisley had a second strategy. She touched her finger to the dot where Glasgow was marked on the map.

Her next option would be to take the A82 north until she reached Crianlarich where she would head west on A85 toward the coast. From there, she would get on a ferry to Ireland.

It wasn't the best backup stratagem she had, but Jason would never expect her to go to Ireland. In order to get as far from Jason as she could, she would have to outwit him.

What if he really is dead? I could be doing this for nothing.

"But what if he's not?" she answered her own question. "Besides, Jason won't stay dead. He's too evil for that."

Jason had already begun to doubt her loyalty before

the battle. As he had told her, she was expendable. If she was going to make a new life for herself, she was going to have to guarantee that Jason would never return to the land of the living.

Aisley looked at the map again. She should have already been out of Scotland, but it had taken her this long to get to all the places she'd stashed the money she'd stolen from Jason and scout to make sure the asshole wasn't waiting for her.

Jason provided her with everything after he had welcomed her into his home. She might have been out of her mind with grief and self-loathing, but at least she had been smart enough to take what little savings she'd stolen and scatter it around Scotland.

She had called it her "Just in Case" scenario. But Aisley knew that even then she had realized going with Jason had been the wrong thing to do.

There hadn't been much of a choice, however. Her days had been numbered, and then Jason found her and gave her a new home. Sleeping in a bed with clean linens and eating freshly cooked meals had been heavenly.

No matter how she might say he forced her to come live in his home, she had been the one to undergo the *drough* ceremony and give her soul to Satan.

There was nothing she could do to reverse the ceremony. Her soul was no longer her own.

A tear slipped out of her eye. Aisley held her hand out, palm up, and let her magic consume her until a ball of bright light filled her hand.

Magic swirled in a beautiful dance of light. As stunning as it was, it was black magic—evil—that allowed her to do that, not the pure magic she once had.

Aisley dropped her hand, and the magic instantly vanished.

"Aissssssley."

She squeezed her eyes shut as the voice sounded in her head. It wasn't the first time she had heard it. It began after she left Jason at the battle.

The voice frightened her. She could feel the malevolence of it, but what terrified her more than anything was that she didn't know if that evil was inside her.

She briefly remembered thinking to betray Jason by contacting Satan herself and gaining more power that way. It had been a hasty thought, yet every time she heard that voice she thought of her intended duplicity to Jason.

"No," she whispered. Then she slammed her hands on the steering wheel. "No!"

The voice retreated once more. But she knew it would return.

It always did.

CHAPTER THREE

Phelan stood on the street outside the hotel in the pouring rain and looked first one way, then the other. Just ten minutes before he had doubled over in the shower by the force of Aisley's magic slamming into him.

She was much nearer than he first realized.

Where was she? And why in all that was holy did she continue to run from him?

Phelan walked to his Ducati motorbike and threw a leg over the seat. He sat down and put his helmet on before starting the engine.

The residue of Aisley's magic made his cock throb with need, but it had been the quick—and sharp—spike of fear he felt in her magic that left him cold.

She might be afraid of him, but there was nothing he wouldn't do to destroy whatever it was that terrified her.

Phelan revved the engine before he pulled out onto the street. He drove slowly to the first intersection, but as soon as Aisley's magic began to weaken, he quickly turned around.

Slowly, street by street, he got closer and closer to her.

He'd only dared this once before. It had been five weeks ago when he'd tracked her to a nightclub.

It was the sheer strength of her magic that led him to her. He had kept to the shadows in the club, which had been easy to do. It hadn't been until he reached the second level that he'd looked down on the dance floor and seen her.

She stood amidst a group of people dancing to some song blaring through the speakers. Men tried to get her attention by dancing close to her, but Aisley didn't notice them. It was the music that pulled her, called to her.

Phelan saw it in the way she moved, in how each note of the music infused her. Her magic seemed to grow and expand until it swallowed him.

He had been rooted to the spot watching the erotic sight of her body twisting, her hips rotating in her skimpy shirt and too-tight jeans, and her black hair pulled away from her face into a braid.

It was then Phelan comprehended how much the music meant to her. The louder it was, the better. When she danced the worry lines on her forehead disappeared, and a smile began to show.

Phelan stopped at a red light and put his foot down to keep the motorbike upright. He recalled that night at the club several times a day.

It hadn't just been the sight of Aisley that was imbedded in his memory. It was the realization that he had nothing in his life he cared about as much as Aisley loved her music.

Was his life so dull?

Three months ago he wouldn't have thought so. He had his bike, his favorite pair of boots, and the open road. He had as many women as he wanted with no one to tie him down.

And on occasion, he found himself helping out those from MacLeod Castle fight evil.

It was a good life.

Why then did it suddenly seem . . . less?

Did this unexpected misery have anything to do with Charon finding the love of his life? Phelan wasn't sure. Charon had always protected his village, but now he had Laura as well, and Phelan saw the difference.

It had been easy to ignore all the Warriors who had found love with the Druids at MacLeod Castle because he was rarely there, but he couldn't disregard it with Charon.

Phelan gunned his bike when the light turned green. This early in the morning with the rain, there were few people about. He swerved his bike around two twenty-something men as they stumbled drunk out of a pub.

"Idiots," he muttered, but looked back to make sure they made it across the street.

He thought of Charon and Laura once again. Charon had nearly lost Laura to Wallace and his crusade to rule the world. Phelan always thought Charon's life was one of the best.

Charon had done what no other Warrior did after escaping Deirdre—he returned to the village he'd grown up in. It had been decades after he was taken and no one knew Charon, but it was his home.

Charon had set about buying up land and property and protecting those who called Ferness home from any evil.

Many times Phelan had found whatever road he'd been traveling leading him back to Ferness. Not because he thought of it as home, but because he was welcome.

The MacLeods welcomed him at the castle as well, yet it wasn't the same. There was Isla who was responsible for tricking him as a young lad and taking him away from his family, to be chained deep in Deirdre's mountain.

No matter what, Phelan couldn't forgive what Isla had done, not even when he learned she had done it to save her own family. Isla thought she was the reason he didn't go to the castle. The truth was, he didn't know how to fit in.

Those who stayed at the castle considered themselves one big family. He didn't remember his mother's or father's face, much less what it meant to be in a family. He had no idea how to act.

So he stayed away.

Phelan pulled his thoughts away from the other Warriors and the Druids as Aisley's magic grew stronger. He slowed the Ducati and pulled over when he found an open parking spot on the side of the road.

He glanced at the buildings around him, trying to determine which one she was in. Four were businesses, one a pub, two restaurants, and one abandoned.

With a flick of his foot, he put the kickstand down and shut off his bike. That's when he heard the music. Even over the din of the rain, with his enhanced senses—thanks to the god inside him—he could hear the telltale dance music.

There must be a nightclub nearby. He fought the urge to find it and go inside to see Aisley, but then he remembered her horrified expression when she'd seen him the last time.

It had been like a knife in his chest, her look saying he had intruded on something private and personal.

So Phelan stayed seated on his bike as the rain fell around him, blurring the visor of his helmet. He could picture Aisley dancing, her arms above her head, her eyes closed as she swayed.

It was enough. For now.

He wasn't sure how much longer he could go on as he

was. If he could just get her in his bed, he'd purge this
unending yearning, this hunger to have her in his arms
once and for all.

Then he could get back to the life he had.

He stood and swung his leg over the bike before he
blended into the shadows. Phelan might want Aisley in his
bed, but he was going to have to approach her carefully.

There would be wooing. First, he would have to earn
her trust. Just as he had with the wounded kitten three
years ago. It had taken Phelan three days, but eventually
he had the kitten curled in his lap. After that, the kitten
allowed him to clean the injured paw.

So all he had to do was think of Aisley as that kitten.

Phelan gave a snort. Aisley had claws like a kitten.
He'd seen that when a man grabbed her butt while she
was dancing. But Phelan knew it was going to take a great
effort on his part to have her purring in his arms.

She *would* purr. And scream in pleasure.

He settled under an awning out of the rain so he had
only to turn his head to see both the right and left sides of
the street. With his helmet in the crook of his arm, he
settled back to wait.

A handful of minutes passed before the sound of a car
door opening caught his attention. Phelan turned his head
to the right and spotted a small car on the opposite side of
the street three blocks up.

A figure got out of the car and ran to the covered sidewalk. Phelan would know Aisley anywhere, even without
his enhanced eyesight.

Those few seconds in the rain plastered her black hair
to her head. She pushed aside the strands sticking to her
oval face, her eyes darting about as she walked into a café.

Phelan stayed on the opposite side of the street as he
kept watch through the café window. She stopped at the

counter and took a seat on a stool while she placed her order.

He started walking, needing to be closer to her. Just before he reached the café, he stopped and faded into the shadows again. He had the advantage over Aisley since she had no idea he was there. Phelan could sense her magic, but Druids didn't have the same abilities as Warriors.

A few minutes later Aisley was handed a large mug of something steaming, which Phelan assumed was coffee, and a pastry.

Aisley smothered a yawn while she wrapped both hands around the mug. He shifted to the right and saw there was a table hidden by a large poster in the window where two men were seated. Both staring at her.

Unease rippled through Phelan. He knew what those men wanted, and it wasn't going to happen.

For the next seventeen and a half minutes he was content to watch her eat and drink. As soon as Aisley was done, she paid and left the café.

Just as Phelan expected, she wasn't alone.

Three steps behind her were the two men. With his speed, Phelan came up directly behind the men without them even knowing it. Their attention was focused on Aisley so they never suspected someone might be watching them.

"Hey!" one of the men called out to Aisley.

She turned around, her magic already gathering around her. Phelan hissed in a breath, startled by the way his body continued to burn with pleasure at the feel of her magic.

Her fawn-colored eyes widened for a split second as she caught sight of him. Phelan didn't give her or the men time to say anything else. He moved his arms up and out between the two men as he stepped between them.

They paused in surprise, and Phelan elbowed them in

the face simultaneously. The two men hit the ground with a thud.

"I suppose you want a thank you," Aisley replied saucily.

Phelan opened his mouth to respond when movement behind her caught his eye. "Duck," he said as a man lunged for her.

Despite his warning, Aisley didn't move quickly enough and the brute's fist caught on the back of the head, sending her out into the rain and down on her knees off the sidewalk.

Inside him, Phelan's god, Zelfor, bellowed for battle. And Phelan wanted nothing more than to give in. But humans didn't know of the Warriors.

Instead of releasing his god, Phelan peeled back his lips and growled as he advanced on Aisley's attacker. He reared back his fist to send a punch to the man's jaw to knock him out, when the brute pulled a gun from his jacket.

Phelan grunted as the impact of the bullet crashed into his chest. He looked down at the gaping hole in his leather biker's jacket and then up at the man.

"This was my favorite jacket."

"What the bloody hell are you, mate?" the man stammered before he turned and ran away.

Phelan glanced at the two unconscious men before he reached for Aisley. She held the back of her head with one hand and braced the other on the sidewalk. He gently lifted her to her feet, but as soon as she was up, she pulled out of his grasp.

"Why did you stop them?"

Phelan frowned. "Do I really need to explain it, lass?"

"Yes," she said and gave a jerk of her head. She winced and leaned against a store window.

"You need to lie down. Let me take you somewhere."

With her face pale, she opened her eyes to stare at him. He wanted to touch her, to run his hands down her face, over her high cheekbones, and across her full lips. He yearned to hold her luscious body against his again, but somehow held himself in check. Instead, he let his gaze feast on her beauty.

From her oval face and midnight hair slicked to her head to her defiant chin. Delicate ebony brows arched slightly over large eyes tilted up at the corners. She had a small nose and a high forehead. It was her lips, full and wide, that were made for sin.

Her legs were long and lean on her trim frame, but she had feminine curves that would make a saint's mouth water with temptation.

As delightful as her body and face were, that's not all that drew him. Besides her magic, Aisley had a quick wit and an even quicker mind.

She fascinated him at every turn. She held him riveted, intrigued.

Beguiled.

One black brow rose. "You're not taking me anywhere."

If she only knew he'd be happy to take her right then and there. Would the knowledge make her blush? Would her skin flush with desire? He was dying to know.

"If you're going to kill me, do it now."

"Kill you?" Phelan took a step back, completely dumbfounded at her words. He had never given her any such notions. Why would she think that? Unless . . . she knew what he was. "Why do you think I'd want to kill you?"

Doubt flashed fleetingly in her fawn-colored depths. "Isn't that why you're following me?"

"If I wanted to kill you, beauty, I'd have done it that night in the club when I kissed you. Or the second time when I watched you dance."

A small frown furrowed her brow. "What do you want?"

"This," he said and closed the gap separating them.

He covered her mouth with his. Phelan couldn't stop

the moan when she responded to his kiss. She opened her lips against his, and he quickly swept his tongue inside to mate with hers.

The kiss was supposed to have been soft and gentle, but the desire for her burned too brightly inside him. He wrapped his arms around her and attempted to deepen the kiss.

The same instant she ducked out of his arms. Phelan opened his eyes to find himself staring at his reflection in the glass before him. He turned his head to the side to look at Aisley.

He had never had to work so hard for a woman before. What did she want from him? And more importantly, why was he having such a difficult time figuring it out?

"Why do you keep running from me? I know you like my kisses, beauty, because you kiss me back."

Aisley rolled her eyes. "If you're really not here to kill me, then let me go."

Phelan turned to face her. He had a tough choice. If he wanted to earn her trust, he had to let her go. But how could he when she was within reach of him now?

With his speed, there was no way she could outrun him. He could have her in a hotel room in a matter of minutes. Then have her undressed and in his bed even quicker.

But he'd been kept against his will for decades. He wasn't about to do that to someone else, especially not Aisley.

"I'm no' your enemy," he told her.

"Prove it. Let me go."

"I'll follow you."

She shrugged.

Phelan blew out a breath and moved aside so she had a clear path to her car. "I'll earn your trust, beauty," he said as she walked past him.

"Doubtful," she replied with a snort.

Phelan waited until she was in her car and drove off before he grabbed his helmet and hurried to his bike to follow her.

CHAPTER
FOUR

MacLeod Castle

"How much longer?" Arran asked the room at large.

Lucan glanced at his elder brother, Fallon, to find him staring into the cold, empty hearth in the great hall. "Aiden and Britt will tell us when it's done."

"It" was the serum Britt had synthesized from their blood. Lucan wasn't the only one uneasy about bringing a mortal with no magic into their battle, but Britt wasn't just an amazing doctor. She had managed to gain Aiden's love.

As uncle to Aiden, Lucan couldn't be happier. He knew his nephew had been floundering about in their world of magic. Not that he blamed Quinn and Marcail for protecting their son. Lucan would do the same thing if he and Cara dared to have children.

Children. He let out a long sigh and shifted his gaze to his wife. Cara sat with some of the other Druids. Her chestnut curls were pulled away from her face in a ponytail. She smiled at something Danielle said, but the smile didn't reach her eyes.

That's when Lucan saw Cara glance up the stairs. She was as worried as the others. Most of last night they had sat in bed talking about Britt's serum and how it could help the Warriors in their upcoming battle.

"What has you frowning?" Quinn asked as he came to stand beside him.

Lucan shrugged before he turned to his younger brother. "I lied to Cara last night."

Quinn's dark brows rose high in his forehead, surprise in his pale green eyes. "That's a first. What was the lie?"

"She asked if the fighting would be over when we kill Wallace. I told her it would."

Quinn crossed his arms over his chest, his small grin vanishing instantly. "I told Marcail that same lie several nights ago."

"Were we wrong to bring them into this, Quinn?"

"Most assuredly. I'm a selfish bastard though, and couldna let Marcail out of my life. She would've been better had she never met me."

"Ah, but would you have been better?"

Quinn had been on the verge of self-destruction. It had only been Marcail's gentle touch and love that gave Quinn a reason to keep living.

"Nay," Quinn answered without hesitation. "I look at all the Warriors in the castle and the women who stand with them, and I know each Warrior is better because of their women."

"You've the right of it, brother. Can we honestly say the same for the Druids?"

Quinn was silent a long time before he shook his head. "Nay."

Lucan tried to imagine life without Cara by his side the last four centuries. He had barely held it together for three hundred years before her, and only because he had to keep himself and his brothers united.

He tugged at the end of one long braid running from his temple. Cara was the only light in the darkness that was his life. The constant battles with *droughs* had taken a toll on him.

Cara was his reason to live through each battle. Without her . . . there would be nothing.

But, like Quinn, he'd been selfish. Even discovering Cara was a Druid and being hunted by Deirdre shouldn't have been enough to tie her to him.

It had been sheer luck that they found Isla. Thanks to her potent magic there was the shield covering MacLeod Castle that didn't just kept it hidden from the world, but prevented mortals inside it from aging.

Every time Cara left the castle she put her life in jeopardy. But it took all of them—Warriors and Druids alike—to battle the *droughs*.

"I hear everyone struck down by Wallace's magic in Edinburgh is healing," Lucan said.

Quinn said, "Aye. We're all glad of that. Marcail was ready to go to Edinburgh with Sonya and try to heal them."

Wallace. Why was it everything they spoke about at the castle was the bastard? He controlled their lives as well as ruined them.

"Will Aiden and Britt remain here once her work is complete?" Lucan asked to change the subject.

Quinn's lips quirked downward at the corners. "I wanted to ask, but Marcail begged me no' to. She's afraid of what the answer will be."

"Britt will be a target when she leaves."

"Which is why Aiden will go with her."

"So you think they'll go?"

"I doona know," he said after he blew out a breath. "I'd feel better if they remained, but Britt had a life before we entered it."

Lucan gave a nod to Fallon as he joined them. "Aiden explained to Britt what she was getting into. She chose this."

"Did she?" Quinn asked angrily. "Aiden could've gone to someone else. Perhaps we shouldna have allowed him on this course."

Fallon grinned at Quinn. "Ah, but he is his father's son. I've never met such a stubborn man as you."

Quinn reached over and hit Fallon in the shoulder, the first real smile in days. "Stubborn? Shall we talk about you?"

Lucan watched the exchange, chuckling as he did. There had been a time when he never thought his brothers would be able to talk to each other again. Look at them now.

Their women had done that.

"What are you smirking about?" Fallon asked. "You're just as stubborn, Lucan. It's a MacLeod trait."

Lucan grunted. "Oh, I know I'm obstinate. I'm the only one who dares to admit it though."

After the laughter died, so did the smiles.

Fallon put his back to the great hall and the Warriors and Druids scattered throughout to face his brothers. "Any word from Phelan or Malcolm regarding Wallace?"

"Charon called and said Phelan had yet to find anything," Quinn answered.

Lucan threw up his hands. "The only one who is able to get ahold of Malcolm is Larena. Ask your wife about him."

"I did," Fallon ground out in a low voice. "She said she's left him a half-dozen messages, but he's yet to return her calls."

"We willna hear from him until he finds Wallace," Quinn pointed out.

Lucan nodded. "True. I'm no' happy with just the two of them looking."

"None of us are," Fallon said.

Quinn ran a hand down his face, showing his frustration. "What do you expect when you tell the women they can no' go looking for him?"

"Me?" Fallon said in surprise. "I seem to recall you ordering Marcail to her chamber. Right before she told you what for."

Lucan grinned as Quinn looked away sheepishly. "We all made that decision."

"Aye," Quinn said.

Fallon gave a shake of his head. "We didna imagine they would in turn tell us we couldna go."

"We could sneak out during the night," Lucan said.

The three brothers exchanged looks as plans began to form.

"Do you think we could get away with it?" Quinn asked.

Fallon said, "Nay, but my being able to teleport us in and out will help."

"There'll be hell to pay when we return," Lucan added.

Quinn glanced around the hall. "It has to be just us three."

"As I said, hell to pay."

Fallon absently scratched his chin. "Quinn's right. Just us three. We'll be gone and back before they know it. We can do small searches in places Malcolm and Phelan have no' gone."

"We go tonight," Quinn said.

Lucan leaned a shoulder against the wall. "Half past midnight. Meet on the north tower."

"This could be for nothing," Fallon cautioned. "Wallace may well truly be dead."

"I want to see his body," Quinn stated.

Lucan glanced at Cara again. "I concur. I need to see his body to believe he's gone from our lives for good. Only then will I be able to breathe."

"It's been two months and nothing. If Wallace was alive, he'd have made himself known by now," Fallon said.

"There was a time we thought Deirdre was dead as well," Lucan said. "That didna turn out so well for us since she was able to use her magic to regenerate her body."

Quinn rubbed his eyes with his thumb and forefinger. "Doona remind me. Wallace was smart. Smarter than Deirdre or Declan. He might've been a little too cocky, but he'll have made plans for his untimely demise."

"Ah, but he wasna counting on having to battle the selmyr," Fallon said, his eyes flashing satisfaction at the memory.

Lucan growled as he thought of the selmyr—ancient monsters who thrived off of consuming magical beings. Druids and Warriors being their choice of meals.

"We've made some powerful friends," Fallon continued. "Without the aid of the Dragon Kings, there's no way we could've fought both the selmyr and Wallace."

Quinn shifted from one foot to the other as Marcail rose from the table and walked up the stairs. "All of that was thanks to Charon. For some reason the Dragon Kings favor him."

"Irks you, does it?" Lucan teased.

Quinn rolled his eyes. "I almost killed Charon while we were in Deirdre's Pit. Now I'm glad I listened to Marcail and stayed my hand."

"Charon has proven a valuable Warrior long before his connection to the Dragon Kings," Lucan pointed out.

Fallon was quick to toss in his agreement. "That he has. No' once has he let us down."

"Should we tell him our plan about our upcoming search?" Quinn asked quietly.

Lucan frowned. "Nay. We tell no one."

"Agreed," Fallon said.

The three ended their talk of searching for Wallace as

Aiden came to the top of the stairs. He looked in need of a shave and a good meal, but the smile on his face said everything.

"Britt is close," Aiden said. "Verra close. It's still going to take a couple of days before the serum will be ready to test."

After a round of clapping and shouts of joy, Aiden disappeared from view.

"This is good news," Quinn said.

Fallon's gaze was riveted on his wife, Larena. She was the only female Warrior, and she had come close to dying when *drough* blood had been put into her wounds.

Just one drop of *drough* blood could kill a Warrior. And somehow Wallace had managed to make the *drough* blood work more powerfully than before in bringing down a Warrior. Of course, the X90 bullets that were filled with *drough* blood didn't help.

In the past, introducing a Warrior's blood to counteract the *drough* blood was the way to save one of their own. Charon's recent injury hadn't been able to be reversed as before. They'd nearly lost him.

Lucan prayed Britt's serum worked. It was just a matter of time before one of them fell to *drough* blood.

"Tonight," Quinn whispered, as if reading his thoughts.

Lucan and Fallon nodded.

Tonight they would begin their hunt. The other Warriors, Druids, and their wives would be angry, but it was worth their fury to find Wallace.

At least they would know something. If he was dead, they could concentrate on finding the spell that would bind their gods for good and allow them to live normal lives.

If Wallace was alive . . . it meant another battle.

Lucan stayed where he was as Quinn and Fallon walked away. Lucan looked over the great hall at the men and women who had become his family. They might not be related by blood, but they were family just the same.

They had lost one already. Duncan.

Lucan's heart was heavy every time he thought of the Warrior. And he couldn't look at Ian without thinking of Duncan since they had been twins.

Their immortality gave them an advantage, but as it had been proven, they could be killed. Lucan didn't want to lose anyone else in his family.

They'd come close recently with Charon and Larena. How many more times would luck favor them?

He feared their luck had run out.

CHAPTER
FIVE

It was just after one when Aisley pulled off the road to eat. The croissant and coffee she had hastily downed at the café had been hours ago.

The lack of food, stress of meeting up with Phelan again, and the worry that Jason could be right around the corner had given her the queen of migraines.

Aisley opened the door and blinked against the blinding light of the sun. She slipped her sunglasses back on and hurried to the small restaurant.

With a nod to the man behind the counter, Aisley walked up to the bar and ordered some fish and chips and a soft drink before sitting down at a table in the far back corner.

Her hands shook when she dug into her purse for her migraine medicine after they brought her drink. At any moment, she expected her head to explode from the pain. She popped the pill into her mouth and took a drink to wash it down.

No matter how much she tried, she couldn't get Phelan out of her mind. He confused her, rattled her, but he excited her as well.

She didn't like that most of all. He was the enemy. She shouldn't want his touch. Or more of his kisses.

She closed her eyes and instantly an image of Phelan filled her mind. Rich, dark hair hung past his shoulders thick and straight. His face was hard lines and angles with a jaw that looked as if it had been carved from granite.

Despite the hardness of his face, his wide lips could tilt in a devastating smile that sent her emotions spinning. But when his blue-gray eyes locked with hers, it was as if the world faded to nothing.

She saw only him, felt only him.

Knew only him.

His tall body with his impossibly hard muscles felt so good against hers. The memory of their fleeting kiss, his heat, and the way she wanted to wrap her arms and legs around him and hang on for dear life revisited her every time she closed her eyes.

Even knowing he was most likely there to kill her, she couldn't resist him or the attraction. He was temptation and danger rolled into one delicious package.

She couldn't look at his lips without thinking of their kisses, of how she craved more. He was impossible to resist. The fact she didn't want to resist him is what caused all the problems.

He couldn't have been more tempting if he were laid out naked on her bed and covered in chocolate. His allure, his seductive eyes, and his damned charm were slowly getting the better of her.

How she wished she could give in to his tantalizing body and inviting arms. His blatant masculine sexuality enticed, tempted, and completely shattered any walls she tried to put up to keep him out.

The food arrived quickly, and she wasted little time in eating. The migraine had begun to let up a tad when she finished.

Aisley leaned back in her chair and closed her eyes, her sunglasses still on. No matter how she tried, she couldn't use magic to stop the migraines. Jason had told her numerous times it was because she was weak.

She didn't know why her magic didn't work that way, only that it didn't. But she couldn't heal herself of anything, even a small cut.

Maybe it was the evil inside her that prevented such things. A Druid with healing magic was rare, and it took pure magic. Pure had never been something Aisley was.

"Certainly not now," she murmured to herself.

As much as she wanted to stay and relax, she had to get back on the road. It wasn't a good idea to stay in one place too long when she was being chased.

Aisley pulled out some money and dropped it on the table next to the ticket before she rose to head back to her car. She blew out a long breath when she was once more behind the wheel.

Sleep was the best thing for her migraine, but there wasn't time for that. She knew without a doubt that Phelan was tracking her.

"Why didn't he kill me?" she asked herself.

No matter how many times she had thought about what occurred in Glasgow, she still couldn't grasp why he hadn't killed her. He almost made it look as if he were helping her.

And he let her leave.

"Another question I won't have answered."

But did she really want answers from the Warrior with the devastating smile and eyes that stripped her bare every time he looked at her?

Yes, God help her, she did.

He was exciting, dangerous, and stirring. Just as he was seduction in a tall, dark package she desperately wanted to rip into.

Aisley shook her head. "He's a Warrior from MacLeod Castle. He's supposed to kill me," she reminded herself.

If only he would wait until she could stop Jason for good. She started the Fiat Bravo and pulled back onto the road. She had a long way to go yet.

Phelan watched Aisley with barely contained desire from a copse of trees as he sat atop his motorbike. He frowned at how she kept her head away from the sun, as if her sunglasses weren't enough to shade her eyes.

It was also the way she held her shoulders that alerted him something was wrong. She looked tired, but also unwell. That's the only thing that stopped him from approaching her again. His seduction was on hold. Again.

Damn, but did the woman know how tempting, how irresistible she was? Could she understand how the driving need to have her in his arms had him in knots?

Phelan waited for her to drive at least twenty minutes ahead of him before he followed. Just as he began to reach for his helmet, his mobile rang.

He pulled it out of his pocket and saw it was a call from Charon. "Aye?"

"Wanted to let you know it looks like Britt's serum is working. It's nearly ready to be tested."

Phelan was glad of the news, and even happier to hear the note of relief in his friend's voice. "Good. How soon until it's ready?"

"Aiden has asked for a couple more days, but I could hear the excitement in Ian's voice when he called."

"Now might be a good time to have Fallon jump you back to the castle."

"Why?" Charon asked suspiciously. "Have you found something of Wallace?"

Phelan briefly closed his eyes, knowing he wasn't doing himself or Charon any favors by following Aisley instead of searching for Wallace. Yet, Phelan told himself that he was searching—as he followed Aisley.

"I would've told you if I had. I assumed you'd want to be with the others at the castle to celebrate."

"I'll celebrate when this shite is finished." There was a pause over the line, and then Charon let out a sigh. "I'd rather be preparing for an unwinnable battle than waiting as we are."

"I wish I had good news, my friend."

"You suspect you'll find him." It wasn't a question.

And Phelan wasn't in the habit of lying, especially to Charon, who was like a brother to him. "Aye, I do. Just as Deirdre resurrected, I think Wallace will do the same if he is dead."

"There wasna a body after the battle was over," Charon pointed out.

"That means nothing and you know it. It's a matter of when and how."

"And how he'll attack us."

"Precisely."

"He'll come after me and Laura first," Charon said.

Phelan wished he had words to reassure his friend, but he didn't. "If he's stupid enough to do it a second time, then we'll be waiting. Would it make you feel better if I was in Ferness to help you guard Laura?"

"Aye, but you need to stay out there. Fallon jumped Isla, Reaghan, and Marcail here a few days ago to set up protection shields around the building and they will alert us to a *drough* getting close to the village."

"That'll give you enough time to get Laura away."

"Like I did last time? We all know how well that went. She nearly died."

Phelan was at a loss how to respond, but that normally happened when he saw or heard Isla's name. He must have sat there in his thoughts too long because Charon began cussing.

"Sorry. I didna mean to say Isla's name."

Phelan shrugged even though Charon couldn't see it. "Doona fash yourself about it. It's fine."

"Nay, it's no', and that's what worries me. After all this time, you have no' forgiven her, have you?"

"I'm trying." And Phelan was, just not as much as he should be.

"Deirdre had all of us in some way, shape, or form. You know what she did to me and what she made me do. Isla explained why she tricked you as a lad to leave your family and go with her."

"I know," Phelan said harshly. He slammed his fist on his thigh. "I can no' talk about it without losing my temper, Charon."

"That's just it, my friend. You doona talk about it, and you should."

"It's better if I doona. Isla is at the castle, and I'm here. The few times I do have to see her is when we're going into battle. That I can handle."

There was another pause on Charon's end of the phone. "She's a good person. She suffered just as we did. Try to remember that."

"If I doona, Hayden is there to protect her from me."

Charon laughed, but Phelan hadn't been joking. The only thing that kept him from attacking Isla was her husband.

"It looks like we need to have that chat again about the differences between *mies* and *droughs*," Charon said.

"There's no need. I know the difference."

"Then you should know Isla isna just a *drough*." Gone was Charon's teasing tone. It had turned hard as steel.

This was something new. Always before Charon had

felt the same as Phelan regarding MacLeod Castle and those within its walls. What had changed?

"She underwent the *drough* ceremony. That makes her a *drough*," Phelan argued.

"There's more to her story than that. You know I'm right."

"What I know is that I kill *droughs*."

Charon gave a wry laugh through the phone. "You know, Hayden used to hunt them as well. He ended up in love with one."

"No' me. And Hayden should never have stopped hunting them. It's *droughs* who keep us in constant battle. You want peace for your life with Laura, my brother, then you need to be hunting and killing the *droughs* as well."

Phelan ended the call before Charon could respond. It wasn't like Charon to defend Isla or those at the castle. Was that what falling in love meant? That he would suddenly change his views on everything?

"No' likely," Phelan muttered as he put on his helmet and started the Ducati.

He waited for two cars to pass before he pulled out of the stand of trees and onto the road.

No matter how many miles passed beneath his tires, he couldn't get the conversation with Charon out of his head. It angered him that Charon was defending Isla.

Isla had had a choice. She decided to take a small lad away from his family to be locked away in a cold, dank prison for years. Chained, lonely, and scared, the darkness never easing away.

There was no forgiveness for Isla.

Not now.

Not ever.

Isla tried to redeem herself when she unlocked him from the magical chains that bound him to Cairn Toul Mountain. He should've killed her then, but her wounds had been severe enough he'd thought she would die on her own. But she hadn't. Somehow she survived and wound up at MacLeod Castle.

Mercy would never come for him.

Retribution, however, would.

That sickening feeling of being betrayed stayed with a person. He had been but a small lad, but even then he realized what happened to him. There was no forgiveness in him for anyone who deceived him.

It wasn't as if he wanted to kill people, but if he didn't they would be fighting *droughs* until the end of time. Druids seemed to be fading away, yet there was always a *drough* ready to take over the world.

Phelan refused to give Isla any more thought. He pushed her from his mind and followed Aisley for several more hours. Phelan made sure to keep far enough back that she didn't realize he was tailing her.

He wasn't surprised when she stopped at a small town around six for another bite to eat. Once more Phelan found a place to keep watch out of sight.

While she ordered, he did a quick search of the town to check for other Druids, especially *droughs*. He wasn't surprised to know that Aisley's magic was the only one he felt.

She had her food by the time he made it back to his motorbike. He began to worry when he saw her take a pill, and then shield her eyes from the lamplight above her.

No matter what she said, Phelan wasn't going to let her go another night without sleep. He crossed the street to the small hotel and paid for a room.

Aisley wasn't sure her food was going to stay down. The migraine hadn't let up. She took another pill and prayed this time it would help.

She kept eyeing the lighted hotel sign flashing Vacancy

from the restaurant window. As tempting as it was, she would sleep for a few hours in her car, and then get back on the road.

Enough time had been wasted driving around Scotland gathering the money she needed to make her escape until she could take on Jason herself. She couldn't explain it, but she felt as if her time was running out. Whether that meant her life, or time to get out of Scotland, she wasn't sure.

And really didn't want to find out.

Aisley ate as much of the soup and sandwich as she could before she paid and walked out of the restaurant. The cool night air felt good on her heated flesh.

She took only two steps when the world began to tilt. Aisley grabbed hold of the side of the building to keep her feet. After several deep breaths, the spinning continued until she knew she was about to fall on her face.

Just before she did, strong arms wrapped around her, and a voice, smooth, sexy, and altogether too dangerous, whispered her name.

"I've got you," Phelan said.

Aisley wanted to demand he put her down, but the world finally stopped spinning. She latched onto his thickly muscled shoulders and leaned her head against him.

It should be a sin for someone to be as handsome and roguishly charming as Phelan. She had no defense for him, but in the back of her mind, she conceded that she didn't want one.

He was sin and seduction, sex and persuasion. He had been perfectly formed to make a woman mindless with desire. He was wild and untamed, just like their land, and that gave him a thread of danger that sent her senses reeling.

It never entered her mind to push away from him. Regardless of whether she liked it or not, she needed him that night.

"You're going to get some sleep, beauty. You'll thank me in the morn."

Her eyelids closed even as she formulated a response. "No," was all she got out.

CHAPTER
SIX

Phelan knew something was wrong the moment he saw Aisley's face. She was too pale, her shoulders held high in a sign of pain.

He reached her in three strides when he saw her grab ahold of the building. It was a good thing, too, or he might not have made it to her in time before she fell.

With a nod to the staring, wide-eyed hotel clerk, Phelan strode past him to the stairs. There was an urgency pushing him to get Aisley inside the room, but he was careful not to jar her, which meant going slower.

He looked down to see Aisley's closed eyes. Her forehead was still creased in a slight frown. Phelan got them inside the room and quickly lay her on the bed.

After removing her shoes and covering her with a blanket, he reached for her purse and the medicine bottle he knew was inside. He didn't recognize the name of the medication, but with a quick search on the Internet with his phone, he learned it was prescribed for migraines.

"Damn," he whispered and returned the pills to her purse.

Phelan knew nothing of migraines. He pulled up a chair beside the bed and simply stared at Aisley. The steady rise and fall of her chest let him know she was sleeping deeply.

He should leave her, but he found he couldn't. Phelan gently moved aside strands of her hair from her face. Her golden skin was as soft as mink, and no matter how he tried, he couldn't stop touching her.

Phelan ran a finger over her forehead to smooth out the lines. She sighed in her sleep and turned her head toward him. He licked his lips, the need to hold her in his arms and taste her sweet mouth again too much to bear.

Control over his god and his urgings had been something Phelan learned quickly. He reined in his desire. Barely.

His cock ached to be inside Aisley, to hear her scream his name as he filled her again and again. And no matter how long it took, he would have her in his bed.

Phelan wound a strand of her midnight locks around his finger. "How long will you make me chase you, beauty?"

While he watched her sleep, he did another search on his phone and learned about migraines. By the time he finished reading the fourth Web site, he was frowning.

He had no idea they could be so debilitating. Was she light sensitive or sound sensitive? He recalled the way she had worn her sunglasses in the eatery at lunch and decided she must be light sensitive.

Phelan rose and hurried to close the curtains to block out any light that might filter in from outside. He didn't bother with a lamp since his enhanced eyesight allowed him to see just as clearly in darkness as it did in the light.

He resumed his seat next to the bed and let her magic wash over him. It wasn't as . . . clean . . . as when he felt *mie* magic. It was almost as if Aisley's magic held a drop of excitement, a punch of attitude, a dash of charm, and a bucket full of seduction.

It was a mixture he'd never encountered, and the more he was around her, the more he craved her magic.

Phelan comprehended all too well that he was treading on dangerous ground. During the first weeks he chased her, he told himself it was because she was the only woman who hadn't fallen easily into his bed.

Now, he was sure it was much more than that. Aisley enchanted him, captivated him . . . enthralled him as no one had in the very long years of his life.

That in itself should be making him run the opposite way. He wasn't the settling-down type. He was a wanderer, a drifter. The life suited him.

The more he thought of Aisley and his confusing feelings, the more restless Phelan became. He paced the room, but it didn't help.

He should walk away, leave and never look back. Charon was counting on him. Wallace had to be found and Aisley was a distraction he didn't need.

Finally he walked out into the hall and drew out his mobile. He stared at the screen wondering if he should tell Charon about Aisley. Charon was always the voice of reason. If anyone would know what he should do, it was the man he called brother.

His finger hovered over Charon's number, but he couldn't dial it. At the last second he chose another number. Though Phelan had never called Malcolm before he'd heard how the others could never get him to answer. So, imagine Phelan's surprise when Malcolm answered on the second ring.

"Did you find him?" Malcolm asked.

Phelan flattened his lips. "Well, hello to you as well."

"Did you?" Malcolm repeated in a flat voice.

"If I did, do you think I'd be so casual?"

There was a slight hesitation before Malcolm said, "Nay."

"Where are you?"

"I'm in the north up near Wick."

Phelan leaned his head back against the wall. "I'm south of Glasgow and have felt nothing of Wallace."

"I have no' either. The MacLeods will be joining in the search soon."

Phelan's eyes snapped open. "All the Warriors?"

"Nay. Just the brothers."

"How do you know this?"

The sound of a hollow laugh filtered through the phone. "Because I know Fallon. He willna stay cooped up for long, regardless of what Larena wants him to do."

"We could use the extra help."

"Aye. I'm going to go back by Wallace's mansion tomorrow and see what I find there."

"That's a good idea," Phelan said. "What do you know of Wallace's associates?"

"The other *droughs*? No' much other than the few that survived scattered."

That was interesting. "How many survived?"

"Maybe two. You wanting to find them?"

"I'm thinking it might be a good start if Wallace does come back."

Malcolm grunted. "Everyone assumes he died in that blast."

"You were there. You know how powerful that was."

"I also know there was potent magic being used by Wallace and the other Druids. That magic could've sent him anywhere."

Phelan raked a hand through his hair and sighed. "Meaning he could be in the future?"

"Or the past, or floating in another reality."

"Bugger it. We could be searching the rest of our lives."

Malcolm blew out a breath through the phone. "Wallace waited a year to get everything in order before he attacked us. If we give him that kind of time again, we may no' win."

"I think we've all realized that. Let me know what you find tomorrow at Wallace Mansion."

"Who is she?" Malcolm asked.

Phelan paused. "Who?"

"The woman who's got you spun around."

Phelan chuckled softly. "There's no woman."

"There's always a woman with you, but more than that, you've never called me, Phelan."

"I was calling about Wallace."

"There's no reason to lie."

"Your power is supposed to be lightning, no' knowing if someone is lying through the phone," Phelan said through clenched teeth, wondering if he was as easy to read as Malcolm made out.

The sound of a car passing came through the phone before Malcolm said, "It's in your voice. You seem preoccupied."

"It is a woman. I want her."

"Then have her as you do all the others."

"It's no' that simple. She doesna want me." Phelan could have sworn he heard Malcolm laugh, but the sound of another car drowned it out.

"I'm no' the one you should be talking to about this. Besides you, I'm the only one without a mate."

"I doona want the others to know."

"They willna hear it from me," Malcolm vowed. "I'll let you know what I find tomorrow."

The phone went dead. Phelan shook his head as he pocketed the phone. Why had Malcolm answered his call when he didn't answer the others? Was it because they were the last two unmarried Warriors?

"Looks like we'll be bonding then because I've no interest in tying myself to one woman," Phelan said as he turned and entered the hotel room again.

Aisley was still sleeping. It took all of ten minutes for Phelan to decide to help her. He couldn't stand to see her in pain, and knowing that the morning might not bring relief solidified his decision.

He turned his arm over to look at the veins on the inside of his wrist. His blood did amazing things. He was able to heal anything. The only thing he couldn't do was bring someone back from the dead.

Not once had he questioned what his blood could heal until Charon had been hit with the X90 bullets and the *drough* blood in them consumed his body. No matter how many times Phelan used his blood in the wounds, it did nothing.

At least Phelan now knew it was something Wallace did to the *drough* blood, but it didn't make it easier to bear knowing not even he could have saved his friend.

Phelan held his left wrist over Aisley's mouth and let his claws lengthen from his right hand. With a flick, he cut his wrist and let three drops of blood fall past Aisley's lips and into her mouth.

She would be healed by the time she woke. And he would be long gone.

It was his decision, but he couldn't make his legs move. If only she would sit with him and just talk he could try to understand why she thought he wanted to kill her.

And why she didna want him.

That wouldn't happen until he earned her trust. No matter what he wanted to do, Phelan knew he had to be out of the room by the time Aisley woke.

Which was damned inconvenient. Need filled him,

making his rod twitch. He flexed his hands, imagining running them over her skin and cupping her breasts.

Phelan rose with a growl. He had to leave now.

Or not at all.

CHAPTER
SEVEN

Aisley slowly opened her eyes expecting to feel the dull, residual headache that always followed one of her migraines. Instead, there was nothing.

She felt refreshed and revitalized. No longer did her eyes feel as if sand had been poured in them. A good night's sleep was all she really needed.

The events of the previous night flashed in her mind as she slowly sat up. Phelan had been there. He had lifted her in his arms. Had he brought her to the hotel? It was the only explanation that made any sense.

"Well, hell," she muttered.

She already found him occupying her thoughts too much. Now she was not only indebted to him, but he'd done a nice thing. She didn't want to thank him.

"He's just messing with my head," she told herself as she threw off the blanket and swung her legs over the side of the bed.

That's when she saw her duffle and purse. Aisley dropped her head into her hands. How could she continue to try and hate a guy who had taken care of her?

"I'm screwed, that's what."

There was a soft knock on her door, which made her jerk her head up. Aisley gathered her magic and padded to the door. She looked through the peephole to see a young man holding a tray full of food.

He knocked again, and this time said, "Room service."

Aisley opened the door to see a redheaded teenager with bad acne give her a bright smile. "He said to wait until eight and then see if you were awake."

"Eight? As in eight in the morning?" she asked in disbelief. She should have been on the road hours ago.

"Aye, miss. Where should I put this?"

Aisley stepped aside for him to enter. "The man. Was he tall with long dark hair?"

The boy straightened from setting down the tray and smiled. "That's him, miss. He's a formidable one. Wanted me to make sure not to wake you no matter what."

"Formidable. That describes him all right," she said with a frown.

Aisley grabbed a few pound notes and gave them to the employee before he left. Then she looked at the tray of food.

"I'd weigh five hundred pounds if I let him feed me," she said as she looked at all the food on the tray.

The smell and her growling stomach was too much. She grabbed a plate full of sausage, eggs, and toast before pouring a cup of coffee and orange juice.

It had been quite awhile since Aisley had eaten so much at one sitting. Her body demanded more, and before she knew it, she'd eaten almost everything Phelan ordered.

There were two pastries and a croissant left, all of which Aisley wrapped in a napkin and packed in her purse to eat during the drive.

A glance at the clock showed it was a quarter to nine. With a curse, she rushed into the bathroom and quickly showered. When she stepped out and stood in front of the mirror she didn't recognize the woman staring back at her.

Aisley ran her fingers through her wet hair, pulling the inky strands away from her face. Where was the young girl who laughed at everything and thought the world was hers for the taking?

It was amazing how life could go along at a good pace, and then so easily get off kilter in less than a heartbeat. She might not have been perfect, but she'd been a good person.

She still didn't know why God had chosen to punish her. Then, she hadn't cared whether she lived or died. She flaunted herself in front of Death every day after that, hoping her life would end and the torment would cease.

It hadn't been Death that had found her but Jason.

Aisley ran a finger over the wrinkles fanning out from the corner of her eyes. They were slight, but a year ago they hadn't been there at all.

At twenty-nine Aisley expected her life to be much different. It was all those wrong choices her mother had cautioned her about.

Aisley turned away from the mirror and dressed in a pair of slim cargo khakis, black shirt, and a pair of black wedges. She then threw her dirty clothes into her duffle. After running a comb through her hair, she grabbed her stuff and walked out of the hotel.

She glanced around the small town looking for Phelan. He was there, she knew it, she just couldn't see him. Aisley tossed her bag into the back of her Fiat and got in.

"Aiiiissssssleeeeeyyyy!"

She squeezed her eyes closed as her heart pounded in her chest. When seconds ticked by with no other evil voice in her head, Aisley started the car and turned up the radio as loud as she could.

The border into England was just a few hours away.

She would make it and leave all of Scotland—and the bad memories—behind forever.

Phelan's elation at seeing the pep in Aisley's step again disappeared when he saw her grip the steering wheel as if her life depended on her hanging onto it.

Just as he was thinking about approaching her, she started the car and drove off.

"Damn woman. If she'd only let me help," he murmured as he put on his helmet.

He started the Ducati, but he didn't immediately follow her. During the night he'd made the decision to let her go and search for Wallace.

Yet, he remained just to get a glimpse of her. That was all he was going to do to make sure she was feeling better. That one look hadn't been enough.

He liked helping her, and he wanted to do it again. If she let him. Which he knew she wouldn't. That in itself had him pulling out behind her and following her once more.

It didn't take long for Phelan to realize Aisley was on her way out of Scotland. And fast. She pulled over only once to get petrol.

As they neared Dumfries, Phelan was trying to think of a way to keep her in Scotland. He couldn't follow her into England no matter how much he wanted to.

His duty was to help his brethren and the Druids in locating Wallace. He had a long time to contemplate his conversation with Malcolm.

There was a chance Wallace could have been tossed through time somewhere, but Phelan wasn't so sure of it. Time travel didn't happen by accident. It was done with powerful magic and the right spell.

The last battle had unfolded, leaving Wallace alone and being attacked by the selmyr. Phelan didn't imagine the bastard had enough time to use the spell to traverse time.

By the time they reached Dumfries, Phelan knew he had to do something. He gunned the Ducati to bypass three cars when the sickening feel of *drough* magic slammed into him, stealing his breath with its power.

Phelan gagged and steered the motorbike off the road. As he did, he heard the squeal of brakes and the crunch of metal as vehicles plowed into each other.

"Aisley," he murmured around the cloying feel of the evil magic.

He pulled off his helmet and put the kickstand down simultaneously before he jumped off his bike and ran to Aisley's car. It was the feel of the *drough* magic that made him move quickly. That and the worry that Aisley had been injured.

Phelan took note of how it looked as if she lost control of the Fiat and spun the front half of it off the road so that the car that plowed into her hit her from the passenger side. He took in the damage to see it was minimal, considering.

He bent to look inside. "Aisley."

She had a death grip on the steering wheel, her chest heaving and her eyes wide. But there was no sign of blood.

"Aisley?" he called again.

When she still didn't respond, he hurried to the driver's side and opened her door. "Talk to me now or I'm going to kiss you right here."

"I need to leave."

"Then we'll leave, but you're in no condition to drive."

She viciously shook her head. "Not with you. You're here to kill me."

Phelan clenched his jaw in frustration. "How many times do I have to tell you? If I wanted you dead, you'd already be dead. Now, there's a *drough* near."

"I know."

That made him frown. "You know? Only Warriors can sense magic, lass."

She pushed him out of the way and started running down the road. Phelan could only stare at her, wondering if he had heard her right when she mumbled the words, "He's come for me," as she rushed past him.

Phelan watched her run as fast as she could in her shoes. He looked around at the chaos of the wreck and quickly pushed Aisley's car off the road. He saw her duffle inside the car and made a quick decision. He grabbed the bag and hurried back to his bike. After he tied her duffle onto the back of his motorbike, he put on his helmet and maneuvered his bike through the cars as he chased her down.

He skidded the Ducati to a halt in front of her and yanked off his helmet as he handed it to her. "Put it on. Now."

"I don't want your help."

"Liar." He kept the helmet outstretched, waiting— hoping—she would take it.

Phelan never allowed a woman in need to go unassisted. He certainly wasn't going to leave Aisley on the roadside alone. If he had to, he'd strap her to his Ducati and drive away.

She stared at the helmet a second before she did as he ordered.

"You need to trust me, Aisley," he told her.

"If I was smart, I'd make you leave me."

"If I was smart, I probably would," he retorted. "Get on, beauty."

Another few seconds ticked by before she threw her leg over the bike and wrapped her arms around him. Phelan drove away as the sirens blared behind him.

He drove them to Holywood where he hid his bike in an alley and walked Aisley into a café. They took a table in the back with him facing the door.

By the look on Aisley's face she was still in shock. And he needed to call Malcolm. "Order me something. I'll be right back."

He walked out of the restaurant and around the corner so he could see Aisley through the window. Then he grabbed his mobile and called Malcolm.

"Two calls in less than twelve hours," Malcolm said as a way of answering. "What's happened?"

"It's Wallace. He's back."

"Are you sure?"

"Aye. I felt his magic. It was powerful, Malcolm. Verra powerful."

There was a string of curses before Malcolm asked, "More powerful than he was before?"

"I believe so."

"I'll let the others know."

"And I'll call Charon," Phelan said.

He ended the call and inhaled deeply. Just when he thought Wallace might be gone for good. He should have known better.

Phelan called Charon, who answered on the first ring. "Phelan."

"He's back," Phelan said and briefly closed his eyes.

"Bloody hell. Where are you?"

"A long way from Ferness. I'm near the border with England."

"What's Wallace doing there?" Charon asked.

Phelan heard the worry in his voice and knew Charon was thinking of ways to get Laura to MacLeod Castle without an argument. "I doona know. I didna see him, only felt his magic."

"Are you going looking for him?"

"Nay. I've got a Druid with me."

"What?" Charon all but yelled. "When did this happen?"

"I've known about her for a few months. I've been keeping an eye on her."

"Is Wallace after her?"

Phelan could hear Charon drumming his fingers on his desk through the phone. "Maybe, but I'm no' sure."

"Bring her to the castle."

"I doona think that'll be easy. She knows I'm a Warrior, and she thinks I'm trying to kill her."

Charon grunted in response. "Obviously she's a *mie* or you'd already have killed her. Perhaps she was led to believe the Warriors are evil."

"Probably. I'll do my best to get her to the MacLeods, but right now my concern is keeping her away from Wallace."

"Good luck with that. Have you called the castle?"

"Malcolm is," Phelan said. "I called him. He's letting the others know."

"Good, good. Call me with regular updates. You doona want me to come looking for your ugly arse."

Phelan grinned. "You'd never find me."

"Try me," Charon said, the smile in his voice.

Despite their teasing, Phelan knew just how worried Charon was. As he disconnected the call, Phelan walked into the café and to Aisley's table.

"There wasna time to check you for wounds," Phelan said. "Were you hurt in the accident?"

She shook her head and stared at the glass of water in front of her. "Was anyone else injured?"

"Minor cuts and scrapes, lass. Doona fash yourself over it."

"How long have you lived?" she asked, raising her fawn-colored gaze to his.

The direct question took him aback for a moment. "I've never had anyone ask, although no one outside of my small circle knows."

"It's not a difficult question."

"Nay, it's no'. I'm a little over five hundred and fifty."

She let out a long breath. "In all that time you've walked the earth, has life ever gotten easier?"

He studied her, wondering if she needed to hear the truth or if he should temper his answer. In her eyes he saw grief, misery, and depression that went soul deep.

Something had happened in her short life, and Phelan found he wanted to comfort her, to lend his shoulder to cry on.

"The truth," she said as if she knew he was debating his answer.

"There are stretches where things are easy and nice, almost peaceful. Then there are those times where everything goes wrong and everyone turns against you."

"So, no. Life doesn't get easier."

"Nay, beauty. Life is as much a bitch as karma is. Only the strong, those like you, survive."

She looked down at the table. "I'm not surviving, Phelan. I'm existing. And I'm tired of it."

CHAPTER
EIGHT

He had no idea where he was, only that he had to get back. There were times he lost track of exactly where "where" was, but then he'd remember.

His memories latched onto one person—Aisley. She betrayed him. She left him to die alone.

And she would pay for it with her life—slowly and painfully.

The longer he held onto his memories the stronger he got. At first it was too difficult. He didn't know how much time had passed, but he was growing stronger.

It would only be a matter of time before he once more walked the earth. His vengeance against Aisley and those at MacLeod Castle would be swift.

They'd never see him coming.

Until it was too late.

MacLeod Castle

"Has Phelan found Jason or not?" Gwynn asked from her seat at the long table in the great hall.

Logan rubbed the back of his neck and looked across the table at his wife as he searched for a different way to answer the question he'd already responded to three times in the past ten minutes.

"As he told Charon," Arran spoke into the silence, "Phelan felt Wallace's magic but didna see him."

Sonya pushed her red curls behind her ears. "Then why isn't he looking?"

"He has a Druid with him," Broc explained to his wife.

Logan exchanged a glance with Galen, who sat next to him. "The point is that Wallace isna dead as we'd hoped."

"Logan's right." Fallon's voice rang out through the hall. He turned from the hearth and crossed his arms over his chest. "Until I see Wallace, I'll hold out that small thread of hope that he's gone."

Thick black lashes lowered over silver eyes as Ramsey frowned. "Are you telling me you doona believe what Phelan felt? We all know how *drough* magic feels. There's no forgetting that."

"That's no' what my brother meant," Quinn said.

Logan stood and looked around the hall. "We could argue this for decades. The simple fact is we need to prepare in case Wallace does return."

"Aye," Hayden said with a nod. "Because if Wallace is back, he'll be wanting revenge."

Isla threaded her fingers with Hayden's and smiled. "Better to be safe, my love. I agree."

Larena rolled her smoky blue eyes and glared at her husband as she sat on the bottom step of the stairs. "And what about us looking for the spell to bind our gods, Fallon?"

"That's put on hold," Lucan said before Fallon could.

"My life has been put on hold," Larena argued angrily. "I've been waiting centuries to have a family. We have an opportunity now to find this Evangeline Walker and see if she knows about the necklace."

Dr. Veronica MacCarrick, or Ronnie to her friends, rose from her seat at the table and walked to Larena. "I've not been a part of the castle that long, and I do understand you want to start a family."

Larena smiled sadly. "You've no idea, Ronnie. None at all."

"But . . . if we focus on finding the spell to bind the gods, how in the world will we fight Wallace?"

Larena raised a blond brow. "We'd obviously wait until he was defeated."

Logan winced at the hard edge to Larena's voice. It wasn't like her, but then again, the strain of the constant battles and her need for a family were taking its toll.

"And what if there's another *drough* to take Wallace's place?" Camdyn asked. "It happens every time we kill one. What do we do then if our gods are bound?"

"I don't give a bloody damn what you do!" Larena yelled as she jumped to her feet.

The silence that followed was deafening.

Fallon walked to Larena and pulled her into his arms. Her silent tears tore at everyone.

"She didna mean it," Fallon said.

Cara nodded from beside Lucan. "We know. As much as we'd all like to be normal, we aren't."

Tara gave an unladylike snort from beside Ramsey. "No, we're not normal. We Druids have magic that sets us apart from others. Whether we grew up knowing our magic or not, we were never normal."

Ramsey leaned over and gave her a quick kiss. "Ah, but I like that you're so different. I wouldna want normal."

"But would you if your god was bound?" Reaghan asked. She glanced at Galen and frowned. "Really? With your god bound, no longer would you be immortal or have enhanced senses. No longer would you hear your gods inside you or be able to call up your god. Each of you would be a regular person. How would we, as Druids, fit into your lives?"

"Quite easily," Galen answered. "I didna fall in love with your magic. I fell in love with you."

Saffron folded her hands atop the table. "Do any of you remember what it was like before you were Warriors?"

"What are you getting at?" Camdyn asked her.

"Answer it," she urged.

Quinn gave a slight shake of his head. "My memories of life are there, but I doona recall much else."

"Memories aren't the same as living it, feeling it," Danielle said.

Ian tugged Dani closer. "What's that mean?"

"It means," Isla said, "that each of you will feel things differently when your gods are bound. Your gods don't just give you enhanced senses, they boost your feelings as well."

Hayden shrugged. "Perhaps, but I know it willna change my love for you."

Marcail rubbed her finger along Quinn's torc around his neck. "You may not, but things will change. No matter how much we hope they won't."

Quinn's lips flattened for a moment. "You think we ought to stay Warriors? You want to continue to live in the castle surrounded by Isla's shield? What about more children?"

Logan's gaze was on Gwynn, waiting to see her reaction to Quinn's question. Gwynn reached across the table and took his hand.

"Do you want me to stay a Warrior?"

Gwynn shrugged. "I want to be with you, wherever

that takes us. There's no doubt y'all are needed, Logan. As Camdyn stated, there is always evil that needs to be killed. Who will do that? The Dragon Kings?"

Arran tapped a finger on the table thoughtfully. "As much as I'm enjoying this conversation, it's pointless to even have such a discussion. We've no' found the necklace that houses the spell."

"We may never find the spell," Broc said.

Larena raised her head from Fallon's shoulder and wiped at her eyes. "I'm sorry for . . . well, everything. The right thing to do is prepare for Wallace."

"There's no need to apologize," Cara said. "We've battled evil for over four centuries. We're allowed to get irritated."

Tara chuckled. "The correct word is *pissy.* And yes, we are allowed."

There was a chorus of laughter, but Logan only had eyes for Gwynn. He rubbed his thumb over the back of her hand. She, Tara, Saffron, Dani, and Ronnie were fairly new to the castle, but that didn't make them any less aware of what their lives were.

The same could be said for Laura, though she and Charon chose to stay in Ferness rather than the castle.

"We can have children," Gwynn whispered so the conversation was just between them while others talked around them.

Logan smiled. "That we can, love. Do you want to spend eternity in the castle?"

"Who knows what the next hundred years will bring? We take it one day at a time. As I've told you countless times, as long as I'm with you, I can face anything."

"And the battles?"

She scrunched up her face. "I'll always worry about you in battle, but you're a Warrior. Then there's Britt's new serum. We'll get through anything."

"I can no' lose you, Gwynn."

"You won't."

Logan swallowed and glanced at the table. "Wallace went after Laura and captured her. He'll come for you and the other Druids as well."

"Are you forgetting that Laura was able to get away, and if she hadn't been able to do it, Charon would have gotten her? I've no doubt you would come for me."

"I'd walk through Hell itself to find you."

Logan had never thought he'd feel so strongly about anyone. Gwynn's answering smile filled him with peace and happiness. She had changed his life. There was nothing he wouldn't do for her.

"We are stronger together." Fallon's voice carried through the hall. "Remember that. Wallace will try to divide us."

Logan's mind began to spin with ways they could protect the castle. "He'll come here."

"And I'll make sure there isn't a place on MacLeod land he can touch without letting me know," Isla stated.

Fallon nodded. "Good. The castle itself has been spelled many times with protection, but let's get on that again."

"Right away," Reaghan said.

Quinn looked at Ian. "We need to get Charon and Laura here quickly."

"Let's no' forget Phelan and his Druid," Ramsey called out.

Fallon pointed to Ian. "Call Charon. Do whatever it takes to get him here. If he and Laura willna come willingly, I'll go get them myself."

Ian smiled wryly. "You doona know Charon at all if you think you can do that. He protects Ferness as you protect all of us here. Charon will stay to ensure none of the town is harmed because he wasna there to fight Wallace."

"He's right," Dani said. "We need to inform Charon and let him and Laura make their own decisions."

Tara lifted her hand in the air. "Laura is still learning her magic, so maybe some of us should go and strengthen the spells in Ferness again."

"I agree," Cara said. "We need to set alarms and spells for protection. There are too many innocents there for us not to do something."

Larena cleared her throat and slid her hands into the back pockets of her jeans. "I'll let Malcolm know the plan and see what he wants to do."

"What about Phelan and his Druid?" Arran asked.

Logan caught Fallon's gaze. "Charon should probably talk to him, but Charon is busy with his own problems. I'll give it a shot talking to Phelan."

"Good luck with that," Camdyn said sarcastically.

Logan ignored Camdyn. Phelan wasn't the most agreeable Warrior, but then again, few had had such a life as Phelan. Logan looked at Isla and saw Hayden whispering something in her ear.

Isla wanted Phelan's forgiveness for her part in his terrible life. Logan wasn't so sure Isla would ever get it. In the four hundred years since Isla had freed him from Cairn Toul Mountain, Phelan hadn't wanted any part of the castle or their little family.

"What are you thinking?" Gwynn asked.

Logan looked into his wife's amazing violet eyes and grinned. "Phelan has a Druid with him."

"Ah, you think he might have found his mate."

"It's possible. It's happened to each of us."

"Did Charon say how long Phelan had been with the Druid?"

Logan shook his head. "Nor did Phelan share her name. He's being secretive."

"Because Phelan wants her to himself," Gwynn said with a sly grin.

"As I want you."

Gwynn laughed as Fallon bade them to begin preparations. Logan watched her leave with the other Druids to being the spells. Already he was counting down the hours until she was in his bed.

CHAPTER
NINE

Phelan watched Aisley pick at her sandwich. He hadn't had a response to her declaration then, and certainly didn't now.

"If you could do anything, what would it be?" Phelan asked.

She lifted her gaze to him and simply stared. "What?"

"It's a simple question," he said with a nonchalant shrug. "If you're too afraid to answer then doona."

"I'm not afraid."

Phelan inwardly smiled. It was so easy to rile her. He shouldn't get such satisfaction out of it, but anything was better than the melancholy he'd been witness to.

"Well," he prompted when Aisley continued to sit there.

She licked her lips and looked over his shoulder, a faraway look coming into her eyes. Her midnight locks hung half in her face, but wherever she'd gone made her happy as evidenced by the small curve of her lips upward.

"I always wanted to be a dancer. My mum put me in classes when I was six. There's always been something about music that allows me to express myself as nothing else can."

Phelan could hear the longing in her voice, and a place in his chest began to ache for her. "Why didna you continue dancing? I've seen you. You come alive with the music."

She blinked and focused back on him. The small smile vanished. "I thought I wanted something else."

"What?"

"You're certainly pushy," she replied testily and reached for her soda.

Phelan moved his finished plate away. "I'm curious about you. More so because it appears as if dancing was your life. What changed?"

"A boy," she said. The forced smile that followed was as hollow as her eyes. "I was in love, you see. I did whatever he wanted."

"Why would you do that?"

"Good question. One my parents asked frequently."

"Was there an answer?"

She shook her head. "I knew I cared for him more than he cared for me, but I was sure it was love. When my parents wouldn't stop haggling us, he told me we should move in together. And we did."

"How did that go?"

"It was everything I thought it would be aside from the run-down place we were able to afford. That lasted all of five months. Then he began to use the money that was supposed to go to rent, food, and bills on alcohol and cigarettes."

Phelan slowly leaned back in his chair. He had a feeling the story was going to end badly.

Aisley tore off a piece of turkey from her sandwich and popped it into her mouth. "We had gotten notice from the landlord that we were to be evicted unless we came up with the three months' rent we owed on the flat. He promised me he'd have the money that evening when he came home from work."

Several minutes ticked by before Aisley raised her gaze to his. "Except he never came home."

Phelan wanted to find the prick who had done this to her and beat him to a bloody pulp. Twice. "What happened?"

"The landlord kicked me out. I barely had enough time to gather my clothes before he tossed me into the street. With nowhere else to go, I went back home. My parents welcomed me for a time."

"For a time?" he repeated with a frown. "What do you mean?"

Aisley rubbed one of her eyes. "It means I left again."

"Did they kick you out?"

"It doesn't matter," she answered cryptically.

Phelan knew there was more to the story. He was surprised she was giving him as much as she was, so he didn't push for more. Yet.

"Where did life take you after you left?"

Aisley shifted uneasily in her chair and looked around her as if she were noticing for the first time where she was. "I need my car."

"I'm sure it's been towed by now. You were in no condition to drive, and I couldna leave you there."

She shoved her hair out of her face. "I've been here too long. I need to go."

"What are you running from?" Phelan asked. "It can no' be me."

Aisley refused to answer. She had left out more of the story, he was sure. What could have happened in her life that was so bad that it sent her on the run?

"I can protect you," he heard himself offer.

Phelan wasn't sure what made him say it, but it seemed the right thing to do. Plus, it would keep Aisley with him. He was sure if he blinked, she'd be gone as it stood now.

"You?" she asked incredulously. "You would protect me?"

He leaned his forearms on the table and smiled. "You're a Druid, Aisley. You're meant to be protected at all costs. There are so few Druids now."

"You wouldn't be saying that if you knew me."

"You mean if I knew the part of the story you'd left out?" he asked. When she nodded, he gave a loud snort. "Lass, give me a little credit. I see the beautiful woman you are, inside and out. Besides, I know evil. I've fought it numerous times, and you are no' evil."

If you only knew.

Aisley didn't say the words aloud. She was being a coward, she knew. The right thing to do would be to tell Phelan exactly who she was. He would kill her, but it would be quick.

Jason would drag it out for days or weeks before he allowed death to claim her.

She opened her mouth to tell Phelan she was a *drough* when she remembered that she could make sure Jason was gone for good. If she had the courage. Phelan pushed his chair back and stood. He held out a hand to her after tossing down some money to pay for the food.

Aisley looked from his outstretched hand to his face.

"I've given my word I'd protect you. You doona need to fear me."

But she did. Not just because he was the enemy, but because of the attraction. Aisley welcomed the memories of the past because it had allowed her to forget the thrumming need for Phelan's touch.

That had only lasted a short time now. He wanted her to get back on the motorbike with him, to wrap her arms around him and not feel the hard muscle beneath.

Impossible.

"Aisley," he said with a frown. "I doona know what you're running from but nothing will harm you as long as I'm near."

It was too tempting of a proposition to pass up. Phelan would protect her from Jason. It would also put her in close proximity to Phelan's amazing body, piercing eyes, and charming tongue.

How long could she hold out against the desire? How long could she pretend her body didn't ache for his touch, that her lips didn't yearn to taste his kisses again?

She put her hand in his, knowing it was a mistake. It was an injustice she was serving him. She knew, and still did it. Because she was tired of running.

Aisley let him pull her to her feet, his rakish smile making her heart skip a beat. She turned in time to see a waitress slip a piece of paper into his front pocket while winking at him.

"Quite the womanizer, aren't you?" she said as she walked away.

His deep laugh followed her outside where she watched him discreetly toss the number in a trash bin. "I like women. I'll no' deny that. I always have. I see no reason to hurt her feelings however."

Aisley didn't want to like him more, but damn, it was difficult. He had helped her numerous times, and now offered his protection.

She hadn't lied earlier though. She was tired of existing. The day her baby died was the day she stopped living.

And now it was time to cease existing as well.

After she took care of one last thing—Jason.

She was going with Phelan for one night of bliss, one night full of pleasure. Then she would tell him who she was. He would be so enraged he'd kill her immediately. She'd have to talk quickly to convince him to wait until she confronted Jason.

Hell awaited her, but Jason wouldn't be able to touch her.

"What is it?" Phelan asked as they stood beside his motorbike.

Aisley put his helmet on. "Can you hide me for a day?"

"I can hide you for longer than that."

"Just a day," she said. "That's all I need."

Phelan's penetrating blue-gray eyes bore into her. He was searching for the truth, but he'd get it soon enough. Until then, her secrets were her own.

"You think one day will be enough to throw off whoever is on your scent?"

Aisley looked down the road to the south where she should be in England by now. "I'll never be free of him. There's only one way out for me."

"And that is?"

"Death."

Phelan grabbed her shoulders and made her look at him. "Have you lost your mind, beauty? There is always another answer before death."

"Is there? Do you have secrets so dear you wouldn't dare share them with anyone else?"

He jerked back and dropped his hands. "Is that what you have? Secrets?"

"I want my life back. I crave it as much as . . ." She trailed off right before she told him how much she wanted his kisses.

Now wasn't the time. But soon, very soon.

"What do you crave?"

His deep voice was smooth, soft. It made her skin prickle with need and her blood burn. He was seducing her with his voice.

It wasn't necessary. She'd been seduced the first time they kissed. Oh, she had tried to deny it, but there was no need to lie to herself anymore.

She wanted Phelan. Her body hungered for his touch, longed to have him against her.

He closed the space that separated them and lifted his hands to her face. Aisley held her breath, waiting for him to touch her. Instead, he fastened the helmet and stepped away.

She wanted to scream with frustration. Her body hummed with need. A need only Phelan could quench.

"Are you coming?" he asked with a twinkle in his eye after he climbed on the bike.

Aisley blew out a breath and got on behind him. She felt the steady thud of his heart when she wound her arms around him. Despite herself, she couldn't stop the grin when he released a laugh as they sped off.

The wind blew his long dark hair away from his face. She peered around his shoulder to see the satisfied smile on his face as he raced down the road.

If she craved him, Phelan yearned for the thrill of the wind on his face and the next conquest in his bed. She should be offended, but instead she found she admired him.

Deirdre had taken him and released his god. He could have given in and became evil, but Phelan persevered and won control over his god.

That's what made him different from Jason. The Warriors could have taken over the world. Instead, they were defending it.

Phelan embraced each day, living life to the fullest while she hid in her memories and pain. It was too bad she hadn't met Phelan before Jason had come for her.

Maybe then she'd have been strong enough to tell Jason to bugger off.

Then again, Jason never took no for an answer.

CHAPTER
TEN

Phelan turned off the paved road onto a back road. He kept the speed down mostly because he quite liked how Aisley's arms hugged him.

The first time he took a turn and her hands flexed against his stomach, he knew she wasn't the adrenaline junkie he was.

With her body plastered against his back, Phelan could think of nothing but divesting her of her clothes and touching every lovely inch of her.

He knew she had an amazing body—her tight clothes revealed a lot as she danced—but he longed to see her naked. Her mocha-colored skin begged to be caressed.

Phelan slowed the Ducati as he neared the loch. Even over the bike's engine he heard Aisley's sharp intake of breath when she caught a glimpse of the water.

He stopped and turned off the motor, simply staring at the sight that had stunned him from the first moment he saw it four centuries earlier and every time he visited since.

Out of the corner of his eye, he saw Aisley pull off the

helmet and run a hand through her midnight hair. Her lips were parted slightly, and her eyes took in everything.

He couldn't hold back the grin. It was a magnificent sight with the trees surrounding the loch and the mountains rising up in the distance.

"I think I could stand here and look at this forever," Aisley whispered.

Phelan grinned at her. "Aye. That's how I felt when I first saw this place."

"Where are we?"

"My home."

She raised a black brow. "Your home?"

"Aye," he answered with a chuckle. "Did you think a Warrior couldna have a home?"

Aisley shrugged, but she looked away hastily, causing Phelan to frown. She had almost said something, but he wouldn't push her.

"Is this where you grew up?" Aisley asked.

Phelan rested a hand on the handlebars and tried to pull up any memories he had of his parents. "Nay," he finally answered.

"It's beautiful and peaceful. And so quiet."

"A good place to escape for a while."

She cut her eyes to him. "Is that what you do when you come here? Escape?"

"Oh, aye. No one knows of this place. No one."

"Do you trust so few people?"

He contemplated her words, wondering why he'd never told Charon. "No one ever asked, and I didna volunteer the information."

"Your own private haven. I'm jealous."

"It's your private haven as well."

Her fawn-colored eyes turned to him. He spotted the uncertainty and trepidation in her gaze. She had said he didn't trust, but she was the one who didn't trust anyone.

Aisley had secrets aplenty, and he worried there wouldn't be enough time to get her to share them all.

Because he had a distinct feeling Aisley didn't plan on staying for long.

"Maybe it's not a good idea for you to take me to your home."

Phelan drew in a deep breath. "Why?"

"It's private. No one even knew you had such a place. Now I do. Aren't you worried I might tell someone?"

"It doesna matter if you do."

"What about me intruding on space that was yours alone?"

"I wouldna be bringing you if I didna want you there."

"Still. I think we should go somewhere else. To keep your place private."

Phelan turned to better see her. "What are you no' telling me, beauty?"

"A lot," she admitted. "A terrible lot, Phelan. Don't bring me to your house. You'll regret it. Trust me."

"It's just a structure. Nothing more."

"Not true. It's your sanctuary. No," she said when he started to interrupt her. "If you didn't care who knew about it, others would. You admitted no one else did. Don't ruin that now."

Phelan straightened. He was irritated at her rationale, mostly because he knew she was right. It hadn't been a whim that made him bring her here. He wanted her to see it. He just wasn't sure why. "Put the damn helmet on."

Just as she took a breath to argue, he started the Ducati and revved it. He glanced over his shoulder to see her quickly put on the helmet and buckle it.

She was a contradiction. One minute he wanted to protect her, and the other he wanted to throttle her. She was ridiculously stubborn, astonishingly beautiful, and grievously broken.

With any other woman, Phelan would bring her to bed, give her a night of pleasure, and leave before she woke. But with Aisley, he wanted to do more.

The crux of the matter was that he didn't know what to do. His only option for the moment was to keep her safe and gain her trust.

As soon as Aisley's arms wrapped around him, Phelan continued on the barely discernable dirt road. After a ten-minute drive that took them around the loch, Phelan caught a glimpse of his home.

Aisley was prepared to continue arguing with Phelan about taking her to his home while she ogled the forest around her. Heavy clouds rolled in, but not even that could dampen the stunning scenery around her.

She was so absorbed in the forest that when Phelan stopped the motorbike it took her a moment to see the house. It wasn't huge, but it was quaint and fit into the landscape perfectly.

Phelan shut off the Ducati and put his hands on his legs while his feet balanced the bike. She watched the pleased look come over his face, the small smile that told her he loved this place.

And she would ruin it by telling him who she was.

No. She refused to do it here. She'd find a way to leave and let him follow her. But there's no way she could let him kill her in his own home, a home he cherished. It was too cruel.

Aisley got off the bike and removed the helmet as she took in the house. It had a steep roof with a chimney sticking up through the far side of the roof. A porch extended off the front of the house and faced the loch that was only twenty feet from it.

There were roses, pansies, bluebells, and violas planted in a glorious array of color around the house and porch. A path led from the parking area on the side of the house around to the porch.

Aisley looked at Phelan, and he gave her a nod to tell her it was all right to go look. With his helmet still in hand, Aisley followed the path to the steps leading to the porch. Then, she turned and looked at the loch.

"How do you ever leave?" she asked as he slowly followed.

He waited until he stood beside her before he said, "It gets more difficult each time."

"If this was mine, I'd never leave."

"Then consider it yours for as long as you want."

Aisley jerked her gaze to his. She was used to being treated with disdain and hatred. It had been so long since anyone was nice that Aisley wasn't sure how to respond.

"I mean it," Phelan continued. "Stay as long as you'd like."

She looked away, her throat clogged with emotion. It was wrong for her to have allowed Phelan to help her in any way, shape, or form. She regretted it now more than ever. "Just one night. I'll stay one night."

He didn't say anything as he turned and pulled a key out of his pocket to unlock the door. Aisley took another few minutes to stare at the calm waters of the loch before she followed him inside.

There she came to a stop. The outside might be quaint and look more like a home built two hundred years ago, but the inside was completely modernized.

"Surprised, I see," Phelan said as he leaned a hip against the kitchen counter.

"Yes." Aisley laughed as she continued inside. "I think you spend more time here than you let on."

Phelan tossed the keys onto the small island. "I used to spend a lot of time here, but lately it seems all I've been doing is going to battle after battle fighting evil."

Aisley set the helmet down on the island and saw three bar stools tucked beneath the overhang of the countertop. She spotted her duffle lying near the couch. When he had brought that in?

"Make yourself at home," Phelan said. "I'm going to go pick us up some groceries."

Before she could form a response, he was out the door and on his bike. She watched him drive away, wondering if she should make a break for it now.

Then she remembered the feel of his muscles, the heat of his body as she'd leaned against him the entire ride. She recalled the feel of his arms as he lifted her when she had the migraine.

She remembered how he had quickly found her after the accident and gotten her onto his bike before the authorities came. Or worse—Jason.

Aisley shuddered. Leaving now would be the best thing, the right thing. But an image of Phelan's blue-gray eyes filled with desire flashed in her mind, and she knew she would stay.

"For just one night," she said to herself as she crossed her arms over her chest.

Though she'd never driven a motorcycle, she was already making plans to steal it in the wee hours of the morning and leave.

Phelan would find her. She knew that without a doubt. That's when she would tell him every sordid, ugly detail of her life. And ask for his help.

It wasn't death she was afraid of, it was the disappointment and fury she suspected to see in Phelan's eyes.

Jason had promised her she would be powerful. Becoming *drough* made her magic potent, but she was still the scared, pitiful, starving girl he'd found waiting for death in that alley.

He'd given her hope. Aisley hadn't realized how desperate she'd needed something to hope for, and she had grabbed it—and Jason's offer—with both hands.

Her father had called her weak.

Her mother had called her amoral.

Jason had called her devious.

Only one person had ever seen any good in her. Phelan.

She longed to believe Phelan when he said she was a good person, but Aisley knew the awful truth. She was evil and what part of her soul remained was destined for Hell.

There was one slim chance to do something good, and she was going to take it and pay whatever it cost to make sure Jason never harmed another person in this life or the next.

Something dropped onto her hand. Aisley reached up to swipe at her face and felt the wetness of tears.

"Damn you, Phelan," she said. "You've made me cry."

Tears—or any emotion—hadn't been possible while in Jason's company. It was a sign of softness, and as *droughs*, any emotion was forbidden.

For so long she kept everything she was feeling inside her. Aisley feared the day she gave in to everything, because it would likely consume her.

She removed the wide leather bracelet she wore on her right arm. It hid the two-inch scar on the inside of her wrist from the *drough* ceremony. Her watch hid the scar on her left wrist.

Keeping them hidden from Phelan would take some doing, but he deserved to hear the truth from her. Not by seeing the scars.

At least she didn't have her Devil's Kiss anymore. The small silver vial *droughs* wore around their necks holding a few drops of their blood had been one thing she refused to do.

Jason hadn't understood it, but he hadn't pushed her.

Aisley hated the Devil's Kiss more than she hated the scars on her wrists.

The scars she could lie about. The Devil's Kiss she couldn't.

Aisley turned on her heel and grabbed her duffle as she walked down the small hallway until she found the bathroom. A large claw-foot tub sat under a wide window overlooking the forest.

She wasted no time in turning on the water to fill the tub. A good soak would wash away the threat of tears. At least she prayed it did.

CHAPTER
ELEVEN

Charon tossed his mobile phone onto the couch as he strode to the floor-to-ceiling windows of the top floor of his building.

"Bad news?" Laura asked as she looked up from her book.

Charon stuffed his hands in the front pockets of his slacks and blew out a harsh breath. "He's no' answering his damned phone."

Laura set aside her book and rose from the couch. She walked barefoot to her husband and slipped her arms around his waist from behind.

She rose up on her tiptoes and whispered in his ear, "He might be busy. Phelan is quite the ladies' man."

"He answers, Laura. He always answers."

"Unless he can't," she reminded him. "If he was in trouble he'd let you know."

Charon turned his head slightly, his chin-length dark locks brushing her cheek. "I hope you're right. I'm concerned about the Druid who's with him."

"Why? Phelan knows the difference between *droughs* and *mies*. What are you worried about?"

"I doona know. Something just doesna seem right."

Laura walked around Charon until she stood in front of him. "Could it be you're upset that he didn't tell you he had a Druid with him?"

Charon pulled her into his arms and rested his chin atop her head. "He was my only friend for a long time. He's no' the settling down type."

"So you're worried about the Druid?"

"I doona know what the bloody hell I'm worried about. He didna tell me anything other than he had a Druid with him. No' her name or anything."

Laura closed her eyes and shrugged. "It could be a male. Not all Druids are female."

"It was a woman," Charon said. "If it wasna, Phelan would've had Fallon bring the Druid to the castle immediately."

"Hm. Then wait a little longer and call Phelan again. If he's on his motorbike, getting ahold of him isn't easy."

"And if he's encountered Wallace?"

Laura's eyes flew open. Just the thought of Jason Wallace made her skin crawl. She hoped she'd seen the last of him when she managed to escape his clutches. All thanks to one black-haired *drough*.

Aisley. Laura had wondered what happened to her during the battle at Dreagan. Her body wasn't with the rest of the dead. There was a possibility that Aisley could have gone wherever Jason went.

"We couldn't get lucky enough for Jason to be blasted into a gazillion pieces, could we?" Laura asked.

"It doesna appear that way."

"Why does evil always seem to win? Why do they always get the lucky breaks while we work our asses off just to stay alive?"

Charon rubbed his large hand up and down her back. "It's the way it's always been."

"Well, it sucks."

His chuckle reverberated through his chest. "That it does, sweetheart."

Laura lifted her head and looked at her husband. "Do you want to go to MacLeod Castle?"

"Only if you do. I willna force you."

"Will it make you feel better if I go?"

He shrugged his thick shoulders, his dark eyes holding hers. "I doona think it matters where we are. Wallace will attack. The other Druids will be here shortly to add their spells around the village."

"You know as well as I no spell will keep Jason out."

Charon smiled, showing her the fierce Highland Warrior she'd fallen in love with. "Nay, but it'll give us enough time to call the others or to get you to safety. I'm eager for another go at the bastard."

"You're not the only one. He did use his magic on me and try to turn me against you."

"But it didna work. You wanted my body too badly," he said smugly.

Laura stepped out of his arms. "Is that so?"

"Aye."

"And you didn't want this?" she asked as she pulled her thin cotton dress over her head, leaving her standing completely nude.

Charon's gaze darkened as desire took him. "You temptress. I didna know you were no' wearing any panties."

"I've got to keep you on your toes."

He reached for her, but Laura sidestepped him and started running for their bedroom. She barely made it through the door before his arms wrapped around her, and he had her pinned against the wall. Charon's mouth took hers in a fiery kiss as she clawed at his shirt until they were skin to skin.

* * *

Phelan put the kickstand down on his Ducati after he shut off the engine and delighted in the feel of Aisley's magic. He'd worried that she would take his absence as a chance to run. Halfway back to the house is when her magic wrapped around him, and he'd breathed a sigh of relief.

He got off the bike, reaching for his mobile in his back pocket at the same time to see who kept calling him. His lips compressed when he saw it was Charon. For several minutes Phelan contemplated returning the call. In the end, he knew he didn't have a choice.

Phelan pressed dial. Three rings later it went to voice mail. He waited for the beep, then said, "It's me. Everything is fine. I'm still with the Druid. There's also been no sign of Wallace. Let me know any news on your end."

He hung up the phone and went to pocket it when it rang. Phelan glanced down to see Logan's name pop up on the screen. He answered with a tight, "Hello?"

"How is everything on your end?"

"That depends on how things are going there."

Logan's chuckle came through the phone. "We've some news you might want to know. Britt is still a few days away from finishing her serum."

"This will combat whatever Wallace has done to the *drough* blood?"

"Aye."

"That is good news. I detect something in your voice though. What else is going on?"

Logan let out a long sigh. By the silence through the phone Phelan knew he was alone.

"Logan?"

"Things are strained here. Half want to believe Wallace is dead and concentrate on finding the spell to bind our gods. The other half are ready for battle."

Phelan rubbed his chin. "Which category do you fall into?"

"I wish I could say I believed Wallace is dead, but I know you wouldna lie about what you felt."

"I didna. It's Wallace's magic. I'd know it anywhere, just as Declan's and Deirdre's was distinctive. So is Wallace's."

"I believe you, Phelan. It's why I'm ready for battle. The Druids have been adding more spells to the castle. A few will be heading to Ferness to do the same there."

Phelan looked out over the loch, hating what Wallace was doing to them. "You know as well as I how easy it is to get through spells. Ramsey did it effortlessly enough at Wallace's mansion. He'll do it wherever he is."

"Aye, but it'll give us time. Isla is setting something up so that she'll be notified if anyone attempts to come through the spells or tries to break them."

It was everything Phelan could do not to growl at the mention of Isla's name. Instead he said, "What do you want of me?"

"We want to make sure everything is all right."

"It is."

"And the Druid?"

Phelan looked over his shoulder at his cabin. For whatever reason, he wasn't ready to share her with anyone else. "She's on the run from someone. I'm no' sure who, but until I am, I'm keeping her safe."

"Where are you?"

He hesitated a bit too long because Logan laughed and said, "You know all I have to do is ask Broc to find you."

"I know it all too well. If you must know, I'm about an hour south of Loch Ness."

Logan made a sound at the back of his throat. "I've often wondered if you had a place you went. That's where you're at now, is it no'?"

"Aye."

"We'll no' be bothering you unless it's necessary. Let me know if you need help with your Druid."

Your Druid.

Phelan hung up the phone with that phrase running through his mind. He quite liked it. He wasn't sure how Aisley would feel about it, which made him smile.

He pocketed his phone before he grabbed the bag of groceries he'd strapped to the back of the bike. Phelan hurried into the house and kicked the door closed behind him.

Aisley had been right. The house was his haven, his sanctuary. The only other people who knew of it were the caretakers he had when he knew he wouldn't return for a while.

There hadn't been a single instance in the four centuries after he built the house that he'd thought to ever bring a woman here.

Now, it seemed right, fitting even, that Aisley was there.

Phelan followed her magic to the bathroom. The door was open, allowing him to see her reclining in the tub staring out the window.

He leaned a shoulder against the door frame and smiled at the bubbles that were up to her chin. She grinned wickedly as if she knew he was watching her.

"I'm all pruny," she said as she lifted her feet from the water and wiggled her toes.

"Maybe it's time to get out then."

"I've been telling myself that for thirty minutes but this feels so good. And the view." She turned her face to him. "I saw a squirrel and there are birds galore. They love your flowers."

Phelan's smile grew. "I've got to check a few things around the place. Give a shout if you need me."

She gave him a little wave and turned back to the view.

Phelan put away the groceries and then went outside. He moved the Ducati to the shed on the other side of the house to keep it out of sight.

After checking the amount of firewood, he examined the plants. With cutters, he trimmed off the dead and wilted flowers in the front before pulling weeds. He walked around back once those were up to his standards.

Phelan loved sitting on his porch and looking over the loch, but the two chairs and small table situated in the middle of his rather large flower garden in the back ran a close second.

He found contentment in getting his hands in the soil and watching the plants grow. One of his favorite things was watching his garden come alive with color in the spring after the winter snows.

Phelan knelt next to one of the flower beds and began to pull weeds. The others would probably laugh if they saw him now, which is one reason he kept so much to himself.

Charon was the closest thing he had to a family, but Phelan didn't share everything with him. It was just in the last few years that he ever called anyone *friend*.

For four centuries he had been his only friend and confidante. After leaving Cairn Toul and Deirdre's clutches, Phelan had searched to discover who he was.

He wandered aimlessly while learning what society was and how he fit in. He had to learn about money, work, family, and relationships.

Phelan squeezed his eyes closed for a moment. Those first fifty years had been awful. He learned the hard way that he fit in nowhere.

When Isla freed him and she lay dying, she'd told him to seek out the MacLeods. Perhaps he should have, but he managed on his own. It had been painful, grim, and difficult most days, yet he'd gotten through.

He still didn't know much about family and less about relationships of any sort. He'd bedded his first woman a year after leaving Cairn Toul.

For the next week, he'd learned everything he could from the woman. Her husband returned from sea, and Phelan moved on to the next woman, and then the next.

He versed himself in how to charm women, to seduce them until they were putty in his hands. While other men studied economics, law, or medicine, Phelan's knowledge turned to carnal pleasures. There wasn't anything he didn't take the time to learn.

Women were his teachers and his studies. For the few hours he was theirs, they shared their bodies and pleasure. But no more.

Never more.

Phelan knew it was because he had a hard time relying on anyone. He'd never felt the need to spend more than one night with a woman, and then not even the entire night. Which is why he was having a difficult time wrapping his head around the fact he had brought Aisley to his home.

He pulled out a dead plant and tossed it aside. Next he checked the roots of the plant beside it and made sure it was covered adequately with soil.

Phelan wondered if Charon knew their friendship was something new to him. Most likely Charon did. It had been him, after all, who had told Phelan the story of how Warriors came to be and the role of the Druids.

For centuries, Phelan assumed all Druids were the same. He'd felt the difference in their magic, but to him, they were all evil creatures using their magic against everyone.

It wasn't until those at MacLeod Castle took a last stand against Deirdre and her new accomplice, Declan Wallace, that Charon convinced Phelan to join in and help the others.

The centuries of peace had been good, but he was a Warrior. He was meant for battle, blood, and death. And it had felt damn good going into the fray.

His god, Zelfor, the god of torment, had been truly satisfied during those skirmishes. There was no getting away from what he was. He could pretend he was just a man, but the lust for death, the joy of using his claws to slice open an enemy felt too good.

He was a monster with a tightly leashed primeval god inside him. His skin might turn a metallic gold when he unleashed his god. With gold claws, gold eyes, and impressive fangs, there wasn't anything tame about him.

Phelan looked down at his hand in the dark soil and saw the gold skin. He pulled his hand from the dirt and flicked off the remains from his claws.

"This is what I am," he murmured.

Zelfor rumbled his agreement inside him.

Phelan ran his tongue over the fangs that sprouted in his mouth. Aisley said she knew he was a Warrior, but how would she react if she saw him now?

That made his chest clench in dread. She was like that frightened kitten he'd found—skittish and afraid of its own shadow.

One wrong move and Aisley would disappear again. Phelan would track her the rest of his life if he had to, but he didn't want it to come to that.

He wanted her.

In his bed.

But more than that, he wanted her to need him.

CHAPTER
TWELVE

Aisley finished drying off. It had been months since she had the chance to soak in a tub without constant fear hounding her. She couldn't sense magic, so Jason could have sneaked up on her at any time. At least with Phelan, he'd alert her to another Druid's presence.

She turned to hang the towel up on the hook and paused to look at the magnificent flower garden. From her vantage point in the tub all she'd caught was a few glimpses of tall flowers, but this was a surprise.

It was probably a good thing she hadn't seen it before she got in the tub, or she'd never have taken the bath. There was a memory she'd held onto of when she was six years old and her parents had taken her to Royal Botanic Garden in Edinburgh.

Aisley smiled, recalling how much she'd loved running up and down the paths, flowers flowing on either side of her. She had felt just like a princess that day.

Phelan's flower garden rivaled the botanic garden. She couldn't believe the array of flowers he had. From white to dark red, bright yellow, vibrant purple, and every color in between. It was like a rainbow had exploded and dripped the colors upon the flower petals. His caretakers must spend hours every day out here.

She was clasping her bra when movement in the garden caught her eye. That's when she spotted Phelan on his knees tending the plants. His hands were quick and thorough, proving he obviously knew what he was doing.

This Aisley hadn't expected. She hurried to dress and went into the kitchen to make some tea. The kitchen window over the sink looked out to the garden, and Aisley found herself watching Phelan instead of the flowers.

She poured two mugs of tea then headed outside. When she came to the steps leading into the backyard from the porch that wrapped around the sides of the house, she paused.

Phelan seemed more relaxed since they'd arrived. She'd seen him in battle, knew how fierce and savage he could be. But the man who was tending the flowers was a contradiction she didn't know how to puzzle out.

His long dark locks were pulled back in a queue and tied with a leather string. She smiled. Phelan might live in modern times, and he might have experienced over five centuries of time, but he was still a medieval Highlander.

That appealed to her on a level that made her take a step back in caution. She thought she'd known the Warrior before her, when in fact she knew nothing other than his ability to fight with deadly accuracy.

Had he been the one to kill Mindy in the woods? She knew without a doubt she'd have met the same fate had she been the one to chase after the Warriors.

That thought was a cold dose of reality.

Phelan, for all his handsomeness, kindness, and strength wasn't someone she could rely on for long. Whether she tried to hide the knowledge she was a *drough* or outright told him of her involvement with Jason, he would find out.

Aisley knew all about trying to keep secrets. She closed

her eyes as a wave of anguish poured over her. Her love and need for her baby, even after all these years, still had the ability to rip through her like the sharpest of blades.

"Aisley?"

She snapped open her eyes to find Phelan staring at her from his place on the ground. Aisley drew in a shaky breath and pushed aside thoughts of her daughter as she held out a mug. "I made tea."

"That sounds good."

She stepped barefoot off the steps and onto the cool grass before walking to the two chairs set in the middle of the garden.

Phelan met her at the chairs and took one of the mugs. "I didn't know how you liked your tea," she said.

"One sugar."

"Good. That's how I take mine."

They shared a smile before they each took a seat in the chairs angled toward each other. Aisley didn't find the silence that followed uncomfortable. The chirping of birds and the rustle of leaves as the wind whispered through the trees was comforting. She leaned her head back against the chair and simply took it all in.

"You really enjoy it here," Phelan said.

Aisley grinned. "I do. My parents lived in Perth. They liked the city life and the noise of it all. I didn't know anything else until later. I prefer country life."

"You're far away from shops and restaurants."

She shrugged and turned her head to look at him. "I'm an awful cook, but I could do without restaurants for the most part. As for shopping, that I couldn't give up altogether. Every couple of months or so would be nice."

"You like it because you feel hidden."

"That's why you chose it." His brows rose at her response, and he smiled before lifting the mug to his lips.

Aisley looked back at the flowers. "You did all this, didn't you?"

"Aye. Surprised?"

"Yes. And, oddly, no."

"What does that mean?" he asked.

Aisley shrugged and wrapped both hands around her mug. She contemplated her answer as she sipped the tea. "I know about Warriors. You're supposed to be the best fighters in your bloodline. I assumed all you thought about was battle."

"In some ways, aye. Especially when there is evil to fight. My God isna satisfied unless I'm in the midst of battle."

She looked at him once more. "Then I'm not surprised. Because . . . well, because this suits you. When we arrived I saw the tension ease out of you. You are part of this land, and it's a part of you."

"Where did you learn your knowledge of Warriors?" he asked.

"My family." Aisley prayed he didn't ask if she had known a Warrior. She couldn't tell him about Dale. The Warrior had saved her several times from Jason and other things. He died saving her from the white-skinned monsters who had gone after Jason.

Aisley barely suppressed a shudder just thinking of the creatures. She missed Dale's quiet presence, how he'd always stood between her and Jason. He had wanted more from her, but had been content with friendship.

"I gather your family didna like Warriors."

She mentally shook herself when Phelan's voice broke into her thoughts. "I wouldn't say that. I know the story of how Warriors were created. I know it took both sects of Druids to bind the gods inside the men."

"So you know it was Deirdre who began to unbind the gods seven centuries ago."

"Yes."

"Do you know there were Warriors who banded together with Druids to fight Deirdre?"

Aisley nodded. "Then she disappeared for four hundred years."

"Do you know why?"

What did she tell him? The truth? She didn't want to lie, but her omission of who she was was also a lie. From what she knew of Phelan, she didn't doubt he would react severely to being betrayed. Aisley took a drink of tea before she said, "Tell me what you think happened."

"A man named Declan Wallace brought her forward into this time. Except he didna take just her. At the time she had just taken the head of one of the Warriors from MacLeod Castle. That Warrior's twin brother knew instantly of his death. That connection, combined with Declan's magic brought Ian forward in time as well."

Aisley listened with interest. She knew of the MacLeods, but only what Jason had wanted to tell her. Dale hadn't said much about them other than that they were damned hard to kill.

But that could be said for any Warrior.

"Since Ian disappeared while inside the castle, surrounded by the Warriors and Druids, they knew they had to do something. Four unmated Warriors agreed to allow the Druids to send them through time to search for Deirdre and Ian."

"The Druids had the magic to move them through time?" she asked incredulously.

Phelan smiled wryly. "I doona think the evil we fight realize how strong the Druids at the castle truly are. *Droughs* use their black magic to battle by themselves, and they are strong. However, a group of *mies* banded together has more magic than a single *drough*."

Jason, the bastard, had never told her that. She was

learning so much she hadn't known. All the times they'd clashed in battle Aisley had thought those from Mac-Leod Castle were just lucky.

Now she knew it was because of their strength and power. It was a sobering thought.

"What happened? Were Ian and Deirdre ever found?"

Phelan's smile held a wealth of satisfaction. "Oh, aye. Ian came across a Druid searching for the MacLeods. That Druid, Danielle, became his wife."

"And Deirdre? I know the tales of the terror she'd evoked across the land." That Aisley wasn't lying about. Jason had reveled in the stories he'd found of Deirdre. He'd admired her beyond anything.

"The MacLeods discovered there were artifacts that, if gathered, could destroy Deirdre."

"You keep saying 'the MacLeods' as if you weren't part of them."

He looked away from her and let out a long sigh. "I wasna."

Aisley's mouth dropped open in shock. "You fight with them now though?"

"I do. When they've need of me."

"I don't understand." The more she learned about Phelan the more complicated he became.

He shrugged and watched a kingfisher land on one of the feeders. "I didna join the MacLeods' fight until a few years ago. There were . . . reasons."

"Tell me about the artifacts." She wanted to know his reasons for waiting to join the MacLeods, but Aisley could tell he wasn't ready to share them. So she turned to the next thing she was curious about. She'd never heard of these artifacts.

Phelan grinned wickedly. "The first artifact was a Druid—Reaghan. She knew the location where Deirdre's twin sister was kept."

"What?"

"She was the only one who could kill Deirdre, so Reaghan and her group of Druids spelled her so she'd sleep, hidden, until someone with all the artifacts woke her."

Aisley was riveted. "Well? What happened?"

"Deirdre was after the artifacts herself. With them, she became unbeatable. It was a race between her and the MacLeods to see who would find them all first."

"You said the first artifact was Reaghan. Who found her?"

Phelan drank more of his tea. "Galen. He and Logan were sent to search for the artifact. No one expected the artifact to be a person, or for Reaghan and Galen to fall in love."

"They're together?"

"Aye."

Aisley ran her thumbnail along the arm of the chair. "And the other artifacts?"

"That was Broc and Sonya. Broc has wings," Phelan said. "The bastard can fly. Sonya doesna just have healing magic, but she also communicates with the trees. Broc and Sonya had to look for an ancient Celtic burial mound for the next artifact."

"Did they get it?"

"They did. I came upon them, though I had no idea who they were. Deirdre was near, and I was willing to help anyone she was fighting. When she attacked, I made sure Broc and Sonya were able to get away."

"Did they know it was you?"

He shrugged one shoulder. "It wasna long after that when Deirdre came across Logan and Duncan on their way to Mallaig to look for the next artifact. Deirdre killed Duncan then."

"And was transported through time."

"Right," he said with a wink.

Aisley couldn't look away from his blue-gray eyes. She knew without a doubt he was telling her the truth. It was no wonder everyone hated *droughs*.

It wasn't just because they gave their souls to Satan for black magic, but because they ruined everything. She didn't want to think about the time Phelan would look at her with hatred. But it was coming.

It was coming all too soon.

CHAPTER
THIRTEEN

Phelan knew something troubled Aisley, and he doubted it was his story. The lost look he'd seen in her fawn-colored eyes vanished for a time. It had returned with a vengeance.

"Logan was one who volunteered to have the Druids move him through time," Phelan continued. "He looked for Ian while on his way to Mallaig for the artifact."

"He expected it to still be there?"

"He hoped it was. Turns out it was. He discovered that with the help of Gwynn. She was a Druid who knew nothing of her magic. She was a descendent of those on Mallaig, and the Keeper of the artifact Logan searched for. She was the only one who could get it."

Aisley's lips lifted in a smile. "And she did. We Druids are strong."

"Without a doubt. Yes, she retrieved it, and Logan and Gwynn returned with it to the castle."

"Are they . . . did Logan and Gwynn get together?"

Phelan stretched his legs in front of him and crossed them at the ankle. "Noticing a pattern, are you?"

"Looks that way."

"It seems Warriors are destined to be with Druids.

Each of the Warriors felt the magic of their woman differently than others."

Aisley crossed her legs in the chair. "Was there just the three artifacts?"

"Nay. In the burial mound Broc and Sonya found there were two, a pendant and a sword. The Tablet of Orn that Gwynn and Logan found was part of it. Ian knew the code to unlock the Tablet, but they still lacked a key."

She chuckled. "Let me guess. The key was the next artifact?"

"They didna know. Turns out, Danielle, who was searching for MacLeod Castle, had the key. With the Tablet fully unlocked they found a map. That map led them to the location Deirdre's twin was hidden."

He paused, wondering how he would have factored in on things had he joined the MacLeods after escaping Cairn Toul.

"Don't leave me hanging," Aisley said. "Finish."

Phelan watched the way the afternoon sun danced over her mocha-colored skin. "They were able to find the opening that led beneath the ground just as Deirdre arrived. It took all the artifacts to get them through the maze. However, the toughest part fell on Camdyn and Saffron."

"Who are they?"

"Camdyn is, of course, a Warrior. Saffron a Seer. Declan Wallace kidnapped her, blinded her, and tortured her to get to her visions. It was when the MacLeods attacked the Wallace mansion that Camdyn found Saffron and brought her back to the castle."

Aisley's forehead was creased in a deep frown. "Is she still blind?"

"Dani was able to use her magic of finding things to search Saffron's mind for the spell Declan used. It took some doing, but Dani, with the help of the others, was able to reverse Declan's spell. When they found Deirdre's twin and woke her, the MacLeods were missing one last item. A Torrachilty Druid."

"Which is?" she asked with a wrinkle of her nose.

"I'd hoped you'd know. They were the most powerful of all Druids. They were also known as warrior Druids. The magic was so unstable and potent, that if it passed to the women, they went mad with it."

Aisley rolled her eyes. "Oh, please. That's the men's way of looking for an excuse to kill the women and keep the magic for themselves."

"Mayhap you're right." Phelan couldn't stop the laugh that bubbled up. "The Torrachilty Druids were wiped out by Deirdre."

"So the MacLeods didn't have the last item they needed."

"No' true. Turns out there is one Torrachilty Druid left. Ramsey. Who also just happened to be a Warrior."

Aisley's eyes grew huge. "And Deirdre didn't know it?"

"She had no idea. With everything in place, there was one last battle. Deirdre was killed, but Declan escaped."

"You make it sound so easy."

Phelan snorted. "It was anything but. Declan brought his mercenaries who had bullets filled with *drough* blood. They were called X90s. Deirdre had her wyrran that she created. By the saints how I hated those yellow-skinned buggers."

"You were part of this battle?"

"Me and Charon both. Neither of us joined the Mac-Leods earlier, and when I discovered there was another Warrior about, I approached him. He convinced me to help the MacLeods with him."

Aisley lowered her mug to her lap. "I gather the battle was bad."

"Any battle is awful. With Laria, Deirdre's twin, now risen, she and Deirdre were locked in combat. Deirdre was betrayed by one of her own, Malcolm, who just happened to be cousins to the only female Warrior, Larena. Who is married to Fallon MacLeod, the eldest of the brothers."

Aisley seemed to retreat at the mention of Larena's name. He frowned as she looked down at her lap, more interested in her mug than the story she had urged him to tell.

"Does it surprise you there is a female Warrior?"

She shrugged.

"Deirdre unbound Malcolm's god and promised him Larena would be spared if he did as she commanded. So Malcolm agreed. In the end, he betrayed Deirdre just as Saffron said someone would."

Aisley lifted her gaze back to his. "Deirdre died then."

"Aye, and her twin with her. None of us could rest, however, since there was still Declan."

"How was he killed?"

"Agonizingly," Phelan said with a smile. "It was Ramsey who ultimately killed Declan. But the magic Ramsey had to use to do it took him. The only one to save him was Tara, his woman, who happened to be a descendent of a Torrachilty Druid."

"Wait. I didn't think women could hold the magic of a Torrachilty without going insane."

"It's true. They can no'. Tara's mother went insane because of it. Tara's entire family are *droughs*, and when she refused to undergo the ceremony, her mother tried to kill her. It was the unstable magic within her that helped bring Ramsey back. If you talk to the women at the castle, they'll say love had something to do with it as well."

Aisley cut him a look. "Are you telling me you don't believe in love? After hearing how all the Warriors are with Druids?"

Phelan sat forward in the chair and shook his head. "I see the love between them. I've never loved anything, so I doona know what they feel."

"Love is wonderful," she said. "Wonderful and amazing. It can lift you as high as the moon in one breath, and then rip your heart out the next. It can save. And it can destroy."

The way her voice faded to a whisper made Phelan want to go to her and take her in his arms.

Aisley cleared her throat and swallowed. "The evil isn't gone, is it?"

"Nay. I fear it never will. There was a year of nothing after we ended Declan. And then Jason Wallace showed up. He's more ruthless than Declan, more cunning than Deirdre. It might take longer than we want, but we'll kill Jason."

"You don't care about your own safety?"

Phelan grinned. "The ancient Celts considered Rome evil. The first Warriors were created to fight that evil. I was made for this, Aisley. Whether I live or die makes no difference."

"That's a load of shit."

He threw back his head and laughed. "Ah, lass. You may be right, but it's the truth. I know each time I go into battle I may never return. It was the way of my ancestors, and it's my way now. What other choice do I have?"

"You said MacLeod Castle had Druids. Let them fight Jason."

Phelan ran a hand down his face. There was no smiling for him now as he thought of the hell Charon had gone through when he'd thought he lost Laura.

"Nay," Phelan finally answered. "The Warriors treasure their mates beyond all else. Every time the Druids leave the castle they chance death. For a Warrior, immortal and powerful, to stand aside and allow a mortal to fight is no' even worth considering."

"The Druids aren't without resources. You said a group of *mies* is more powerful than a *drough*."

He cocked an eyebrow at her. "You're Scottish, beauty. You know how we Highlanders protect our family. A Warrior couldna call himself a man, much less a Highlander, if he allowed his woman to fight instead of him."

"How many Warriors have been killed fighting evil?"

"Too many to count."

She licked her lips. "You spoke of the X90 bullets. The evil you battle doesn't have to get close to use them."

"I know. It's a chance we take to protect the world. A chance I willingly take, regardless of the consequences."

Aisley sat there looking lost and so damned beautiful that Phelan had to fight to stay in his seat and not reach for her. He could turn her mind off their conversation with pleasure. She might have willingly come with him to his home, but he wasn't sure if she was ready for more.

Phelan shifted in the chair to ease his aching cock. It seemed strange that he was even contemplating going to bed alone.

It had been over two months since he'd had a woman. Two months of following Aisley. Two torturous months of needing her, longing for her. But never having her.

Here she was, sitting just feet from him, and instead of seducing her, he was trying to think of ways he could gain more of her trust.

What the hell was wrong with him?

Before he would have charmed and seduced her, and had her in his bed before midnight. But it wasn't just sex he thought about with Aisley.

He worried if she was warm enough, if the food he bought was to her liking, and if she felt safe with him.

Phelan contemplated calling Charon. His friend would

know how to handle Aisley, but then Phelan couldn't imagine sharing her with anyone else.

"Where were you going?" Phelan asked to take his mind off the constant flow of questions he kept asking himself.

Aisley's fawn-colored eyes turned to him. "When?"

"Before the accident. It appeared you were headed out of Scotland."

"I was," she answered softly.

"How far were you planning to run?"

"As far as it took."

Her evasive answer told him a lot. "You had a plan."

"Yes. I was going to try and disappear in London for a bit before heading into France."

He watched her thumb trace the top of her mug. Phelan thought of the accident. There had been no one in front of Aisley. No car she could have hit.

Phelan looked at her profile. She trusted him enough to be there with him, but not nearly enough to tell him what she was running from.

"How did the accident happen? I was several cars behind you and couldna see."

For long moments, she sat there in silence. Phelan didn't push her. If he knew who she was running from, he could better protect her.

As it was, he was probably putting her in more danger just by being with her. Wallace was back. He'd already made it clear he had no problem attacking anyone close to a Warrior for ultimate damage.

Phelan's gut clenched thinking of Wallace harming Aisley.

"I heard a voice," Aisley said.

Phelan was pulled out of his thoughts. "A voice?" he repeated with a frown. "I doona understand, beauty."

"In my head. I heard a voice in my head."

Phelan leaned forward and braced his forearms on his knees. All his attention focused on her. "What did this voice say?"

"My name."

CHAPTER
FOURTEEN

Ullapool

Malcolm stood in the overgrown hedges and looked at Wallace Mansion. It hadn't been repaired since their last battle there. Still, there was something evil about the house.

But just like Declan, Malcolm knew Jason would return to the mansion. It was in his nature. The question was, would Malcolm wait for him?

Malcolm's feet crunched on the rock as he walked toward the front door that lay upon the ground. He took the few steps and paused at the doorway.

Dirt and dust littered everything. The smell of rotting food reached him from the back of the house where the kitchen was. But the only occupants in the house were animals, not human.

Malcolm sent Phelan a quick text and turned on his heel. He would go looking for Wallace's associates.

MacLeod Castle

"Nothing more from Phelan or Charon?" Hayden asked from across the table.

Ramsey blew out a breath and shrugged. They hadn't moved from the table in the great hall. A mug of ale sat in front of him, but Ramsey's mind was too occupied with thoughts to want to drink it. "Nothing."

"What now?" Arran asked from beside Hayden. "I'm no' going to be able to sit and wait much longer."

Ramsey motioned to the adjoining room with his chin. Aiden sat on the couch with Britt snuggled against him. They had both fallen asleep during the previews of the movie they put in. "We let Britt rest, and then hopefully she'll have good news for us."

"Isla wants Broc to find Phelan."

Ramsey shifted his gaze to Hayden. The lines bracketing Hayden's mouth showed the worry his friend was under. "Has she asked Broc yet?"

"Nay. She wants me to do it."

Arran set down his mug after a long drink of ale. "I gather you're no' too keen on the idea."

Hayden's black eyes met Ramsey's. "No' at all. Phelan has made it clear he wants nothing to do with my wife. I doona want her near him."

"Who says she has to get near him?" Arran asked.

Ramsey shoved his ale toward Hayden when Hayden emptied his. "If Broc does as Isla asks, then she'll want Fallon to teleport her to him. She willna rest until Phelan forgives her for what she did to him."

"Which isna likely to happen," Hayden ground out and wiped his arm over his mouth. "I willna put Isla in harm's way, and with Phelan near, she's always in danger."

Arran narrowed his golden eyes. "Phelan fights with us. He wouldna harm Isla."

"He would," Hayden argued. "He hunts *droughs* as I once did. I remember all too well the hatred that burned inside me. It pushed aside all reason until only vengeance and retribution remained. As long as Isla is no' alone, Phelan will leave her be."

"The moment she isna," Ramsey said, "there's no telling what he'll do."

Arran raked a hand through his dark brown hair and slowly shook his head. "I almost miss the days when we only had Deirdre to worry over. Now it's Wallace, the selmyr, finding the spell to bind our gods, and a multitude of other things."

"I gather Ronnie isna sleeping well either," Ramsey said.

Arran grunted. "She's a worrier. She worries endlessly about things she can no' control."

"I think most of the Druids are concerned," Ramsey replied.

Arran looked from Ramsey to Hayden. "We were no' here during those four centuries while we were tossed into the future. How were things?"

"Do you mean were there arguments?" Hayden asked. At Arran's nod, Hayden said, "Oh, aye. We're like any family. There were bickering, tears, laughter, anger, joy, hope, and every other emotion you can think of. Why?"

"I think Ronnie is having second thoughts of being here."

Ramsey squeezed the bridge of his nose. "This is what Wallace wants. He wants to fracture us. He wants to make the Druids doubt their lives with us."

"Isla hasna said anything about children, but I see how she looks at little Emma, I remember how she held Aiden when he was an infant." Hayden sighed deeply. "The fact she hasna said anything cuts me deeper than if she had. I just want her to be happy."

"She is," Arran answered. "She's with you. You may see how she looks at Camdyn and Saffron's baby, but we see how Isla looks at you. You, you stubborn fool, are her entire life."

Hayden's frown turned into a goofy grin. Ramsey gave a nod of approval to Arran. "He's right, Hayden. Isla has no' said anything because it does no good."

"You're probably right," Hayden said and lifted his mug for a long drink. "Arran was correct. It's different for those of us who lived the four centuries without any evil. All of us considered growing our families, but we knew what awaited us in the future. We saw how Quinn and Marcail constantly fretted over Aiden."

Ramsey nudged Arran's foot beneath the table to get his attention. "Why do you think Ronnie has changed her mind?"

"She seems restless. I rarely see her smile anymore. And at night when she thinks I'm asleep, I hear her cry."

Ramsey looked around the hall. One of their greatest strengths was the love each of them shared. Had Wallace managed to do the unthinkable and crack what was unbreakable?

"Next time, idiot, reach for her instead of listening to her," Hayden told Arran.

Ramsey found Tara standing in the kitchen doorway. Her pale brown locks fell in waves over her shoulders. She nodded to something someone said, and then her blue-green eyes turned to him. She smiled, and as usual, his heart missed a beat.

"How are things between the two of you?" Arran asked.

Ramsey drew in a long breath. "Tara is afraid to have children and pass on her unstable magic. Mixed with my magic from my Torrachilty roots, there's no telling what could happen if the child is female."

"Ah. But if it's male," Hayden said. "Tara's magic is

diluted several times over, and no' a direct line to that potent magic as yours is. We could have another powerful Druid."

Ramsey looked down at the table, the wood worn smooth from centuries of use. "You didna see what became of the females who tried to control the magic. It's fifty times more powerful than what our Druids are used to. It's addictive and wonderful. We were known as the warrior Druids because it took a warrior's control, strong mind, and even stronger body to harness the power. I'm no' saying women can no' do it, only it's more difficult for them."

He paused when he felt Tara's magic near him. She wrapped her arms around his neck and kissed his cheek. "That, lads, is the reason we won't be having children. The Torrachilty people did what they had to do, but I'm not willing to kill my daughter just because she's born a girl."

"You could help her harness the magic," Hayden said. "Look at Larena. She's strong. You're strong."

Ramsey smiled at Tara. This is a conversation they'd had many times. He respected her thoughts on it, and he agreed with them.

He pulled her into his lap and held her tightly. Together they were whole.

"No," Tara said. "None of you realize what I grew up with, the damage I did because I didn't know what I was or what to do with my magic. Even if we were able to teach our daughter, the chances of her going insane from the sheer power of the magic is too great a risk. I was given Ramsey. That's enough," she finished and looked at him.

Ramsey's blood surged with need. At Tara's smile he stood with her in his arms. "You'll have to excuse us. I need some alone time with my wife."

Arran watched Hayden silently get to his feet and walk

to Isla. After a few whispered words, the two started up the stairs.

It didn't take Arran but a second to locate Ronnie in the kitchen. He stood and walked into the kitchen to find her with her hands and front covered in flour.

She lifted her head when he walked in and gave him a smile. "I'm learning to bake a cake."

He strode to her and pulled her into his arms for a deep kiss. She melted against him, her arms sliding around his neck. His body burned for her. It had from the moment he'd first seen her, and it would until his heart beat its last.

Arran ended the kiss to see her lips swollen and her eyes dazed. "Let someone else bake the cake."

Ronnie nodded. "Yes. Someone else can bake the cake."

Arran took her hand and quickly led her up the stairs to their room. When the door closed behind him, he turned and pushed her against it while covering her body with his.

"I want you."

"I know," she said with a laugh as she reached between them and wrapped her hand around his arousal.

"Nay, Ronnie, listen to me. I want *you*. Always you. It's enough for me, but I'm no' sure if it's enough for you."

She blinked her hazel eyes, the smile sliding from her face. "You've heard me crying."

"Aye."

"It's not what you think, Arran. Before you my work was my life. I knew the chances of finding a man and having a normal life weren't for me. That meant no children."

"You doona want bairns?"

She put her hand covered in flour on his chest over his heart. "I'd love to have your children. If it happens, it happens. If it doesn't, as you said, we have each other. And that's enough for me."

"Then why the tears?"

"Because I know others aren't all right with that. Larena for one. She's barely holding it together. She's obsessed with finding the spell to bind your gods."

Arran pushed a lock of her wheat-colored hair behind her ear. "And you?"

"I've told you what I think of it," she replied with a roll of her eyes. "I fell in love with who you are now. If you want to live as a mortal, then I support that. If you want to remain a Warrior and continue to fight against evil, I'll be standing beside you. Either way, Arran MacCarrick, you'll not be rid of me."

"Never," he said and kissed her slowly, thoroughly. He heard the seams rip as he yanked off her apron, but her sigh was all the encouragement he needed to divest her of her clothes as soon as he could.

Their laughter filled the room as they helped each other out of their clothes and fell in a tangle of limbs upon the bed.

Arran ran his hand down the side of her face. "I love you beyond words, beyond meaning . . . beyond anything, Ronnie."

"And I love you, husband."

They shared a smile as he kissed her again.

CHAPTER
FIFTEEN

Phelan stood on the porch and leaned his hands on the railing as he looked out over the loch. The evening had been wonderful. The most perfect evening he'd ever had.

Dinner had been a simple affair of steaks, bread, and carrots. Turns out Aisley has a particular hatred for carrots. Phelan smiled as he recalled her story of how her parents made her eat her helping of carrots when she was six.

He and Aisley had talked of nothing and everything. Phelan noted how careful she was not to bring up her past or much about herself. She didn't ask questions of him either.

Not that he had anything to hide. There wasn't any kind of pressure to dazzle her with witty conversation or do one of his many tricks to seduce.

Phelan couldn't remember the last time he had such an enjoyable meal. The desire for her never dissipated. To his chagrin, it grew.

The brush of their hands as he'd passed her the wine-glass singed him, causing a bolt of something primal and urgent to zing through him.

Phelan inhaled a breath of Scottish air and looked up at the moon. It was full, its light glowing like a beacon in the sky. The clouds drifted in front of the moon, causing a faint haze to appear like a ring around it. The real beauty was how the moonlight hit upon the clouds, outlining them.

It was nearing midnight. Aisley had been asleep for a couple of hours. Already Phelan had checked on her twice. Each time it was more and more difficult to leave her room.

How easy it would be to climb in bed beside her and arouse her body while she slept. By the time she woke, she'd be in such a state of need that she wouldn't turn him away.

"What have I come to?" he asked himself in a soft whisper.

An owl hooted from a nearby tree in answer.

Phelan needed something to cool his lust. He briefly thought about a swim in the loch but didn't want to be that far from Aisley. He opted for a cold shower instead.

He straightened and entered the house. He tugged off his shirt and unbuttoned his jeans by the time he reached the bathroom. Phelan shut the door quietly before he quickly removed his boots and jeans. Only then did he turn on the water.

He stepped into the shower and gritted his teeth as the cold water hit him. It did very little since he hardly felt the cold thanks to his god.

Phelan put his hands on the tiled wall and let his chin drop to his chest as the water fell down his neck and back. He looked at the floor of the shower, suddenly thankful it was six feet long, since he had a suspicion he'd be spending the night there.

*   *   *

Aisley stared at the ceiling, one hand over her forehead and the other across her stomach. She hadn't lied to Phelan when she claimed exhaustion and went to bed. At the time she couldn't keep her eyes open.

It wasn't long after she fell asleep when the dream that had plagued her for months returned. Except this time Phelan was doing much more than kissing her.

His hands, his big, calloused hands were caressing her body. Touching her in just the right places, making her moan and squirm with need.

She'd woken just before the orgasm.

After that, sleep had been far from her mind. The last time Phelan had come to check on her, she had almost asked him to stay.

He wanted her. She could see the desire in his eyes. Mostly he tried to hide it, but it was there. What she couldn't understand was why he hadn't made a move toward her.

At the club two months ago he hadn't taken no for an answer and kissed her before she knew what was happening. Today he'd treated her with kid gloves. Almost as if he expected her to break at any moment.

The worst part was when she told him she'd heard the voice in her head whispering her name. Instead of asking her questions about who it could be, he'd simply gotten to his feet and began to talk about dinner.

Just when she thought she understood Phelan, he changed. No matter how he kept her mind in knots, her body knew what it wanted.

Him.

She looked to the door when she heard the shower turn on. He was still awake. The question was, did she have the guts to go to him?

Aisley sat up and wrapped her arms around her legs,

which she'd drawn up to her chest. It had been years since she'd slept with anyone.

She imagined him naked in the shower, the water running over his tall, muscular form, and her mouth went dry.

Without another thought Aisley threw off the covers and rose from the bed. She opened her door and walked to the bathroom. There was a moment's hesitation when she placed her hand on the doorknob.

Her lips tingled, reminding her how much she had enjoyed his kiss. That's all it took to give her the courage to open the door.

But being in the bathroom was altogether different than stepping into the shower with him.

Aisley watched his silhouette through the shower door as he stood still as a statue. She drew the shirt over her head and slid her panties down her legs.

Phelan knew Aisley was in the bathroom. He'd felt her magic come toward him as soon as she left her room. He held his breath, waiting to see what she would do.

And then the shower door opened.

His gaze clashed with hers as he straightened. He might have seen her in skimpy clothes at the club but nothing prepared him for the sight of Aisley nude.

Phelan let his eyes travel down her face to her dark-tipped nipples and full breasts to the narrow indent of her waist and her flared hips. His balls tightened when he saw her lean legs and the triangle of black curls hiding her sex.

His gaze jerked back to her face. A silent question lurked in her eyes. There was desire and need, but a hint of fear as well. Not fear of him, but fear of rejection.

He held out one hand to her and turned on the hot water with his other. As soon as her hand was in his, Phelan gently tugged her into the shower, her free hand pulling the door closed behind her.

It seemed like an eternity since he'd last tasted her lips. No longer could he wait. He drew her against him, turning her to push her against the shower wall.

Her soft sigh at the first brush of his lips against hers was nearly his undoing. He wanted her too desperately. He was on the brink of spilling his seed, and he had just touched her.

Phelan cupped her face in his hands, angling her head so he could kiss her. He slipped his tongue past her lips and her fingers clutched his shoulders.

He deepened the kiss and felt her body shudder. With the water running around them, Phelan couldn't stop touching her. He cupped her breast and ran his thumb over her nipple.

Aisley tore her mouth from his, her chest heaving. "Please. I need . . ."

She trailed off as he stared at her. Phelan kissed her jaw and then down her neck. "What do you need, beauty? Tell me."

"You. I need you."

He looked at her, the truth shining in her eyes. This wasn't how he wanted to make love to her for the first time, but neither could he deny her.

Phelan gripped her hips and lifted her until her legs wrapped around his waist. Her arms wound around his neck while her fingers delved into his hair.

Normally Phelan knew what his partner needed or wanted. He knew neither with Aisley, and it didn't matter. His heart pounded like a drum in his chest while his blood burned hot with a hunger like no other.

He held her above his cock as he looked down to watch their bodies join. Dimly he heard her suck in a breath. Phelan squeezed his eyes closed at how tight and wet she was.

Inch by agonizing inch, he filled her. Her nails dug

into his neck. Her legs tightened and tugged his hips closer to her, urging him onward.

When he was fully seated, Phelan opened his eyes to find Aisley with her lips parted and watching him.

"More," she begged.

He smiled and bent his head to take one pert nipple in his mouth. She moaned as his tongue teased the turgid peak mercilessly.

She rocked her hips, sending a jolt of pleasure through him. Phelan lifted his head and pulled out of her before thrusting deep.

A soft cry fell from her lips. But Phelan wanted so much more from her. He wanted her screaming, her body no longer her own.

Again and again he plunged within her taut channel. Faster, harder, deeper. The more she took, the more he gave. He pounded her body, claiming it as his own, even if she didn't know it.

He took her lips in a kiss meant to claim. He plundered her mouth, their tongues dancing together just as their bodies were.

As soon as he felt her body tighten, he stopped moving. She was so close to climaxing that he could've had her peaking a few strokes after entering her.

The longer the pleasure was held off, the stronger the orgasm. Inwardly Phelan smiled when she tried to move against him. He held her still with his hands on her hips.

"Please," she begged breathlessly.

He began to move again, slowly at first and then building to a rhythm.

"Don't stop," she whispered in his ear. "Please, don't stop."

He had every intention of doing just that until he heard her breath hitch. Then she screamed his name, her body convulsing around his cock with such force that with one more thrust he climaxed as well.

For long minutes, they remained as they were, under the water, foreheads touching.

Phelan lifted his head to see her eyes closed. Gently he pulled out of her and sat her on the teak stool. Then he grabbed a sponge and lathered some soap.

He began washing her arms then moved to her shoulders and chest. When he came to her breasts he took extra time, making sure each one was thoroughly washed.

It was the smile on Aisley's face that made something move in his chest. Phelan quickly washed the rest of her, and then pulled her to her feet to wash her back.

Only then did he turn her to face him. He lathered his hand with soap and gently washed away his seed from her sex. His cock stirred when she rocked her hips against his hand.

He rinsed her, but before he could open the shower door, she had the sponge in her hand. Phelan looked into her eyes, wondering what such a beautiful woman was doing with him.

Her hair was plastered to her head as she scrubbed the sponge over his chest and arms, and then turned him around to do his back.

She made quick work of his butt, and then turned him once more. Aisley knelt in front of him and began washing his legs from the feet up.

Phelan fisted his hands at his sides, refusing to move the closer she came to his cock. When she finally touched him, his rod jumped in response. Her gaze flicked to him.

"I'm no' through with you yet," he told her.

A small smile played about her lips as she washed his cock, now fully aroused once more. He grabbed her shoulders and pulled her to her feet. After rinsing off in record time, he shut off the water and opened the shower door.

Phelan stepped out, but when she tried to follow, he lifted her in his arms.

"I'm capable of walking, you know."

He shrugged. "I like carrying you."

"Are you afraid I'll change my mind and run off again?"

"The thought has crossed my mind," he said as he shouldered open the bedroom door.

"Put me down," she demanded.

Phelan narrowed his eyes on her, and then unceremoniously tossed her onto the bed. Before he could find a response, she leaned forward and grabbed his hand. He wasn't sure what she was about until she cupped his hand around her sex.

"Feel that?" she asked him. "I won't be running from you."

Phelan sucked in a breath at the dampness he felt on his fingers. He pushed a finger inside her and watched as her eyelids slid shut.

"I'd find you," he whispered before he kissed her neck. He moved his finger in and out of her. "You know I would."

"Yes."

"You wanted me to."

"No. Yes. I don't know. Just don't stop touching me."

"Never, beauty."

Phelan kissed down her chest until he was at her breasts once more. He pulled a dark peak into his mouth and suckled as her hips bucked against his hand.

If she thought he prolonged her release in the shower, she was in for a surprise. Or he'd try. When it came to Aisley, he discovered he had no control. He might want to declare her body as his, but she owned him.

It was just a good thing she didn't know that already.

Phelan added a second finger inside her, but didn't increase his pace. Beads of water fell from their skin and hair that neither paid attention to.

He shifted his mouth to her other breast and ran his tongue around her nipple before gently scraping his teeth across it. She cried out, her hands clawing at the blankets.

"No' yet," he told her when he felt her legs squeeze his hand.

"I can't help it. It's coming," she cried out.

Phelan pulled his fingers from her and played with the hair surrounding her sex. "I said no' yet."

Fawn-colored eyes glared at him. "Why?"

"It'll be better."

"Show me."

With a smile he began to kiss down her stomach.

CHAPTER
SIXTEEN

Aisley held onto Phelan tightly. She feared as soon as she let go he would disappear, just like her dreams. Her hands itched to run over his sculpted chest and washboard stomach again, to marvel at the width of his shoulders and his muscular arms.

She dragged in a breath, her body quivering as he settled between her legs. He kissed and licked her hip bone before leisurely kissing across to her other hip.

He was torturing her in the most wonderful, sensual way. Her senses were heightened, her blood like lava in her veins. He was the center of her world.

For a second fear flared through Aisley. Phelan had given her release in the shower. It had been quick and amazing, but even then she'd felt whatever was between them almost . . . strengthening.

That was one thing she couldn't allow to happen.

To herself.

Or to Phelan.

He suddenly lifted his head, deep lines furrowing his forehead. "What is it, beauty?"

Aisley blinked away the tears that threatened. Why

did he have to be so damned nice? She was used to callousness. She could handle cruel.

"This . . . you . . . scare me." It felt good to speak the truth. And she wished she could tell him more.

Like telling him she was Jason's cousin. It would shatter what was between them—even if it was just attraction. A heavy weight settled on her as she realized just what a disaster she had created by allowing Phelan close.

It was then she comprehended that she needed him to keep Jason at bay long enough for her to do whatever magic she needed to kill Jason once and for all. Making Phelan understand that before he killed her would be the problem, which is why she had to keep it from him.

She should have refused Phelan's help. But then he was difficult to resist.

His blue-gray eyes held hers. She caught a glimpse of his ancient soul, jaded and yearning. Her heart thundered in her chest.

Because in that instant, that millisecond of time, the connection between them was irreversible.

The fear should have frozen her. Instead, she saw in Phelan the same things she felt. It was selfish of her, but she wanted a few hours of peace. A few hours to pretend that she wasn't a bad person and her soul didn't belong to Satan.

She wanted to pretend she had the life she'd once dreamed of and a man who cared deeply for her. Even if in the end she would pay for it all with her death.

"Doona fear me," Phelan whispered and kissed her stomach, his eyes still on her. "Doona fear this. Most of all, beauty, doona hold back from me. Let me take you away."

Aisley's eyes slid shut as his kisses took him closer and closer to her center. She raised her hips, needing contact with him, with the pleasure she found in his arms.

His large hands skimmed all over her body, touching, learning. She could feel herself come alive, almost as if she had been waiting for his touch her whole life.

Then his mouth was on her. Aisley moaned when his tongue licked her sex. He licked and laved her clitoris until she was trembling with need.

He brought her to the brink, only to leave her breathless and begging for more.

"No' yet," he murmured against her thigh.

He tongued her again, teasing her clit mercilessly. She cried out when his hands reached up and cupped her breasts. Instantly her breasts swelled.

She bucked against him when he pinched her nipples. The pleasure pain was too much. Desire was tightening low in her belly with each flick of his tongue.

The climax slammed into her, taking her breath as her body trembled with the force of it. She was sailing, floating, drifting on a sea of utter contentment.

Her sex was still clenching when Phelan rose up on his knees and grabbed her hips to lift them up. She watched as he held her steady while the blunt head of his arousal brushed against her.

She moaned. Her sensitive flesh ached to feel him inside her once again. Aisley met his gaze as his thick, hard cock filled her.

The position he had her in prevented her from moving. He was in complete control. And she loved it.

She needed it.

She craved it.

Just as she needed and craved him.

It should frighten her, but it didn't. Nothing could as long as Phelan was touching her.

He buried himself deep, a satisfied moan rumbling in his chest. She locked her ankles at his waist and fisted the covers when he rotated his hips. He gave her a moment to accommodate his thick length before he began to move.

Aisley groaned at the feel of him thrusting inside her. She arched her back and tightened her legs, but he refused to loosen his hold on her hips.

His fingers dug into her flesh as he continued to plunge inside her, going deeper, harder each time. Already her body was building toward another orgasm.

A cry of pleasure fell from her lips when Phelan's strokes grew faster. He set up a driving rhythm that she was powerless to ignore.

Her body was on fire. Every fiber of her being was attuned to him, waiting for the next time he would take her to paradise.

She might not be able to move her hips, but she met each of his thrusts by squeezing her legs and clamping down on his staff. He whispered her name and thrust harder.

"Phelan," she murmured when she felt herself about to peak.

Suddenly he released her hips and leaned over her, his hands on either side of her head. Their gazes clashed, held as he relentlessly pounded her body with his.

Aisley grabbed his waist as she felt the first wave of her orgasm. She screamed his name when the climax took her. With one more thrust, Phelan buried himself deep.

Pleasure swept them, expanding and increasing until it coalesced into a dazzling glow of ecstasy.

It was becoming easier and easier to hold onto his memories. Whenever he'd forget, a name would suddenly appear in his mind.

Aisley.

He felt the power run through his body, felt the magic

consume him with each moment. But there was no heart-beat, no breath.

If only he knew where he was, he could get back. There were things he had to do. Things like . . . and just like that, his memory faded.

Whatever awaited him was important. He knew that without a doubt. It drove him to continue to explore his mind and search for the answers.

Aisley.

She wasn't far. If only he could reach her. She would help him. He was certain of it, just as he was certain that he would get back.

But where was "back" exactly?

It was on the tip of his tongue, but the more he struggled to grasp the name, the further it slipped from him.

He wasn't giving up though. There was just a little more to do, and then he'd have everything he needed.

Aisley.

CHAPTER
SEVENTEEN

Phelan never considered himself the type to cuddle after sex, but then again, he'd never had Aisley in his bed before. And it was his bed.

Another first.

He rose up on an elbow and caressed the valley between her breasts and then down to her stomach. She smiled, her eyes closed.

"That tickles," she murmured.

Phelan opened his mouth to respond when he saw the four-inch scar on her lower stomach. He slowly traced the scar, wondering why she hadn't told him she'd had a baby. Then wondering where her child was.

"It's numb there."

He glanced at her to see the smile gone and her eyes still closed. She was motionless, as if she could barely get the words out. Her sorrow was obvious, and Phelan didn't like how much that bothered him. "This is one of those secrets you didna want to tell me."

"Few people know of it. It's my burden to carry."

"Was the bairn a lad or lass?"

Her head turned to him as she opened her eyes. "A

girl. Remember when I told you I went back to my parents and then left?"

"Aye."

"I was there six weeks before I learned I was pregnant. We thought it was the flu or something because nothing I ate stayed down. Mum took me to the hospital where the doctor told me I was expecting. The entire ride back home, Mum didn't say a word."

Phelan heard the anguish in her words, the barely leashed anger and disbelief. By the way she spoke in hard syllables, he knew the ending couldn't be good.

"It took another two days before I could keep a piece of toast down. I didn't see or hear my parents during that time. After the second piece of toast, I grew bold and put a wee bit of butter on it. Then I got crazy and ate some jam."

She smiled, but it didn't meet her eyes. Phelan wasn't sure why, but he took her hand in his and simply held it.

"I went to tell my parents," she said. "That's when my father threw me out. Mum just sat there crying. She wouldn't even look at me. I was allowed to pack a small bag. I had no money, and God forgive me, but I swiped Dad's wallet on the way out."

"What else were you to do?" he asked. "I'd have done the same thing, beauty. Where did you go?"

She blew out a breath. "Edinburgh. I had a schoolmate there. She had a live-in boyfriend who didn't like me, but she gave me the couch for a few weeks. I found work. The money was pitiful, and I was always hungry. There was never any food in the flat. The few times I saved up enough to buy a decent meal, the bastard would steal the money or take the food."

"Tell me his name."

That brought out a slight grin. "I might take you up on that. There was no way I could afford a flat on my own, and I was wearing out my welcome. So, I waited another two weeks, keeping my money hidden in my shoes that I wore when I slept. Then I made my way to Pitlochry. I'd just arrived and was looking for somewhere to eat when I met a man who worked at the nearby distillery. I was hired as the store clerk that day. They even found me a small flat to rent."

"Sounds like things were working out."

"They were. It was while I was there that I felt my baby move for the first time."

Her watery smile was radiant and made his breath catch for the love he saw in that smile and her memories. In all his travels, Phelan couldn't say he had ever seen anything so full of love.

He didn't trust anyone enough to get close to him to have any deep emotions. With Charon he could lower those walls he put around himself because Charon was a Warrior and had been in Deirdre's mountain.

But never with a woman.

Until that moment he hadn't cared to feel the dangerous emotion of love. He didn't want to experience it, but he couldn't deny he wouldn't mind having someone love him. No one ever had.

Or ever would.

"I was watching the telly and drinking a glass of milk when she moved," Aisley continued. "I worked harder to get our life set up after that. Everyone at the distillery was so nice and helpful. When my babe grew restless, I'd sing to her. She'd push her little fist or foot against my stomach, and I'd place my hand atop it."

Phelan swallowed. He was afraid to move, afraid to speak lest he break the spell and Aisley stopped talking. He wanted, needed to hear more, to see that other side so many took for granted.

"For months my life kept improving. I was making a

fresh start. The past was far behind me. I managed to pick up an extra shift for more money one Saturday. It was late, and the tourist crowd was all but done for the day. A couple came in and asked for a specialty blend that was kept below the store. My ankles had been swollen for weeks, and my belly was so huge I couldn't see the lower half of my body."

Phelan closed his eyes, no longer wanting to hear any more.

"I'd walked those stairs many times," Aisley said. "I took them slowly down and found the bottle. I was half-way back up when my foot slipped or I didn't quite place it on the step properly. I don't remember falling. I remember the pain that exploded in my body. Then everything went black."

He looked at her to see her eyes on the ceiling. Her body was stiff, her words barely above a whisper.

"Apparently the fall triggered labor. For six hours I was in labor before they realized my little girl had the cord wrapped around her neck twice. There was an emergency C-section. When I finally woke from the surgery the doctor was standing by my bed. He told me my baby was dying. Something about a defect with her heart. I stopped listening when I learned I was going to lose her. It didn't matter why, only that I was."

Phelan watched a lone tear fall from her eye to disappear in her hair. He couldn't understand how anyone could suffer so, and yet still want to love. "You doona have to tell the rest."

"I convinced them to bring her to me," Aisley continued as if she hadn't heard him. "I held her in my arms and told her all the things I'd planned to tell her while she was growing up. She looked up at me with those pale brown eyes as she gripped my finger in her little fist. Then she took a breath and was gone."

Phelan had no words. He drew Aisley into his arms and held her. He didn't know how long they lay there. All he knew was that it felt right, Aisley felt right.

She had revealed one of her deepest secrets. He had the feeling she had never told anyone what she just shared with him.

He swallowed as he thought of his secret. Phelan wanted to tell her, needed to tell her.

"My friends think I was stolen from my family as a lad of six. The truth is I wanted to go with Isla."

CHAPTER
EIGHTEEN

Aisley smoothed a lock of Phelan's dark hair from his face. She was glad Phelan was talking, because then she wouldn't have to think about the past. "You were just a child."

"Aye. A child who was angry at my Da and my older brother. I walked away from the house to sulk, I suppose. It's difficult to remember. When I looked up there was this woman with the mesmerizing ice-blue eyes."

"What did she want?" Aisley asked.

He leaned back against the headboard, his hard muscles moving and bunching. "Me. I didna know that at the time. I doona believe she worked too hard to convince me to go with her. There is one thing I remember above all others. I didna look back. No' once, Aisley."

"You're being too hard on yourself. How were you to know what she wanted?"

"That's no' the point, is it? I was angry. I agreed to leave with a woman I didna know. I didna even ask where we were going. It wasna until we reached the foot of Cairn Toul that I hesitated."

Aisley didn't want to know this. She already cared too much for Phelan, and the more she cared, the more she put her plan in jeopardy. If she learned more, her heart was going to be in serious danger.

She hadn't meant to tell him so much about her baby. When she began, it all spilled out in a tumble. She told him things she had never shared with another soul, never wanted to share. They were her private tortures, her misery.

"Isla must have used magic, because the next thing I recall was being inside the mountain. That's the first time I saw Deirdre."

Aisley sat up and turned so that she faced Phelan. He laid his hand on her leg with one side of his mouth tilted upward. "You joke about meeting one of the most powerful Druids ever?"

"Never," he said with vehemence. "That woman was the Devil's daughter and deserves to endure her death a thousand times a day."

Aisley ran her palm over his muscular stomach, remembering how his body had moved over hers, bringing her untold pleasure and unimaginable carnal indulgence. He was sin and sensuality, wickedness and sex.

He was everything she needed and wanted.

Everything Jason could use against her.

"Were you scared?" Aisley asked.

"Out of my mind frightened. She hadna even spoken, but I knew she was evil. Beautiful, but evil. It wasna her floor-length white hair that made my skin crawl. It was her white eyes. They seemed to see right into my soul. She smiled, then told Isla to take me away.

"I was foolish enough to try and run. One of Deirdre's Warriors stopped me. After that, I knew there would be no escape. I followed Isla down a long corridor that led to a hidden door. From there we went down stairs that seemed to never end. The lower we went, the darker it became. She held a torch to help light our way, but that only made everything scarier."

Aisley threaded her fingers with his. "Where was she leading you?"

"As far below Cairn Toul as they could. Deirdre had magical chains waiting for me. Isla clasped those manacles around my wrists. She wouldna look at me, but she told me the shackles would grow as I did so they wouldna chafe too badly."

"She regretted bringing you," Aisley said.

Phelan blew out a harsh breath. "It didna matter. I was there. She locked the manacles. Then left me in the dark. I was brought three meals a day, but the Druids sent to me were Deirdre's slaves and never spoke. Every day Deirdre would have my blood drained from me, enough to fill a goblet. For almost twenty years I had only myself to talk to. Then the real hell began."

"She released your god."

He nodded slowly. "Inside me is Zelfor, the god of torment. No' even being a Warrior got me released from that dungeon. Instead, she continued drinking my blood."

"I don't understand," Aisley said in confusion. "Why would she want your blood? Did she drink all the Warriors' blood?"

"Just mine," he said wearily. "My blood can heal anything, beauty. The only thing it can no' do is bring someone back from the dead."

She thought of her baby, of how her infant daughter had suffered needlessly. Phelan could have saved her.

Aisley shoved aside such thoughts. That would lead to insanity. Her daughter was gone. The only good thing about that was Jason couldn't harm her.

"And your power?" she asked.

Phelan stroked her hand with the back of his thumb. He said nothing as he looked into her eyes. Aisley turned her head when she saw something flare out of the corner of her eye.

There was a large fireplace with a giant blaze where the window used to be. A second later and the entire bedroom looked like something out of a medieval castle. She looked around in awe.

And then in a blink, it was gone.

Her head jerked to him. "You can change someone's perception of reality?"

"Aye. It's how I stayed sane. It's also how I gained control over Zelfor."

"What an amazing power."

"It's come in handy a few times," he said with a grin.

She nodded. "I bet. Did Deirdre eventually let you go?"

"One of the MacLeods was taken by Deirdre. The other two brothers came for him. They brought other Warriors with them. Quinn met Marcail in that place since both were prisoners. Other Warriors who had befriended Quinn then joined in the battle. It wasna long before Deirdre was killed."

Aisley rubbed her forehead in confusion. "I thought you said it was Laria who killed Deirdre?"

"I did. Deirdre was killed in this battle, but it was just her body that died, no' her soul. Her magic was powerful enough that she regenerated her body."

A shiver of dread snaked down Aisley's back. Her thoughts instantly turned to Jason. It was a tangible fear she had that he would suddenly appear. Now, it seemed, she was right to worry.

"Isla, gravely wounded, came down to my dungeon and released me."

Aisley set aside thoughts of Jason for the moment. "She did regret bringing you to Deirdre. How long were you in Cairn Toul?"

"I doona know exactly. Fifty years? A hundred? It matters no'. I couldna remember my parents or where they lived. I couldna even recall their faces or names."

She leaned forward to cup his face. "You couldn't keep the memories and fight your god for control. It was one or the other. Besides, you were just a small child. How could you remember everything?"

"I doona know what it means to have a family. I have one person I call friend. One. I've never had any kind of relationship."

"I can't remember the last time I had a true friend."

He flashed a boyish grin. "Looks like we're two of a kind."

"That we are. What happened after you left Cairn Toul?"

"I wandered. Endlessly. I walked the entire breadth and width of Scotland several times over. I learned about coin and how to count it. I learned to read and write. I learned how to make love to a woman. I learned . . . everything."

Aisley couldn't believe all he overcame. She had taken for granted the things she learned from her parents while growing up.

Phelan had nothing but a dark prison and himself to talk to. Yet, he survived. He was strong and stubborn. He could endure anything.

She knew he wouldn't have fallen for Jason's false promises.

"What?" he asked.

She lifted a shoulder in a shrug. "I'm thinking that I'm in awe of you. I'm not sure many could have come out of what you did sane, much less in control of their god."

"I focused on one thing."

"Which was?"

"Killing *droughs*."

Aisley's stomach fell to her feet like lead. Her heart thudded painfully in her chest as she tried to focus on Phelan's face.

She knew he would be the one to kill her, but after they

had made such sweet love, she had allowed herself to believe things might turn out differently.

Phelan had just put it all into perspective once more.

"At first it was all Druids," he went on, unaware of her thoughts. "Then I learned there was a difference. My focus shifted to *droughs*."

"Do you kill all *droughs*?"

"Aye."

He answered without hesitation. How then did he not realize she was the very thing he set out to kill? Didn't he feel it in her magic?

"Doona feel sorry for them," he said. "They're evil, beauty. They give their soul to Satan."

"I know." She shifted to the side and heard him release a curse. "What is it?"

His finger ran over the jagged scar on her left side. "What's this?"

"A lesson," she answered and tried to hide it.

But Phelan pushed her hands aside. "From who?"

Aisley looked away from his probing eyes. "Someone from my family."

"And the lesson?" Phelan bit out.

"That I learn my place."

He sighed. When he spoke again, his voice was soft. "This is more of your secrets you doona want to share."

Aisley couldn't look at him. If she did she was liable to tell him everything. He would kill her on the spot as soon as she said Jason's name. She knew how he loved his home, and to taint it with her death seemed too cruel.

"It is."

"I willna push. Tell me when you're ready."

"I will tell you," she promised.

His finger traced the wound. "Did you no' get this seen to properly?"

"I wasn't allowed. I stitched it myself as best I could."

He grasped her chin and gently turned her head back to him. "You're one hell of a woman, beauty."

For the second time her eyes welled up with tears. "I'm just a person who has done unspeakable things."

"So have I. As I said earlier, we're a pair."

She didn't stop him when he pulled her onto his chest. Aisley liked the feel of his body next to hers and the sound of his heart beating beneath her ear.

If things were different, she could see a life with Phelan. Not even the prospect of his immortality and her mortality bothered her.

She'd known Phelan was bad news the moment she spotted him while dancing at the club months ago. It was the way he watched her with his compelling eyes filled with desire and longing.

"No running," he whispered in the darkness as if he knew she might be contemplating it.

"No running," she repeated.

There will be no more running. Ever.

Phelan promised to protect her. And he would. He didn't know it yet, but he would be the person to set her free.

She closed her eyes and snuggled against his chest. Freedom. She'd forgotten what that was like until Phelan. He had shown her another world.

It was beautiful and tragic at the same time because she was only getting a taste of it. Just as she only had a taste of being a mother.

All of this was punishment for her past sins. She knew that now. She accepted it.

Of course that was easy to do in the arms of a handsome Warrior who knew exactly how to touch to bring about the most exquisite pleasure.

Phelan's hand caressed her back, lulling her to sleep. She tried to fight it. Sleep isn't what she wanted. She wanted to live each minute to the fullest for the next few hours.

He kissed her forehead and whispered something she couldn't make out in her foggy brain. In the next heartbeat, she was asleep.

Phelan stared at the ceiling as he held Aisley in his arms. Every time he thought of getting up, he found a reason to stay. His usual habits weren't in play around Aisley for some reason.

And he stopped caring.

He thought of the jagged scar on her side and seethed with rage. Who would do that to her? More importantly, why? He would find out the story. He'd discover who dared to mark her.

Then he'd killed the bastard.

Slowly.

CHAPTER
NINETEEN

It was the birds singing that woke her. Aisley opened her eyes to see a pretty bunting sitting on the sill of the open window. It gave another chirp before it flew away in a flurry of yellow feathers.

Aisley snuggled against the pillow she had her arms wrapped around as she lay on her stomach. The memories of the night before brought a smile to her face.

Phelan wasn't just a superb lover, he had given her things she hadn't known she needed. Things like a warm smile, a comforting squeeze of his hand, and the safety of his arms. She still couldn't believe she had told him of her daughter.

That time of her life she never shared with anyone. Jason had somehow found out, but no matter what he asked, she never gave Jason details.

It had been different with Phelan. He hadn't pressed her for anything.

She lifted her head and found the clock on the bedside table. "Oh," she cried and sat up as she saw it was almost noon.

Aisley tossed off the covers and grabbed the first piece

of clothing she found as she rushed out of the bedroom and into the kitchen.

After a quick look for Phelan, she tugged on the shirt and saw the front door open and his bare feet crossed at the ankle on the porch railing. She smiled and walked to the doorway to see him wearing a pair of jeans and a smile.

He held out his mug of tea. "Did you sleep well?"

"Thanks, and I did," she said and took the mug. "You should've woken me."

"Why?"

She sipped the tea as she stepped to the side of the door and leaned back against the house. "There wasn't a need for me to sleep so long."

"Exhaustion had nothing to do with it, right?"

She ignored his pointed look and continued drinking the tea.

"That shirt looks better on you than me."

Startled, she looked from him down to the shirt she wore. Aisley bit her lip when she saw the black tee with a large Celtic emblem on it. It came down to her thighs and smelled of Phelan—all man, wind, and pine.

The fact she was enjoying wearing his shirt made her realize how attached she was becoming. She'd wanted a night in his arms, and she had gotten it.

Now, it was time for the next step in her plan. It wasn't that she was afraid to die. Oh, she was terrified of Hell, but death was a certain kind of freedom from Jason. But first, she had to stop Jason.

"Is there a town near?" she asked.

Phelan's forehead puckered as he lowered his feet to the porch and sat up. A breeze off the loch ruffled his dark hair, making her want to slide her fingers into the cool, wavy locks. "Do you need something?"

"I thought we might go to dinner." When she saw he

didn't immediately take the bait, she added, "And I've so little in my duffle, that I'd like to pick up a few more things."

"Do you always pack so light?"

She shifted her gaze to the loch. Aisley couldn't stand to look into Phelan's blue-gray eyes and lie. "I've never been on the run before. I packed what I could as quickly as I could. Turns out I brought things I didn't need."

"And left things you did," he finished.

"Precisely. Apparently there's a fine art to packing when you're running for your life."

She glanced over to find Phelan watching her intently. She knew his mind was processing what she said and trying to come up with a way to ask her who it was she feared.

All too soon she would tell him everything. The desire in his gaze would vanish, replaced with fury and retribution. She wasn't ready for that. Not yet at least.

So Aisley decided to turn the conversation. In a manner. "You said evil was still out there."

"It is."

"Am I taking you away from something?"

He rose to his feet and stood in front of her. Aisley had to tilt her head back to look into his face. He gently moved her hair behind her left ear. "I'm here because I want to be."

Damn, but the man knew just what to say to make her melt. Which made her feel even worse because of her deceit.

Jason had wanted to kill all the Warriors fighting him, but she knew Phelan was a good man, a man needed in this world to keep the balance of right and wrong.

Aisley swallowed to moisten her suddenly dry mouth. As much as she wanted him with her, she also knew how important his work was—and what she needed to do. "Phelan, I don't want to be responsible for any more deaths."

As soon as the words left her lips, she inwardly cringed while she waited for him to demand to know what lives she was talking about.

"You can no' be responsible for your daughter's death," he said. "But you're right. After lunch, I'll take a look around."

He walked into the house, and Aisley released a breath she hadn't known she was holding. She looked down at the mug and saw the scars on her wrists. How Phelan hadn't noticed those last night she didn't know.

It was better if she told him the truth before he could ask. She had already lied enough. He deserved better. Yet, she couldn't feel too badly because the hours she spent with him had been some of the happiest of her life.

She followed him into the house and set the mug on the island, careful to keep her hands from view. He moved about the kitchen wasting little movement as he got out the makings for sandwiches.

Her stomach rumbled loudly, and they shared a smile.

"The dark circles under your eyes are almost gone. You should sleep more," he said as he began cutting a tomato.

Aisley shrugged, recalling the awful need that consumed her to get as far from Jason and his evil as she could. "You don't fear anything. You don't know what it's like."

"I recollect fear all too well, beauty." He paused in his cutting to look at her. "It's true I've no' feared anything in some time, but I do remember it."

"Remembering and experiencing it aren't the same thing."

"Who do you fear? Tell me his name, and I'll put an end to your fear today," he said and pointed the knife to where his motorbike sat.

For a split second Aisley almost told him everything

right there. She wanted to share it all. Then she recalled how he'd looked at this place with love.

His home was a paradise for her—one she wanted to leave as she had found it.

She already tainted the place by being there, but that he could get over. Staining the ground with her blood could well ruin it for him.

Or help him get over what you've done to him.

Aisley hated her conscience.

"What will it take for you to tell me?" Phelan demanded.

She covered his hand that held the large knife with hers. "I will tell you, Phelan. I promise."

"When?"

"Take me to dinner tonight. I'll tell you then."

He placed his hands flat on the counter and dropped his chin to his chest. "I can cook here. And you can tell me now."

"I shared my body and part of my past with you last night. I'm asking for just a few more hours." She needed them to gather all the essentials she required to fight Jason.

His head jerked up to pin her with his gaze. "You make it sound as if I'll be angry when you tell me. Are you married?"

"No," she said with a soft smile. "I'm not married."

"But I'll be angry."

"The truth is rarely what we want it to be."

"That's no' an answer, beauty."

"Don't make me lie. Please," she begged. She was so tired of lying.

He picked the knife up and finished slicing the tomato. Aisley sighed and wondered if she made a mistake in not telling him right then.

Phelan admitted to killing *droughs*. What would make him stay his hand against her? The fact they'd shared their bodies? She doubted it.

After what Deirdre and Isla had done to him, she knew exactly how he would react to her betrayal. And how swiftly he'd bring death to her.

She couldn't take her eyes off him. His muscles moved, bunched, and shifted as he made their lunch. The easiness from earlier was gone, and Aisley found she missed it.

"I'm sorry," she said.

He threw the knife into the sink and glared at her. "Have I given you any reason no' to trust me?"

"No."

"They why do you no'?"

"Because I like you."

He gave a loud snort. "That's no' an answer."

"Give me today. I'll tell you everything over dinner in town."

"Why does it have to be in town?"

"It's my tale to tell. I get to choose where."

He shrugged and grabbed the sandwiches. "All right."

Aisley was almost giddy with relief. If he pressed harder, she might tell him. It was such a burden to bear. And she did like him. More than he realized probably.

It was the attraction, the pull, which drew her to him that told her she was getting too close. But she didn't care. Her life was about to be over. There would be no heartache for her, no tears or wondering why he had left her.

By the time lunch was finished, things were almost back to normal. Phelan left to do a patrol, and she promised to be there when he returned.

"Where would I go?" she asked as she watched him drive away.

She couldn't believe there'd been a time she hated him chasing her. Besides Dale, Phelan had been the only man to be there for her without wanting something in return.

"Too bad I didn't meet you sooner, Phelan."

When he was out of sight, she shut the door and walked

into the bathroom. Her body was deliciously sore from their lovemaking. Just thinking of the previous night made her burn for his touch.

Aisley stepped into the shower and sighed as the hot water ran over her. She began to hum, something she hadn't done since she was pregnant. Phelan had changed her in ways he couldn't possibly understand.

She smiled and lathered the shampoo in her hair. As she leaned her head back to rinse it the steam around her changed, morphed.

Into Jason's face.

Aisley screamed and stepped to the side. Her foot slipped on the soap pooling at the drain, and she fell, slamming her shoulder against the floor of the shower.

She looked up with her heart in her throat, but the steam had shifted. No longer could she see Jason's face.

"Stop it!" she screamed. "Do you hear me? Leave me alone!"

She slapped her hand against the shower floor but couldn't stop the tears that came. For a few minutes she let herself wallow in pity, then she climbed to her feet and finished her shower.

Aisley was still shaking when she stepped out of the shower and reached for the towel. She expected Jason to jump out at her at any moment.

That's when she got angry.

"No," she said aloud. "I refuse to live the last few hours of my life scared witless. You've done that to me enough. I'm going to stop you!"

She took a deep breath and refused to give her bastard of a cousin the satisfaction of her fear. Aisley toweled off and walked back to the bedroom for a fresh change of clothes when she spotted Phelan's mobile phone. Had he left it on purpose?

It suddenly rang, flashing CHARON across the screen.

She stared at the phone. Her time was running out in more ways than one.

Tonight. Everything would end that night.

She glanced at the clock to find it was half past one. A few hours was all she had left. There was relief, but also remorse that she'd have to leave Phelan.

More than that, guilt weighed on her for deceiving him. He was a ladies' man. She knew without a doubt he would find a new woman quickly enough.

A stab of jealousy ran through her. What else did she expect from him? It wasn't as if they were falling in love.

She was the enemy—his enemy.

And he would bring her death.

CHAPTER
TWENTY

Northern Scotland

Malcolm stood against the brisk wind atop the mountain with his hands in the front pockets of his jeans and his eyes closed. The wind buffeted him much as life continued to do.

Drops of sleet began to land on his face, but still Malcolm remained. He should be looking for Wallace or his associates, but he was questioning the why of it. Just so another *drough* can take Jason's place as he'd taken Declan's, and Declan had taken Deirdre's?

The only way to end it all was to wipe out all Druids. He could do it. There was no feeling, no emotion inside him that would give any remorse.

The others at MacLeod Castle wouldn't feel the same. It was their wives he would be killing. It wasn't that he necessarily *wanted* to kill them, only that with their deaths the evil they fought would cease.

A sizzle of magic, odd and unique slammed into him like a punch to the gut. Malcolm withdrew his hands from his pockets and whirled around.

To find Guy staring at him with a knowing grin.

"Are you looking for a tussle, mate?" Guy asked and nodded to Malcolm's hands.

He looked down to find his claws glistening in the sleet. For just a second, he stared at the maroon claws before he shoved his god back down and they disappeared.

Somehow Malcolm wasn't surprised to find one of the shifters there. He wasn't too far from Dreagan, but after the last battle where the Warriors and dragons had joined forces, Malcolm knew the Kings would always be around.

"What do you want, Dragon King?"

Guy shoved back his damp shoulder-length honey-colored hair and narrowed pale brown eyes at him. "Do I need a reason?"

"Aye." Malcolm stepped to the side and watched Guy's black-ringed eyes follow him. "Are you tracking me?"

"I saw you last night."

Malcolm lifted a brow. "I was here last night."

"I know."

There was a hint of laughter in his words. Malcolm crossed his arms over his chest. "I didna sense you."

"Nor would you, Warrior. I had taken to the skies."

Malcolm needed to remember that in the future. The Dragon Kings may only be able to shift at night to stay hidden, but they could climb high in the skies. And apparently their eyesight was rather good.

"I take it from your mood things are no' going well," Guy said.

They stood side by side in the freezing rain looking out over the glen below. Malcolm shook his head. "Phelan felt Wallace's magic."

"Damn. No' good news. I'd hoped we had seen the last of that bugger."

"We all had."

"Even you? I thought you rather enjoyed battle."

Malcolm cut him a look. "I do. All Warriors do."

"But you more than the others, aye?"

Why deny it? It wasn't Larena or Fallon asking. It was another immortal who knew what it meant to go into battle. "Aye."

"It makes you feel alive when you're all but dead the rest of the time."

Guy's remark hit too close to home. Malcolm was a Warrior. He had been created to fight. The longing for death, craving blood covering his hands, it's what he was.

"If you're no' careful, you could lose yourself," Guy warned.

Malcolm snorted and dropped his arms to his sides. "I'm already lost. The only difference is I realize it while everyone else still hopes for the best."

"Larena willna give up on you."

"My cousin is stubborn that way. I doona want to hurt her, but eventually I will."

"Is that why you stay away?"

Malcolm turned to the Dragon King and clenched his jaw. "Why the questions, King? What do you want from me?"

"Con has taken an interest."

Malcolm growled at the mention of Constantine. He was the king of the Dragon Kings and seemed to stick his nose in places he shouldn't. "Tell Con to get uninterested."

Guy chuckled and said, "Obviously you doona know Con. He saw something in you, Malcolm. Larena does as well. Perhaps if you did you wouldna be lost."

"Are you trying to anger me for a reaction?"

"Is it working?"

Malcolm released a breath. "You're irritating. Go back to your wife, dragon. I'm done with you."

"You shouldna push everyone away, Warrior. One day you're going to need friends."

"I doona need anyone or anything."

"Keep lying to yourself," Guy said as he turned and walked away.

Malcolm wanted to dismiss Guy's words, but long after the Dragon King left his statement continued to run through Malcolm's mind.

"Damn interfering dragons," Malcolm grumbled.

Phelan finished his scouting on foot and hurried back to his bike. The forest wasn't exactly the spot he expected to find Wallace, but Phelan knew firsthand what a great place it was to hide.

He was thankful he didn't sense Wallace's magic, but at the same time, a niggle of worry wouldn't relent. What did it mean that he felt Wallace's magic so keenly? And now nothing?

It was enough to make him want to haul Aisley to MacLeod Castle. At least he would find out who she was running from. Phelan smiled as he started the bike.

On the drive back to the cabin, he glanced at the sky to see the rain clouds coming in. He might not mind riding in the rain, but he didn't want to take Aisley out on the motorbike in such weather. Anything could happen. She'd catch a chill or they could wreck and she might die.

It didn't go unnoticed by him how he worried over Aisley now. Even before he knew of her parents kicking her out, being pregnant and alone, and then her daughter dying, he had an uncontrollable, undeniable need to protect her.

Not once had he thought to fight it. Nor did he want to.

He chuckled as he imagined what Charon would say if he knew. Phelan reached his hand to his back pocket and discovered he'd left his mobile phone at the house. He would check in with Charon when he returned.

The closer he came to the cabin the more he felt Aisley's

magic, except it was stronger than normal—as if she was using it.

Wave after wave washed over him as her magic pulsed across the land. He gripped the handlebars tightly when his body responded in an instant.

When the cabin came into view he simply followed the feel of Aisley's magic to see her standing at the shore of the loch. As soon as she saw him, her magic dimmed to the regular hum of when she wasn't actively calling it forth. She waved as he drove to the shed and parked the bike.

It began to drizzle as he walked to her. She started running to the house. The storm grew stronger with each step she took. Phelan met her halfway and wrapped his arm around her as they rushed to the porch.

Her laugh was rich and amazing. And he wanted to hear more of it.

"I thought the storm might miss us," she said.

Phelan drew her into his arms and kissed away any more words she might have. At the first taste of her, he tightened his arms and deepened the kiss. She moaned into his mouth as their tongues mated.

He couldn't get enough of her. His splayed hand ran up her back over her damp shirt and into the long, thick length of her midnight hair. He fisted his hand in her tresses and bent her back over his arm. Her nails sunk into his shoulder. The kiss turned fiery, furious as their passion ignited into an inferno.

She ended the kiss and pulled out of his arms. An impish grin showed on her face as she unbuttoned her shirt and tossed it aside.

Phelan's balls tightened when her jeans followed. Her fawn-colored eyes danced with desire when she undid her white lace bra and let it fall from her breasts. But it was when she hooked her thumbs in her panties and, with agonizing slowness, slid them over her hips and down her legs that he moaned in need.

She threw the black-and-white polka-dot panties in his face. Her laughter filled the air as he watched her run into the rain. She threw her arms out and spun around and around in the storm.

Phelan dropped her panties and shed his clothes in record time. He followed her into the rain and jerked her against his body. "You're a siren come to seduce and enchant me."

"Is it working?"

"Aye, beauty. From the first moment I saw you."

His gaze dropped to her kiss-swollen lips. He covered her mouth with his. With her bare breasts pressed against him, he couldn't get close enough to her.

When he considered lowering her to the wet ground, he ended the kiss and drew in a shaky breath. "You'll catch your death."

"If I get a cold, you can heal me. Besides, I never get sick." She reached between them and wrapped her hand around his cock. "Stop worrying about me and enjoy this."

His lids slid shut as she ran her hand up and down his length. She paused at the tip of his arousal and ran her thumb around it.

Longing and need burned through him. Phelan dropped his head back and let her have her way with him. He groaned when she cupped his sac and gently massaged his balls.

"You're killing me," he murmured.

"As you did me last night. It's time for your pleasure."

He grabbed her wrist to halt her and looked into her eyes. "Seeing your pleasure is enough for me."

"Why couldn't I have met you before?"

The sadness in her eyes made him ache inside his

chest. He slid his hands to her neck until he held her face in his hands. "We're together now. For as long as you want."

"I thought you didn't do relationships."

"I don't. Teach me, Aisley."

Aisley didn't know who was more surprised by his statement: he or she. She blinked through the raindrops falling from her lashes. "I'm not the one for you."

His blue-gray eyes narrowed with anger. "What?"

"I'm not the one for you," she repeated and tried to step out of his arms, but he wouldn't release her.

"We can no' go into town in this weather," Phelan said. "I'll no' endanger you that way."

She let him change the subject because she knew how ridiculous it was for them to talk of a relationship. There would never be one between them. "Why are you saying that as if you're trying to convince me?"

"Because I know you were going to leave tonight."

She swallowed and lowered her eyes to his chest. "Phelan, if you knew the truth—"

"I doona care," he interrupted her.

"You say that now."

"Then tell me now, beauty. Tell me this secret you fear. Just promise you'll stay with me."

Aisley knew what he asked was impossible. Yet, it was what she wanted. She wasn't ready to give up this slice of paradise she'd found with Phelan.

In the middle of the forest, it was just the two of them. No pasts, no worries. Just the pleasure in each other's arms.

That wouldn't stop Jason, however. He was coming for her. She knew that now. And she knew she had to stop him. Phelan hadn't given her enough time that day. She needed several hours, and he had given her barely one.

She wanted to tell him about Jason that night, but she

didn't have all she needed. And if she was going to have a chance, she needed everything. Or Phelan might not give her the time to gather it once he learned the truth.

"Or keep your secret," Phelan said when she hesitated. "I . . . I've never spent this long in the company of a woman I've made love to. This is new, and I'm sure I'm saying this all wrong."

Aisley put her finger to his lips to silence him. "You're saying everything right. That's the problem. I'm not good for you."

"You are," he said as he moved her finger. "Why else would I want you here?"

No matter how much she knew she needed to leave, her heart had already made the decision. There was no fighting it, no denying it. No one had ever asked her to stay.

No one except Phelan.

"No. I can't." It killed her to say the lie, when inside she was shouting *Yes!* at the top of her lungs. "I asked for one night. You gave that to me. There can't be any more."

He stared at her, unmoving. She memorized every detail of his blue-gray eyes, his heart-stopping lips, and the rugged planes of his handsome face.

This is what she would remember of Phelan. Not what she knew was to come.

When she tried to step out of his arms again, he let her go. Whatever part of Aisley that had been healing died that instant.

CHAPTER
TWENTY-ONE

Phelan couldn't believe Aisley didn't want to stay. He knew she had enjoyed their night together. The mere thought of her leaving left him anxious and . . . ill. He'd never experienced anything like it before. And he didn't like it.

Gone was the contentment that had soothed him. Gone was the cheerful mood he had awoken with.

In their place was anger, unease, and sadness.

What was he doing? He'd never had to chase a woman before, not like he was with Aisley. He certainly never had to talk a woman into staying with him. Usually he was the one who left when they fell asleep.

He took a step back, ignoring the pounding rain. The desire from earlier hadn't left him, but he refused to touch her, refused to let her know how much her words cut him.

Ever since he'd kissed her two months ago at the club he'd known she would change his life. He just hadn't expected this.

He was done with her, finished trying to make her see him. Whatever had begun between them was over. If she wanted to leave, he wouldn't stop her.

Phelan's lips parted to tell her to leave when he paused and recalled how Aisley had opened up to him the night before. She'd told him of her child and her hardships. Why had she done that if what they shared was just a quick pleasure for them both?

She wouldn't.

He blinked the rain from his lashes. "I'll drop you off in the morning."

"It would be better if I left now."

"Since there is only my Ducati as transportation, and I doona feel like getting out, you'll have to wait."

He turned and walked away then before he gave in and pulled her into his arms. Aisley had been hurt badly. The scars from her past weren't just physical, they were embedded deeply in her very being.

Since he wasn't sure whether to give up on her or not, he wasn't ready for her to leave. The rain gave him the perfect excuse to keep her with him a little longer.

Phelan turned back to the house and walked to the porch where he gathered his discarded clothes. A few minutes earlier he had been anticipating Aisley's body in his arms again. And just like before, he was headed for a cold shower.

He didn't look behind him to see if she followed. The keys to the Ducati were with him, and he seriously doubted if she would take off in such a storm.

Once inside, he chanced a look through the windows and spotted Aisley with her arms wrapped around her and her head hanging down.

Phelan continued into his room where he positioned himself to look out the window at her. "Come inside," he urged her.

If she walked away now, he would let her leave for good. Or he would try. He had tasted her, knew her wonderful body and what it felt like to be inside her. Phelan wanted her again. This insatiable hunger for her alarmed him, but not enough to make him run.

"Trust me, Aisley," he said.

When she started toward the house, he let out a sigh before he walked into the bathroom and turned on his cold shower.

MacLeod Castle

Larena stood in the dark with her arms crossed over her chest staring out one of the large windows in the bed-chamber she shared with Fallon. Since neither she nor Fallon were Druids, they had no sense when the other left.

Yet, she'd known the moment he departed the castle.

She hadn't gone looking to see who else left with him. She knew who the other culprits were. Larena was furious with her husband, but the melancholy that had taken her wouldn't allow her to show it.

A glance at the digital clock on the bedside table showed it was 4:16 in the morning. Fallon had been gone for over five hours.

Her enhanced hearing picked up a scrape of a chair on the stones downstairs. They were back. How long would Fallon sit with his brothers and talk before he made his way up to their room?

A year ago Larena would have gone down to him and given them all an earful.

A year ago she would've confronted him the first night he left her bed without telling her where he was going.

A year ago she would have demanded to go with him.

She no longer knew the person she was. What confused her more each day was why none of the Druids were as upset about not being able to start families as she was.

Many times she evaluated her need. She wasn't sure why the need to have children was so strong when she'd been—not exactly content, but understanding—about having to wait four centuries.

She could only surmise that after Declan's demise, she had a year where she thought she and Fallon could begin their family.

Then the search for the spell to bind their gods had taken precedence. Now there was another *drough* to fight.

The door to the bedroom opened. She knew the sound of Fallon's footfalls as well as she knew her own. He paused for just a moment before he closed the door and walked toward her.

"Baby, what are you doing out of bed?" he asked as he wrapped his arms around her.

"How many more nights are you, Lucan, and Quinn going to search for Jason? How many more nights do you think can pass before the other Warriors learn what you three have been about?"

There was a soft sigh before Fallon said, "I doona know. How long have you known?"

"From that first night."

"Why have you no' said anything?"

She shrugged, since she had no response.

It didn't surprise her when Fallon turned her to face him. His forehead was deeply furrowed as he looked at her. "You're no' angry."

There was no need to answer, since his words weren't a question.

"Why?"

She dropped her arms to her sides and wearily inhaled. "I don't have an answer. I should. Something is wrong, Fallon. I'm not myself. It's not just the fact we're putting off having children again. It's more. It's as if part of me is missing."

"For how long has this been going on?"

"Since I died this last time."

He pulled her against him and rested his chin atop her head. "We'll figure it out, love. I promise."

"I fear there isn't an answer. I should be yelling at you for searching for Jason on your own. Yet, I'm not. It's like there's some kind of . . . veil," she said for lack of a better word, "that's covering me. It's dulling the world. I find no happiness, no laughter, no joy in life."

"We need to talk to Charon then." Fallon rubbed his hands up and down her back. "He died from the X90s as well before we could bring him back."

She lifted her head to look into the deep green eyes of her husband. "The difference is he was brought back by healing magic. I wasn't."

"Then what brought you back to me?"

"I don't know. I was dead. We both know that, though we've never spoken of it. You never asked what it was like."

"Because I refuse to believe I truly lost you. You came back to me, so you couldna have been as dead as you think you were."

She grinned and stepped out of his arms. "We had Jason to battle, so I allowed you to ignore the fact that I had truly died. Not come close as I have before, but died, Fallon. You know it. There was nothing the Druids could do to heal more, and no amount of Warrior blood reversed what the X90 did."

"Stop," he said and turned away.

Larena understood then that she had done wrong by letting Fallon ignore the truth. Everyone had. She'd been so happy to be back that she hadn't wanted to question it.

However, that's all she'd been able to do for the past several months. If she had been dead, just who had brought her back? And why?

"No," she stated. "I'll not stop now. We need to address this. All of us, not just you and me. If this happened to me, it could happen to one of the others. Charon might not have spoken to you about it, but that doesn't mean it didn't happen."

Fallon raked a hand down his face and turned to lean against a chair. He propped his hands on the chair back and shook his head. "You know I'll do anything for you."

"I know."

"What is it you need?"

"This damned depression is like mud. I'm knee-deep in it and can't get out. I haven't the will to fight it."

"Then let me."

Her heart fluttered as it always did when he looked at her with longing, love, and desire. A tear fell down her cheek. "I'm a Warrior. I should be able to do this on my own."

"Warrior or no', you're my wife, Larena MacLeod. We stand together, fighting, loving, and living. I've faltered in my promise to you. I'll no' falter again."

She let the thin straps of her silk gown fall down her shoulders. With just a little wiggle of her hips, the gown pooled at her feet.

"Then start by making love to me."

Fallon straightened and yanked her against him. "I doona need to be told twice."

They shared a smile before he kissed her, backing her to the bed as he did.

CHAPTER
TWENTY-TWO

Aisley might be in dry clothes staring out the living room window of the cottage, but in her mind she was still standing in the rain with Phelan. What might be happening now if she had said yes?

Would they be making love? Laughing? Sharing more secrets?

How she wanted to believe he would be understanding when he learned she was Jason's cousin, but she knew all too well what would happen.

If only he had given her more time that afternoon. She might have been able to find the magic she needed. Her last resort was contacting Satan, and she refused to do that with Phelan near. He would be able to feel the evil. And all her plans would be for naught.

A glass of red wine was placed in front of her. Aisley lifted her gaze to find Phelan beside her, his expression unreadable.

"You look like you could use a drink," he said before he walked back to the kitchen.

Aisley did need a drink. She needed the entire bottle, actually, but she would settle for the glass. Her hand wrapped around the stemless glass as she brought it to her lips and took a drink.

"Will the storm last long?" she asked.

His chopping paused as he asked, "Can no' wait to get out of here, can you?"

She never wanted to leave, but she couldn't tell him that. "I told you it was a bad idea to bring me here."

"You're the one making this complicated, beauty. Why can you no' trust me?"

Aisley turned in the chair and rested her arms on the back while she looked at him. "Do you trust me?"

His lips parted, but no sound came out. It was just as she expected. Not that she blamed him. He was right when he called them two of a kind. They had both endured betrayals, and their lives had been altered by that fact.

"It takes me awhile," he finally answered.

She nodded and got to her feet when she saw him put the meat in the skillet to cook. "So you can take all the time you need to trust, but you want me to do it now?"

"Aye. Nay." He gave a quick shake of his head. "Stop putting words in my mouth."

"I'm not," she said and slid onto the stool to watch him cook. "It was a question derived from what you've asked of me."

He turned slightly and looked at her over his shoulder. "I doona trust easily."

"Neither do I. We both have our reasons. Can't you just leave it at that?"

He went back to cooking. "Nay, I can no'. You are in need of help."

"Ah. And you want to be my hero." The sad part was, she very much wanted him to be her hero and save her from all of it. If only her story could be altered as it was in books and movies.

"Perhaps."

She had hurt him again. It wasn't her intention, but if she didn't keep him at arm's length she would never be able to accomplish her goals.

Because if she let herself, she could easily fall in love with Phelan. He was that kind of guy, wonderful and kind and intense.

The kind she knew she could always count on.

The kind who would see to whatever need she had.

The kind who would gladly hurt anyone who harmed his family.

He was the kind of guy she had always wanted and feared didn't exist. If only she had waited for him. If only she'd had the strength to get past her grief and get on with her life she might have been able to tell Jason no.

But she hadn't.

There was no sense in wishing for things that could never be. This was her life, and she had to accept that.

"Is there anything in your life you would change?" she asked.

He flipped the meat and nodded. "I wouldna have left my family. Deirdre might still have gotten to me, but it would've been later. What about you?"

"I would have said no."

"To the man who got you pregnant and left you?"

She winced. "Well, yeah, I'd have said no then as well. I was thinking of something else, but if I hadn't moved in with him, I wouldn't be where I am now."

"And we wouldna have met."

She lifted her eyes to find Phelan staring at her. "That might be for the best."

"I doona regret our meeting."

He didn't now. He would later. She would bet her soul on it—if she had a soul to wager. "You really would keep things the way they happened to you just to meet me? I don't believe that."

Phelan shrugged and went back to cooking. His statement rattled her so badly that Aisley rose and walked onto the porch. Her emotions were running too high for her to respond to Phelan as she should.

She remained on the porch drinking her wine until he announced dinner was done. Aisley sat at the table and refilled her wineglass before she filled Phelan's.

It wasn't until he sat down with her that she realized it was the first time since her parents kicked her out that she had sat down with anyone for a home-cooked meal.

Instead of commenting on that fact, Aisley ate in silence, a wall coming between her and Phelan she couldn't seem to tear down.

It saddened her tremendously, but even as she wanted to change things, she couldn't seem to find a way.

Emotion clogged her throat, making it difficult for her to have an appetite. She ate as much of the meal as she could before she pushed her plate aside.

"Was it no' to your liking?"

His words were hard, brittle. "It was delicious. I'm just not very hungry."

Aisley gathered her plate and walked to the sink to begin cleaning. They worked side by side, and all too soon the kitchen was clean, leaving her with nothing to do.

And a six-foot-two-inch immortal Highlander to remind her of the pleasure they had shared the night before.

She glanced outside to see it was still raining.

"I willna stop you."

Aisley jerked her gaze from the window to Phelan. His blue-gray eyes were steady, daring as they watched her.

"Nor will I follow."

After all the time he had taken tracking her, his words were like a punch in the gut. "You've done enough."

Phelan wanted to hit something. How could such a

beautiful woman be so infuriating? "You would walk away so easily?"

"It's for the best."

"Ballocks."

She shrugged and backed up a step. "I wanted one night."

"Well, I want more."

"We don't always get what we want."

He smiled, though he knew it was cold and calculating. "I do."

"Not this time," she stated and squared her shoulders.

Phelan hadn't taken centuries to learn the art of seduction for nothing. He took a step toward Aisley only to have her retreat. It was easy enough to maneuver her so that she was trapped in the corner of the countertop.

He leaned forward as if he were going to kiss her, and at the last minute shifted so he could lick the lobe of her ear. Then he whispered, "Tell me you didna enjoy last night."

"You know I did," she said, though her voice was unsteady.

"And you doona want to be pleasured so again?"

She put her hands on his chest and tried to push him away. "Stop. I know what you're doing, and it won't work."

"Then you have nothing to worry about," he said as he took her hands and gently lifted them to his mouth so he could wrap his lips around one of her fingers.

"Phelan," she said breathlessly. "You'll regret this later."

"Then I'll regret it later. I want you now. Tell me you doona want me, beauty. Tell me, and I'll walk away never to bother you again."

Her fawn-colored eyes darkened and her body leaned into him. "God help me, but I want you."

Her lips parted and her pulse at her throat grew erratic.

He inwardly smiled at her reaction. This amazing Druid, this beautiful woman was turning him inside out. Yet he couldn't get enough of her.

Zelfor roared his approval inside Phelan. And Phelan agreed. There was no other woman like Aisley. Phelan had walked the land for four centuries and never met another like her.

He could walk the world until the end of time and never find anyone who could compare to her.

His fingers plunged into her hair and held her head as he kissed her. Phelan poured all of his passion, all of his yearning into that kiss.

She molded her body to his, open and accepting of anything he demanded of her. The more she gave, the more he wanted. That want became a burning need.

His body was ablaze with desire. The flames licked at his soul, urging him to make her his. Now. Forever.

He moved his arm between them and palmed her breast. When he encountered material, he let a claw extend and then he ripped her dress down the middle and jerked it off her.

In seconds he had her bra removed, and with two swipes of his claw, her panties followed her dress. His hand found her breast again. She moaned into his mouth when he tweaked her nipple. Phelan had never felt such lust flare in his blood before. If he didn't get inside her soon, he was going to explode.

For the second time that day, Phelan jerked off his clothes, this time with the help of Aisley. When he was naked, he jerked her against him and stared into her eyes.

"Tell me again," he demanded.

She kissed his chest before she looked up at him. "I want you."

Phelan tightened his hold around her. He dropped to

his knees, pulling her down with him. There was a smile on her face when he fell onto his back and looked up at her.

She splayed her hands on his chest and straddled him. Phelan watched in spellbinding awe as she rose up on her knees, her gaze fastened on him. Then she took his aching cock in hand and brought it to her entrance.

It took a herculean effort to remain still instead of raising his hips and plunging inside her, but somehow he managed it. Barely.

Aisley's head dropped back when she lowered herself onto his rod. He gritted his teeth together and let her remain in control. She impaled herself on him slowly, her wet heat surrounding him.

She rocked forward, wringing a low moan of satisfaction from him. Phelan gripped her hips so he could urge her faster or slower, but his hands itched to touch more of her.

Her breasts jostled as her movements grew quicker. She was wanton and passionate, beautiful and reckless. And all his.

Something primal, primitive grew inside him as he stared at the woman who had fascinated him from the start. He didn't care about her past. His only thought was of the now.

And the future.

He cupped her breasts. Each time she rocked her hips, he raised his. The movement was taking each of them higher, the pleasure calling them onward.

The turgid peaks of her nipples grazed his palms as he massaged her breasts. He rolled her nipples between his thumb and forefinger adding pressure as he did.

She cried out and lifted her head. With her hands once more braced on his chest, she met his eyes and rode him hard and wild.

There would be no holding back for either of them, no prolonging the exquisite release. The need was too great, too intense to be denied any longer.

Only Aisley, beautiful, mystifying Aisley, could bring him to the edge of a climax so easily.

"Come with me," he urged.

She gave a small nod in response. Phelan ducked his head and took her nipple in his mouth while his hands palmed her fine ass. He held the peak gently between his teeth and ran his tongue back and forth over the nipple.

Her legs tightened a moment before her body clamped around his cock. Phelan dimly heard her scream as they climaxed together.

The force of it sent him reeling. The world was twisting, turning as indescribable rapture flooded them, besieged them.

Suffused them.

Their souls touched, connected. Merged.

There was no turning back for him, no walking away from the woman in his arms. She was his, and he would do anything and everything to keep her.

Phelan wrapped his arms around Aisley as she collapsed on his chest, their ragged breaths drowned out by the rain.

Phelan couldn't quite grasp the tranquility, the serenity that had him firmly in its grip. Though he knew it couldn't possibly last, he was going to enjoy it while he had it.

He rubbed his cheek against the side of Aisley's face, careful not to scratch her with his whiskers. He was in bad need of a shave, but he was loath to move.

She sighed softly in sleep and huddled farther down in the blankets he wrapped around them. After their lovemaking, they had rinsed off in the shower. He smiled, remembering how he couldn't keep his hands off her.

He refused to allow her clothes. Instead, he'd grabbed the tartan blanket from the couch and pulled her outside. There he sat on the swing with the blanket around him and his arms held wide.

Even now he could recall the sight of her sad smile as she nestled her firm arse between his legs and leaned back against him. He'd wrapped the blanket around them as they watched the rain fall.

That was hours ago. If he wasn't certain she was warm, he'd have brought Aisley inside when she fell asleep.

He glanced at the sky to see it turning from black to a steel gray. Dawn was coming, and with it the rain tapered off to a faint drizzle.

What would the new day bring? Would Aisley still want to leave? Could he let her go?

It hadn't taken long during the hours of the night for Phelan to realize he needed to fill Charon in on Aisley. And not just Charon. Fallon needed to know there was another Druid. Though Phelan was certain Charon had already mentioned it to Fallon.

Phelan wasn't looking forward to answering all the questions he knew would come about Aisley. He wanted her kept away from Wallace and whoever else hunted her, but he didn't want to share her.

Nor did he want to break the peace they had found.

It was their own world here in the middle of the forest. Nothing and no one to bother them. It was near perfection.

Which in itself brought ice to Phelan's veins. Perfection had a way of dissolving quickly, as he learned yesterday.

"You let me sleep," came Aisley's muffled voice.

He smiled against her hair. "You needed it."

"Did you stay awake all night?"

"Aye."

Aisley yawned and quickly covered her mouth with her hand. "What are you thinking about so hard?"

"I need to go patrolling again."

"Hmm. I figured as much. There's something else though."

Phelan kissed her temple, hoping she didn't ask him to take her into town. "Those at MacLeod Castle need to know about you. There is always celebrating when another Druid is found."

He didn't miss the way her body tensed, though she tried to hide it. "Why do they need to know?" she asked.

"As I said, protecting Druids is what they do."

"It's what you're doing."

He happened to agree, but Phelan also knew if Wallace attacked him, Aisley wouldn't have anyone to back her up. Wallace was too powerful of a *drough* for Aisley to try and fight on her own.

"Aye, but for how long will you let me?" Before she could answer, he asked, "Have you used your magic in a fight before?"

"You mean against someone?"

He nodded.

She hesitated in answering, which made him frown. "Yes."

"Then you know what you'll have to do if Wallace attacks here."

"Let's not talk about that."

Phelan took one of her slim hands in his. He marveled at her long fingers. With his thumb, he caressed her palm, trying to calm her. It wasn't until he turned her hand over that he saw the scar running down her wrist.

Blood pounded in his ears while his gaze was riveted on the scar. He tried to draw in a breath, but his lungs seized. Phelan needed to be rational. He knew she didn't wear a Demon's Kiss, but that didn't mean she wasn't *drough*.

But he'd know if she was *drough*.

He'd *know*!

She put her other hand atop his to cover the scar he was tracing with his finger.

"Aisley . . ." He had to pause and clear his throat. He was afraid to ask, afraid she would admit to being *drough*. But she knew he hunted them. Why would she have willingly come to his cabin if she was a *drough*? Was this her secret? Had another betrayal come?

"Ask," she said quietly.

"Did you try to kill yourself?"

She drew in a deep breath. "Many times."

"Why?" The truth was in her eyes, boldly daring him to ask how.

"I couldn't face the days after my baby died. I sat in the flat that was supposed to be ours looking at a crib that would never hold her. The tears stopped coming and life became . . . unbearable. I walked away from Pitlochry and the future I had there. It didn't take me long to fall into the wrong crowd and use what little money I had on drugs. I prayed the Reaper would come for me."

He drew her wrist to his lips and kissed the scar. "You survived."

Aisley squeezed her eyes shut to hold back the tears. What a coward she was. She hadn't been entirely truthful to Phelan, but she had tried to kill herself when she used the drugs.

But not by slitting her wrists.

Phelan had given her so much and offered her even more. He was a good man who deserved better than she was giving him. It was time she came clean.

"Phelan, about the scars—"

The sound of his mobile ringing interrupted her. Aisley sat up so he could rise from the swing and hurry into the house. She grinned when she caught sight of his bare ass before he disappeared through the doorway.

She stood, wrapping the blanket around her. A chill settled into her soul, a chill that had nothing to do with the weather and everything to do with her.

Aisley walked into the house to see Phelan listening intently to whoever was on the other end of the phone. She ran her hand through her hair and wrinkled her nose.

A shower was in order. She could use that time to determine how she would tell Phelan what he suspected when he found the scar on her wrist, as well as her plan.

She shut the door to the bathroom and let the blanket fall when she turned on the shower. The warm water didn't thaw the casing of ice around her soul. And the more she thought about telling Phelan, the sicker to her stomach she got.

But this is what she deserved for not being honest with him from the start.

She could have told him that night at the club when he kissed her. Of course, she'd thought he knew, but it was obvious now he hadn't.

Instead of him chasing her to kill her, he'd been following her those two months trying to get closer to her.

Aisley couldn't believe her luck. To finally find someone who was caring, honest, good-looking, and incredible in bed, and not be with him was a hard pill to swallow.

Who was she kidding?

It wasn't hard, it was damned impossible.

"Why?" she asked anyone in the cosmos who would listen. "Why did Jason come looking for me? Why wasn't I strong enough to tell him no? Why couldn't Phelan have found me earlier? Why do I have to be his enemy?"

Aisley mentally shook herself. There was no use fighting the inevitable. She was ready to die. Wasn't she?

Sadly, the answer to that was no. She'd found something good with Phelan, and she wasn't ready for it to end. Eternity wouldn't be long enough in his arms.

He was a true hero.

And she was the enemy he would vanquish to save the world.

Because whatever she might think of herself, Phelan had the right answer in killing all *droughs*. The evil within a *drough* was too powerful.

Whenever they succeeded in killing Jason—and they would eventually—someone else would take his place. It might take months or even years, but it would happen.

Aisley loved being a Druid. She enjoyed the feel of her magic, even that smidgen she'd had, race within her veins. Becoming *drough* had given her magic a huge boost, but it wasn't worth the price.

No longer did her magic give her joy. She could feel the evil inside her, feel it infest her magic and turn it from pure to something grotesque and corrupt.

She finished her shower and shut off the water. As she toweled off, she thought the house seemed quiet, but she assumed Phelan was outside.

With the towel wrapped around her, she stood in front of the mirror, but couldn't make herself look at her reflection. The anger Phelan would feel when she told him— she deserved a thousand times over.

He had been betrayed again. She might have had a good reason for doing it, but it didn't matter. A treachery was a treachery no matter what kind of spin was put on it.

Aisley swallowed and made her eyes lift to look in the mirror. She hated what stared back at her. While she combed her hair, she looked anywhere but directly into her own eyes.

Her hand shook by the time she set down the comb. She hurried out of the bathroom to find some clothes. Aisley put on the first thing she found, which was a pair of yoga pants and a thin, oversized sweatshirt she had cut the neck out of.

After all, it didn't really matter what she wore for her death, did it?

"Phelan," she called when she walked out of the bedroom.

There was no answer.

Aisley looked all over the house, and then searched outside. Only when she happened to glance at the shed and saw his Ducati gone did she realize he'd left.

It must have been an important phone call. She'd gotten a reprieve, but one she wasn't happy about. Aisley feared that by the time Phelan returned she would lose her nerve.

"I'm a damned coward," she mumbled.

All because she was falling hard for Phelan Stewart. A Warrior, a hero, an amazing lover, and all-around good guy.

"Oh, hell. I'm so screwed. I want him."

She wanted him so badly it hurt to breathe. Because she wasn't *falling* for Phelan. She'd already fallen.

Completely, utterly.

Totally.

"Oh, dear God. I love him," she whispered in shock.

When had that happened? How had that happened? Hadn't she been guarding her heart?

Phelan was charming and seductive, and somehow he'd snuck past all her defenses. Then she had gone and made everything worse by agreeing to stay with him. That couldn't happen now. She had to leave.

She could run out into the woods, but he'd find her since not only did he know the forest, but he could follow her magic. She'd end up going in circles since she was directionally challenged.

Still, it was better than staying, and she might have enough time to delve into her magic to learn how to stop Jason for good.

Aisley ran into the bedroom and began to toss her few

meager belongings into her duffle. She jammed her feet into her tennis shoes, and just as she was reaching for the duffle a shiver of something evil slid over her.

"No," she said.

"Aissssssleeyyyyyyy!"

She fell to her knees and clutched her head. The voice filled her mind to an earsplitting crescendo as it repeated her name over and over again.

The voice was stronger than before, as if each time it said her name it grew in power.

"Stop it!" Aisley screamed. "Leave me alone!"

"Aisley."

This time it seemed the voice whispered right beside her ear. She jerked her head around and saw mist swirling. Dread filled her, freezing her in place.

Was it Jason? Or was it the gray-skinned creatures that she'd barely escaped from?

She had seen how the monsters moved by turning into mist and disappearing. If it was them, it was pointless to use magic. That would only make them attack her sooner.

Aisley watched as the mist grew thicker and thicker. She knew without a doubt that whatever appeared out of the mist was there to kill her.

She scooted back on her hands and feet until she hit a wall. The mist began to fill the room, creeping closer and closer to her.

"Aisley."

CHAPTER
TWENTY-THREE

Trepidation and restlessness settled in Phelan's chest after his phone call with Fallon. Phelan gunned the Ducati as he drove faster, hoping that somehow the speed would dissolve the worry over Charon from his chest.

He put on the brake as he came up behind a car. Phelan saw the Slow Now sign, but the driver didn't heed it as they reached the almost 90-degree turn.

They were either locals or tourists. The sudden brakes flaring and the car's skidding of tires told Phelan they were tourists.

He had to come to a stop and waited for them to take the turn at a turtle's pace. Phelan glanced ahead and saw he had a small portion of road in which to go around them.

It wasn't something he would chance in a car, but he wasn't in a car. He was on the Ducati.

Phelan revved the motorbike and squealed his tires before he raced around them. He easily cleared them and got back into his lane right before he saw the Yield sign as he came to the one-lane stone bridge.

He often heard tourists complain about the bridges, but few of them realized they had been built when people used carriages. The bridges were wide enough for one carriage to cross at a time.

When Phelan had gone another ten miles he pulled off the main road onto a dirt road. As soon as he found a good spot, he pulled into the grass and shut off the motorbike.

It wasn't that he couldn't sense Druid magic from his bike, but sometimes being on the Ducati when he was searching for someone made things more difficult. It was better if he did his search on foot.

Phelan put the kickstand down and got off the bike. He removed the helmet and placed it on the seat. Just as he turned he spotted a pine marten on a nearby log.

The animal made him think of Charon and how one night they'd had too much to drink and raced to see who could be the first to catch one of the quick-footed animals.

Needless to say, neither came up with the prize.

"Damn you, Charon."

Phelan ran a hand down his face and sighed. He ran over Fallon's conversation again. Something was wrong with Larena, and she suspected it had to do with the *drough* blood in the X90 bullets that had been used to kill her.

The same blood that had nearly taken Charon's life.

Or so Charon said.

Phelan recalled all too well being in the backseat of the car as they drove away from Wallace's mansion after the battle. Charon's limp body was covered in blood from the knife wound.

They had gone to Wallace's to help Arran get Ronnie back after she was captured. They hadn't expected Wallace to have *droughs* working for him. *Droughs* were notorious for doing things alone, but Wallace thought differently.

The *droughs* did their work and stopped their attack. For the most part. Charon and Phelan had gone undetected by the *droughs* and turned the tide back in their favor.

Yet, Charon stepped in front of a dagger dipped in *drough* blood meant for Arran.

All the Warriors' powers were affected by something at the mansion. Fallon couldn't jump them back to the castle. They had no choice but to pile into the car and drive back.

Every Warrior in the car had given their blood to Charon, but nothing had helped. Phelan still remembered the helplessness he felt when, for the first time, his blood failed to heal.

He long suspected the power in his blood had nothing to do with the god inside him. If that was true, then it should've healed Charon instantly. But it hadn't. The blood of the Warriors helped to slow the *drough* blood inside him, but it didn't stop it.

Halfway back to the castle their powers returned and Fallon took Charon. Phelan had waited anxiously to know Charon had recovered with the help of the Druids.

What Charon failed to mention was that the pain of the wound continued to bother him. It had never happened before. It reinforced everyone's suspicion that Wallace had done something to the *drough* blood to make it stronger somehow.

The *droughs* they fought continued to get more powerful and attack in new, unconventional ways. How could the Warriors keep up? They were constantly one step behind. At that rate, the *droughs* would win the war.

Phelan's thoughts turned to Aisley. The mere mention of her in a world of evil and darkness made his stomach hurt. She was meant for so much more.

He had always wanted to kill Wallace, but now he had a very specific reason. Aisley.

Was this how Charon and the others with mates felt?

The anxiety, fear, and dread was swallowing him whole. He wanted to find Wallace, but at the same time he wanted to be with Aisley to protect her.

He couldn't be in both places.

"Fuck," Phelan growled angrily.

What a damned predicament. He took a deep breath and looked around him. Clutters of trees dotted the ground, and in between was tall grass swaying in the wind.

Droplets of water fell from the leaves above him from the storm the night before. He slowly moved his gaze around him. There were few places Wallace could hide in this area, and with Phelan's enhanced vision, he didn't need to go search every grove of trees.

When he was satisfied he didn't see anything out of the ordinary or feel *drough* magic, he climbed on the Ducati and got back on the road.

There were hours of searching ahead of him.

He could only hope Aisley was at the cottage when he returned.

Aisley had to tamp down the magic that surged through her. It was instinct for a Druid to call upon her magic in a crisis. It had taken her seeing the gray-skinned creatures' frenzied attack on Jason as he used his magic that stopped hers cold.

The first brush of the mist touched the tip of her shoes. A feeling of defeat and despair consumed her. It swept over her, swallowed her.

Drowned her.

Aisley closed her eyes and waited for the mist. There was no use running, no point in trying to get away. She was a useless, pointless Druid. She deserved the agony about to befall her.

Phelan's blue-gray eyes filled with desire flashed in her mind.

She grasped his image and held onto it. The more she concentrated on him, the more she was able to throw off the feelings crushing her.

"No," she whispered as she jumped to her feet and ran out of the house.

She raced into the forest with no clear thought to where she was going—only that she had to get away. Aisley ran until she couldn't breathe, and then she ran some more.

A rabbit darted in front of her. She smothered a gasp and leaped over it, only to land awkwardly on her ankle. It brought her to a halt as she collapsed on the ground.

Aisley looked over her shoulder thinking Jason or the monsters would appear at any moment. Seconds turned to minutes, minutes turned to hours, and nothing came for her.

A red squirrel sat on a limb in a nearby hawthorn tree eating a nut and watching her. Blackbirds and finches flew around as if she didn't exist. The sway of the limbs in the breeze lulled her.

The forest was a comfort she had never known before. She assumed it was being with Phelan, and he did have something to do with it.

Now that she was by herself however, she could feel it. The forest was alive with life. And magic.

Aisley scooted toward a fallen tree and straddled it so that she leaned back against the trunk of another tree. The rough bark of the pine scraped her palms. At her feet were clusters of ferns, a bright green against the brown of the earth and pine needles.

How had she never ventured into a forest alone before? How had she never felt the pull?

She closed her eyes and simply existed. It wasn't long before she heard a flutter of wings near her. They were too slow for a bird. A butterfly perhaps?

A sound to her left drew her attention. She listened to

the scrape of claws on a tree and recognized it was a pine marten. Rabbits called out behind her. Two squirrels chased each other from tree to tree.

Aisley froze as she heard the distant sound of drums. The beat was slow, rhythmic. She focused on it, trying to determine where it was coming from. It didn't frighten her, because somehow she knew it came from magic.

Her heart began to beat in time with the drums. Aisley had no idea how long she drifted in a strange space of time with the drums. All she knew was that it felt right, as if she should have heard them years ago.

The drums grew louder, and suddenly chanting began. She instantly retreated, but they wouldn't let her loose. The thousands of voices chanting in words she couldn't make out urged her to them, beckoned her.

She knew no fear. Only . . . a strange sense of peace and rightness. She drifted toward the chanting, though she knew it wasn't really her body. It was more like her conscience, or her soul.

"Aisley," the thousand voices said in unison.

"Who are you?"

"He's coming for you. He's growing stronger."

"Jason," she said.

"Yesssss."

"Can I escape him?"

"Only with the one you trust."

Aisley knew they referred to Phelan. He was the only one she trusted. "Phelan won't help me when he learns I'm a *drough*."

"Betrayal."

"Are you telling me I'll betray someone?"

"Betrayal and death."

She tried to remain calm. "Is there a way I can kill Jason so that he never returns to the land of the living?"

"You have a choice coming. A choice, Aisley."

"What choice? Please. Help me with Jason. Let me do this to make up for my bad choices."

Even as she asked the question the chanting and drums began to grow faint. She tried to follow them, but they were gone as suddenly as they had come.

Aisley opened her eyes and sighed. She wasn't sure who the voices were, but the magic that had surrounded her didn't feel evil. If felt pure.

She frowned as her thoughts turned to what their voices had told her. Jason was coming for her. Betrayal and death awaited her. And the only one who could help her escape Jason was Phelan.

It was the choice they spoke of that kept running through her mind. Were the voices telling Phelan she was *drough*? Or was it something else?

"Bugger. I hate cryptic messages," she whispered.

Aisley looked down at her watch to see it was nearing four in the afternoon. She couldn't believe she'd been gone almost eight hours. It was time to get back.

She gingerly stood on her injured ankle. There was only a twinge of pain that dissipated after a minute. With her shoulders squared, she turned in the direction she had come and started back.

Amazingly enough, she managed to reach Phelan's cabin in an hour without any mishap. Which was a first for her since she had ran blindly into the forest.

She also thought she ran much farther. There was definitely something going on, she just wasn't sure what.

When she reached the cabin, she paused before she stepped onto the porch. The door still stood wide open from when she'd flung it on her way out.

Aisley swallowed past the lump in her throat and walked into the house. Room by room she searched and found nothing. She ended up in the bedroom where the mist had come.

There, on the mirror hanging on the wall, written in what looked like a mix of blood and dirt was her name.

CHAPTER
TWENTY-FOUR

Despite his dismal day of searching for clues to Wallace's whereabouts, Phelan was anxious to get home. He'd been away from Aisley all day. Normally that would have suited him just fine, but that wasn't the case anymore.

He found he needed to know she was close, yearned to have her beside him. It wasn't just that he wanted her in his bed. He simply wanted . . . her.

All of her. From her laughter to the way she left clothes all over the room. From the feel of her soft midnight hair running through his fingers to tripping over her shoes. From her amazing body to her awful cooking skills.

There wasn't a part of her Phelan didn't like, or a part of her he didn't want to know better.

He pulled the bike into the shed, and found himself hurrying to the house. A wave of her magic washed over him like a warm, comforting blanket.

Phelan saw her on the porch leaning against the wooden pillar next to the steps. He stopped with one foot placed on the porch and wondered at the peculiar look she gave him.

"What is it?"

She shrugged. Aisley wasn't exactly smiling, but she wasn't frowning either.

Phelan thought back over the day and realized what he had done. "I should've told you I was leaving."

Aisley gave a nod. "That would've been the courteous thing to do."

"I've never had to answer to anyone before."

"You don't have to answer to me."

"I didna think." That bothered him. He should have thought of her. He'd been too upset over Fallon's call, but that didn't mean he should have forgotten Aisley.

"How did your patrol go?"

There was no anger in her fawn-colored eyes. Phelan wrapped a strand of black hair around his finger and marveled at the silky feel of it. "Unproductive. How was your day?"

"I took a walk in the woods."

He opened his mouth to tell her that might not have been a good idea, when she continued talking.

"And before you tell me it might not be safe, let me remind you I'm a Druid."

Phelan flattened his lips. "There are creatures out there your magic will draw. They're called selmyr."

"Selmyr."

"Aye. Ancient creatures that have been locked away but were accidentally released."

"By?" she asked.

Phelan tugged her into the cabin behind him. He shut the door when she faced him. "By Arran and Ronnie. It was an archeological dig site. The selmyr feed off magic."

"Just magic?"

"Aye, but they'll kill anything. I fought them recently. The more magic a Druid used, the more frenzied they became."

Aisley walked to the couch and sank down on it. "Where are these selmyr now?"

"I doona know. They travel on the wind and look like man-sized tornadoes of dust before they appear. They move with lightning speed. And no amount of magic can kill them."

"Do you know anything about how they were originally captured?"

"It was Druids from the Isle of Skye who managed it the first time, but I know nothing more than that."

Her gaze looked away as she bit her lip.

"Aisley? Do you know any Druids from the isle?"

She gave a small nod. Slowly, she returned her gaze to him, her pallor now a shade of green. "Me."

Phelan stood in stunned silence. "You?"

"Me," she repeated. "My family dates back six generations from Skye. My great-grandparents moved to Glasgow for a job after they were newly married. I've never been to Skye."

"Have you heard of the selmyr?" he asked as he sat beside her, his body angled to better see her.

"When I was a small girl, my grandfather used to tell me stories of a creature that could travel on the wind. He said it would come and get me if I wasn't a good lass."

Phelan rubbed his jaw. "Did he describe them?"

"He said they were vampires, except they were ash-colored and hideous to look at."

"That's the selmyr. Is your grandfather still around?"

She shook her head. "He died many years ago."

Phelan got to his feet and began to pace. "These selmyr are a force we Warriors were barely able to contain. It was only with . . ." He trailed off, wondering how much to tell her.

The Dragon Kings stayed hidden throughout history

because no one knew who they were. They showed themselves to the Warriors and Druids of MacLeod Castle because of Charon.

Phelan couldn't tell Aisley about the Kings no matter how much he wanted to. Not without the Kings giving their approval.

"It's all right," Aisley said. "You don't have to tell me more."

"We had help. I can tell you that much."

Aisley put her hand on her stomach. She was getting nauseated the longer she sat there listening to Phelan talk of the selmyr and the last battle.

She had been at the last battle. She now knew the name of the gray-skinned creatures who had killed Dale and nearly gotten to her. Selmyr.

They were the monsters of nightmares. They fed by biting with their long fangs and drinking their victim's blood. No wonder her grandfather called them vampires.

But she wanted to know who had helped the Warriors. If there was something as powerful as the Warriors out there, then Jason's chances of winning were dimming considerably.

"We need to go to the Isle of Skye."

Aisley jerked at Phelan's suggestion. "No."

"You have no' seen the selmyr. I have. I've battled them, been bitten by them. They may take just blood, but a Warrior's power is in that blood. We're weakened with each bite."

She thought of Jason, the mist that had formed in the bedroom earlier that morning, her name written on the mirror, and the voices from the forest.

Was this the choice the voices told her she had to make?

"There are so few Druids nowadays," Phelan continued. "Many doona even know they have magic. I doona know if we'd ever find another Druid with a connection to Skye."

Aisley swallowed and knew she couldn't tell him no. The selmyr attacked indiscriminately. They didn't care who was *drough* and who was *mie*.

Maybe going to Skye, the place of her ancestors, would help her find something in her magic to stop Jason. She was sure he was dead, but he wouldn't remain that way.

"All right."

He smiled and pulled out his mobile phone.

Aisley put her hand over it to stop him from calling anyone. "We do this alone."

"It's going to take more than just the two of us."

"I know. But let's do our searching together."

He stared at her for several tense moments before he said, "If that's what you want. My friends willna hurt you."

How could she tell him that his friends would know what she was? How could she tell him that when his friends arrived, whatever was between them would end?

Aisley stood. "We can leave tonight and reach Skye in a few hours."

He grabbed her hand as she started to walk away. Aisley looked back at him to find him frowning. "You want to leave?"

"No." *Never.* "But you're right. We need to find out how the selmyr were contained before they attack again."

"They've no' attacked in three months."

"That you know of," she said.

Phelan stood and blew out a harsh breath. "I wasna ready to leave yet."

"The selmyr could track me here and attack when you're out hunting for Jason Wallace. If I can't use my magic to defend myself, what am I to do? We don't have a choice but to get these monsters put in the darkest hole that can never be found."

"I like your thinking, beauty," he said and kissed her.

Aisley leaned into him, loving the feel of his heat and hardness. She wanted to tear his shirt off and feel his skin beneath her hands, but it would have to wait.

She might not be able to reverse the fact she was a *drough*, but she could help Phelan with the selmyr. It seemed fate had given her a prime opportunity.

Or hated her enough to put her in a no-win situation.

But she had been in that no-win situation from the moment Phelan kissed her that first night.

In less than twenty minutes, she stood on the porch looking out over the loch with her duffle in her hand. For the briefest of moments she thought she had found a place where she could live out her last few days in relative peace and happiness.

The fact she was leaving the tranquility of the forest and the cabin she'd come to consider home made her blood turn to ice. For she knew in her gut that she would never return.

"We'll be back," Phelan said as he came to stand beside her. "As soon as we can."

She didn't bother to respond as he took her duffle and strapped it onto the back of the Ducati with the small bag he carried.

Aisley put on the helmet and climbed behind Phelan on the bike. She looked at the cabin surrounded by a rainbow of flowers. Jason tried to ruin it by showing up, but Aisley had erased any evidence of her name written on the mirror.

For a second, she thought she heard drums, but before she could listen again, Phelan started the bike. He revved the motor and drove away.

She watched the cabin as long as she could before they turned the corner and it faded from sight. Her throat clogged with regret.

The cabin had not just given her incredible nights with Phelan, it had also shown her a side of herself she hadn't known was still there. A side that had been hidden, waiting for her to be strong enough to face it.

She turned her head forward. For good or worse she was on a course she hadn't planned on. It wouldn't make up for the evil she'd done—or the evil she was.

It was a start, however.

Aisley wasn't fool enough to believe Phelan would think it proved she was on his side. The outcome between her and Phelan hadn't changed.

And wouldn't.

He was smart. If she didn't come clean soon, he would figure out her secrets on his own. Or his friends would tell him. Neither of those scenarios benefited her.

Not that telling him was her best option. There wasn't a best option. Yet, she'd found inner strength after her time in the forest and the magic that had found her.

That inner strength would help get her through the next few days. It had been a silly dream to think she and Phelan could remain forever alone at the cabin.

Jason would find her. Phelan's friends would push to meet the Druid he had found. All of which would destroy their paradise. Jason would ensure Phelan suffered while making her watch, and then Jason would turn his wrath on her.

Aisley closed her eyes when Phelan's hand came up to cover hers that was wrapped around his waist. It was a comforting gesture, one she would hold in her heart through the long eternity of Hell.

CHAPTER
TWENTY-FIVE

Phelan slowly inched the Ducati onto the ferry before turning off the engine and resting his hands on his thighs.

"Mallaig," Aisley said. "This is where Logan came searching for . . . the Tablet of Orn, right?"

"Aye. He and Gwynn met on the dock behind us."

"Can you feel Druid magic?"

He nodded slowly. "Oh, aye. No' so much on Mallaig. Here the magic is . . . residual. This was once a great stronghold of Druids that even Deirdre feared nearing. I suspect there are still a few Druids residing here, but their magic is almost gone."

"That's sad," Aisley said as she removed her helmet and got off the bike. She turned to look at Mallaig. "Is there no way for the Druids to get their magic back?"

"Too many years mixing with those that have no magic have diluted things. I doona know if there's an answer, beauty."

"And Skye? Are there Druids there?"

Phelan's gaze turned to Armadale, where they would be docking. It was considered Skye's back door. Armadale was located on the low-lying Sleat Peninsula, but his gaze was drawn to the startling jagged peaks of the Cuillin mountains that towered above Armadale some fifteen miles farther inland.

"There are Druids," Phelan finally answered. "I've been to Skye a few times over my years, but no' once did I encounter a Druid."

Aisley's head swung to him with her forehead furrowed. "Why is that? Are they frightened of you?"

"Most likely. Which begs the question, beauty. Why are you no' scared of me?"

"It's your eyes," she said softly.

Phelan tugged her against him so their conversation wouldn't go beyond them. "You've no' asked to see me in Warrior form."

"Should I have?"

"Aye." He studied her fawn-colored eyes. He had seen the marks on her wrists. She had an explanation for them, and he hadn't found a Demon's Kiss. But how could he have missed that she hadn't asked to see his Warrior form?

Was that because she'd seen a Warrior before? If that was the case, that could only mean she was involved with Jason Wallace.

Phelan's hand tightened on her hip. "Tell me why you've no' been curious to see what I look like."

"Do you think I'll run from you?" she asked with a grin that didn't quite reach her eyes.

"Stop, Aisley. Doona jest. Tell me the truth."

She glanced away before she placed her hand atop his arm. "I feel the devastating power inside you. You fairly hum with it. The way you move, the way you take everything in. You're a predator, Phelan. You're dangerous and ferocious. I know your skin and eyes change. I know you'll have claws and fangs, but I don't have to see that change to know the fierce, untamed man before me is a Warrior."

It wasn't exactly an answer. She was hiding something, and a part of him knew he wouldn't like what it was. But he couldn't push her.

What he found with her was too pleasant to shake up. If her explanations of her past didn't make sense, he would think she was a *drough*.

But he knew that couldn't be the case. He'd have felt it in her magic. Aisley's magic was too thrilling and wonderful to be anything but *mie*.

So whatever was in her past they would face together when she trusted him enough to share it. Until then, he would take each day they had as a gift that she hadn't run from him.

Twenty minutes later they docked at Armadale. Instead of taking the road leading to Skye, Phelan drove them left from the ferry terminal.

"Where are we going?" Aisley asked.

"I'm hungry."

She held onto him as he drove them slowly down the landward end of the pier to The Shed. He stopped in front of the tiny café and once more shut off the engine of the bike.

"I hope it's better than its name," Aisley whispered.

"It is. Trust me. We can spend a little time here," he said when he saw her looking at the Ragamuffin shop, a clothing store.

She looked back at him and smiled when her stomach growled. "Food sounds good."

He grabbed the door to the café to open it for her when his phone rang. "Grab us a table. I'll be right there."

She hesitated a minute before she walked inside. Phelan watched her find a table as he pulled his mobile phone out of his back pocket.

As soon as he saw Charon's name on the screen he answered it. "Are you all right?" he asked.

There was a choked laugh on the other end. "Aye. Should there be anything wrong?"

"Have you no' spoken with Fallon?"

Charon was silent for several seconds. "What's going on?"

He blew out a breath and walked away from the café door. "Are you feeling any effects from the wound you suffered at Wallace's mansion?"

"You mean the wound that your blood couldna heal?" Charon asked tightly, softly.

"Aye," Phelan ground out. "I need to know if it's doing more than just bothering you. Laura and I've both seen you rubbing your chest where the blade entered you."

Charon let out a string of cussing. "There's something different with the *drough* blood on that blade. I knew it felt odd. What is it?"

"I doona know. Fallon told me Larena says there's something wrong with her."

"Shite. I'm beginning to miss the days when it was easy to battle Deirdre."

"When was that ever easy?"

"It wasna at the time, but now it sure seems like it." Charon let out a long breath. "The wound still bothers me sometimes. I'll admit that. But I'm myself."

"Larena isna."

"She died."

"You practically did as well," Phelan stated.

Charon laughed wryly. "Ah, but then you were there. Your blood saved me."

"You doona know that."

"I do. Sonya told me how everyone in that car put their blood in my wound, but it didna do much. Until you added yours."

"Mine should've healed you instantly."

"Which tells me, my friend, that Wallace has been busy."

Phelan pinched the bridge of his nose with his thumb and forefinger. "I think I despise Wallace more than I ever did Deirdre."

"I never thought I'd hear you say that."

"Me neither. The truth is, this bastard is conniving. We never see how he's going to hit us."

"Until it's too late. I know. Is Fallon talking to Britt about Larena? Britt might be able to help."

Phelan glanced inside the café to see Aisley staring absently at the menu. "He has her focused on finishing her current work. When that's complete, she'll turn to Larena."

"I saw how he reacted when he thought Larena was dead. I wouldna want to see what becomes of him if he loses her a second time."

"It's good that Aiden found Britt then."

"Speaking of finding things," Charon said conversationally. "How is your Druid? What's her name again?"

Phelan saw Aisley rise from her chair and look to the door. She was thinking of running, he knew it. "Charon, I've much to tell you about her, but it's going to have to wait. I'll be in contact soon."

He ended the call and strode into the café. As soon as she saw him, she sat back down. "You were going to leave," he said as he joined her.

"I . . . yes."

"Why?" After all they'd been through he couldn't believe she would start running again.

She dropped her head into her hands. "I don't know," came her muffled reply.

Phelan pulled her hand from her face and intertwined his fingers with hers. "You'll feel better after you get some food inside you."

"I shouldn't be here."

"What are you talking about?"

"Here. On Skye. With you. I thought I could help and do something good. I don't belong. I need to go."

He kept a tight hold of her when she would have risen. Her magic swelled, fear edging it. "Tell me what's going on, beauty."

"It's this isle. I feel . . . I can't explain it. I feel out of place."

"Take a breath." Once she had he said, "Good. Now, here comes the waitress. Order something. We can talk after you eat."

He didn't release her hand until the waitress left. Aisley's magic pulsed in confusion, like it couldn't decide whether it was happy about where they were or not.

Something was going on though.

Corann stood on the docks hidden by a boat as he watched the Warrior and Druid in the café. What was a Druid doing with a Warrior? And more importantly, what did the *drough* want?

The fact she remained despite his use of magic to get her to leave showed she was powerful. But how powerful? His experience watching over the Druids on Skye told him to observe the two for a time. He would see where they were going.

Isobel's head surfaced from underwater. "Corann, did you find them?"

"Aye, lass."

"Shall we question them?"

He looked down at the fair-haired Druid and drummed his fingers on his leg. "No' yet. Return to the others and tell them to await my word."

"We're ready for battle."

"Let's hope it doesna come to that. Now go, Isobel."

He waited until she disappeared below the water before

he turned back to the Warrior and Druid. By the way the Warrior watched the female, it was obvious he cared. The Druid, however, was nervous, agitated.

She kept looking around, almost as if she knew she was being watched. And that magic was being used on her.

"Good," he murmured. "You need to know I'm here."

When the Warrior's gaze turned his direction, Corann stood steady. This Warrior had been to Skye before. He always came on his own.

He would roam the land for a few days and then leave. This time was different. The Warrior had a purpose. Corann might have wanted to stay hidden, but he suspected he'd be confronting the Warrior soon.

Corann grinned when he saw the Warrior trying to see him. Corann didn't use magic. He didn't have to. The ship in front of him offered a shield that not even a Warrior's enhanced eyesight could see through.

The Warrior's attention turned back to the black-haired Druid. The last time a Warrior had sided with a Druid had left its mark on the land.

Deirdre had killed many of Skye's Druids for their magic. She'd taken even more and made them slaves to do her bidding. Corann refused to allow anything like that to happen again.

He rejoiced to find another Druid, even one that was a *drough*. But he'd kill her if she dared to follow in Deirdre's footsteps.

CHAPTER
TWENTY-SIX

Aisley wanted off the Isle of Skye. It didn't matter what argument she tried to give Phelan, he kept telling her he would protect her.

If she knew *what* it was that put her on edge, she would be able to tell him. As it was, since she couldn't name it, he was confident he could take care of whatever it was.

"Stubborn."

"What?" Phelan asked as he turned to look at her over his shoulder as he drove the Ducati along the road.

She didn't bother to answer him. Instead, she studied the ruins of Armadale Castle before it went out of sight.

It wasn't long before they reached Broadford, which Phelan told her was Skye's second largest settlement. Despite her uneasy feeling, the views were dramatic and stunning. This was the home of her ancestors, the place where her magic came from.

She wished she had visited sooner. Even now she could feel her magic swelling, as if it knew where she was.

"Broadford lies in the shadow of the Red Cuillin mountains. The village origins date back to the cattle market that was held here in the 1700s. After the Napoleonic war, many veterans came here after 1815," Phelan said when they slowed to go through the town.

She shook her head. "You're like an encyclopedia. Is there anything you don't know?"

"The bay is Broadford Bay. Oh, and there's a serpentarium."

"A what?" she asked. "You don't mean snakes, do you?"

"Oh, aye, beauty. It's home to snakes, lizards, and frogs. Want to see it?"

She shuddered. "I'll pass, thanks."

His laughter brought a smile to her face. Life with Phelan was certainly never boring.

They stayed on the A87 that hugged the magnificent coastline offering staggering views of the water and Skye's many peninsulas as they twisted and turned with the road north.

When they reached Portree, he didn't stop as she expected. Instead, he drove them to the Cuillin Hills Hotel and parked.

"We'll get a start in the morning," he said as he shut off the bike and waited for her to get off.

Aisley handed her helmet to Phelan as she took in the view of the harbor from the hotel high up a hillside. When she glanced at the hotel, she found the whitewashed brick to be a beautiful collection of gables. Then she caught sight of the mountain range. What had Phelan called them? The Cuillins.

"They're the wildest and most jagged mountain range in all of the UK," he said as he stood beside her.

"They're beyond spectacular."

"Have you mountain climbed before?"

She raised a brow as she looked at him. "Not exactly. Why?"

"That's where we're headed tomorrow."

Aisley blinked. "You must be joking."

"Afraid no', beauty. Now, let me tell you about the hotel," he said as he helped her off the bike and guided her toward the entrance. "Cuillin Hills Hotel was originally a shooting lodge called the Armadale Lodge in the 1880s. They've continually added onto the structure through the decades."

Aisley could only marvel at his knowledge as they walked into the hotel. He held both of their bags, and with a smile at the older woman behind the counter, he sauntered over to her.

He was amazing to watch. Women practically fell over themselves to get his attention. Aisley stood to the side and observed as the older woman's faded blue eyes crinkled in the corners at something Phelan said.

She giggled, just like a schoolgirl, her lashes fluttering. Phelan leaned an arm on the counter and flashed a bright smile Aisley knew the older woman wouldn't be immune to. A moment later and he was handing her a stack of pound notes.

Aisley shook her head as he walked over to her. He gave her a smile. "What?" he asked innocently.

"Do you charm everyone?"

"What can I say? I like women."

"And they like you."

He winked. "I know."

Aisley laughed while she followed him up the staircase to their room. The laughter died when she took sight of where they would be sleeping.

"You doona like it?"

She couldn't tear her gaze away from the window and the breathtaking views of the Cuillin mountain range. "It's spectacular."

Firmly clamping her mouth shut, she turned to find a massive four-poster bed with a dark tartan comforter. The bed faced the windows, and she could only imagine what kind of view she'd wake up to.

"Rain is coming," Phelan said.

Aisley glanced out the window to see dark clouds gathering over the mountains. "I've often heard that Skye's weather changes daily."

"The weather here changes by the hour, beauty. We'll need to be prepared for anything."

"Don't worry about me. I don't get sick."

He moved with lightning speed to stand before her and grab her arms. "You'll have everything you need before we get on those slopes. You're mortal, beauty. You doona know what that means."

"You forget, I know exactly what it means. I watched my daughter take her last breath in my arms."

His lips pressed into a firm line. "I willna argue with you about this."

"Fine. I just don't understand why you think we need to go to the mountains. Can't we just ask around any one of the villages we've been through?"

"It willna be that easy. We can ask, but we'll no' discover anything. What we want will be in those mountains."

She narrowed her eyes at him. "All right. Spill, Warrior. What do you know?"

He dropped his arms and raked a hand through his hair. His gaze moved behind her to the window and mountains beyond. "That range of mountains isna treacherous for nothing. I've seen Celtic markings there before."

"Celtic markings doesn't mean Druids."

"It does if you know what to look for. We'll find whatever clues we need in those hills."

"I'm glad you're confident."

He pulled off his shirt and tossed it in a nearby chair as he crossed to the bathroom. "Somewhere on this isle is a Druid who has the answers we seek. We just need to find that Druid."

"Are you sure that's such a good idea?" she asked as he shut the door.

"Aye," he yelled through the door.

She rolled her eyes and fell back on the bed when she heard the shower turn on. A moment later the sound of something hitting the window made her raise her head.

"Rain."

Just a few minutes ago the sun had been out.

She grinned when she recalled hearing a tourist complaining about the lack of darkness during the summer months. They didn't know that during the winter there were only a few hours of sunlight.

Aisley leaned up to grab her iPod from her purse. She missed hearing the music. Once her earbuds were in, she hit play, closed her eyes, and let the music soothe her. The agitation she'd felt while having dinner diminished.

She wasn't sure what it was about Skye that set her on edge, but it wasn't a place she felt comfortable in. Phelan was right though. There was magic everywhere.

It came through the land and filled the air. It was in every flower petal, every blade of grass. It was in the rain, in the sea, and in the clouds.

The only thing that came close to feeling like this was the standing stones throughout Scotland. Aisley, like any Druid, was drawn to the stones.

It had been her ancestors who erected the many standing stones across the land. The power of those Druids had been so great, the magic could still be felt, centuries later.

Skye was similar, except the magic felt . . . more solid. As if it wasn't an echo of magic, but the magic itself.

Corann stood on a peak of the Cuillin mountains and stared at the hotel where the Warrior and Druid had gone. A curtain of rain fell over Portree, cloaking it in gray.

"They're getting closer," Ravyn said.

He glanced down at Ravyn and gripped his walking stick tighter. "Aye. What has the wind told you?"

She shrugged and played with the ends of her waist-length black hair. Her bright blue eyes were trained on the hotel. "The wind tells me to help them."

"Hmm." Corann had never known Ravyn to misunderstand the wind. She was a Windtalker. Unlike the Druids on the mainland, those on Skye retained the full strength of their magic, but only by being selective and careful.

"You don't want to help them?" Ravyn asked.

"I worry about the *drough*."

Ravyn dropped her hands and turned her gaze to him. "The wind only tells me that she's in danger."

"From the Warrior?"

"That I don't know. Maybe Isobel will know more."

Corann grunted. Isobel was his Waterdancer, and she had learned nothing more than Ravyn.

"That means she hasn't," Ravyn said with a smile.

"Doona get cheeky with me, lass."

Ravyn nudged him with her fist. "You like me being cheeky, old man."

Corann's smile faded as he thought of the Warrior and Druid again. "Have everyone ready, Ravyn. Whether these two are just visiting or no', I'll no' have us unprepared."

"I'll see it done."

"Good."

She turned to leave, then paused and put her hand on his shoulder. Corann turned his head and met her gaze. Ravyn had an old soul. As a natural born leader, she had no problem taking her place among the Druids of Skye.

It was her future he fought for. It was hundreds of generations to come that he would die for.

"There's been no sign of Jason Wallace," she said.

"Nothing our magic has been able to pick up anywhere in England or Scotland."

"Perhaps he left the country."

"That's a possibility, but I don't think so."

Corann sighed wearily. "I've a feeling we'll know the answer soon enough."

"There are Warriors fighting evil. The wind has told me."

"Aye. Those at MacLeod Castle. Warriors and *mies*."

"They killed Deirdre."

He gave a nod. "And Declan. This I know, Ravyn. What's your point?"

"Maybe that's why this Warrior is here?"

"With a *drough*?" Corann pointed out.

Ravyn let her hand slide from his shoulder. "No one knows of us. We've kept hidden. If there is an attack here, they'll not be prepared for our assault."

"And if that happens, lass, there'll be no more hiding for us. Everyone will know our location. There is more evil out there than Jason Wallace."

She folded her arms over her chest and planted her feet. "You've said that since I was a little girl, except you used Deirdre's name. Give over, old man. What evil are you talking about?"

"Pray, Ravyn, that you never find out."

"Corann—"

"Enough," he said with finality. "Go to the others. I'll keep watch."

Only when Ravyn had walked away did he slump against his walking stick. He was running out of time. If things didn't work out, he'd have to tell his Druids everything he knew.

They had to be prepared.

CHAPTER
TWENTY-SEVEN

Aiden rubbed his eyes and blinked several times before he looked back under the microscope. The celebratory feeling that had rushed through the castle was gone.

He couldn't help but wonder if it would ever be there again.

Aiden leaned back in his chair and looked at the ceiling. The shock from what Fallon had told them of Larena still left him reeling.

Any joy he felt at Britt making headway in countering Wallace's X90 bullets came to a screeching halt, leaving him cold and furious.

So many had been lost in their battles. Duncan, Braden, Fiona. Malcolm and Charon had come close to dying. Larena had died.

Now they had discovered that while magic might have brought her back, the *drough* blood used to kill her was changing her.

Britt threw the pencil she'd been holding across the

room. It bounced off the stone wall to land with a quiet brush on the rug.

She slid off the stool and shoved the piles of paper beside her off the table and onto the floor. They scattered, floating upon the air as if her anger couldn't touch them.

Aiden rushed to her. He wrapped his arms around her as he stood behind her. "It's all right."

"No," she said with a sniff. "It isn't. Time is running out for us, Aiden. I can feel it, and I don't even have any magic."

He turned her to face him and smoothed her blond hair away from her face to look into her blue eyes. "Then we'll work until we do run out of time. My parents, my aunts and uncles, didna put their life on hold to give up now. No one is giving up."

"If Larena would've told us sooner," Britt said and closed her eyes.

Aiden pulled her against him so that her head rested on his chest. He held her close, because he couldn't help but wonder when things were going to come crashing down around them.

No amount of magic, no amount of Warrior strength could help Larena. The Druids had been with her all day to no avail. How they missed something was wrong he couldn't begin to guess.

Everyone, including himself, had assumed she hadn't been herself because she didn't want to wait to start a family anymore. Now they knew the truth.

The castle stones that had always seemed so alive and vibrant now seemed dull and lifeless. Magic lived and breathed through the very stones and earth surrounding the castle. But even the magic seemed to shrink away in fear of what was coming.

"I don't know what to do," Britt said.

"Neither do I. All we can do is stay on course. If Wallace attacks, let's have something to use against him he willna see coming."

Britt lifted her beautiful tear-streaked face. Her lashes were spiky from crying, but she inhaled deeply and squared her shoulders. "You're right. I'll only be in the way during a battle, but I can help in other ways. It's just . . . it's your aunt."

"Larena and Fallon will get through this. Larena is a fighter. She wouldna have a goddess inside her if she wasna. Fallon would walk through Hell itself for her. Doona underestimate their love."

A ghost of a smile tugged at Britt's lips. "Let's not forget Lucan and Cara or Quinn and Marcail."

Aiden grunted at the mention of his parents. "As soon as Dad leaves the room, Mum will take Larena's emotions."

"That makes Marcail ill."

"Which is why Dad will stay with her as much as he can."

"Your mother is smart. She'll figure out a way."

Aiden knew it without a doubt. He didn't stop Britt when she stepped out of his arms and bent to pick up the papers. The smile he directed at Britt was to help her. There was nothing that could help him, not until Jason Wallace was dead.

Wallace's magic was strong, but Aiden had never expected it to tear them all apart. But it was. Slowly, deliberately.

Intentionally.

Aiden might have chafed under the watchful eye of all the Warriors and Druids while he grew into manhood. He might have fought against the need to strike out on his own for the four centuries he watched time move without him.

Yet MacLeod Castle was his home. The people inside it his family. Wallace couldn't win. After everything they had sacrificed it seemed too cruel for Wallace to win.

"Aiden?"

He looked at Britt to find her blue eyes watching him intently as she knelt on the floor, the papers in her hands. "Aye?"

"I'll find out what's wrong with Larena. Just as I will finish this work on the X90s. I won't let you down."

He pulled her up and into his arms. Then he claimed her mouth in a kiss that was savage and fierce. His blood sang with the need to bury himself in her. "And that is just one of the thousands of reasons I love you."

"You always know what to say, Aiden MacLeod," she said with her eyes unfocused and her lips swollen. "Kiss me again."

Aiden quickly complied.

Phelan stepped out of the bathroom toweling off his hair to find Aisley asleep. He smiled when he saw she was listening to her iPod. It shouldn't have surprised him.

He dropped the towel and walked naked to the bed. They'd be leaving early. It was probably wise to let her sleep regardless of how much he wanted her.

With gentle hands he removed her shoes and shifted her so that her head rested on the pillow. For several minutes he simply stared at her.

He might have enjoyed the women he shared his body with over the years. He knew he'd more than liked having them in his arms. Not once had he wanted them around after the pleasure was done. He hadn't wanted to hurt them, which was why he always left while they slept.

What was it about Aisley that changed his way of thinking? He needed to know. The why of it he understood. She scared the shit out of him.

For a woman to touch him so deeply was a once-in-an-eternity deal. Aisley could be his mate, the one woman in all the lifetimes who was meant for him.

He wanted to be with her. But a part of him, the part that was unsure of the feelings assaulting him, wondered why he was still near her.

A Druid. He had not only been with the same woman for several days now, but with a Druid. At one time he considered all Druids worthy of nothing but death.

Charon had set him right. Good thing, too, or he'd have missed out on Aisley.

Phelan glanced out the window to see the rain. He dressed and quietly left the room. There were things he needed to get before they set out for the Cuillins in the morning.

As soon as he reached the lobby he felt it. Magic. Druid magic. He slowed his steps and searched the room. Whoever it was wasn't in the hotel. Outside perhaps?

It was the same magic he'd felt a brush of earlier when he and Aisley stopped to eat after the ferry. Phelan had searched but never found the Druid.

"Following me, aye?" he whispered to himself.

Phelan ignored the rain as he walked out of the hotel and down the street to the shops. Some had already closed. He reached one just as the young woman was turning the lock. Phelan flashed her a smile, and she twisted her wrist the other way.

"I just need a few things," Phelan said when she opened the door for him.

She smiled, showing dimples in both cheeks. "Of course. Anything I can help you with?"

"Actually, you can."

Aisley woke to the smell of hot tea. She cracked open an eye and cringed when she saw Phelan dressed and smiling as he held the cup of tea out to her.

"I need a few more hours," she said and threw an arm over her eyes.

"I let you sleep those hours."

This got her attention. She moved her arm and sighed. Then she pushed herself into a sitting position to lean back against the headboard and reached for the mug. She took several sips before she asked, "I thought you wanted to get an early start."

"I do. I went out last night and gathered everything you'll need for the hike."

"You mean everything *we'll* need."

He simply smiled at her statement. "Of course."

She rolled her eyes. "Ah. I see. You're a Warrior, so you don't need the things a poor mortal does."

"Something like that."

"I am a Druid, you know. I do have magic. I can use it if need be."

"I've seen you use it. I know."

Aisley stilled, thinking he was referring to the battles between the Warriors and Jason. Then she relaxed when she recalled the two men attacking her in Glasgow.

"I just want you safe," Phelan said.

She looked at the dark liquid of the tea. "Why do I keep feeling as if I need to get as far from Skye as I can?"

"I think that's the Druids doing it."

"You've seen them?" she asked as her gaze jerked to him.

He shrugged one thick shoulder. "No' seen exactly. I've felt them. They're here and watching me."

"Us."

"Us," he agreed.

She scooted to the edge of the bed, careful not to spill her tea. Her feet dangled over the side. "Aren't you worried that they haven't approached us?"

"Nay. They're waiting to see what we'll do."

"I thought you said you'd been here before."

"I have. Several times."

Aisley rolled her eyes when he didn't elaborate. "All those times you didn't sense Druids?"

"I did." His smile was slow, telling her he knew he was being difficult.

"Phelan," she warned.

He chuckled. "Everyone I've encountered on this isle has been mortal without a touch of magic. The Druids keep to themselves. I've felt them, but always from a distance. Whoever is watching us now has gotten closer."

"You're not worried."

"Nay."

"Nay," she mimicked as she slid off the bed and walked to the window to look out on the mountains shrouded in mist. "You do realize with all your powers as a Warrior that a Druid can still stop you in your tracks."

"We'll see."

Aisley set down her mug on the small table and glanced at the hiking shoes, thick socks, waterproof jacket, and gloves laid out for her. But that wasn't all. Besides a light-weight, waterproof pant there were four long-sleeved thermal shirts in black and two sweaters, one a cream color made of thick wool. The other was a charcoal gray and lighter weight, but still made of wool.

"The weather can change by the hour," Phelan said as he came up beside her. "You'll be prepared for anything."

She lifted her gaze to him. "And you?"

"I'm always prepared for anything."

He gave her a quick kiss before he slapped her butt. "Hurry. I'm anxious to get moving."

Aisley shook her head as he walked out of the room to do whatever it was Phelan did. She didn't waste any more time getting dressed.

CHAPTER
TWENTY-EIGHT

Aisley held her gloves in her hand as she walked to the lobby. She wasn't shocked to find Phelan talking with two other women who were hanging on his every word.

One of the females, a buxom blonde showing enough cleavage that Aisley could make out the red of her bra, placed a hand on Phelan's arm.

Phelan kept talking, but he angled himself so that he moved away from the blonde's touch. It was obvious, and it was done in such a way that if Aisley hadn't been watching him, she wouldn't have known what he did.

His gaze slid to her. The smile he gave slammed into her, nearly knocking her on her ass. He might be charming those other women, but his look told her he only wanted her.

Aisley fisted her hand as she recalled the way his thick, defined muscles moved beneath her hand, how warm his skin was. How wonderful his weight felt atop her as he filled her body with his arousal.

Her breath hitched and her body flushed with need. Phelan wasn't just sex appeal and rugged masculinity, he was magnetic, hypnotic.

Irresistible.

And for the moment, he was hers.

As if he knew what she was thinking, his blue-gray eyes darkened. His desire was as palpable as her own. The invisible bonds between them strengthened, grew. They tugged at her, drawing her down the last two remaining steps.

Aisley couldn't stop her feet from moving her toward Phelan. He was a force unto himself, and like gravity, she was powerless to resist his call.

She ignored the nasty looks from the two women as she came to stand in front of Phelan. He wore a black long-sleeve thermal shirt that molded to his bulging muscles. Instead of the same waterproof pants she wore, he had on jeans.

"Ready?" he asked.

She thought about the need pulsing within her. "No."

"Doona tempt me, beauty," he said in a low, seductive tone that made her heart race.

"Consider this tempting."

He stared at her for the longest time before he shook his head. "I can no' believe I'm no' throwing you over my shoulder and taking you back to the room."

"You're not?" she asked incredulously.

"This is a first for me. Just as leaving you sleeping last night was."

"Then you shouldn't have let me sleep."

His smile made her roll her eyes. "You needed your rest for today."

Aisley decided then and there that the next chance she got, she was going to tease Phelan mercilessly. Let him writhe in need as she was then.

He handed her a backpack before he slung his own over his shoulder. "Ready?"

"Not really," she said and followed him out of the hotel.

They were halfway to the Cuillins before she asked, "What about our stuff in the hotel?"

"I've paid a week in advance. Our things will be fine," he answered from in front of her.

Aisley hooked her thumbs in the straps of the backpack and kept pace with Phelan. The sky was clear. For now. How long it would stay that way was anyone's guess.

"They're near," Phelan said when he reached back to help her up over a large boulder.

"Great."

"We're no' the only hikers. They willna approach us for a while."

"I'd rather they didn't approach at all."

"Why do you fear them?"

Aisley glanced at him and shrugged. "Unknown Druids, remember?"

"They are no' *droughs*, beauty. There's nothing to fear."

"Have *mies* always been so welcoming when they meet a Warrior then?"

He grinned, a wickedly teasing gleam in his eyes. "Nay."

"Oh, so nothing to be concerned about," she said sarcastically. "I feel so much better."

His laughter only made her grit her teeth. She didn't want to see these Druids. They could know what she was. Then they would tell Phelan and everything would be ruined.

Aisley looked up at the Cuillin mountains as they started walking again. The mountains rose up to jagged, imposing peaks, some with snow.

"Those are the red hills," Phelan pointed out as he slowed for her to get even with him. "They can be differentiated because of their soft rounded contours to their steep sides. The black hills are another matter entirely."

"How?" she asked, intrigued. She might joke that Phelan

was a walking encyclopedia, but she loved the information he stored in his mind.

"The peaks of the black hills are connected by a continuous ridge that twists and plunges its way from north to south. Mountaineers from all over the world have come to climb the Black Cuillin."

"It's a good thing we aren't going there." When Phelan didn't comment, she inwardly groaned. "We're going there, aren't we?"

"Aye."

"Just a simple 'aye'?" She tried to hold back the frustration to no avail. When he looked at her over his shoulder with a grin he was trying to suppress she found herself smiling. "You're laughing at me."

"Never, beauty. Just remembering how you told me you were a Druid, and that I shouldna worry over you."

"Well, I'm giving you permission to worry. I'm not exactly an experienced climber."

"Good thing I am."

She adjusted the backpack. "Of course you are. Is there anything you aren't good at?"

"Relationships?"

Aisley liked how he could admit something so personal. "You phrased it as a question."

"It is. I'm asking you."

She elbowed him. "I think you're doing pretty good for a guy who claims he's not had a relationship before."

"I've a good teacher."

That made her grin falter. "Phelan, you shouldn't take my word for everything. My relationships were disasters. I don't even know if I understand what constitutes a real relationship."

"You know," he said as if his declaring it were true.

They walked in silence for several minutes, taking in the scenery. The closer to the mountains they got, the more dramatic the landscape. It was no wonder people flocked to Skye, she mused.

Aisley couldn't help but wonder what her life would have been like had she grown up here.

"You have family somewhere on this isle," Phelan said.

"How do you always know what I'm thinking?"

He winked and sidestepped a rock. "I know you."

"And yes, I know I've family here."

"Do you want to find them?"

"No. I remember when I was about five that I met an aunt and uncle who lived here, but I don't remember their names."

His hand reached out and quickly steadied her when her feet slipped on the damp grass. "I thought mortals kept in touch with their families."

"Some do. Some don't. My mother was an only child and didn't know her relatives. My father was the second out of five. All his siblings but one moved away from Skye. I suppose everyone lost touch."

Phelan stopped when they reached the crest of a small foothill to the mountains. "You know you have family. I doona think you should pass up getting to see them again, beauty."

He didn't try to hide the longing in his voice. Aisley reached for his hand. "If I could, I'd take you back in time and let you see your family."

He gently squeezed her hand.

They started walking again, this time hand in hand. Aisley surreptitiously glanced at their hands. It seemed so natural and felt so right, that for a second she'd forgotten that the only other time she had held a guy's hand was when she was still in school.

It was a simple gesture, but one that meant so much to her. Phelan had no idea that with every word, every move she was falling deeper and deeper in love with him.

When she was with him he gave her the courage to think what life could be if she sided with the MacLeods and stood against Jason.

Then she would recall she was a *drough*. The death she wanted was being pushed further and further away. Phelan was doing that to her. His kisses, his smiles.

But it was temporary, however much she might want it to be permanent. She needed to remember that. It was becoming more and more difficult though. Phelan had changed everything without even meaning to.

Never far from her thoughts was Jason. He would come for her. She knew it as she knew the sun would rise in the east. Jason killed with merely a thought.

What he had in store for her would be a hundred times worse. Not just because she had left him, but she was blood. He'd been suspicious of her long before the last battle.

How many times had he told her she was expendable? He had no qualms about killing her, regardless that she was family. How she hated him. That deep, true hatred that burned in her gut.

The weather suddenly shifted as the wind began to howl around them. Aisley was glad she had ahold of Phelan. He kept her anchored in more ways than one.

After an hour of walking against the wind, it halted as quickly as it had begun. None of it fazed Phelan. He kept walking, moving them closer and closer to the Cuillins.

Fifteen minutes later he stopped and reached into his pack for a bottle of water that he handed to her. Aisley eagerly accepted it while she sat on a boulder and he leaned against another.

The weather was cool, but she was sweating from her exertion. The layers of clothes Phelan had bought were definitely coming in handy. Nothing she'd had in her duffle would have sufficed.

"Each mountain in the black hills has a name," Phelan said as his gaze fastened on them.

"What are they?"

"Am Bastier, which means 'the Executioner.'"

"Oh, that makes me feel safe."

He chuckled and took a drink of his water. "There's Sgurr a Ghreadaich."

"And that one translates to?"

"The Peak of Torment."

Aisley's brows lifted. "Wow. They keep getting better and better. Is that all?"

"Then there's Ah Garbh-choire."

She held up her hand when he started to talk. "Let me guess. It means 'Doorway to Hell.'"

Phelan tossed back his head and laughed. "Nice try, beauty. It translates to 'the Wild Cauldron.'"

"That's so tame compared to the others."

"Names can be deceiving," he warned.

Aisley looked at the mountains. "You think we'll find answers there to the selmyr. What if we find more?"

"That's what I'm hoping for."

"More isn't always good."

Phelan's blue-gray eyes scanned the surrounding area. "Throughout my long years, I've learned there is verra little that ever turns out to be good."

Aisley inwardly cringed. She was going to turn out to be one of those things. And that saddened her as nothing else had since losing her daughter.

It was almost time. He had taken form. It had been but for a moment, but it had happened.

Aisley.

She drew him. He'd felt her presence. It was his hatred that guided him to her time and again. It's what would lead him to her once more.

He stretched out his mind, searching for her through time and space. There was someone else he wanted to look for, but her name kept slipping from his mind. When he found Aisley, she'd tell him all he wanted to know.

Where he was, time didn't exist. He simply . . . was. With no form, he wasn't sure how his magic stayed with him. Instead of questioning it, he gathered his magic close.

The words of a spell he'd learned . . . he wasn't sure when he'd learned it. The words were just there. They fell through his mind like raindrops on a loch. His magic rippled through time until he found Aisley.

CHAPTER
TWENTY-NINE

Phelan wasn't astonished to find Aisley could climb better than she'd said. They reached the first slope of the Cuillins an hour ago. The climb was steep and slippery in places. He stayed behind her in case she fell, but he let her choose the best path for her.

The Druids he'd felt in Portree were near. They were getting closer to them, he knew. Aisley's apprehension of meeting them gave him an uneasy feeling—about all of it.

Phelan realized that giving Aisley the room she needed to trust him could well turn against him. What he had learned of her past were things she hadn't shared with anyone else.

It was the rest of her past that concerned him. Like who she was running from. And who in her family had told her about being a Druid and magic as well as Warriors but hadn't told her the story of Deirdre.

He braced a hand on Aisley's hip when she reached a steep part of the mountain that required her to get a firm handhold to pull herself up. Only when she had gotten past the roughest section did he use the strength his god gave him and jump to stand beside her.

Her lips twisted. "I'm thinking I should just hop on your back and you do that all the way up the mountain."

"I can," he said with a grin. "Then you'd miss some great views. And we could miss the Druids."

"This is a long shot we're taking. The Druids that bound the selmyr are probably long gone. You said yourself Druids are becoming scarcer and scarcer. Do you really believe the ones here will know what to do?"

He turned her to unzip her pack and take out the jacket he'd packed for her. After he zipped her pack back up, he pulled it off her and handed her the jacket. "You're going to want to put this on."

Aisley looked from him to the sky. Without a word she got it on and zipped it as the first drops of rain started. Phelan then handed her a fleece beanie.

"Thank you," she murmured as she slid the beanie over her head, making sure it covered her ears.

"The rain is going to make the climbing that much more difficult."

She shrugged. "I'll be all right."

"Aye, but I willna be worrying about you. There's a place a few hundred yards up that will give us protection."

Aisley's flattened lips told him she hated being coddled, but he couldn't help it. He wouldn't chance her life just to get a little farther.

Not to mention the rain could last all day. He hadn't mentioned spending the night on the mountain, but he had come prepared for it.

Phelan pointed her in the direction they needed to go. As if on cue, the rain quickly turned from a drizzle to a downpour. It could last as little as a few minutes or as long as an hour. The weather on Skye adhered to its own rules.

The slope evened out as they neared the hollowed part of the mountain. But it also grew narrow. Phelan was opening his mouth to tell Aisley to be careful when her foot slipped on a loose rock.

His instincts and quick reflexes grabbed her before she could go over the side. Phelan tightened his hold on her wrist before he pulled her up beside him.

Aisley was visibly shaken as she looked over the side to where she would have fallen had he not caught her. He couldn't even think about it.

"Slowly," he cautioned.

She nodded and started forward with one hand on the mountain. Phelan watched every move she made like a hawk. It was an eternity later that they reached the hollow.

As soon as they were inside he pushed her up against the wall and kissed her long and hard. It was meant to distract them both, but her answering moan turned his blood to molten lava.

He angled his head, deepening the kiss. His hands delved into her wet hair, feeling the coolness of it. Instantly it was like cold water doused on him.

Phelan ended the kiss and looked down at her. "Are you cold? You feel cold."

"I am a little."

"You need a fire," he said and looked outside hoping to find something to burn.

There was a loud sigh behind him. "What I need is for you to calm down," she shouted over the rain.

Phelan turned his head and glared. "You're cold."

"And so is your skin. It's raining and the temperature dropped. I've been in colder weather than this, and I survived."

He was handling the situation all wrong, but how could he explain to her the terror that gripped him? She was mortal. It took the smallest thing to end her life. He'd witnessed it through the centuries, and the idea of it happening to Aisley left him feeling as if the iron grip on his chest would never let up.

"Besides, there isn't room for a fire," Aisley said. "There's barely enough room for both of us to sit."

Phelan ran a hand down his face and shook the water from his hair. "Do you have the magic to heal yourself?"

The silence that followed made the fist around his chest tighten until he couldn't breathe.

"No," she replied in a soft whisper.

He turned to her. "You're strong. You willna get sick."

"I won't get sick," she repeated, a small smile tilting up the corners of her mouth.

Phelan dropped his pack to the ground and smoothed his hair away from his face. He couldn't take his gaze off Aisley. She slowly set her pack down before she removed her jacket.

With her gaze locked with his, she held her hands out with her palms facing down. Her magic, warm, elegant, and provocative engulfed him.

Claws lengthened from his fingers that he buried in the granite of the mountain. If he went to Aisley, if he neared her he'd take her savagely, brutally. His hunger was that great.

Fire erupted between them. Phelan tore his gaze from hers to look at the red and orange flames. Heat instantly filled the small space.

"I might not be able to heal myself, but I can do other things."

Phelan swallowed hard. "You really have no idea what your magic does to me, do you?"

"If you mean, can I see that your eyes are flashing from blue-gray to gold, yes, I can tell."

"Does it frighten you?"

"Only if you don't come here so I can kiss you."

Phelan was in front of her the next second.

MacLeod Castle

Larena stood on the shore with her arms wrapped around her. The wind battered her while the waves rolled toward her, landing in foam upon the rocks at her feet.

For centuries she had been a part of this land. She'd given blood, sweat, tears, and her soul to protect it—to protect those within the castle walls.

The woman she was when she first met Fallon had been shaped by years of fighting *droughs* and the love of the one man in all the world who was meant to be hers.

Yet, she was changing. She could feel it inside. The things that used to matter—family, laughter, love—were things she had to work to remember.

She held out a hand and called up her goddess. Her skin shimmered as it turned iridescent and long, sharp claws extended from her fingers. She ran her tongue along her fangs.

Her goddess, Lelomai, called for death.

Larena struggled to take in each breath. Lelomai was taking control. Bit by bit Larena was losing the battle she'd won hundreds of years ago.

Lelomai's call to let go was tempting. Larena was tired of fighting, tired of giving up everything for the safety of mortals who didn't know she existed.

All she had to do was relinquish the last grip of her control. It would all be over quickly.

Hands, firm and strong, spun her around. She found herself looking into the dark green eyes of her husband. Fallon's long, dark locks were dancing about his head in the wind, and the stricken look on his face told her he knew exactly what she'd been about to do.

"Doona go where I can no' follow," he begged.

She placed a hand over his heart after she tamped down her goddess. He'd had his own demons to fight when she first met him. She had helped him fight his addiction to alcohol, but she wasn't sure he could help her. "It's getting too hard to fight my goddess."

"You've had control for five centuries, my love. The only way Lelomai gets to rule you is if you let her."

"If I let go, all of this craziness inside me will cease."

"If you let go, I'll lose you."

Anguish, sharp and true, rang clear in his deep green eyes. She had loved this man through centuries. How could she think of giving up on that? They had shared laughter, heartache, battles, long nights of steamy lovemaking, and a bond that couldn't be reversed.

Larena closed her eyes and gave a vicious shake of her head to clear it. When she looked at Fallon again, whatever had taken hold of her was gone.

"I'm fading," she told him. "I can feel it. One day you'll come to me and I won't know who you are."

He pulled her into his arms and held her tightly. "We'll always know each other, Larena. Our love is solid and formidable. Evil isna strong enough or brave enough to try and touch us."

"It's not safe for me to walk freely in the castle. You need to lock me in the dungeon."

"Never."

She lifted her head and traced his lips with her finger. "Always so stubborn."

"I'm protecting you."

"Then let the Druids spell me into a deep sleep."

He shook his head. "Nay. I wouldna be able to reach you then. You must stay with me. You have to fight this.

I'll be here. You know I'll help you, but you have to do this, Larena."

He didn't finish. But there wasn't a need. She knew if she didn't fight she was already lost to him.

She looked out across the turbulent sea. Engaging whatever was inside her was going to be the most difficult battle of her life. How could she refuse Fallon, though? She couldn't. It seemed a daunting trial before her, but with Fallon beside her, she could get through anything.

Larena faced her husband and smiled. "Then let's fight this thing."

Relief flooded his eyes. He held out his hand, and together, they jumped to the top of the cliffs to walk back to the castle.

CHAPTER
THIRTY

It was after lunch before the rain stopped. Kissing Aisley had been a mistake. It took everything Phelan had not to make love to her right then and there.

He settled for heated kisses and having her straddle his lap as he sat on the ground. She drew his attention away from everything, which he couldn't allow right then.

Phelan sensed not just the *mies* but something else as well. Danger was in the air. It crackled around him, putting him on instant alert. Whether the danger was for him or Aisley, he wasn't sure yet.

And until he was, he didn't want Aisley to know anything.

He looked out over the land. The sun was already breaking through the dense clouds, shining beacons of light over the rugged terrain of Skye. The rain coating the mountains sparkled like diamonds in the sunlight. It didn't seem to matter what weather was on Skye, the place was truly enchanted.

"That was good," Aisley said as she swallowed the last bite of her sandwich and reached for her water.

Phelan swiveled his head to her. "I think we should wait for the sun to dry the rocks before we proceed."

"We could be here for an eternity. Do you think I didn't grow up with the damp Scottish weather and don't know how to keep my footing?"

"The Cuillin mountains are different. They were aptly named for a reason."

She rose to her feet, dusted off her bottom, and then shrugged on her backpack. With a small movement of her hand, the fire she created disappeared. "We go now."

Phelan couldn't hold back his smile. The woman was spectacular when her fawn-colored eyes flashed with determination.

He used the rocks behind him to gain his feet. "Aye, we'll go. But slowly."

"Slow it is, then."

He followed her out of the hollow and averted his eyes while trying not to smile when she'd taken two steps and her foot slipped on some loose pebbles.

"Fine," she said with a huff after she righted herself. "Go on and say 'I told you so.'"

Phelan instead cupped the back of her head and kissed her. He gazed into her eyes and whispered, "Be careful, but keep moving. Slow and steady."

"What is it?"

"I want off this narrow section before you give me gray hair," he lied.

She puffed out a breath, but when she took her first step, Phelan saw she was being more cautious than before. Thankfully, a half hour later they came to a wider portion of the mountain.

Phelan took the lead again. His eyes were always searching, looking for a sign of the Druids or the danger. If the threat was to Aisley, he could easily defend her and get them both to safety.

If he was the one at risk, he hoped Aisley could use her magic to get herself away.

He glanced at her and was met with a smile. Phelan knew it was the right thing to do to come to Skye. If they could contain the selmyr, then it was one less thing they had to battle.

Coming to Skye alone might not have been so wise. Yet he wanted to do something for the group of men and women who had welcomed him at MacLeod Castle. Maybe it would make up for not going to them four centuries ago.

Maybe it would help heal the wound that cut through his soul.

Aisley knew something was bothering Phelan. It was the subtle differences in the way he moved and looked around them. He'd gone from hiker to predator in less than a heartbeat.

There were no trees on the mountains. Just rock as far as the eye could see. Bright green grass carpeted the lower hills and valleys and sometimes even halfway up a mountain.

The peaks of the mountains looked imposing and daunting. She wondered how far up they'd have to go before Phelan found what he was looking for. Which made her frown. What exactly was he looking for?

"Phelan, where are we going?"

"Deeper into the mountains."

She suppressed a frustrated sigh. "Why?"

"The Druids," he said over his shoulder. "I told you that."

"Yes, but you didn't tell me where we were going."

He slowed until she was even with him. A grin pulled up one corner of his mouth. "I doona know where the Druids are, beauty. The farther we go into the mountains the more of a chance we have of finding them."

"And if we don't find them?"

"We will."

His confidence should have bolstered her own. Instead it irritated her. "I don't like being kept in the dark about things. It makes me feel untrustworthy."

Phelan halted instantly and his eyes pinned her. "This isna about trust, beauty. It's about keeping you safe. You bring up trust at every turn."

She swallowed nervously, wondering if he would press her for answers about who she was running from. Aisley looked away because she knew Phelan was right. She did have trust issues. Big ones.

"The Druids are here," Phelan said, his deep voice softened. "I can no' see them, but I feel them. I've no answers for you other than that. I hope they'll talk to us with you beside me."

Aisley looked into his blue-gray eyes. "You think they know what you are?"

"A Warrior? Aye. It's why they're watching us. I'm sure they also want to know what you're doing with me."

"Surely they know of those at MacLeod Castle?"

He raked a hand through his hair and shrugged. "They may no'. You have roots here, Aisley. Your blood links you to Skye. If the Druids talk to anyone, it'll be you."

"Phelan, look, I'm sorry," she said and licked her lips. "I just . . . it's just . . . so—"

"Shh," he said over her. "There's no need for an apology, beauty."

"There is," she insisted when he continued walking.

It took her more energy to climb up the steep slope behind him. Her breath came in great gasps, and the cool air that had come in with the rain was gone.

Sweat covered her brow. Aisley couldn't get her jacket and sweater off fast enough. She stuffed them, as well as her beanie, into her pack and sighed with relief.

She grabbed a bottle of water and lifted it to her lips when she spotted a face in the rocks below and to the left of her. The vibrant blue eyes blinked up at her without fear, without alarm.

It took Aisley a moment to make out the face belonged to a female. A stunning one at that with long black hair. Aisley parted her lips to call to Phelan, and in that instant, the girl vanished.

Aisley jerked her head to Phelan to find him watching her with furrowed brows. "There was a girl there," she said and pointed to where the face had been.

"I knew they were close," Phelan said. "We need to keep walking."

"Why didn't she speak?"

He lifted one shoulder. "They're getting closer to us a wee bit at a time."

Aisley slid her pack back onto her shoulders and started after Phelan. His long strides ate up twice as much distance as hers could. She thought he would be happy that a Druid of Skye had been so near, but it was the exact opposite. He was worried, and it didn't take his searching gaze or the gold claws extended from his left hand to tell her that.

It was in the way he walked, as if he were looking for something to kill.

Aisley imagined this was how he would be when he came for her. His jaw tight, his eyes devoid of emotion. A Warrior through and through.

She took in a deep breath when they reached another plateau. Turning around slowly, Aisley took in the views.

"Wow," she murmured. Her eyes landed on Phelan to find his lips flat and a frown marring his forehead. "What is it?"

"I—"

She didn't hear the rest as pain exploded in her head.

Aisley clutched her head with her hands and bent over. Agony shot through her like small pieces of glass cutting into her brain.

"Aisley."

No. It couldn't be. Her stomach fell to her feet with dread.

"You're mine!"

She screamed when something cut into her upper left arm. The force of the attack sent her off balance as it spun her. She tried to pry open her eyes to see where she was, but the pain was too much.

"Mine!" the voice bellowed in her mind.

Another cut, this one deeper, toppled her onto her back. Something was pressing on her chest, the weight of it blocking her air. Her lungs couldn't expand to draw in breath. She was suffocating.

She knew who was attacking her. And Jason wouldn't make her death quick.

Phelan couldn't make his body move fast enough. He dropped his pack and launched himself from the edge of the mountain as Aisley fell off the side.

Something, someone had pushed her. He knew it, just as surely as he knew that he wasn't going to let her die.

He caught her against him and reached out with his other hand to grab hold of anything he could find. His fingers came in contact with a rock protruding from the side of the mountain, and they came to a bone-jarring halt that jerked his shoulder out of place.

Phelan gritted his teeth. He forgot all about the pain when he saw the blood dripping from Aisley's arm, and the trickle that fell from her nose. She was breathing but unconscious.

He glanced down to see a small outcropping about thirty feet below him. Phelan released his hold on the rock. He landed on the outcropping with Aisley cradled in his arms and his knees bent.

In one jump, Phelan had them back atop the plateau. He removed her pack and gently lay Aisley on the ground, then knelt to look at her wounds. There were three slashes across her arm. One was so deep it went to the bone.

With one claw lengthened, he cut his wrist and let his blood flow into her wounds. As soon as he saw the injuries heal, he released the breath he'd been holding.

But Aisley wasn't out of the woods yet. Phelan let his blood drip into her mouth. It took her a minute before she swallowed it, but as soon as she did, he could see her body healing.

He wanted to search for whatever had attacked her, but he couldn't leave her. The longer she lay unconscious, the more agitated he became.

There had been something in the air, something evil and malicious. He'd felt Wallace's magic an instant before Aisley grabbed her head in pain.

But if it had been Wallace, why hadn't he also attacked him? Wallace made no secret of his hatred for those fighting against him. It would have been the perfect opportunity for Wallace to capture or kill him.

Instead, the assault had been on Aisley.

Phelan jerked his shoulder back into place and then pulled out his phone. His finger was about to press Charon's number when Aisley's eyes opened. She drew in a long breath, and her gaze found him.

"You're all right now," he told her.

A lone tear fell from her eye to fade into her hair. "You aren't safe with me, Phelan."

CHAPTER
THIRTY-ONE

Aisley waited for Phelan to question her. Instead, he ran the backs of his fingers along her cheek tenderly. His blue-gray eyes studied her solemnly.

"How do you feel?"

She took stock of her body and was amazed to find there wasn't a twinge of pain anywhere. "Like nothing happened. Did I dream it?"

"Nay, beauty," he said dejectedly.

That's when she understood what he had done. "You used your blood to heal me."

He gave a single nod. "It was Wallace. I doona know why he attacked you and no' me, but I've put you in grave danger."

"You don't understand," she said as she sat up, even as he tried to keep her lying down. Aisley pushed his hand away. There could be no more secrets. Phelan had to know everything. She couldn't live with herself if he blamed himself for what was her fault.

"I do," he said over her. "We need to head back to the hotel. I'll call Fallon. He can teleport some Warriors and

Druids here to protect you while the rest of us search out the Druids here for answers on the selmyr."

Aisley rolled her eyes. Damn but Phelan was stubborn. "First, I'm not turning back. We're here. And the Druids can help you defend against Wallace."

Phelan got to his feet in one smooth movement. "Do you even know what happened to you? I saw it all, Aisley."

"And I felt it." As horrible as it was. She suppressed a shudder just thinking of the agony she'd endured for just a few minutes.

If that's what Jason had in store for her, she was determined not to let him get close again.

Aisley climbed to her feet and stood in front of Phelan. "The part of my past I didn't want to tell you. It's time you knew. Everything."

"What was that?" Phelan asked, his forehead furrowed as he narrowed his gaze over her shoulder.

In a blur of movement, he was gone, chasing after whatever he saw. Aisley retrieved her pack and his and started after him as fast as she could.

She lost sight of him when he went up and over one of the mountains. Carrying two packs made climbing difficult. She'd had no idea Phelan put so much stuff in his pack. It weighed twice as much as hers.

Aisley grunted as her thigh muscles screamed in protest from the strain as she trudged up the incline. The rips in her sleeve allowed the breeze to cool her heated skin, but it also reminded her that Jason was back.

And Phelan deserved the truth.

Even if she wasn't ready to attack Jason herself.

Out here in the middle of the Cuillins was the perfect place to die. It was the home of her ancestors. It would be her final resting place. It was fitting, in a morbid sort of way.

She brushed hair out of her face that had come down

from her ponytail. The ascent up the mountain was the most challenging climbing she'd ever done. As much as she hated to do it, she had to stop and rest.

Aisley gave herself five minutes. She used that time to relieve the weight of the packs from her shoulders and to drink as much water as she could.

Then she was back to climbing. She didn't see another soul for the next forty-five minutes. Though she tried not to notice the time, she couldn't help but wonder where Phelan was. What would make him leave her like that?

"Bugger it," she ground out when her foot slipped for the third time on a bit of rock she was trying to get a foothold on.

The rock wasn't big enough to take even the tip of her foot. She tried for a fourth time only to have her foot slide off again.

She was about to find another place to climb when a hand appeared in front of her face. Aisley looked up to find Phelan. She took his hand, and he effortlessly pulled her up beside him.

"I saw a Druid," he said as way of explanation.

Aisley set down the packs and grabbed the water as she tried to get her breathing under control. She drank half a bottle before she lowered it and glared at him. "You could've told me that before you raced off."

"Aye. I need to work on that. I'm used to being alone."

"It's courtesy," she said, winded.

Phelan pointed to the valley below. "We need to go there."

"Did you find the Druids?"

He smiled sheepishly. "No' exactly."

"Lead the way then."

Phelan took his pack and tried to grab hers as well. Aisley jerked it out of his grip and reached for a bag of nuts she'd seen. She slid the pack onto her shoulders and tore open the package of cashews to munch on as they walked.

The entire way down the mountain all Aisley could think about was spilling her secrets. She could be a coward and tell him as they walked. But she wanted to look him in the eye so she could gauge his reaction. It was how to start that was the problem. She couldn't just blurt out that she was Jason's cousin.

If she told him she was looking for a way to fight Jason, then Phelan would want to know how she knew him. It was all so damned convoluted.

More clouds rolled in to block the sun. It helped to lessen the heat, but fortunately, there was no more rain. The weather had changed so many times that Aisley wouldn't be surprised if it began to snow.

They finally reached the valley. Bright green grass stretched in an endless sea before her, only broken by the occasional boulder that protruded from the ground.

Aisley turned in a slow circle looking at the valley, the mountain peaks against the white clouds, and the shadows those same clouds cast on the mountains.

Phelan's hand brushed hers. His pull on her was so great she was incapable of ignoring him. Her eyes slid closed when his fingers brushed her jaw and gently turned her face to him.

His lips grazed hers in a whisper of a kiss. He murmured something in Gaelic she didn't understand, and then he claimed her mouth.

Roughly, fiercely. Savagely.

Aisley's body came alive under his touch. She moaned, answering the demand in his kiss. Her arms wrapped around his neck as he molded her body against his.

His arousal was pressed against her stomach. Her hips rocked against him, wringing a groan from deep within him. He whispered her name as he kissed down her throat.

"I need you," she said.

She dropped her head back while his mouth moved to her neck. His hand cupped her breast and squeezed. She knew it was wrong to make love to him right before she told him she was *drough*, but Aisley couldn't help herself.

There was no denying her body—or Phelan.

"They're watching," he said.

"I don't care. I need to feel you inside me."

He dropped his head against hers. "As much as I want to lay you down and strip you while making love to you in this place, I'd rather no' be watched while I do it."

Aisley couldn't help but grin. She plunged her fingers in his dark locks and held him. If only she had the magic to stop this moment in time.

The Druids who dared to control time paid a hefty price. Not only did Aisley fear the consequences of trying, but she didn't have the magic for it—even with her black magic.

"Do you hear that?" Phelan asked and lifted his head.

Aisley listened carefully, but heard nothing. "No."

He took her hand and pulled her after him as he walked deeper into the valley. They walked another ten minutes when she heard it.

"Water," she said.

Phelan smiled. "A waterfall, if I'm correct."

A laugh bubbled within her as he started running. She followed, their hands still linked. The sound of the water grew the closer they got to it until it was a deafening roar.

They came to a halt when they reached a cliff that dropped off into the most beautiful emerald-green water Aisley had ever seen.

The waterfall was below their feet coming from a stream to her right. The water tumbled over rocks before plummeting into emerald depths. Surrounding the water were sheer walls of rock and more boulders protruded in the water below.

"In all the times I've been here, I've never found it," Phelan said.

Aisley glanced from the water to him. "Found what?"

"This is the Fairy Pool."

"I've heard of this. It's a tourist destination."

Phelan squatted down and looked over the side to the water. "Nay, beauty. No' this one. This is the real Fairy Pool."

"Meaning?" she prodded.

His gaze lifted to hers. "You've magic. Do you think you're the only one who has it?"

"Well . . ." Aisley trailed off because she didn't want to admit she had thought that. Then she lifted her chin. "I knew there were Warriors."

"Ah, but our gods were pulled from Hell by magic. We doona have magic."

"You're magical enough for the selmyr to want to eat you."

Phelan chuckled. "True enough, beauty."

"So, what other magical beings are walking about?"

He pointed to the water. "Why do you think they call this the Fairy Pool?"

"Surely not for fairies. They don't exist."

He didn't argue with her, just smiled patiently.

"Tell me," she urged.

"Scotland has many myths and legends about magic and magical beings. Druids were real. What makes you think none of the others are?"

Aisley looked at the water. It looked so inviting. She turned on her heel and began looking for a way down to the water.

It didn't take her long to discover a narrow trail that was nearly covered by the tall grass. Aisley was about to take her first step when Phelan's arm wrapped around her waist.

"Hold on, beauty," he said just before he jumped off the side.

Aisley's gasp caught in her throat as the air whooshed around her. Phelan landed softly before he let her feet touch the flat stone he stood upon.

"You come in handy," she said with a laugh.

His blue-gray eyes dropped to her lips. Heat filled Aisley as her breasts swelled and her nipples hardened. Her body ached for his. The hunger filling her was primal, unadulterated.

Raw.

Before they could kiss again, Phelan's head snapped up. Aisley looked to where he was staring to find an older man with a gray beard hanging to his chest and penetrating black eyes.

"What do you want here, Warrior?" the man demanded.

Phelan moved so that she stood behind him. She leaned to see around his shoulder and get a better look at the old man. His shoulders were slightly bent, and he held a large walking stick in his right hand.

Gray hair was pulled back in a neat queue at the base of his neck. He wore a plain, dark green military-like jacket over a tan shirt. Black pants and boots completed his outfit.

Phelan let out a slow breath. "We're looking for you, actually."

"Why?"

"We've found information that the Druids of Skye could help contain the selmyr."

At the mention of the creatures, Aisley saw the old man's body give a slight jerk. So they knew what the selmyr were. Maybe Phelan had been right in wanting to come here.

"Who are you?" the man asked.

"Phelan Stewart. I bring a Druid descended from your line—Aisley. And your name?"

The old man's gaze came to rest on Aisley. She refused to look away. Why should an old man cower her when Jason hadn't been able to? Somehow she stood her ground.

"Corann," the man answered. "You've found us, but whether we help or no' remains to be seen, Warrior."

Phelan squeezed her hand and started to follow Corann when he walked away. Aisley hesitated a moment wondering why Corann had looked at her so strangely.

"Don't do it," came a female voice behind her.

Aisley turned to see the same vivid blue eyes from earlier staring at her. Up close she could tell the Druid was only in her early twenties. "Don't do what?"

"Tell Phelan your secret."

"He needs to know," Aisley whispered. She scrunched her face as she looked at the woman before her. "Who are you? And how did you know?"

"I'm Ravyn. I know because the wind told me."

"Then you understand he has to be told. He has a right."

Sadness came over Ravyn's face. "I know, but you can't do it here. If you do, Phelan will kill you as you've guessed. Then we'd have to kill him for harming you."

"I don't understand." Aisley rubbed the back of her neck where a dull pain had begun. "You know I'm *drough*. I'm connected to Jason Wallace. I can stop my cousin, if I give in to the evil. And then my death is the answer."

"Perhaps. But you'll not tell Phelan on Skye. Not if you want our help with the selmyr."

It was blackmail plain and simple. Yet, Aisley accepted Ravyn's threat. After all, Aisley wasn't ready to tell Phelan anything and spoil what they had.

Aisley turned to look at Phelan and Corann. Phelan stood head and shoulders above those around him. He commanded attention with his good looks and the self-assured way he held himself.

He could have been a great lord or even a powerful ruler had Deirdre not taken him. But it didn't matter what century Phelan was in. He was a man others took notice of and respected.

"You love him," Ravyn stated. "But you must wait to share your secret. Phelan is needed."

"I know he's needed. He's important in the fight against evil. To harm him just because he'd be doing the right thing in killing me is absurd."

Aisley had heard enough. She started after Phelan only to feel Ravyn move up behind her. Her voice, when it reached Aisley, was barely above a whisper. The wind swept through her hair at the exact moment, sending a tingling along her skin.

"He's a prince."

CHAPTER THIRTY-TWO

MacLeod Castle

Camdyn MacKenna tapped his finger on the table absently. The evening meal was over, but no one left the great hall. He missed being in his own home, a home he and Saffron had built outside the shield protecting the castle.

He'd brought his wife and daughter to the castle to keep them safe, but he was beginning to wonder if there was such a place. Before, there had never been a question. Everyone gathered at the castle.

The combination of magic within the stones and the magic of the Druids, along with the Warriors' powers made the castle a stronghold few could get through.

That no longer held true.

He could see the strain of that knowledge on the face of every Warrior. The Druids weren't immune to it either, but the women were better at hiding their anxiety.

"I'd rather no'," Broc's voice rose to echo through the hall.

Camdyn's gaze swiveled to where Broc, Fallon, Arran, and Ramsey stood at the other end of the long wooden table. The conversation in the hall quieted as everyone turned their attention to the four men.

"I'm no' asking you to get him," Fallon argued.

Broc crossed his arms over his chest, his dark brown eyes narrowing dangerously. "That's exactly what you want. Phelan told Charon he'd call when he had news."

"That's no' good enough!" Fallon bellowed.

Arran held up his hands between the two men. "Easy, lads. We're all testy here. Remember that."

Fallon inhaled deeply, never taking his eyes off Broc. "I need to know where Phelan is."

"Give a good reason then," Ramsey stated calmly, his voice laced with a hard edge. "You've no' told Broc why."

"Why do I need to?" Fallon demanded.

One black brow rose in Ramsey's forehead as his silver gaze coolly watched Fallon. "Common courtesy for one, my friend. You've never had a problem trusting Phelan before. Why are you concerned?"

Camdyn rose from the bench and walked toward the group. "That's easy to answer. Larena. I just doona understand why you need Phelan."

"His blood," Fallon said as he began to pace. "I want his blood to try and help my wife."

Camdyn glanced at Saffron who stood with the other women near the hearth. He'd do anything for Saffron, so Camdyn understood why Fallon was so insistent on finding Phelan.

"You need to leave Phelan out there," Arran said into the silence.

Fallon snorted. "Why? So he and Malcolm can continue to find nothing?"

"Have you, Lucan, or Quinn discovered Wallace?" Broc asked angrily.

Camdyn and Ramsey exchanged a glance. When Fallon

looked at Camdyn he said, "It's true. We've all known what you three have been about."

"So much for secrets," Quinn mumbled from his position leaning against the wall.

Ramsey looked around the hall. "There are no secrets here. Everyone should know that."

"Leave Phelan alone," Broc said. "We need him out there searching for Wallace."

Arran lowered his hands. "Phelan has a Druid with him now, so it willna be long before he brings her to us. We'll talk to him then about helping Larena."

"It may be too late," Fallon said as he stalked away.

Camdyn watched him leave. He took a step to follow when Saffron's sweet magic washed over him. Camdyn reached her just as her eyes began to swirl white with a vision.

He caught her in his arms, holding her tightly against him. She was a Seer, which was a rarity in the Druid world, but he never got used to her having the visions.

When Saffron finally blinked, tawny eyes stared up at him once more. "I know," she whispered.

"Know what, love?"

"I know why Britt can't finish her research on the *drough* blood." Saffron swallowed hard, her fingers digging into his arm. "It's Jason."

"What about him?" Lucan asked from beside them.

Camdyn waited as impatiently as the others while Saffron let her mind wander through the flashes of scenes her magic gave her. The visions weren't always clear. Sometimes it took Saffron days to work out exactly what her visions had been trying to tell her.

Saffron stood with Camdyn's help, though she didn't let go of him. "Britt can search for all of eternity for a marker in the blood that will tell her what's different about it and never find it."

Gwynn handed Saffron a glass of water and asked, "What do you mean?"

Camdyn could feel the turmoil rolling off Saffron in waves through her magic. She was angry, frightened, and worried. He kept an arm around her to offer her as much support as he could.

"There's nothing scientific for Britt to find," Saffron said. "Jason added more evil."

Hayden frowned and shook his head. "That doesna make sense. *Droughs* are already evil."

"So are the gods within us," Logan pointed out. "If you go by that theory then the *drough* blood shouldna harm us."

Saffron moved out of Camdyn's arms when Emma began to cry. It wasn't until Saffron had their nine-month-old daughter in her arms that she was able to take a deep breath.

"*Drough* blood is evil. What Jason has done is add in more evil." Saffron kissed Emma's head and met Camdyn's gaze. "I saw it. I saw Jason asking Satan for help bringing us down. The answer was to make it that none of the Warriors would recover fully from *drough* blood."

Camdyn took Saffron's hand and looked at his fellow Warriors. "Britt needs to stop looking for the marker and finish whatever she's doing so that we can counter this new *drough* blood."

"That's going to be damned difficult without the marker," Britt said from the top of the stairs. "I need that marker to make an antidote. Whether magic was used on the blood or not, there is a marker. And I'll find it."

Saffron stood and handed Emma to Camdyn. "Then I'll help."

Camdyn waited until Saffron was out of sight before he turned to Fallon. "You're no' the only one wanting to protect a wife. We need to know where Wallace is."

"And I've been no help," Broc said, his voice laced with anger. "Wallace is no' on this world, no' yet anyway."

Quinn rubbed his chin. "Between worlds maybe? That's where Deirdre was."

"Does it matter?" Isla asked.

Galen watched the green claws extend from his fingers. "Nay. Wallace will die like the *droughs* before him."

Broc clapped Galen on the shoulder. "We may no' know where he'll strike, but we know he's coming. We've known less and won the battle."

"We'll win this one as well," Ramsey stated.

Agony sliced through him, sharp and intense. He cried out, though he had no voice, as his bones began to knit together. The anguish of it was borne because he knew he would have it all in the end.

The torment of his muscles and tendons reforming was more torturous than his bones. Then came his flesh. It was horrific, the stinging of new skin tightening over his body made his lungs seize.

It took a moment for him to realize he had organs once more. Before he could enjoy it, he was ripped from the nothingness.

Rain pelted his skin as he opened his eyes to find himself squatting, his fingers braced on the ground. He dug his fingers into the wet grass and threw back his head.

He let loose a bellow that had been locked inside him for what felt like eons. Slowly he stood and looked down at his hands.

His bones cracked as he opened and closed his fingers. He drew in a deep breath and released it. His eyes were unfocused, and it took several blinks before he could see.

A smile formed when he found himself standing in the backyard of his home. What remained of his mansion were black pillars and rubble everywhere.

With a flick of his hand the mansion was restored to its former glory. He strode to the back door and walked in. A mirror in the long hallway caught his attention. He stopped and glanced down at his naked body before he met the blue eyes of his reflection.

A smile that didn't have an ounce of kindness or mercy turned up his lips. "I'm back."

His first order of business was Aisley. His cousin owed him her life.

CHAPTER
THIRTY-THREE

Phelan wanted to look around the Fairy Pool more. It was the real Fairy Pool, not the tourist pools on Skye that were named after this one.

Aisley's gaze was trying to take it all in as Corann led them toward the cliff facing. Corann waved his hand in a wide sweeping motion and the rocks began to shimmer. Phelan's body raced with excitement when the entrance to a cave appeared.

Corann stepped through without looking back at them. Phelan put his hand on Aisley's lower back and urged her forward when she hesitated. Phelan wasn't sure how many Druids surrounded them since they remained hidden, but a young black-haired Druid that had spoken to Aisley earlier was the last to enter the cave.

Phelan caught sight of hundreds of Celtic symbols marked along the walls of the narrow entrance before it opened into a low-hanging cavern.

"This is as far as you go," Corann said as he stopped and faced him.

Fire flared between Phelan and Corann, the flames

hopped erratically and danced in Corann's black eyes that watched him. Phelan had nothing to hide. He remained still while Corann finished his inspection.

"You could've done this outside," Phelan said.

Corann grunted and lowered himself to a log that had been cut to make a stool. He kept his hand on the walking stick and placed his other on top of his thigh. "I could've. I preferred no' to."

"You wanted to see if I could enter the cave," he said as realization hit.

A smile flitted across Corann's aged face. "Aye. Does that anger you, Warrior?"

"Should it?"

"Hmm." Corann ran his left hand down his beard. "Sit. We'll talk."

Phelan lowered himself to another log stool. When Aisley didn't follow, he turned his head to find her staring at Corann. Phelan took her hand and tugged her down to the stool beside him.

"What is it?" he asked in a whisper.

Aisley shook her head, not meeting his gaze.

"You've been attacked," Corann said to Aisley.

She covered the tears in her shirt with her hand. "Phelan healed me."

"We saw."

"You watched as I was attacked and did nothing?"

Phelan was glad Aisley asked the question, because it had been on the tip of his tongue.

Corann shrugged. "We were too far away."

"Ballocks."

Aisley said it softly, but the impact was like a punch. Phelan inwardly smiled at the spirit of his Druid.

"Would you rather hear that we didn't want to help you?" the black-haired girl said.

Corann's head whipped to her direction. "Ravyn."

That's all it took. One word and the young girl didn't say another.

"You doona trust us," Phelan said. "We understand this. As I told you, we've come for your help and nothing more."

"Is that right?"

Phelan felt Corann's question was directed at him, but the old man's eyes were on Aisley. Phelan leaned forward to brace his elbows on his thighs. "You know of the selmyr."

Corann gave a single nod.

"Can you tell us nothing of them?" Aisley asked.

"I can tell you that you'll be safe on Skye. For a time. The selmyr will feed elsewhere until there is no more. Only then will they dare come to Skye."

Phelan ran a hand down his face, his mind running with possibilities. "How do magical beings fight the selmyr?"

"You can no'. No' unless you're a Warrior."

That wasn't what Phelan wanted to hear. "So Druids are at risk?"

"Aye," Corann said.

"How did you contain the selmyr last time?"

"It took my ancestors years. The selmyr should've remained trapped. What happened?"

"You seem to know everything else," Aisley said. "Why don't you know this?"

Corann said not a word as he looked from Aisley to Phelan.

Phelan cocked his head to the side. "Things happen. We were busy fighting *droughs*. While we were searching for a spell that could bind the gods within us once more, a Druid accidentally released the selmyr."

"That is unfortunate." Corann stood and began to pace in slow strides. "As I'm sure you've known since arriving on Skye, Warrior, our Druids are powerful. We doona have the same potent magic as my ancestors, but we're still a force."

"Aye," Phelan agreed.

"Even with our magic, I doona know if it's enough to capture the selmyr again."

"I see." And Phelan did see. Corann was fearful of the selmyr, which told him that it had taken an incredible amount of magic and skill to trap the creatures before. "Is there any way Warriors can help capture the selmyr?"

Corann halted and faced him. "We lost hundreds of Druids the first time. We doona have those to sacrifice now."

"I know where there are more Druids."

"Those at MacLeod Castle, you mean?"

Phelan nodded, not surprised Corann knew. "It seems you know quite a bit, old man."

"No' as much as you may think. I know of MacLeod Castle. I know there are Druids who live with Warriors there."

There was something in Corann's tone that set off alarms in Phelan. He narrowed his eyes on the Druid. "You might want to watch your tone. Those Warriors you're so ready to hate are the ones who've kept Deirdre and Declan from taking over the world. Those Druids you speak of have done the same while finding mates with the Warriors. For centuries some of them have lived waiting for the time when Deirdre would reappear and we could kill her."

"Which they did," Aisley added.

Corann seemed unimpressed. "Be that as it may, Warrior, the last time a Druid teamed up with one of your kind havoc reigned."

"You're referring to Deirdre." Phelan fought to keep calm. "That bitch had set her plans in motion long before she unbound our gods."

Corann sneered. "That is a story told to young Druids. Deirdre never had the magic for such things."

Phelan came to his feet. It was only Aisley's hands on his arm that held him still. "Doona tell me what you *think* happened, old man. I know the truth. I was there. She unbound my god and kept me locked in that awful mountain for over a hundred years."

Aisley tugged on him to leave, but he remained rooted to the spot.

"There have been Druids who have refused the offer of help from us," Phelan continued. "Those Druids are no longer. Deirdre wiped them out. Declan did his share as well. The new *drough* who has been playing havoc with things is Jason Wallace. He'll know I've been here. He'll come for you. Without our help, how long do you think you and your Druids will be able to stay alive?"

"Is that a threat?" Corann asked.

"It's a statement. Do with it what you will."

Corann slammed the end of his walking stick into the ground. "You're evil."

"The god inside me is, aye. I didna allow my god control. I'm in control. I call up my god when I need him."

Corann lifted his walking stick and pointed it at Aisley. "What's your excuse for being with a Warrior?"

Phelan glanced down at her to see Aisley's pulse beat wildly in her throat. She feared these Druids. That in itself infuriated him. She was one of them. They should be welcoming her, not condemning her for being with him.

"He's a good man. Not only has he helped me, but he's protected me," she answered in a clear voice.

Corann returned his stick to his side and leaned upon it. "What do you need protection from?"

Phelan had heard enough. If she wouldn't tell him, she certainly wasn't going to tell Corann. "There are things in her past. That's all you need to know."

"She's a Druid," Corann said. "She has magic to protect herself."

That same thought had gone through Phelan's mind. He knew how powerful of a Druid Aisley was, but that didn't deter him from wanting her. "She's . . . special."

Corann's bushy gray brows rose in response. "Is that so?"

"I didna come to give you a history lesson of my life or to validate what my friends and I have done to protect this world. I came for your assistance in trapping the selmyr. If you willna help, then just say it and stop wasting our time."

"I'll think on it. Stay here for the night. If I'm no' back in the morning, you have your answer." Corann then walked into the back of the cave with the black-haired Druid and both promptly disappeared.

"Wow," Aisley said.

Phelan grunted. "I think we already have our answer."

"So let's start back now."

He tugged on a lock of hair that hung next to her cheek. "We've had a long day. Let's stay. Besides, I want a closer look at the Fairy Pool."

"I knew you were going to say that," she said with a sly look.

Together they set down their packs and looked out over the water. The sun was low in the sky, casting everything in a deep orange glow.

"What's the legend?" Aisley asked.

"The Fae, of course."

"Seriously? Fairies?"

"Fae," he corrected. "And they are no' what has been depicted in movies. They're our size and doona have wings."

She walked to the entrance and leaned a shoulder against the rocks. The waterfall was so loud she had to raise her voice when she asked, "So I gather they're very magical?"

"Aye," he answered from beside her. "Verra. But no' all of them are good. There are the dark ones."

The light faded a bit from her eyes, almost as if his words had saddened her. "There is evil everywhere."

"In every dimension. There is also good."

She slid her hands into her back pockets. "People think you're evil. I know you're not. How do you deal with that?"

"I ignore them." When that didn't bring a smile, he tried another tack. "Every person, every animal has the ability to be good or evil. They choose which side to feed the most."

"How did you decide?"

He sighed and thought back to those long, lonely, dark-filled days. "I'm stubborn."

"Do you think people can change?"

"Of course. I've seen it."

Her tongue ran over her lips as she turned to look at him. "I'm not proud of my past or most of my decisions. I've not always done the right thing."

"No one has. You can no' expect to be perfect."

"Others would disagree. Tell me more of the Fae," she urged.

He let her change the subject. "It's said the Dark Fae like to capture young girls. They'll either terrorize and torture them, taking their innocence until nothing is left but a shell. Or they'll kill them. The Dark Fae also like to tempt men."

"Do I even want to know what they do to men?"

"The females use them for sex. They become slaves to the dark ones until their only way to survive is by sharing their bodies with the Fae."

"And you want to get a closer look at these things?" she asked incredulously.

Phelan smiled. "Oh, aye. I do."

CHAPTER
THIRTY-FOUR

A prince. Phelan was a prince.

The words kept repeating over and over in Aisley's head. She wanted to dismiss what Ravyn had said, but something inside Aisley hesitated.

There was a very real chance Ravyn was right and Phelan was descended from royalty. It would explain the innate self-assured attitude and his confidence.

"Want to go for a swim?" Phelan asked.

She choked on a laugh. "Are you serious?"

"Aye, beauty." His eyes shone with a wicked light that made her blood quicken. "Are you afraid it's too cold for you?"

"I'm Scottish, remember?"

He simply smiled at her response before he lifted a brow and took off his boots.

Aisley half expected him to be joking. As his second boot hit the rocks and he pulled off his shirt, she knew he was all too serious.

In a matter of seconds, he was naked. He winked at her before he ran the few steps to the edge of the water and dove in.

She gasped when she spotted the rocks, then let out a rough breath when he cleared them. "Insane. That's what he is," she mumbled to herself.

He surfaced and turned to look at her. Phelan jerked his head, sending his hair out of his face while he treaded water. There was no doubt she'd wanted to touch the water since she first saw it.

But Phelan's explanation of the Dark Fae made her hesitate. She might be a Druid, but she had no idea how her magic would work in the Fae realm. Or if it would at all.

Her gaze locked with Phelan's, and all thoughts vanished. Nothing mattered. Not Jason, not the Druids, not the Fae.

Only Phelan.

Aisley's hands shook when she started to disrobe. It was her love of Phelan that frightened her the same time it gave her strength. She doubted anyone would understand it because she didn't.

She pulled the ponytail holder from her hair and felt the thick weight of her hair fall against her back. Phelan swam closer to the edge, waiting for her. He held his hand out to her, his blue-gray eyes darkened with yearning she understood all too well.

Aisley took his hand and allowed him to gently pull her into the water. The emerald-green liquid was cool against her heated skin, but not nearly as cold as the icy depths of most lochs.

"I've never known a woman like you."

Aisley enjoyed the compliment, but she knew what kind of man Phelan was. "In all the centuries of your life you expect me to believe I'm one of a kind?"

"Aye."

She swallowed. The truth of his words shone in his

eyes. Aisley backed away from him, suddenly unsure of where he was going with the conversation. She knew what she felt, and though she craved for him to return her affections, Aisley could never allow him to love her.

"I'm not who you think I am."

"Ah, but you are, beauty."

She shook her head. "I've seen the worry in your eyes when I bring up the secrets of my past. You're scared of what I'll tell you."

"Forget the past," he said as he swam toward her. "The past is the past."

"Easier said than done." She didn't push away when he reached for her and tugged her into his arms. "I didn't tell you at first because I didn't want to. Then I didn't tell you because I knew what you would think of me."

"And now I doona care."

"You need to ca-"

He cut off her words by placing a finger over her lips. She was backed against rocks worn smooth by the water. Her heart raced, her blood burned.

And her body ached.

All for Phelan.

He could turn her into a wanton with simply a look. His blood might heal, but it was his touch that she considered life for he had made her feel something good and right again.

Aisley had forgotten what that was. She suffered, she endured, but not once had she ever been so cared for as she was in Phelan's arms.

His fingers slid around her neck to cup the back of her head. The water moved sensuously between them. Aisley's lips parted on a sigh when Phelan's body glided along hers, rubbing against her nipples.

"So damned beautiful," he murmured.

Blue-gray eyes stared at her from beneath thick black lashes. His large hand held her head steady while he lowered his face to hers.

Her eyes slid closed at the first brush of his lips. The kiss was slow, pleasing, and altogether romantic. Aisley had never had a single romantic thing done to her, and Phelan's kiss took her aback.

He didn't let her retreat. Instead, he deepened the kiss, demanding more. She didn't hesitate to give him everything she was, even a part of her she'd been holding back—the smallest part of her that was still the little girl with big dreams for her future.

Aisley released her hold on herself. She gave him all that she had, including what was left of her soul. Phelan would never know he held her heart and soul in the palm of his hands. It was her gift to him—and herself.

His other hand splayed over her back, holding her tightly against him. It wasn't until the waterfall fell over her head that she realized he had moved them.

She broke from the kiss and laughed while the water washed over her. A moment later he shifted them so the water fell like a curtain behind her.

"Behind the waterfall lies the door to the Fae. Shall we go?"

Aisley shook her head. "There have been too many interruptions for us today already. The Fae can wait."

"Just what I wanted to hear," he murmured before he kissed her again.

Their legs tangled beneath the water. Aisley's arms wrapped around him while the muscles in his back shifted beneath her palms.

He was seduction, persuasion, and temptation. He was desire, excitement, and decadence. All rolled into one mouth-watering, heart-racing, gorgeous package no one could resist. Least of all her.

His hand moved between their bodies. She moaned when he slid a finger inside her before teasing her clitoris in small, rapid circles.

Her breathing became ragged, but every time she tried to wrap her legs around him he wouldn't let her.

"No' yet, beauty," he whispered between kisses.

That wasn't what she wanted to hear. Her body wanted release. Every kiss they shared, every touch throughout the day had been like a slow, tantalizing enticement.

They'd made love fast and frenzied. They'd made love savagely. But they had never tread where they were headed. The unhurried caresses, the languid kisses were taking Aisley to a place she feared she'd lose herself in.

A place where she forgot who—and what—she was.

When she clamped a hand around his wrist and met his gaze, Aisley knew she couldn't deny him anything he wanted. Even if what he wanted broke her.

There was no exchange of words. There was no need. The hunger, the passion between them was enough.

Aisley delved her fingers into his wet hair and kissed him. This time when he swam through the water, he took her to a large, flat boulder that was half submerged in the emerald depths.

She found herself placed carefully on the stone so that only her lower legs hung in the water. He leaned up over her before he bent to kiss first one nipple and then the other.

Her fingers dug into his sides as she tried to bring his lower half out of the water. But he had different ideas.

He moved one of her legs onto his shoulder. Her hands fell away to grip the rock while he shifted down her body. A second later and her other leg was propped on his shoulder as well.

Aisley's sex clenched when his head lowered toward her thighs. He held her hips in his steely grip, glanced at her with his beautiful blue-gray eyes, and then licked her.

Her back arched off the boulder.

Phelan couldn't take his eyes off Aisley. It wasn't just her beauty or her magnificent body. It was her passion. She left him breathless with need and aching for more. It didn't matter how many times he had her, it was never enough.

That thought should give him pause. The things that would have had him on his Ducati for the next bed partner just a few months ago is what kept him next to Aisley.

She knew what he was and wasn't trying to change him. Her acceptance for everything he was staggered him. Phelan assumed he'd walk the earth until the end of time and never find such a woman.

How wrong he'd been.

Satisfaction coursed through him when her moans filled the air. She looked like a goddess splayed out on the boulder with the light fading in the sky and the emerald waters of the pool lapping at her skin.

He loved the taste of her, but he craved more. Phelan rose out of the water and leaned over her. Aisley's fawn-colored eyes opened. Her pupils were dilated as she looked at him. Immediately her hands were on him, urging him over her.

Phelan filled her with one thrust. Her nails raked down his back while she quivered beneath him. He briefly closed his eyes and savored the feel of being surrounded by her hot, tight walls.

It was the closest thing to heaven he'd ever found. He looked down as he slowly pulled out of her. Her lips parted, her chest heaved while she waited for him to fill her again.

He set up a leisurely rhythm to prolong their pleasure. There was no way he would allow this to be over quickly.

Aisley's skin tingled everywhere he touched her. She

was coming apart at the seams, waiting for Phelan to take her to paradise.

His thick arousal thrust into her again and again, stretching her, filling her. He rotated his hips as he drove inside her causing a cry to burst from her.

Her hands roamed over his back, feeling the muscles move and constrict with him. She wrapped her legs around him and sighed when he slid deeper.

He moaned and thrust harder. She saw his arms shake as he held himself over her and watched their bodies meeting. Aisley lowered her gaze just as his thick rod pushed into her. The sight ratcheted her desire by several degrees.

As if sensing her heightened need, he bent and scraped his teeth over her hard nipple. Aisley lifted her hips to meet his next thrust.

She felt the water rise around them, but she was too caught up in Phelan to care. His hips pumped faster, harder. Her body was his. All she could do was hold onto him.

The climax was explosive when it claimed her. Aisley screamed Phelan's name while a luminous light engulfed them.

He gave a final thrust and buried his head in her neck as his seed filled her. Aisley held him tightly while the pleasure wrapped around them, enveloping them.

Surrounding them.

When Phelan was able to lift his head, he knew something profound had happened. Aisley hadn't just touched his body as no other, she had touched his heart as well.

He knew in that instant that there was nothing in this world—or any other—that would tear her from his arms.

CHAPTER
THIRTY-FIVE

Phelan might have wanted to see the Fairy Pool to find the Fae, but he found all he ever wanted in Aisley's arms. She was as limp as a rag doll when he lifted her from the water and carried her into the cave.

After he lay her down, he stretched out beside her and pulled a blanket over them so she wouldn't get chilled. The fire blazed on her other side. It was then he spotted food that hadn't been there earlier.

She rolled toward him with a sigh and rested her head upon his chest. It seemed so natural that he would wrap his arm around her.

"What are you thinking?" she asked after a moment.

Phelan grinned and played with the damp strands of her hair. "You have no' asked me to wear a condom. Are you using a spell to prevent getting with child?" When she didn't immediately answer, Phelan looked at her. "Aisley?"

"I didn't finish telling you everything about what happened after I had my daughter."

By the tone of her voice, he inwardly steeled himself for more bad news. Phelan was having a hard time imagining anyone as wonderful as Aisley suffering so much. "You doona have to say."

"It's all right," she said without looking at him. She drew patterns on his chest with her finger. "I want to. I need to."

She took a deep breath and said, "There were complications. I don't remember all of it because of the painkillers they had me on, but it had something to do with my fall and the operation. I can't have any more children, Phelan. So there's no reason for me to ask you to wear a condom or to use a spell."

To have lost her daughter and then learn she couldn't have any more children. It seemed fate had it in for Aisley. Phelan just couldn't figure out why.

He kissed her forehead. "I'm sorry."

"It's for the best, I'm sure. These things happen for a reason."

Her valiant attempt to shrug off what happened made his heart ache. "Magic may be able to fix whatever is wrong."

"It's better this way. Trust me."

Phelan didn't exactly care for kids. They were noisy, loud, and smelly. But sometime between the last time they'd made love and then, he suddenly found he wanted to see her stomach swell with their child.

What was happening to him? Even more frightening was that he wasn't concerned about his attitude change.

"Do you think Corann will return in the morning?" she asked.

"Nay. He doesna trust me. I hoped having you here would help."

"You were wrong."

"Aye. It appears he's mistrustful of any Druid no' part of his clan."

"It could be more than that."

Phelan grunted. "No' likely. I know the type of man Corann is. He's been in charge a long time. There's been some history here between Deirdre and these Druids that no one knows about. It's because of that event that he is so protective."

"You found the Fairy Pool though."

He could feel her smile against his chest. "Aye. Corann didna like that at all. That means the Fae wanted me to find it."

"But why?"

"Good question. Maybe we should go through the waterfall and find out."

Aisley rolled onto her back, smiling. "I'll pass, thanks. You go and tell me what it's like."

"What?" Phelan rolled onto his side and propped his head up with his hand. "You're the adventurous kind, beauty. Why would you pass up such an opportunity?"

She shrugged, but he saw a sliver of dread in her eyes she couldn't quite hide. "I might not be able to use my magic in their world."

"Ah." Now it all made sense. "We wouldna know until we went."

"Why do you want to go?"

Phelan thought about it a moment and shrugged. "I doona know. It seems as if I've always known about the Fairy Pool. I've been looking for it since I left Cairn Toul and Deirdre."

"Four hundred years is a long time to be looking for something."

"There were times I couldna get to Skye."

Her eyes widened. "What do you mean?"

"Whether it was the weather preventing the ferry, or currents refusing to let me swim, whatever forces were at work kept me away many times."

"And when you did get here?"

He glanced through the cave entrance to the water. "I've walked these exact hills, this exact valley dozens of times and never found anything. I think you brought me luck."

She sat up and pushed her hair back from her face. Sadness was etched around her eyes, and her lips were pressed into a tight line. "I didn't bring you luck. Trust me on that."

"We'll have to agree to disagree," he said and sat up with her. "Why is it when I try to give you a compliment you knock it down? I thought women liked compliments."

She smiled wryly. "I want you to remember I'm just a person. I make lots of mistakes that I'll have to pay for. So don't go thinking I'm perfect."

"Pay for?" he repeated. "Beauty, I think you've paid a damned steep price. There is nothing else for you to pay for."

"That's the stickler, Phelan, because there is."

He inhaled and slowly released it. "This is what you've been trying to tell me."

"Yes."

"I doona care, but if it's that important to you, then tell me after we leave Skye. I doona want your mind on anything other than the pleasure I give you and the wonder of this place."

Relief pooled in her eyes. "I'd like that."

"Good. Now how about we eat?"

He was glad when the smile was back in her eyes as she reached for the food to set between them. She might be happy not to have to tell him her secrets, but he was being selfish. He didn't want her to have to relive more unhappy memories, and he wanted to fill her with good things while he had the chance.

Maybe the time they spent together would erase some of the awful things that had been done to her.

* * *

Aisley wasn't surprised to find Phelan already up and about when she woke the next morning. She stretched and yawned before she sat up. A smile broke when she saw her clothes neatly folded in a pile near her.

She dressed and combed her fingers through her hair. It was the first time she was thankful she didn't have a mirror to know how awful she looked.

It was just as she finished pulling her hair into a ponytail that Phelan walked into the cave. "Morning," she said.

"Morning. Did you sleep well?"

"As if you need to ask. Do you sleep at all?"

"I doona need to, but I did last night."

She sat and put on her hiking shoes. "No sign of Corann, huh?"

"Nay. We've got a hike back to the hotel and with the weather, we might want to leave soon."

"You mean before I had a chance to talk to you," came a voice behind them.

Aisley jerked around to find Corann. She rolled her eyes and got to her feet. "What is it with the grand entrances?" she mumbled.

Phelan covered his grin by clearing his throat. "I didna expect you."

"Obviously," Corann said. "There was much discussion during the night. The fact the Fae allowed you to find their pool played a heavy part in our decision."

Aisley asked, "Why did the Fae allow him to find the pool?"

Corann's black eyes shifted to her. "The Fae allowed both you and Phelan to find the pool. As to why? We doona know, lass. It has been over six hundred years since anyone outside of my clan has seen the pool."

"Then why do the Fae no' make an appearance?" Phelan asked.

Aisley hated to admit she was just as curious as he. "Do you see the Fae often?"

"No' in many years," Corann said. "But neither of you came here to talk of the Fae."

Phelan scratched his jaw. "Nay. We came for help with the selmyr. Do you have good news for me?"

"In a manner."

Aisley didn't like the way Corann stared at her. He knew she was *drough*, but it was more than that. It was like he knew what was to come for her in the days ahead.

"Then tell us," Phelan said, his voice low and menacing.

Corann hesitated a moment before he said, "The only way we could best the selmyr again is if all the Druids in the UK converged here."

Phelan let out a string of curses, but Aisley wasn't going to let it go so easily. "There has to be another way. We're Druids. There are powerful Druids out there."

"True. Verra true, lass." Corann ran his hand down the length of his gray beard. "The problem lies in finding the one who can call up the spell."

"What?" Phelan demanded.

"The spell was created by the magic of a certain family here on Skye. It's said that family line died out generations ago, but there's been no proof. There could still be one out there who could wield the spell."

Aisley lowered herself to a rock. "Is the spell that difficult?"

Corann gave a single nod. "It takes the blood of that family in order to call the selmyr. The selmyr have no choice but to come. When they do, they can be trapped."

"So you just need the blood of that family," Phelan said. "What's the name?"

"The name was Hunter, but it'll be impossible to trace since this was long before names were recorded. But it's more than that. The Druid who uses the spell has to be strong enough. If not, the selmyr will drag the Druid with them to be feasted on for eternity."

"Bugger," Aisley whispered.

Phelan looked at Aisley. "I've seen the selmyr drain a Druid in seconds. I've been bitten by the bastards. I can no' just wait around for their next attack."

"No," she agreed. "We have to find the Druid."

Suddenly Phelan smiled. "Broc. He can find anyone, anywhere. Broc can find who we're looking for."

"They must have magic," Corann reminded them.

Aisley stood when Phelan slung his pack onto his shoulder. "And the spell?" she asked Corann. "Will the Druid know the spell?"

"Nay."

"Of course not," she said to herself.

Corann smiled. "You've spunk, Aisley. That'll help you in the days ahead."

She stilled at his words. A glance showed her Phelan was talking to Ravyn. When Aisley looked back at Corann it was to find the elder Druid's black gaze watching her intently. "What do you know of my future?"

"The same thing you know."

"Regardless of what you might think of Warriors, there are good ones. Phelan is one of those. So are the ones at MacLeod Castle."

Corann leaned both hands on his tall walking stick. "You tell me to trust them, but you fear them."

"You know what I am. You know what they'll do to me."

"Hmm," he said ambiguously. "It's your fighting spirit that's kept you alive in the harshest times, Aisley. There is a choice coming to you. Make the right one, lass."

CHAPTER
THIRTY-SIX

Phelan tried to pretend he didn't know Corann and Aisley were deep in conversation. By the frown marring Aisley's forehead he could tell she wasn't happy with whatever Corann told her.

It wasn't until he felt Ravyn's magic billow around them that he knew the Druid was trying to stop him from hearing Corann's conversation.

"Resorting to magic now, aye?"

Ravyn smiled. "Corann warned me that your hearing was excellent."

"It is."

"I had no choice then."

"You've some cheek."

The Druid's intense blue eyes sparkled with merriment. "It's not every day I get to meet a Warrior. I'm curious to see just how much power your god gives you."

"I could show you, but I'd much rather you tell me why Corann has such an interest in Aisley."

Ravyn's smile fell. "Corann fears any kind of alliance between Druids and Warriors."

"Because of Deirdre?"

"Yes," Ravyn said and looked away as if struggling to come to terms with something. When she met his gaze again she had obviously resolved whatever concerned her. "I like Aisley, and I know you do as well."

"Your point?" Ravyn didn't immediately answer, and it set Phelan on edge. "Do you have a Seer? Has someone seen something of Aisley's future?"

Ravyn put her hand on his arm. "There is no Seer here. It's just . . . the ancients. They told us of Aisley."

"What else did they tell you about her?" Phelan knew Ravyn to be no more than twenty, but she let the veil fall from around her and he saw there lived a very old soul in the body of a young girl.

"There is evil after her."

"Wallace," Phelan said between clenched teeth. "He's going to hurt her to get to me. It's what he promised the last time we fought him. Those who fight him are in his way. He's resorted to all sorts of unspeakable acts to take us out."

Ravyn licked her lips and stepped closer to him. "If this Wallace is everything you say he is, be careful."

"You're telling a Warrior to be careful."

She rolled her eyes. "Stop teasing. Corann told us all about Deirdre."

"But do you know all of it? Do you know she was brought forward to your time by another *drough*? Do you know how we killed her?"

Ravyn slowly shook her head, her eyes bright with interest. "The elders discovered Deirdre's death through the ancients. The wind told me."

"How many of you are there?"

She raised a black brow. "You don't seem surprised that I can speak to the wind."

"Why should I? I know another Druid who has that ability. She's at MacLeod Castle. Gwynn is her name."

"She's a Windtalker?"

Phelan glanced at Aisley to see her conversation ending with Corann. "She is that. Gwynn thinks she's the only one. She'll be happy to know there is another."

"Do you have a Firewalker or Waterdancer? What about a Bleeder or Healer? Or a Skinwalker, Treewhisperer, or Timebender?"

"Slow down," he said with a grin. "Do you have such Druids here?"

"Of course."

He hid a smirk at her derision. "I know of a Healer. I also know a Treewhisperer."

"What are their names?"

"It's the same Druid. Sonya has been at MacLeod Castle for four centuries. She's also married to a Warrior."

Ravyn's eyes widened. "Married?"

"All the Druids at the castle are married to Warriors. Why does that bother you?"

"Are the Druids *droughs*?"

Phelan snorted. "Nay." Then he thought of Isla. Her story was too complicated, and if he told it he'd have to tell part of his story. It was better if they knew nothing of Isla. Yet.

"That's good," Ravyn said.

"Why? What would happen?"

"Do you no' know the prophecy? A powerful *drough* will mate with a Warrior and produce a child that holds all the evil of the world."

"First, lass, that prophecy has come and gone since it involved Deirdre when she tried to get Quinn MacLeod to become hers. Second, the child couldna hold all the evil since there is evil everywhere."

Aisley walked up then. She looked from Ravyn to Phelan. "What's going on?"

"I gather Ravyn spoke of the prophecy," Corann said as he joined them.

Ravyn shrugged and leaned dispassionately against the stone wall. "He asked. I told."

Phelan heard the enthusiasm in her voice. She was lying to Corann. But why? "And I was telling her we all knew of that prophecy. It involved Deirdre and Quinn MacLeod. Quinn rejected her, of course. Even when Declan Wallace brought Deirdre to this time and our Seer—"

"You have a Seer?" Corann interrupted.

Phelan blew out an exasperated breath. "Saffron. Declan kidnapped her and kept her for his own. She was saved by those at MacLeod Castle, and she saw Deidre heavy with Declan's child. But we killed Deirdre. The prophecy is no more."

"Unfortunately you're wrong," Ravyn said quietly.

Phelan felt Aisley stiffen beside him. He edged closer to her and asked Ravyn, "What do you mean?"

"The prophecy states that a *drough* with potent magic will mate with a Warrior and produce the child of the prophecy."

Corann said, "And now you understand one reason we're so leery of Warriors."

"You've nothing to worry about," Phelan said. "There isna a Warrior I know who would dare to sully themselves with a *drough*. When I see one, I kill it."

"It," Aisley said. "A *drough* is an 'it'?"

"Aye," he answered without looking at her. He looked to Corann. "We killed Deirdre and Declan. We'll kill Jason. We'll make sure no more gods can be unbound. Then you willna have to worry about your prophecy."

Corann's grunt was full of doubt. "How many Warriors are at the castle?"

"They're married."

"You're not," Ravyn pointed out.

It took great effort for him not to turn to Aisley and

claim her right then. Instead, he grinned. "As much as I loathe *droughs*, you doona have to worry."

A few words later and Phelan was leading Aisley out of the cave. He didn't like how Corann looked at him as if he'd be the one to fulfill the prophecy—a prophecy no one at the castle had worried about in years.

Damn. He wanted to leave Skye with good news. Instead he had semi-decent news regarding the selmyr and bad news about the prophecy.

He lifted Aisley in his arms when they reached the steep path up the cliff. She wrapped her arms around him a second before he jumped them to the top.

"That just never gets old," she said with a wide grin.

"Glad I can be of use."

"Oh, I've plenty of uses for you," she said with a wink.

He linked hands with her and glanced down at the Fairy Pool. The Fae had allowed him to find the pool once. Would they do it again?

"We can stay longer if you want," Aisley said.

Phelan shook his head. "There are more important matters to tend to. I'll be back though."

"But you're concerned they won't let you find the pool again."

"Aye."

She rested her head against his arm. "There's a reason they showed you this time, and I don't think it has anything to do with the Druids or the selmyr."

"What then?"

"That I can't answer. Do you . . . do you think it might have something to do with your family?"

He jerked his head to her and frowned. "My family? If that was the case, why wouldna they let me find this place the many times I've tried to come to Skye?"

"It was just a suggestion. Nothing more," Aisley hastily said.

Phelan regretted his outburst, but it was always the case when he thought of his family. He was angry at them for not looking for him. More than that, he carried a huge weight of guilt for leaving them and remembering nothing of them.

"I'm sorry," he said and kissed her.

"There's nothing to apologize for. We all have parts of our past that are touchy."

He led her away from the Fairy Pool and the Druids of Skye. Each step made him doubt his insistence to leave.

"How do you know the Druids weren't really Fae?" Aisley asked some time later.

"I doona, though I felt the Druids' magic. I know they were Druids."

"But you've never met a Fae. You don't know what they look like."

Phelan chuckled as he wrapped an arm around her waist. In three jumps he had them atop the mountain. He could have done it in two, but he was being careful with Aisley. "True. I've learned all I could about them through the legends and myths, but I've no' talked to anyone who actually met a Fae."

"I'd bet the entire royal fortune that you talked to one who know the Fae."

"Corann." Phelan rubbed the back of his neck. "You're probably right. I was so caught up in answers for the selmyr that I didna even think to ask him."

"So go back and ask."

He looked back down to where the Fairy Pool was, but it was no longer visible. "I think our time is done. We need to get back to the mainland quickly."

"Back to reality."

There was no mistaking the distress in her words. Phelan could get them back to the hotel in about an hour. If he went at Aisley's pace it could take all day.

"I can take you back to my cabin," Phelan said. "Wallace didna attack you there."

She wouldn't meet his eyes, preferring to stare at his chest instead. "I don't think it matters where I am. If Jason Wallace wants to find me, he will."

"Do you know protection spells you can put around my cabin? If so, I can leave you there while I meet up with Charon and tell him all we've learned."

"I know spells. I don't know how effective they'd be however."

He put his finger under her chin and lifted her face until she looked at him. "If you're worried about telling me this awful secret you have once we get back to the mainland, then forget it. I know the person you are now. That's enough for me."

"You're a good man, Phelan Stewart. A very good man. It's because of who you are that you need to know all there is about me."

"Why? What's so damned important about your past?"

"It's shaped who I am."

"You say I'm a good man. I know you're a good person, Aisley. Let that be enough."

She looked away and let out a long, slow breath. "Will you leave me at your cabin?"

It had been his plan, but he suddenly realized she could run from him again. He didn't mind chasing her. It was the thought that Wallace could get to her before he could that froze his blood.

"You wanted a nice dinner. I think I'll give you that. Inverness has one of my favorite restaurants. I think you'll enjoy it."

He didn't give her time to answer as he picked her up in his arms and used his speed to get them back to the hotel.

CHAPTER
THIRTY-SEVEN

Jason Wallace stared at his reflection in the mirror of his room. His skin felt too tight over his body. After being nothing more than mere consciousness for so long, he felt small.

And he didn't like it.

It didn't help that he'd returned to an empty house. No servants, no Dale, and no Druids. Had Dale and all the Druids died in the last battle with those ugly white-skinned creatures?

Jason ran his hand over his clean-shaven jaw before smoothing back his short blond hair. The blue eyes stared back at him. He might look the same, but he was far from the man he had been.

He wasn't even sure if he was a man.

The corners of his mouth lifted in a smile. What exactly he was he couldn't be sure. Not that it mattered. The potent black magic running through him could barely be contained. He could feel it moving through his veins hot as lava, scalding him the same time it empowered him.

There was a violent need to release his magic on anything and everyone. The ferocious, vicious necessity couldn't—wouldn't—be ignored.

He craved to unleash his magic. Because with every bit of magic he used, it helped to feed him. It seemed odd, this newfound magic.

The resurrection spell he used had worked far beyond his expectations. If he'd known what could happen to him, he'd have done it sooner.

"If only I'd been this strong when I first fought the MacLeods. They'd be dust in the wind now."

But there was still time. Right after he found Aisley.

"Ah, cousin, do I have something in store for you," he told his reflection.

With his magic it wouldn't take long to locate her. It's too bad he didn't know where she'd been when he attacked. He had hurt her, but he was sure she wasn't dead.

If she was, he'd simply resurrect her. She had to suffer for what she did.

He turned away from the mirror as he struggled to remember what he'd experienced when he found Aisley. It had been just a day since he attacked her then been made whole again.

Where had she been? And who was she with?

Jason grabbed his suit jacket as he walked out of his room. He put it on as he made his way down the stairs to his office. It was the same office Declan had used, the same office where Gwynn and Logan had destroyed things when they came to see Declan. The same office where he had held Ronnie and tried to convince her to become *drough*.

The same office where the MacLeods attacked and destroyed the house again.

He stood in the middle of the large office and looked at the wall of books behind the large mahogany desk. Magic had restored the house. Again.

The mansion had been in his family for generations. It had been remodeled and added onto with each owner, but over the course of several years there had been more death and destruction than in the entire history of the Wallaces.

Jason walked to the burgundy leather Chesterfield couch and sat. He stared at the glass-topped coffee table before he glided his hand about six inches over the top.

Instantly a landscape rose up like a 3-D model. Craggy mountains with jagged peaks surrounded by thick mist came into view.

There was no doubt he was looking at a place in Scotland, not with such rugged appeal and untamed beauty. But where?

"What am I looking at?" he asked.

The land blurred into a mass of green and brown as it changed from the mountains to a welcome sign near a port.

"Welcome to the Isle of Skye," Jason read the sign. "So, cousin, you're on Skye. What would bring you there?"

He leaned his forearms on his thighs and clasped his hands together. For several minutes he looked at the port trying to think why Aisley would venture to the isle.

"Show me Aisley," he demanded.

Again the landscape blurred, but for only a second before it stopped in front of a hotel. Now that he'd found her, he could begin.

He raised his hand to dismiss the image when something made him pause. "Who is Aisley with?"

A small replica of Phelan Stewart replaced the scenery of Skye.

"Now this is too fucking easy," Jason said and leaned back against the couch.

There was much he could do now that Aisley was with Phelan. Once he discovered why she was with him. She could be using him, but then again, Aisley was weak.

When he originally asked her to be a *drough*, he'd expected her to be so much more than the weak woman she'd become.

Just because she lost a babe. Jason snorted. He'd made sure she'd lost much more than that. Her parents had died horribly. All while Aisley watched, unable to do anything about it.

That should have made things right. Instead, the silly bitch had tried to leave him. It had taken his resorting to inflicting physical pain upon her to get her on the right track.

Which had done the trick. Then something else happened. Jason wasn't sure when, but Aisley had changed, softened again.

He'd planned to kill her before the last battle with the MacLeods, but then Mindy died and he needed all the Druids he could get.

His mistake was giving Aisley the opportunity to betray him. And no one betrayed Jason Wallace. Those who did paid the ultimate price.

Jason waved away the image of the Warrior. He rose and poured himself a dram of whisky as he contemplated his next move.

He could approach Aisley on Skye, kill Phelan, and then deal with Aisley as he'd dreamed of doing. It was a simple enough plan, but he was curious why a Warrior had teamed up with a *drough*.

After all the battles they'd been in, surely Phelan knew who Aisley was. If he somehow didn't, he'd be able to feel her *drough* magic, which would tell him everything.

So what was going on?

Jason drained the amber liquid in one swallow and set down the crystal glass. There was an opportunity here, and he wasn't going to allow it to pass by.

He didn't need other Druids to find Aisley. However,

they would come in handy should he need something. Jason closed his eyes and released a burst of magic into the air.

Any Druid within a three-hundred-mile radius would feel his magic. It was those inclined to the dark side that would seek him out.

He grinned and poured himself another whisky. Things couldn't be going easier.

Aisley stood in the shower and let the hot water fall over her head. The disappointment she felt when they arrived at the hotel had been staggering.

She tried to play it off, but she failed. Phelan had known something was wrong. He just hadn't tried to pry after asking her the third time.

The water hid the tears she allowed herself to cry. To have had such a glorious few days with such an incredible man made leaving Skye and facing the future even more difficult.

But it also gave her the courage to do whatever she had to in order to fight Jason.

Her finger traced the scar on her lower stomach as she thought of her precious daughter. No one knew the name she'd given her baby. She hadn't allowed it to be carved on the headstone.

"Gillian," she whispered.

She'd been unable to think of anything but Gillian ever since talk of the prophecy before they left the Fairy Pool. Phelan showed her the depth of his hatred for *droughs*. Though Aisley shouldn't have been surprised.

Their time together, the way he smiled at her, touched her, kissed her had altered her perception of being a *drough*.

Phelan brought it all into crystal-clear focus.

But the prophecy worried her. Obviously it concerned

the Skye Druids as well if they brought it up to Phelan. It hadn't gone unnoticed by Aisley how Ravyn and Corann glanced at her when they spoke of a Warrior sleeping with a *drough*.

She couldn't exactly tell them that they needn't worry since she couldn't have children. Her only choice was to remain silent and learn as much as she could.

"Aisley?"

Her head jerked up when Phelan said her name outside the bathroom door. "I'm all right. I'll be out in a minute."

"Take your time. We'll leave in the morning."

One more night. Maybe two, if she was lucky. But luck had never been something she could claim was hers.

If she were in a city, Aisley would find the nearest club and let the loud music take away her worries. If only for a few hours.

She shut off the water and wrung out her hair before reaching for the towel. Her movements were jerky as she dried herself.

A glance in the mirror showed red-rimmed eyes. The last thing she wanted was to explain to Phelan why she was crying. She didn't hear him moving about in the room, so maybe he'd gone out for something. Aisley wrapped the towel around her and opened the door.

To find Phelan leaning his hands against the doorjamb.

"Tell me what's wrong." He stared at her with his blue-gray eyes, his voice soft but firm.

She was so tired of carrying the burden of lies that she knew now was the time to share her secrets.

"I doona care about your damned past," he said before she could utter a word. "If that's what is bothering you, then let it go. If it's something else, then tell me so I can fix it."

"You can't fix this."

"Try me."

"Over the past few days I've been given the world. With you. I . . ." She paused to swallow past the lump in her throat. "I don't want to lose that."

He cupped her face and let his thumb caress her cheek. "We doona have to. The only ones who can tear whatever this is between us is . . . us."

"This is the longest time you've spent with one woman, isn't it?"

"Nay."

She cocked her head to the side. "A lover then."

"If you need to be specific, then aye. There's nothing wrong with that."

"There is," she argued. "You'll get tired of me. That's why you left those other women."

He yanked her roughly against him and lowered his voice to a seductive whisper as he said, "I left those others because they were no' you."

Whatever argument Aisley had died on her lips. She let the towel drop and rose up on her toes to kiss him. His kisses were like a drug. They could give her unimagined pleasure with just one touch.

"I'm no' letting you go," he said between kisses. "You can run from me again. But know this, beauty. I'll hunt you down. No matter how far you go, no matter how long you run . . . I'll find you."

She shivered at his words. They could hold a double meaning. He might proclaim to want her now. How drastically would things change when he learned she was *drough*?

Would he give her a head start in order to hunt her down like a rabid animal? Aisley wouldn't allow that to happen because she wouldn't run.

"Make me forget," she begged him.

"What do you want to forget, beauty?"

"Who I am. Make the world fall away, Phelan. Please."

He carried her to the bed where he lowered her to her feet. Together they divested him of his clothes until they were skin to skin, mouth to mouth.

Heart to heart.

"I'll make it all go away," he promised as he kissed her with abandon.

CHAPTER
THIRTY-EIGHT

MacLeod Castle

Britt puffed out her cheeks before blowing out a breath. She was well past exhausted. Her back ached from bending over the microscope, and her head hurt from trying to work around the problems of the *drough* blood.

"Just think. Months ago I was bored outta my mind and looking for something challenging," she said to Aiden.

He was never far from her. She was thankful, because many times she'd wanted to chuck it all in and give up. Then she'd look at him and remember why she gave up her life to live in a magical castle.

"You need a break. You've been at it for days, sweetheart."

She relaxed when he came up behind her and massaged her shoulders. Tension eased out of her as she sighed in pleasure.

"There are other ways I can make you sigh," he whispered in her ear before he kissed her neck.

Britt spun around on the stool so that she faced him. "When this is over—and it will be over—we're going to take a trip. I don't care where we go because we'll be in bed the entire time."

"The entire time?" he asked, his green eyes gleaming with wicked promise.

"The entire time."

"Then get that pretty arse in gear."

She loved how he could make her laugh. Despite the threat that constantly surrounded them, Aiden always knew the right thing to say and do.

Britt was leaning in to kiss him when the analyzer beeped. She slid off the stool and hurried to it as the findings were printed on paper.

"Good news?" Aiden asked as he came up behind her and looked over her shoulder.

For a minute Britt couldn't move. Her heart was beating so fast she thought she might pass out. Finally she turned to Aiden and looked from the paper to him then back to the paper in her hands.

"I found it."

"What? What did you find?"

Britt blinked to keep the room from spinning. It had been a chance she took by doing the testing. So far she'd been unsuccessful at finding the marker that made the *drough* blood more evil. She'd held out no hope for this last test either.

"The marker. I found the marker we've been looking for."

Several seconds ticked by as she and Aiden stared at each other. Then he yanked her into his arms and hugged her tight. She was shaking with relief and only staying on her feet thanks to Aiden's strong arms.

"You did it," he said. "I never had any doubt."

"I did. Buckets and buckets of doubt. Oh God, Aiden, I can't believe I found it." She buried her face in his neck while he rubbed his hands up and down her back.

"Are you ready to tell the others?"

She shook her head. "Not yet. Finding the marker is the first step, and I don't want to give anyone false hope. Especially Fallon."

"You're probably right. I'd just like to give them some good news."

Britt swallowed and stepped out of his arms, the paper clutched in one fist. "You're right. They need hope. We all do. Tell them. I'm going to keep working. Between this and finishing the serum, I've got lots to do."

"Come down to dinner. You need to eat."

"I'll eat in a bit. Go have dinner with your family."

He grabbed her hips and pulled her flush against him. "You are my family now, too. I'll bring you up some food, stubborn wench."

"Ah, but you like me being stubborn."

"Aye," he said and rubbed his nose against hers. "You know I like it verra much."

It would be so easy for her to fall into his arms. But work called. "Share the good news while I try to finish this."

Britt waited until Aiden had left the tower before she turned back to her equipment with a sigh. She was a step closer, but they needed a miracle. In a big way.

"Think, Britt," she told herself. "Everyone is counting on you. Nothing like pressure to get things done."

She resumed her spot on her stool and smoothed out the crumpled paper in her hand to read over the results again. While more tests were being done on the synthetic blood she'd created that would combat any *drough* blood entering a Warrior, she was determined to find a way to eliminate the marker from Larena's blood.

This work out in the world could earn her science and medical prizes, but that no longer mattered. Helping those in the castle fight evil was her priority now.

"So, let's see what my first test with the new marker will be."

Ferness

Charon signed the last of the checks and gathered them to take to Laura. She sat at her desk outside his office answering e-mails and keeping the books for the many properties and businesses he owned around the small village.

"Here is the last batch," he said.

She smiled as she took the checks. "I thought work might help ease your mind about things. Especially Phelan."

"A good try, and it did for a bit. The bugger is purposefully no' answering my calls. After several texts, he finally responded with a curt 'Talk to you soon' response."

"He could be busy."

"I hope that's the case. We've just heard nothing more about Wallace."

Laura rose from her chair and took his hand to lead him to the couch. With a little shove to his chest, she pushed him down. "As much as you might not like hearing this, I'm glad there's been no sign of Jason. Because as soon as there is that means another battle."

"Hopefully one final battle where we kill the bastard."

"And then?" she asked. "When does the next *drough* rise up to take his place? You know as well as I that Jason has several *droughs* following him."

"Had," Charon corrected.

Laura crossed her arms over her chest and sighed loudly. "You don't know if it's past tense. They could be waiting for him. I know there was one who was his cousin. Aisley was her name."

"We found bodies of Druids after the last battle, love."

"I know who you found. I was there. There were two bodies we didn't find, Charon. Jason and Aisley."

"You think wherever Jason is Aisley is as well?"

Laura's lips flattened into a line. "I don't know. She was with him, but there were times I thought she wanted to help me. She did help me."

"So you're saying she's no' with Wallace?"

"I don't know," she said and threw her arms out. "If she wasn't with Jason she could've run away with me. She didn't. She stayed."

Charon grabbed Laura's hand and pulled her down next to him. He hated to see her so upset. "Perhaps Aisley wasn't at Dreagan and the last battle because she left Wallace. Family or no', maybe she came to her senses."

"You could be right. It's just . . . you didn't see how he looked at her. It was as if he thought he owned her, Charon. And he doubted her loyalty."

Charon ran his thumb over the back of her hand. They had gone over her time with Wallace countless times, but she'd never said as much as she was now. What was it about this Aisley that concerned his wife so? "Anything else you remember?"

Laura turned her moss-green eyes to him. "The Warrior, Dale. He put himself between Jason and Aisley, as if he were protecting Aisley. He cared for her. Deeply."

"But Aisley's *drough*?"

"I can't feel magic as you can. Based on what Jason said, yes. She's *drough*."

"There's no turning back from becoming *drough*, love. Her soul belongs to Satan."

Laura's brow furrowed. "I know. Why are you telling me that?"

"Because I know you. You want to help her."

Laura turned and scooted until she was reclining back

against his chest. "She seemed so . . . lost. I was that way once."

"Aye, but you didna become *drough*."

"We don't know the circumstances."

"A *drough* is a *drough*. You need to remember that, love. Aisley is lost. There is nothing that can turn the evil from her."

"Isla is *drough*."

Charon ran his hand over Laura's shiny dark hair. "She was forced. Because she didna freely give her soul to Satan, he never had a true claim. Had she given in to the evil of the black magic, she would've been Satan's."

"Instead she's been able to channel the strength of her black magic."

"Precisely. Isla is a mix of *drough* and *mie*, a first any of us ever encountered. I doona believe it could happen again."

Laura rested her hand upon his thigh. "If it happened once, it could happen again. We don't know if Aisley was forced or not."

"You're right, of course. I just want you to understand the possibility of what you're saying is verra slim. You've got a soft heart, my love, and I doona want you hurt."

"I know. I don't know what I want or how I feel about Aisley. One minute my heart aches for her because she seemed trapped with Jason. Then the next I despise her because she didn't help me escape."

Charon glanced at his mobile phone sitting on the table. "I can call Broc. He'd find Aisley for you."

"No. I don't think that's necessary. I'm feeling sorry for a *drough*. How silly is that?"

He chuckled and kissed her temple. "You've a soft heart, remember?"

"It's a pain in the ass, is what it is. I shouldn't feel

remotely sad for a *drough*. Like you said, she made her choice. She has to live with being what she is."

As much as he agreed with Laura, Charon found himself wondering if his wife had been right to question Aisley's motives.

"Did Aisley help Jason capture you?" he asked.

Laura shook her head. "It was just Jason and Dale. Why?"

"Just thinking. Where were the other Druids?"

"Around me. Wait. There was another Druid with Jason. Her name was Mindy. She and Aisley hated each other. Mindy was Jason's lover."

Charon recalled that Laura had mentioned Mindy's name before. "Do you know why Mindy and Aisley didna like each other?"

"It was pure loathing they felt toward each other. I don't know the reasoning, though. It seemed as though Mindy felt threatened by Aisley. Whereas Mindy was always near Jason, Aisley hung at the back of the group usually by herself."

"Interesting. Did Aisley retaliate against Mindy with magic?"

"No. Then again, neither did Mindy. Jason repeatedly tried to intimidate Aisley. He whispered something to her about reminding her what he did the last time she thought to do something to him. I couldn't hear exactly what he said."

The more Charon heard about Aisley the more he wondered if he should have Broc find her. She was *drough*, but maybe she could give them information about Wallace.

There was just one catch. Would they believe anything she said?

CHAPTER
THIRTY-NINE

Phelan reached for Aisley in the bed, only to find the sheets cool to the touch. It was only the feel of her magic that kept him from panicking.

He opened his eyes to see her standing next to the window already dressed for the day. The sky was filled with low-lying gray clouds. The sadness surrounding her made his gut clench.

They'd passed the night making love again and again. She asked him to make her forget, and he made sure she had. Through it all, she clung to him as if it had been their last time together. Every kiss, every touch had felt like she was saying good-bye.

He wasn't sure what to do. He might know how to make love to a woman a thousand different ways, but he couldn't find the words to help Aisley.

Telling her to forget the past hadn't seemed to work. Not even when he told her he didn't want to know about her past. She was determined to tell him whatever her secret was.

He sat up wishing she was naked in the bed with him. Spending the day making love to her sounded like a great plan. Then he thought of Charon and the others, Wallace, and the selmyr.

The time for sorting through what was bothering Aisley would have to wait until he let the others know what he'd learned.

"It looks like rain again," Aisley said.

Phelan rose from the bed and scratched his jaw. He was in desperate need of a shave. "We might beat it."

"I'm ready to leave whenever you are."

The fact she wouldn't look at him worried Phelan. "Give me ten minutes."

The entire time he was in the shower he kept a feel out for her magic in case she tried to run. When he emerged from the bathroom, she stood in the same spot she'd been earlier.

"Have you eaten?" he asked while he dressed in his favorite pair of jeans and a dark-blue-and-white-striped button-down.

"I'm not hungry."

Phelan walked to her and took her by the shoulders so he could turn her to face him. "You know if I could take you back to the cabin I would. I'd be content to spend the rest of my days there with you."

A smile spread over her face. "I know. Your friends need you though. We need to let them know everything."

"Why do I feel like last night was your way of saying farewell?"

She took his hand and rubbed it against her cheek. "You slept again."

"Aye. You're the only woman I've ever done that with."

"You're the only man who has wanted me for me."

"Who else would I want you to be?"

She shrugged and looked away. "I miss the music."

Phelan realized it had been some time since she'd gotten lost in her music. He knew of a place in Inverness where he would take her. With the music blaring, she could dance and leave her troubles behind.

"I know a club," he said. "I'll take you there tonight."

Her fawn-colored eyes looked at him. "Thank you."

"The sooner we get to Inverness, the sooner we can get to the club."

"Let's get moving then."

Her smile was a little forced, and she couldn't quite hide the sorrow in her beautiful eyes. But Phelan was determined to show her she had nothing to be worried about.

She wouldn't believe him. He'd have to prove it to her. And he was looking forward to it.

They encountered a small section of rain on their way back down to the port. Their timing was perfect, however. When they reached the port, they pulled right onto the ferry.

Five minutes into the ride and Aisley's laugh filled the air when she spotted dolphins swimming alongside the ferry. Phelan stood beside her, but his gaze was on her, not the dolphins.

He grinned as she tried—and failed—to contain her midnight locks from getting in her face. The wind whipped around them, gulls squawked for food, and the dolphins jumped and played in the water.

But the most beautiful sight he ever beheld in his very long years was the woman beside him. She opened herself to him and showed him a part of life he had missed out on.

She was pulling away from him now, but he'd be damned if he didn't hold onto her. It had been just a few days, and he knew there was much more to learn than what she had shown him. He wanted to learn from her. Only her.

Aisley turned to him then, her eyes dancing with delight. "Aren't they wonderful?" she said of the dolphins.

"Magnificent." He was speaking of her, but she didn't know it.

She didn't search out compliments, didn't try to push him to give more than he was willing. Aisley was unique in that she offered him . . . everything.

He felt it each time they made love. She readily, eagerly gave her body to him. But she'd given much more than that. He hadn't wanted to admit it before. Even now it caused the carefully constructed wall around him to crack.

It was the realization she had freely opened her heart and soul to him that made his breath catch in his throat.

For the first time he wanted her to demand to spend more time with him instead of being content with whatever he gave her.

The thought of not having her in his life caused him to become restless and unsettled. He wasn't ready for her to leave.

His mind raced with thoughts about how he could help his friends and still have time with Aisley. It wasn't that he didn't want to bring her to the castle. There was something about protecting her himself.

Though he was the first to admit he couldn't do it all. There was only one man who he trusted enough to share his responsibility of Aisley with.

Charon.

Phelan pulled out his mobile and sent a quick text to Charon while Aisley was occupied with the dolphins. The band that had constricted his chest loosened once Charon responded to the text. Phelan knew Laura and Aisley would get along well. If Aisley wasn't comfortable with going to MacLeod Castle then she could stay with Laura in Ferness.

Why hadn't he thought of all of this sooner? Phelan

was feeling rather proud of himself as they docked in Mallaig and started the drive to Inverness.

Aisley grew worried at how close she was to Wallace Mansion when Phelan drove into Inverness before lunch. Of course, she could be on the other side of the world and still be too close to the house.

Instead of finding a hotel, they grabbed a quick bite to eat before Phelan drove them to an Internet café to do a search on the Hunter bloodline. At least that's what Phelan was looking up.

Aisley was searching for anything to do with a young prince that had gone missing in the sixteenth century. Records were sketchy from that time, but she knew if Ravyn was right and Phelan was truly a prince, there would be something about it.

She searched every major nation during that time but found nothing. Her eyes burned from staring at the screen for several hours. It wasn't until she did another search to find what countries existed at that time that she broadened her search to include little-known countries.

And that's when she got a hit.

Her fingers were shaking as she moved the cursor to click the first link. There, among the timeline of events for Saxony, was a small notation of the king's brother taking his family out of the region.

There was nothing more, but Aisley couldn't leave it at that. She did another search and found some obscure text mentioning that the people of Saxony were trying to kill certain members of the royal family because of something to do with their blood. Bathing in the royals' blood could heal whatever a person suffered from.

Aisley sat back and looked across the table at Phelan who was gazing intently at his screen. It wasn't enough to tell him. She had to have definite proof.

She took a deep breath and expanded her search. That's when a dozen or so links popped up mentioning the legend of some Saxony royal family living in Scotland.

No matter how many of the links she checked, nothing mentioned anything more. She was about to give up when she saw a paragraph from a student who wrote a paper on the lost Saxony royals.

In it, the woman wrote that the family had been searching for their son who they suspected was kidnapped. No ransom was ever asked for, and no body was ever found.

Aisley knew she was reading about Phelan's family. They had searched endlessly for him. He hadn't been forgotten. She didn't know where they had been headed, but they remained to look for him.

She knew firsthand what his blood could do. The healing properties of his blood had nothing to do with his god and everything to do with who he was.

How many other members of his family had the same blood? It obviously hadn't extended to the king and his children. Only to the king's brother. Or perhaps only Phelan.

Phelan looked up at her then. "What is it?"

"Nothing," she lied. She wasn't certain if he wanted to know what she found. Nor was she sure she could tell him how she learned he was a prince. It was something saved for another time.

"I found where the surname Hunter was changed to Johnson and MacDonald. After that, things get lost. It took too long for the common surname to take root within a family. If it had, things would be easier."

"It's a start."

"No' much of one." He logged off and pushed back his chair. "I promised you a nice meal and the club I told you about."

Aisley didn't have to be prompted twice. She hurried to log off and stood. "Let's go then."

At the hotel she showered and changed into a silver sequined tank top and short black skirt. Phelan whistled when she walked out of the bathroom.

Her stomach was in knots. Not because of what she had discovered about Phelan and his family, but because she knew she was going to take on Jason and possibly die by Phelan's hand that night.

"Ready?" he asked.

Aisley took his arm, noting the crisp button-down of the deepest burgundy and the black trousers. His long dark brown locks were combed away from his face and secured in a low queue at his neck.

He looked dark and dangerous. Aisley almost stopped them from leaving so she could have another night in his arms. But already she had held off the inevitable. The weight of her secret wouldn't last another night.

The restaurant Phelan chose was but two blocks from the hotel. There was a small smile about his lips that looked boyish, as if they held a surprise he couldn't wait to tell.

"What is it?" she asked with a laugh.

He halted them outside of the restaurant and looked around. "I've a surprise for you."

"Really? What is it?"

"I invited Charon and Laura to meet us for dinner."

Aisley's stomach fell to her feet like lead. She couldn't breathe, couldn't stop her entire body from shaking as realization set in. "No. I didn't get a chance to tell you myself. Phelan, I'm a *dr*-"

"There they are," he said over her as he waved.

Aisley turned to find Laura and Charon at the corner of the street staring at her as if she were the Devil himself.

CHAPTER
FORTY

Phelan didn't understand the way Charon and Laura stared at Aisley, or why Aisley's nails were sunk into his arm in a death grip. He looked at Aisley to see she was as pale as death, her chest heaving as she watched his friends.

It seemed to take forever before Charon and Laura started toward them. He wanted to reassure Aisley that she could trust Charon, but there was something in the way his friend looked at him that gave Phelan pause.

Unease snaked down his spine. There was recognition in Laura's eyes as she looked at Aisley.

"Phelan," Charon said.

Phelan nodded to his friend, then to Laura.

Laura, however, was looking at Aisley. "Hello, Aisley."

Aisley swallowed twice before she managed a weak, "Hello."

"You two know each other?" Phelan asked.

Aisley's fawn-colored eyes were large and filled with tears. "I tried to tell you so many times. It's why I asked you to take me away from the cabin. I didn't want to tell you there."

"Tell me what?" He didn't like the fear he saw in her

eyes or the way her lips trembled as she spoke. Nor did he like the way her magic quaked around him. He also didn't like the way Charon was looking at her as if she were his next kill.

Aisley jumped when lightning flashed above them followed quickly by thunder. "I thought you knew at first. I thought you'd come to kill me."

"What?" He was getting more confused as the minutes ticked by. "I thought we'd already been through this. I doona want to kill you."

"Ask her what her surname is," Charon said.

Phelan cut him a glare before he turned back to Aisley. He recalled when she had told him she thought he would kill her. At the time he'd thought she was fearful of Warriors. Now he was beginning to suspect something else entirely. "Who are you?"

Tears streamed freely down her face now. "Please understand that I planned to tell you tonight. I had valid reasons."

"Tell me what, dammit!" he bellowed, uncaring of the looks the passersby gave him.

"I'm *drough*."

He gave a snort. "That's ballocks. I'd know."

"It's true," Charon said. "I can feel her *drough* magic."

Phelan looked from Charon to Aisley's tear-streaked face. Her eyes were filled with regret and sorrow so deep he wanted to pull her into his arms. It was the knowledge that he hadn't known she was *drough* that made him step away from her.

"I'm sorry," she said and tried to cling to him. "I thought when you found me in Glasgow you were going to kill me. You didn't. You kissed me." She shook her head as the rain began to fall. "Then you took me to your cabin. I knew then there was a chance I could stop Jason myself, and I knew he was after me. I wanted to see if I could stop Jason before I told you. But not at the cabin. That place is too beautiful to be sullied with my blood."

"You're damned right," he said between clenched teeth. He took another step back and jerked his arms away from her. "I took you to my house. My house! No one has ever seen that. No one even knew of it. You let me make love to you. I told you my secrets! And you betrayed me."

She jerked with every word that left his mouth. His anger was so great he didn't care what it caused her. He could barely stand the thought that he had shared his body with a *drough*.

"I . . . I know it was wrong. But I went with you because I knew you could keep Jason away until I could fight him. Then, I knew you'd kill me."

He blinked and recoiled from her. Everyone knew he sought out *droughs* to kill, but the thought of ending Aisley's life was too sickening to even consider.

"I'm sorry," she murmured.

Phelan shook his head, thankful the rain had sent most people indoors. There were few on the sidewalk to overhear what they were saying. "Just leave."

"I'm Jason's cousin."

Phelan's eyes closed at her words. Would the hits ever stop coming? When he opened his eyes he looked anywhere but at her. He had made love to a *drough*. "Get out of my sight. I can no' even look at you."

"I can stop Jason. Please," she begged as she grabbed his arm.

Phelan tugged away from her, which sent her off balance and crashing to her knees on the concrete. He fisted his hand to keep from reaching for her when he smelled the blood from her skinned knees.

Despite all she'd told him, he couldn't stop his feelings for her. But he must. The idea that he had willingly bed-

ded a *drough*—and Wallace's cousin—several times made
his stomach roil.

To think he'd considered taking her back to his cabin
so they could spend weeks, months together. He was
crushed, utterly shattered.

Would there ever come a time someone didn't betray
him?

"Was everything you told me a lie?" he demanded.

She shook her head, her black mane of hair hiding her
face. When she looked up at him after settling back on her
heels, she said, "No. None of it."

"You just conveniently left out the part about being
Wallace's cousin and a *drough*. Even when I asked about
the scars on your wrists! Did you get the information you
wanted from me?"

"No! I stayed because you asked me to, and because
for the first time in my life I'd been given something
good."

"Fuck that. You know how I hate *droughs*. How could
you even look at me?"

"Because I knew in the end you would end my suffering."

Phelan was so taken aback he couldn't respond for
several seconds. "You want me to believe that your suffering will end with your death? Are you too stupid to
realize your torture will only begin once you're in Hell?"

She got to her feet instead of answering. Blood coated
her knees and palms, but she didn't seem to notice. "It's
your loathing of *droughs* that I've been counting on."

"Where is Wallace?"

"I don't know."

"Bullshit. Where is Wallace?" he shouted.

"I don't know! I don't care!"

Aisley watched Phelan's lips that had kissed her so tenderly and brought her unimaginable pleasure peel back in

a sneer. Her heart tore in two at the betrayal she saw in his blue-gray eyes.

She'd known it would be this bad, but she'd hoped she would be the one to tell him on her terms, not have his friends interrupt things.

Regardless, it was done. And it was past time. The weight she thought would be lifted with her secret only grew heavier. She knew that was because of Phelan. It was because of her love for him.

The way he pulled away from her, as if he couldn't stand to have her near made her heart splinter into a million pieces. She'd just thought she was broken before. Now she truly knew what that statement meant.

He turned and walked away from her without another word. Charon and Laura followed close on his heels. Aisley was left all alone in the rain.

She turned in the opposite direction Phelan had gone and began to wander the streets. There would be no returning to the hotel for her clothes or money. Nothing mattered anymore.

The sound of drums echoed dimly in her mind, but she quickly shut them out. She wanted no part of magic anymore. She wanted no part of anything anymore.

She couldn't even think of Jason or fighting him, because she didn't have the strength for it now. Phelan had been her strength. She was as weak as Jason had always claimed.

When she came to the suspension bridge over the River Ness, she stood on the side and looked over the long drop to the water below. If Phelan wouldn't kill her, she'd have to do it herself.

Aisley let go of the metal and jumped.

A punishing grip on her wrist jerked her to a halt. She looked up into the familiar blue eyes of Jason.

"Hello, cousin," he said with a terrifying smile.

* * *

Phelan sat on the corner of the bed in the hotel room staring at Aisley's bag with her clothes hanging out of it and spilling onto the floor.

"What all did you tell her?" Charon asked from his position leaning against a wall.

Phelan shrugged. "Nothing of importance. I told her the story of how Warriors came to be. She'd never heard it. I told her of Deirdre and Declan."

"You told her how you were taken, didn't you?" Laura asked softly.

Phelan nodded and dropped his head into his hands as he leaned forward. How had he not known what Aisley was? "I doona know why I couldna feel her magic was that of a *drough*."

When Charon and Laura didn't respond, Phelan lifted his head to spear Charon with a look. "You know, I bet."

Charon cleared his throat and glanced at Laura. "I do, but I doona think you want to hear it."

"Just tell me."

"You've heard all of us speak of how we feel the magic of our mates differently than others."

Phelan could well imagine the horrified expression on his face. "You think Aisley is my mate?"

"It would explain why you didn't know she was *drough*," Laura answered.

Phelan snorted angrily. "It could be magic she used on me."

"I don't think so." Laura sat beside Phelan. "You were too angry, and rightly so, while Aisley spoke to notice the pain she was going through. She could've walked away. She could've let me or Charon tell you what she was. Instead, she did. I believe her when she said she was going to tell you."

Phelan couldn't wrap his mind around all of it. "It

makes sense now why she didna want to leave Skye. She knew I'd find out."

"Nay," Charon said. "She knew she was going to tell you. She expected to die."

"You believe her, too?" Phelan asked as he got to his feet to pace the room.

Charon nodded. "I do. Whatever her motivations for getting close to you, she wasna going to keep her secret. I could see it in her eyes."

Phelan stopped and dropped his head back to look at the ceiling. "I didna give her a choice. She was in an accident when I felt Wallace's magic that first time. I was following her. I put her on my bike and drove her to my cabin."

"Your instinct was to protect her, and I don't think you were wrong there," Laura said.

Phelan looked at her and frowned. "What do you mean?"

"It's as I was telling Charon yesterday. Wallace doubted Aisley's loyalty. He threatened her with something."

"He cut her," Phelan said. "Left a nasty scar on her left side. I'll bet my immortality it was Wallace. She never said, but it makes sense."

"So maybe she's innocent."

Charon walked to sit beside his wife. "Or maybe she isna. Wallace is devious. Who knows what his plan is for any of us?"

"You think it includes Aisley?" Laura asked.

"Without a doubt."

Phelan wanted to argue in defense of Aisley, but he couldn't find the words. It didn't matter what Laura told him that Wallace had done to Aisley.

The simple matter that she and Wallace were linked by blood sealed her fate. She'd been right in thinking he would kill her. He should have.

He would.

Whenever he saw her again.

Phelan squeezed his eyes closed when he felt a spike of fear in her magic. His first instinct was to run to her. It was only by sheer will alone that he remained rooted to his spot.

He was only able to breathe again when her magic faded completely. It had diminished steadily but quickly. Had she stolen a car and left Inverness?

The idea that she might be dead was one he couldn't even contemplate. Phelan focused on where she might have gone. Anything to stop the awful emptiness that filled his chest like the deepest winter.

He didn't want to think about Aisley or her treachery. Zelfor bellowed for vengeance deep in Phelan's mind. Battle was what he needed. Blood and death coating his hands and the ground. That would stop the desolation he felt.

"Wallace attacked her on Skye," he said to fill the silence. "I thought he was after me at the time."

"Was he after her?" Charon asked.

Phelan shook his head. "Nay. I think it was a ploy to get me to feel deeper for her."

"Wait," Laura said. "Aisley mentioned fighting Jason herself."

Phelan snorted. "Doona believe it. Wallace is around. I think it's time we found him."

CHAPTER
FORTY-ONE

"We need to call Fallon," Charon said.

Phelan knew he would eventually have to go to the castle, but he wasn't ready. Looking at Isla would only make him think of Aisley.

For all of them, it was better if he stayed away for the time being.

"I need to do something other than sit around a damned hall talking. I need to find Wallace."

Laura began to pick up Aisley's clothes and neatly fold them before putting them in her duffle. "You don't even know where to find Wallace. You've been looking for months."

"Have I?" he asked sarcastically. "I'm no' so sure I was. I was more concerned with Aisley. She led me on a merry chase while Wallace did whatever he did."

Charon leaned his hands back on the bed. "Broc has been trying to locate Wallace since the battle. Wallace hasna been anywhere to be found. You and Malcolm searched for months. Even Fallon, Lucan, and Quinn snuck out of the castle at night to search. No one has found anything. I doona believe Wallace was here."

"Where has he been then?"

"That I doona know. You and I left Cairn Toul and never looked back. I snapped Deirdre's neck with my own hands. She was dead. Her body was destroyed, but no' her essence. She was able to come back. I think Wallace has done the same thing."

Laura walked out of the bathroom with Aisley's toiletry bag. "I really don't like hearing that. Will Jason be the same or different if he comes back?"

"That's a big if," Phelan said. "We doona know if Wallace died."

"On Skye, tell me what happened when Aisley was attacked," Charon urged.

Phelan hated the way his friend was watching him as if he were looking for any cracks in his armor. "It was similar to what happened when I was following her. I felt a wave of *drough* magic. It was unmistakably Wallace's."

"Wait," Laura said. "Back up and tell us about the first time you felt Wallace."

"I did." Phelan raked a hand through his hair and briefly squeezed his eyes shut. "I'd been following Aisley for weeks. It's true what she said. I kissed her at a club. I knew she was a Druid, but I didna sense black magic about her. I kissed her, she asked me what I was doing, and then ran off. I trailed her after that hoping to get close to her."

He paused, hating himself for being duped. Again. And by another *drough.* "She was on her way out of Scotland when I felt Wallace. I was several cars behind her. Her car swerved and she was hit by the car behind her."

"She swerved?" Laura asked.

Phelan struggled to find any measure of patience. "Aye."

"Why did she swerve? Was there a car in front of her?"

"Nay."

Charon sat up and turned his head to his wife. "What are you thinking?"

"I'm thinking Jason may have been trying to get to Aisley. She maybe felt him and it surprised her enough that she jerked the wheel of her car."

Phelan bit back a smirk. He wasn't sure why Laura was trying to find the good in Aisley. There was no good. A *drough* was evil to the core of its black soul. They could wield magic with barely a thought and make people do anything they wanted.

Charon rubbed his chin thoughtfully. "What happened after the wreck?"

"I knew it was Wallace, and I feared he might come for her because of me," Phelan explained. "So I put her on my motorbike and got the hell out of there."

"Did anything like that happen again?" Laura asked, some emotion Charon couldn't name shining in her eyes.

He leaned back against the wall. "On Skye. We were hiking to look for the Druids when Wallace's magic slammed into me. It was stronger than before. I expected an attack. Instead, I heard Aisley scream."

"What happened?" Charon asked.

Phelan closed his eyes and remembered seeing the blood run down her arm, the panic that had gripped him. "She was cut deeply on her left arm, and then it was as if something knocked her over the side of the cliff. I caught her and pulled her up, and she had more injuries than I realized."

"You healed her," Laura stated into the silence that followed.

He opened his eyes and nodded. "Aye. I healed her."

"Was she frightened?" Charon shrugged at Phelan's look. "It's a valid question."

"She was. I thought it was because Wallace was trying to get to me through her. Now I think it was because she went over the side of the cliff."

Laura crossed her arms over her chest. "No. Aisley

wanted to die. It wasn't her near death that frightened her."

"And you would know how?" Phelan demanded. "Do you know something about her I doona?"

Charon got to his feet and stood between them. "Laura thinks when Wallace captured her that Aisley looked . . . well, lost."

"Dale protected her," Laura added.

Phelan frowned. "The Warrior Wallace had? He protected Aisley?"

"Yes. I think he cared for her."

He didn't like hearing that someone else had watched over her. Despite his hatred, he couldn't stop what he felt for her, convincing liar or not. "It doesna matter now. None of it does. She knows who we need to stop the selmyr. Or more importantly, she knows how to stop us from wiping out the selmyr."

Charon blew out a deep breath. "Shite. It's time to call Fallon."

In two strides Phelan stood in front of his friend, his hand covering Charon's mobile. "Nay."

"Why? It's going to take all of us. You know that, my friend."

"I need to know what Aisley has done before anyone else gets involved. Wallace already tried to get Laura. I'll not be responsible for other Druids hurt or dead because my cock led me to Aisley."

Several tense minutes ticked by before Charon gave a nod and pocketed his mobile. "All right. Where do we begin?"

"The Internet café we were at earlier. I thought we were both searching for the same thing. I doona think so now."

Charon took Laura's hand in his. "I'm no' a computer genius. If you willna bring in Gwynn to do a search, I can only think of one other place we could go."

"Dreagan." Phelan wasn't sure it was a good idea, but then again, the Dragon Kings were incredibly powerful. Without them, he was sure they'd all be dead in the last battle.

Charon raised a brow in question. Phelan glanced at Laura before he gave a nod. Charon got his mobile and pressed a button.

Somehow Phelan wasn't surprised to know his friend had Dreagan on speed dial, and he was sure it had nothing to do with the business of stocking their exceptional scotch in Charon's bar.

"Con, I need a favor," Charon spoke into the phone. There was a moment of silence as he listened to whatever Con said. "I need someone who can hack into a computer."

Phelan looked down at his small bag. His life was in that bag. He could go anywhere at any time and have all he needed. Aisley had been the same way. It had felt so good to have someone who understood his lifestyle and hadn't tried to change him.

Now he knew why she hadn't demanded anything or altered his life. She was content to string him along until she had her claws in him so deep he wouldn't know up from down.

"Let's go," Charon said, jerking Phelan out of his musing.

Phelan grabbed his bag and reached for the door when Laura called his name.

"Do we bring Aisley's stuff?" she asked.

He opened the door and started walking out as he said, "Burn it for all I care."

In no time at all they were on the road headed to Dreagan Distillery. Phelan followed behind Charon's sleek charcoal-gray Mercedes CL AMG Coupe.

The rain fell in a steady stream while lightning lit up

the sky in a dramatic and beautiful display of artistry. Any other time he'd be watching the storm.

But as the tempest raged around him, it was nothing compared to what he was feeling inside.

All the women he'd bedded, all the women he'd charmed, not a single one of them touched him as deeply as Aisley. And many had tried.

How foolish he felt acting the besotted lover doing anything for her. How utterly ridiculous he was to believe the story she told him of her parents throwing her out, being pregnant, and then the baby dying.

He accepted every word she spoke.

She was a consummate deceiver. Not once had he questioned her. As for her secret, he knew it had all been a ploy. Every action, every emotion, every touch had all been to get him to fall for her.

It was a good thing he hadn't or he really would be in trouble. He cared for her. Or rather, he *had* cared for her.

He should have killed her as she asked. Now he would have to hunt her down. The only good thing about that is he was sure he'd find Wallace when he found her.

Taking both their lives would go a long way to soothing his hurt pride. Never again would he trust a woman. Now he remembered why he charmed them, seduced them, and left them.

It was something he'd never forget again no matter how long he lived.

By the time they turned off the road onto the long, winding drive between mountains that led to Dreagan, Phelan was so angry he had to fight to keep Zelfor under control.

When they came to the rock-lined parking area of Dreagan there were two men waiting for them beneath the large overhang of the distillery. Phelan got off his bike and walked to Rhys.

Rhys's long, dark hair was wet from standing in the rain. His unusual aqua eyes ringed with dark blue were crinkled at the corners as he smiled. "Good to see you."

"Likewise."

Rhys cocked his head. "Why do I no' believe you, Warrior?"

"Because you're a pain in my arse, Dragon."

Rhys threw back his head and laughed. "We didna know you were tagging along with Charon."

"He's no' tagging," Charon said from beside Banan. "We're here so hopefully one of you can help him."

Rhys's gaze jerked back to him, all laughter gone. "What's happened?"

"I'll explain everything as we make our way inside. Time is of the essence."

Banan opened the door and waved them in. "I think you all know your way to the manor."

Phelan nodded to Banan as he passed him. The manor was hidden from view of visitors that came to see the famous distillery. But it was more than privacy those at Dreagan wanted.

It was the fact they were dragons who could shape-shift that had to be kept a strict secret.

Phelan relayed the story, leaving out key points that were no one's business, by the time they reached the manor. Laura hadn't said a word, but he saw the way she frowned at a few choice words he used for Aisley.

"That's quite a story," Banan said. He turned gray eyes to Rhys. "Want to give the hacking a try?"

Rhys strode up the stairs and into a small office where he sat behind a desk with five computer monitors surrounding him. Phelan shared a surprised glance with Charon.

"I didna realize you were a computer guru," Phelan said.

Rhys snorted. "This room is for anyone at the manor.

We've a lot of time on our hands, Phelan. We like to . . . mess . . . sometimes."

Banan chuckled from the doorway. "That's a good way of saying we've accidentally taken down sites because we were . . . messing."

"That's how you learn," Rhys said and began to pound on the keyboard. "Where were you at?"

Phelan gave him the location of the Internet café in Inverness and shifted around the desk so he could see what Rhys was doing. Surprisingly it didn't take long for Rhys to gain access.

"Where was she sitting?" Rhys asked.

Phelan leaned forward to look at a picture of the café that Rhys pulled up on another monitor and pointed to where Aisley had sat. "There."

Rhys keyed in more information, his eyes moving from one monitor to another before his fingers moved over the keyboard again.

"What time did the both of you log onto the computers?"

Phelan gave him the information and watched him enter more information.

The process was repeated a couple of times before the other four monitors flashed Web sites about Saxony on their screens. Phelan glanced at each of them, not understanding what he was seeing.

"Did you get the wrong terminal?"

Rhys slowly shook his head. "Nay. If that's where she was sitting, then this is the information she looked up."

"This has nothing to do with the name Hunter."

Laura, Charon, and Banan moved around the desk to see what they were looking at.

Banan pointed to one of the screens. "It mentions here that the Saxony royal family had special blood that could heal others."

Phelan felt the room spinning around him. "What? What did you say?"

Banan began to repeat it when Phelan slashed a hand through the air. "I heard you. Why would she do a search on that?"

"She didn't," Rhys said. "She searched for a lost prince. These sites are the last ones she looked at." He turned his head to look at Phelan. "She was searching your history."

Phelan rubbed his eyes with his thumb and forefinger. The day kept getting crazier and crazier. "I doona understand why."

"You're a damned prince?" Charon asked, his voice pitched high in surprise.

Phelan shook his head. "Nay."

"You might want to rethink that," Banan said and lifted his head from the screen he was reading. "It looks like Aisley found information about your family."

"That's no' possible. I doona even have that information or know what to look for. How would she?"

Rhys rolled his chair back so Phelan could get a closer look at the monitors. "I think you'll have to ask her. Regardless, if you didna know of your family before, she found it for you. You might want to thank her."

"Over my fucking dead body," Phelan said as he stalked from the room.

CHAPTER
FORTY-TWO

Phelan spewed a mouthful of curses when he ended up for the third time in the kitchen. The manor was a damned maze. He just wanted out.

"That way," Jane pointed.

He gave a nod of thanks to Banan's wife and hurried out of the manor. A fine mist of rain swirled around him. He could see it dancing on the air as he stalked into the open field.

Sheep scattered as he drew near, their baas growing louder in their hurry to get away from him. He ignored them and continued to the trees he saw.

When he reached the grove, his anger still hadn't cooled. Phelan took a look around and started up the incline. Sweat beaded his brow and rolled down his back as he ran up the mountain.

Rocks slid beneath his boots, but he paid them no heed, not even when he slipped nearly a hundred yards down the mountain. Phelan kept his gaze focused on the summit until he reached it.

After he got to the top he simply took in the magnificent view. The clouds hovered around the peaks while the thick mist rolled leisurely down the mountains and swallowed anything that stood in its way.

"Feel better?"

Phelan whirled around at the sound of Rhys's voice. "Sod off."

"What's bothers you more, Warrior? The fact that Aisley knew something of your past and didna tell you? Or that she was *drough* and you didna know it?"

"Leave," Phelan said between clenched teeth. He was looking for a fight, and anyone would do. Including the dragon next to him.

"I'm saying what Charon willna." Rhys ran his hand through his hair to get it out of his face. "Can you admit the truth to yourself?"

Phelan turned his head to glare at him. "What do you want from me?"

"To admit that you care for her."

"Why? Does that make you feel more powerful that I got played?"

"Did you?" Rhys asked. "We doona know for sure."

Phelan put his back to him. If he ignored Rhys then maybe he'd go away.

Rhys, however, didn't seem to understand as he said, "Tell me, Phelan, have you wondered why you didna feel her black magic? The real reason? The one you willna even consider?"

"She used me."

"Perhaps. But you felt something for her."

"Nay. I was mistaken."

"Denying it willna make it go away. Admit you loved her."

Phelan growled and spun around the same time he released his god. He bent and barreled his shoulder into Rhys's gut. Rhys wrapped his arms around him as they tumbled over the side.

They rolled in a mass of arms and legs, banging into boulders and smashing into trees until they were jerked to a stop. Phelan lifted his head to see it was Rhys who had grabbed hold of a tree to halt them.

Phelan jumped to his feet and bared his fangs. It felt good to have Zelfor released. It would feel even better if he could spill blood.

Rhys swiped the back of his hand over his lip and looked down at the blood smeared there. "If you were looking for a fight that's all you had to say."

"Why say anything when I can show you?"

"Give it your best, Warrior," Rhys said and beckoned him with his fingers.

Phelan knew it wasn't wise to attack when anger burned through his veins as it did, but he couldn't stop himself. He swung his arm at Rhys's face with his claws extended.

Rhys leaned back in time, but Phelan's claws sank into his shoulder. A satisfied roar sounded inside his head from Zelfor. Phelan smiled and jerked his claws out. He readied for another swing when Rhys landed a punch to his jaw.

The force of it sent Phelan on his ass. He shook his head to clear the ringing and looked at Rhys. The Dragon King stood with his fists held in front of him and a cocky smile on his face.

"I bet it's been awhile since anyone set you on your arse."

Phelan climbed to his feet. They circled each other while he spread his fingers wide looking for an opening to cut Rhys again.

Yet when Phelan looked, the injury he'd given Rhys was already healed. As a Warrior, Phelan's god healed him, but not that quickly.

"There is much you doona know of us Dragon Kings," Rhys said when he caught Phelan looking at his shoulder.

Phelan shrugged. "So you heal faster than we do."

"Is that all? Or is there more?"

He hated the smile on Rhys's face. "Are you going to talk me to death or fight?"

Phelan grinned when he and Rhys clashed again. He lost count of the hits he gave and the ones Rhys landed. A tree groaned ominously when Rhys threw him into it. In the next moment Phelan tossed Rhys against a boulder.

Their fighting had them rolling down the mountain again until they landed in the valley. It was Rhys's laughter that made Phelan pause.

He was on his back and looked over to find Rhys had risen up on his elbow staring at him. The curious sheep drew closer to them, and that's when Phelan felt one sniff his face.

Phelan shooed away the animal and sat up. He drew his knees up until he could put his heels in the ground. Then he wrapped his arms around his knees and clasped his hands together.

"I'm game for that anytime," Rhys said as he sat up.

"As am I."

"Do you feel better?"

The smile Phelan had slipped. He looked away from Rhys's probing aqua gaze. "I swore no *drough* would ever get the better of me again after what Isla and Deirdre did to me."

"Let the past go, Phelan."

It didn't go unnoticed by him that Rhys was giving him the same advice he'd given Aisley. "Isla took me from my family."

"A family that was no' only on the run to save your life, but a royal one at that. You're royalty, Phelan. A prince. And your family never left Scotland. They remained, searching until death took them."

"Why did she look into my past? What could've been there that Aisley wanted to use against me?"

"Maybe it wasna to use something against you but to help you."

Phelan looked up to find Rhys standing above him with a hand held out to help him up. He took it, and Rhys pulled him to his feet.

"Contain your fury until you've captured Aisley, Phelan, or Wallace will get the better of you."

He knew Rhys gave solid advice, but he couldn't get Aisley out of his head. How could he set aside his anger if he couldn't stop thinking of her?

Consciousness came to Aisley slowly. She realized she was sitting up and opened her eyes to a distortion of colors. It took her blinking several times before she was able to focus on what she was looking at.

A cold, sinking feeling filled her when she saw the iron bars. She didn't need to look around to know where she was.

Jason's prison below the mansion.

"So you're finally awake."

She hadn't dreamed him preventing her from jumping. He really was there. Aisley couldn't stop her racing heart, but she'd be damned before she let Jason know how much just the sound of his voice frightened her.

"No quip, cousin?" Jason shifted from outside the bars and moved out of the shadows. "What happened to your cheeky comments always at the ready?"

The one thing she hadn't wanted to happen had. She was in Jason's clutches. Whatever death Phelan planned to give her would be nothing compared to what Jason would do.

She looked at her cousin. "You disgust me."

"You were no' so disgusted when I pulled you out of that gutter."

"Believe me, you slimy bugger, I wish I'd have refused you."

"As if I'd have let you." Jason narrowed his gaze on her. "You think you control your destiny, Aisley, when in fact it's in my hands."

She lifted her chin in a show of defiance. "Do you still feel like that bullied weasel of a boy from school, Jason? Do those lads who used to push you around still give you nightmares?"

"You've no idea, do you?"

A ripple of terror rolled down her back. "What do you mean?"

"You doona know what I've become. You doona yet comprehend what I can do to you. But you will, Aisley, you will."

His eyes flashed solid black before magic slammed into her, breaking several ribs.

CHAPTER
FORTY-THREE

"What now?" Phelan demanded when he walked into the large room to find Rhys, Banan, and Charon playing pool.

Charon called his play before the ball rolled into the pocket. He slowly straightened and held his pool cue beside him. "While you and Rhys were . . . letting off some steam, Banan and I did a little research on what Aisley discovered."

"Doona say her name." Phelan couldn't stand to hear it. Already she invaded his every thought. Everything reminded him of her. It was too much.

His hands itched to hold her against him, to run his hands through her midnight hair. It had only been a few hours without her. How could he face eternity?

Banan walked around the table, never taking his eyes off the burgundy felt and the balls scattered on it as he decided on his play. Finally he stopped and leaned over the table to call his shot, carefully holding the cue as he lined up his play and took his aim, knocking a solid yellow ball in a pocket. "So we willna say her name. Are you going to comment on the fact we found something?"

"What do you want me to say?" Phelan looked out one of the many windows on the opposite wall at the mountains that urged him to walk their craggy slopes and get lost in the wilds of Scotland.

Rhys chuckled from an overstuffed leather chair he reclined in, sipping the famous Dreagan scotch. "I told you, Banan. Phelan doesna want to know."

"You want to know," Charon told him. "Trust me."

Phelan rubbed his hand over his jaw thinking he needed to shave so he wouldn't scrape Aisley's skin. Then he recalled she was no longer his. He remembered the betrayal and the lies.

And his heart shattered all over again.

"Tell me," he said when Banan missed his second shot.

Rhys rose and poured two glasses of whisky before turning and handing one to Phelan. "You look like you could use this."

"Ais—" Banan stopped and cleared his throat. "She was on the right track. With more time I think she would've discovered what we did."

Charon eyed a striped purple ball and lined up his pool cue. "She found where you're from, and she learned your family fled in order to save you. What she didna learn was about your blood."

"What do you mean my family left to save me? Didna everyone have the same kind of blood?" Phelan asked.

"Nay," Charon said and took his shot. Two stripes found pockets. He moved to line up another play. "It seems your blood was rare, even for your family."

Phelan absorbed that info as Charon's next shot bounced off the eight ball and hit the side of the table before colliding with a blue stripe that rolled into a side pocket.

Charon stood and caught his gaze. "In other words, you were precious to the entire royal family. It seems your uncle let it be known about your blood because of jealousy. Your parents left Saxony that night, though they were unlucky enough to run into a group of peasants who tried to take you."

"Your younger sister was killed in that attack," Rhys said.

To know that his family had gone to such lengths to protect just one of their children left Phelan ashamed of himself for the hateful thoughts he'd had of them over the centuries.

"How many siblings did I have?" he asked.

In two more shots, Charon finished off the billiards game. "Five. Three brothers and two sisters. You were the second to the youngest."

Phelan walked to the closest chair and sank into it. He stared at the whisky in his hand, not really seeing it. "What's so special about my blood?"

"That we doona know yet," Banan said. "The history we found on it is verra obscure. The word *magic* is used a lot, but in those times, people used magic to describe a great number of things that had nothing to do with it."

"Isla said my family was in northern Scotland near Oykel Bridge. Are they still?"

Rhys shook his head. "No' any longer. They were for a time. Two of your remaining four siblings survived long enough to marry and have children. Your sister's line, unfortunately, was wiped out by clan wars."

"Your brother's line survived," Charon said.

Phelan drained the whisky in one swallow and felt it burn down his throat and into his stomach. "The name Stewart Isla gave me. It isna my family's name, is it?"

Banan set his pool cue on the table and leaned against it. "Your family surname was Albertine. You are a prince, Phelan."

"A prince with no country, no throne, and no family." He smiled humorlessly. "I'm the envy of everyone."

Charon placed his pool cue alongside Banan's and retrieved the decanter of whisky. He walked to the three of them and refilled everyone's glass. "If it wouldna been for Aisley, we wouldna know as much as we do. How did she find out?"

"I doona know. Maybe she's always known. Perhaps that's why she was with me."

"Did she try to take any of your blood?" Rhys asked.

Phelan frowned. "Nay."

"Then I doubt that's the case."

Banan scratched his cheek. "I agree with Rhys. I suspected she was either telling you the truth or had an ulterior motive."

Phelan's gaze narrowed on the King. It seemed they had done more than dig into his past. They'd dug into Aisley's. "What did you do?"

"We found out the truth about her," Charon said.

Phelan set aside his glass and struggled to control his rising anger. It was then he noticed how quiet the manor was. There was no laughter from the three women who had found mates with the Kings, no smell of food from the servants in the kitchen. And no other Dragon Kings. "Where is everyone? Where are Laura and Jane and the other Kings?"

"Out."

Rhys's one-word response sent warning bells ringing in Phelan's head. He jumped to his feet and fisted his hands at his side. Zelfor screamed to be released, but Phelan still had control—by a thin thread, but it was control.

"Calm down," Charon said as he too got to his feet.

"Keep whatever information you found on that *drough* to yourself."

Rhys stood and met Phelan's glare with one of his own. "Are you afraid we'll tell you she lied so the pain you're feeling will only double? Or are you more scared of knowing that she told you the truth?"

Phelan could no longer hold back his rage. He released his god and let out a growl. "I must no' have beat you enough, Dragon, for you to still be running your mouth."

"Aw. Does the little Warrior have anger problems?" Rhys replied in a small, whiny voice.

It sent Phelan over the edge.

He lunged for Rhys only to have Charon and Banan jerk him to a halt.

"Enough, Rhys!" Banan bellowed.

Rhys snorted and tossed aside the crystal glass that landed with a thump on the rug. "You handle him with kid gloves. He's an immortal. He needs to know the truth."

"The truth willna help him now," Charon stated.

Phelan shoved both men off him and tamped down Zelfor. "I'm right fucking here. Stop talking about me as if I'm no' in the room."

"Then start acting like an adult," Rhys replied.

Phelan's lip lifted as he growled.

"Oh, I'm shaking," Rhys said sarcastically. "The big bad Warrior might get me."

Banan shoved him hard. "If he doesna, I will. Stop agitating him, Rhys. We wanted him calm."

"Then just tell him." Rhys slumped back into his chair.

Phelan's gaze shifted as he caught Banan and Charon exchange a look. Whatever they were about to say wasn't going to be good. He didn't want to know if Aisley lied to him, or worse, told the truth.

Either one was going to crush him, and, frankly, he'd had enough.

"Nay," Phelan said.

Charon let out a sigh. "I know why you doona want to know, but it can help. Either way, it'll help."

"Will it? How can you be sure? Have you had someone betray you as she did me? Have you questioned everything someone said wondering if it was a lie to lead you further into whatever trap they've set for you?"

Charon shook his head. "Phelan, as your friend, I'm begging you to let us tell you."

"Oh, for fuck's sake," Rhys said with a roll of his eyes. "Aisley was kicked out of her home. She was pregnant, and the baby died. The infant girl is buried in Pitlochry."

Each word Rhys spoke was like a knife twisting in Phelan's heart. It was worse hearing the deeds a second time, but only because he'd heard the suffering in her voice when she had told him.

"So?" he forced himself to say when Rhys finished. "That doesna excuse her for becoming *drough*."

Banan ran a hand through his hair. "You're one cold bastard."

Phelan didn't bother to respond. He turned to Charon. "You've had your fun here. It's time to contact Fallon."

"I suppose it is." Charon hesitated a minute too long.

Phelan walked up until he was in Charon's face. "You doona feel sorry for her, do you?"

"Nay. I feel sorry for you."

"Well, doona. I'm fine."

One dark brow rose. "A wee bit delusional, are we?"

"Honest, no' delusional."

Banan said, "You're no' being honest. Someone you cared about lied and you're pissed."

"You're damned right I am," Phelan said, not taking his eyes off Charon.

Charon shoved him away and growled long and low. "You want to take your anger out on someone, then I'm game."

"Why do you want to defend her?"

"I'm no' defending her! She told you the truth!"

"For what purpose?" Phelan asked, his vexation running deep. "She's a *drough*. They're evil. You can no' trust anything they say or do."

Rhys chuckled dryly. "And you're no' evil, Warrior?"

Phelan looked at the Dragon King. "The difference is I didna have a choice about the evil inside me. Deirdre let it loose. I'm the one who contained the god and control it. A *drough* makes the decision to give their soul to Satan for black magic. The evil controls them."

"You didna answer my question."

Sometimes Phelan really hated Rhys. "I'm no' evil."

"But you just said you had evil inside you, same as a *drough*."

"No' the same!" he yelled.

Rhys stretched his legs out in front of him and crossed them at the ankle. "Evil is evil. You say you control yours. Do you really?"

"Rhys," Banan said in a low, warning voice.

Phelan smiled, claws sprouting from his fingers. "You looking for another fight, Dragon?"

"Unlike you, Warrior, I doona go looking for a fight everywhere."

The truth of Rhys's words hit Phelan like a brick wall. Whatever anger he had evaporated in an instant. The old fury that burned so bright while Deirdre held him captive is what kept him going through each horrible day.

Once he was free, he thought to let it go. He thought he had let it go after Deirdre was killed. Now he realized it had remained, banked, but waiting for something else to fuel him.

Aisley had taken Deirdre's place. It sickened him. What kind of person was he to have such wrath inside him? Was that why he was always alone? Is that why he had such few friends?

He looked at the two Dragon Kings and the Warrior who were trying to help him. Too late Phelan comprehended that was their intention. Rhys was the only one who had dared to tell him straight.

Phelan retracted his claws and took a step back, and then another. He didn't deserve friends. He didn't deserve anything if he treated friendship with threats and rage.

He caught Charon's worried look. When his friend took a step toward him, Phelan turned on his heel and strode away.

Charon had seen many sides of Phelan, but this was a new one. The bone-deep, soul-crushing suffering he glimpsed made him want to go after his friend.

But he knew Phelan well enough to know he needed time alone.

"Well. That went splendidly," Rhys said flatly.

Banan slammed his glass on the table. "Shut up, Rhys."

"Why? Because I dared what neither of you would think about doing?"

"He's right," Charon said. "Rhys did what was necessary. I didna realize—nor do I believe Phelan fully understands—just how much what Aisley has done has affected him. He's never let anyone in."

Rhys rose and walked to the door. "He's a pain in the arse, but he's a good man."

"Aye," Charon agreed. "I worry he'll close himself off for good now."

"If he survives this," Banan said.

Charon knew Phelan. He would survive it—what he was at the end of it was the question.

CHAPTER
FORTY-FOUR

Aisley drew in a ragged, painful breath. There wasn't a part of her that didn't scream in agony. She no longer held back the tears, nor could her screams be contained.

She was alone. For the moment. There was no telling when Jason would return, or what new punishment he would inflict on her.

The damp ground she was lying on helped cool her heated skin. Aisley had a cramp in her leg, but she couldn't move from lying on her side without passing out from the pain. So, she suffered through the cramp.

Jason had healed her ribs. Sort of. They were healed just enough that she couldn't take a deep breath. Jason had broken and mended other bones in her body, and the suffering had sent her body into overload.

She couldn't even use her magic to defend herself. Somehow Jason had taken away her ability. She was defenseless, vulnerable.

Helpless.

Her mind drifted to the only place of happiness she had—Phelan. She relived the precious memories to help her get through the worst of the pain.

Aisley would have to be careful though. If Jason realized what she was doing, he could use it against her. Phelan was hers and hers alone. He might hate her now, but she would always remember the taste of his kiss, the feel of his body sliding inside her.

"Ready for more?"

She jerked at the sound of Jason's voice whispering in her ear. The movement caused agony to explode up her legs from her two broken femurs.

"You didna seriously think of falling asleep and finding a place of calm, did you?" Jason asked. He made a tsking sound as he walked around her.

Aisley took a deep breath and tried to prepare herself for the onslaught of his magic.

Yet, when the first wave barreled into her, she couldn't hold back the screams.

Phelan blew out a breath as the voices echoed in the massive great hall of MacLeod Castle. Charon said nothing more about what had happened at Dreagan, and Phelan wanted it that way. It was better that way.

He leaned his head back and laced his fingers over his eyes while Charon and Laura added their account of what had transpired with Aisley.

He didn't want to relive that moment again. At least not aloud. Phelan was tired of telling others what had happened when he had barely digested the thing himself.

It was no surprise when Isla took Aisley's side. That is until Ronnie mentioned it was Aisley who had shot Larena. That's when the hall erupted.

Phelan could feel his soul withering bit by bit. He'd made love to and protected the *drough* responsible for Larena's death and her predicament now.

"Ronnie said she stopped Dale from beheading Larena," Isla's voice said over the others.

He cringed. Would it make Aisley smile to know there were Druids defending her?

Twice now he bit his tongue to keep from telling them he'd seen the pain of her past in her eyes as well as the good inside her. But how could there be good? She was a *drough*. She belonged to the Devil.

But damn his soul, he wanted her. He craved her like the desert craved moisture.

He hungered for her, yearned for her.

Ached for her.

When he could stand it no more, he stood and walked from the castle. The cool sea air rushing against his face helped to calm his racing heart.

He didn't stop walking along the cliff's edge until the castle was a speck on the horizon. Only then did he let the full extent of Aisley's duplicity show.

In less than one heartbeat, he released Zelfor. With a roar he slashed his claws through the thick oak log at his feet. It didn't make him feel any better. In fact, he felt worse.

He walked farther. When that didn't help, he raced back to the castle as fast as he could. When the castle was a mile away, he jumped down the cliff, stopping midway. Then he climbed and leaped his way to one of the many caves in the cliffs.

Phelan stood at the entrance and looked out over the sea feeling more alone than ever. The ground was several hundred yards below, and the wind howled as if it knew the confusion inside him.

He was being ripped apart from the inside out. To have finally let someone in, only to be reminded of the treachery and dishonesty of people.

"Stop feeling sorry for yourself," said a soft, feminine voice behind him.

Phelan whirled around to find a woman of impossible

beauty sitting on a rock looking at her nails that were painted a pale lavender with some design on them he couldn't make out. Her shimmery blue-black hair hung well past her hips. She lifted unusual, swirling silver eyes to his. With her almost translucent skin, he knew she wasn't mortal.

"Who are you?" he asked.

"You know." She looked back at her nails before she let out a long sigh and got to her feet. She wore skintight jeans that tucked into black stiletto boots and a willowy shirt of pale purple that he swore he could see her nipples through.

He shook his head to clear it. "I know what?"

"Who I am. Or rather . . . *what* I am."

Phelan studied her for a moment, scarcely able to believe what he was about to say. "You're Fae."

"Bingo, stud."

He frowned at language coming from such a sweet face.

"Ah, let me guess," she said with a roll of her eyes. "You were expecting elegant and otherworldly."

"Aye."

"Well, get over it. Stud." She looked him up and down. "And you are a stud. But that's not what I'm here for. Unless," she trailed off and smiled wantonly.

As attractive as she was, Phelan couldn't believe the idea of touching her repulsed him. "Nay."

"Can't blame a Fae for trying." She shrugged. "Alrighty then. Down to business."

"Why do you talk so . . . modern?"

She smiled and tossed back her hair. "I love it. My queen, not so much. But I'm not at court now, am I? So I can talk however I want. So, spill your guts, stud."

"Stop calling me that."

"Why? You know your appeal to the opposite sex.

Hell, I'm sure you also could've had any man you wanted. You ooze sex appeal, stud."

Phelan blinked. He looked away from the Fae. "What do you want with me?"

"Haven't you guessed? I've come to torment you."

"You're succeeding."

"Aren't you going to ask me my name?"

He blew out a frustrated breath and leaned a hand against the side of the cave. "Will it make you go away? Never mind. What's your name?"

"As if I'd tell you."

She was going to make his head explode. This wasn't how he'd pictured a Fae. That wasn't exactly true. He'd expected them to have unearthly beauty, but the quiet elegance he imagined wasn't even in the vicinity.

"It was your pain," she said quietly from beside him.

Phelan glanced over at her to look at her profile. When had she moved? "Why did you allow me to find the Fairy Pool and no' let me see you then?"

"We were there." She smiled and cut him a look. "You were otherwise occupied. *Stud*."

He briefly closed his eyes and chuckled. "Can you tell me why you let me find the pool?"

"How do you know it was you we wanted to find it?"

That drew him up short. "You wanted Ai . . . You wanted the woman to find it."

"Perhaps it was both of you."

"She's evil. You're no' a Dark Fae. Why would you want her?"

The Fae laughed, the sound bouncing off the sloping cave walls. "You've never seen a Fae. You don't know what one looks like, much less one of the Dark."

"I'm right." He knew he was, he was just waiting for her to admit it.

Her grin grew. "You're right."

"Tell me why you'd have interest in a *drough*."

"I could ask you the same question."

Phelan spun around and stalked the short distance to the back of the cave. "Stop it! Stop answering my questions with questions."

"Then stop being a wanker."

"Just give me an answer. Please."

There was a soft exhale before she said, "It won't matter how I answer you. Whatever I say, you'll question it further. Sometimes, stud, it's better when there isn't an answer."

"I doona believe that."

"If you can answer me with truth—the truth you've barely allowed yourself to understand—as to why you had interest in a *drough*, then I'll answer your question."

Phelan sank onto a nearby boulder and dropped his head into his hands as he leaned forward. "I can no'."

"You can't say the words because hearing them out loud will make it more true than hearing them in your head."

He nodded. He wanted to deny everything she said, but he couldn't. It was as if with her, he could admit to things he couldn't even admit to himself.

There was a crunch of a boot as she nimbly made her way over rocks to sit beside him. "Tell me. Why were you with a *drough*?"

"Because she stirred my blood. Being without her seemed impossible."

The Fae patted his shoulder. "If we hadn't wanted Aisley to see the Fairy Pool we would've waited until you returned alone. We wanted the two of you to see it together. And before you ask, I can't tell you why. Not yet at least."

"Does it have to do with the Druids on Skye?" he asked as he lifted his head to look at her.

She nodded her head, her beauty shining even in the

dark cave. "I'm not sure why it involves the Druids, but it does. We aren't all-seeing, though some of us claim to be."

"Why wait until now to come to me? You could've come while we were still on Skye or in Inverness, or even at Dreagan."

She lifted one arched blue-black brow when he mentioned Dreagan, her gaze full of revulsion she didn't try to hide. "The Fae don't mix with the Dragon Kings. Ever."

"All right." The finality in her voice made him want to ask what had happened between them, but he knew she wouldn't answer. "So are you here to comfort me?"

"Not exactly, stud. I'm here because I could never resist a hunky man who needed a good, swift kick to his perfectly formed ass."

"What?"

She grinned widely. "I knew that would get your attention. Seriously though, you need to stop thinking of the woman and focus on your enemy."

"Wallace." Phelan sat up straight. "What do you know?"

"I know he's more powerful than ever before. He holds more magic than Deirdre collected in her thousand years."

"Shite."

"That's certainly one way of putting it, stud."

Phelan got to his feet and started toward the entrance. He halted after a few steps and looked back at her, her silvery eyes almost glowing in the dark. "Is that all you came to tell me?"

"No."

He waited as she stood, her tall, thin body gliding effortlessly over the jumbled rocks upon the floor until she stood beside him.

"The surname you search for who can end the selmyrs is Bennett."

"Thank you," he said and exited the cave.

Rhi watched him leave with a heavy heart. She had only given him half the clue he would need to discern the only person who could bring down the selmyr.

He wouldn't have believed her anyway if she'd given him the truth.

She walked to the edge of the cave and watched Phelan's form reach the top of the cliff. "Be careful, prince. Someone you care about is going to die very soon."

CHAPTER
FORTY-FIVE

Phelan threw open the door of the castle. "We need to look at the surname Bennett."

Everyone just stared at him except for Laura who jumped up from her spot at the long table. She rushed to Gwynn who had her laptop out.

"What are you talking about?" Arran asked.

There was a grin on Charon's face when he said, "It's for the selmyr."

"The selmyr?" Cara repeated.

Phelan closed the door behind him as he walked into the great hall. "We were so caught up with Wallace that I forgot to mention we . . . I went to Skye in search of a way to defeat the selmyr."

"Why Skye?" Isla asked.

He didn't want to answer her, but her question was valid. "We already knew it was the Druids on Skye who contained the selmyr the first time. I knew it was the only place to start."

Quinn frowned and leaned his elbows on the table. "Are there any Druids left on Skye?"

"No' just left, but able to help," Charon added.

Phelan looked around at all the faces waiting expectantly. He had looked forward to the time he could really help those at the castle. Finally, that day had arrived.

"Aye, there are Druids there. They followed us . . . me," he corrected, hating that it seemed so natural to include Aisley in everything. "I spoke to their leader, Corann, as well as one young and powerful Druid, Ravyn."

Broc leaned a shoulder against a wall as he stood behind Sonya. "How many are there?"

"That I doona know. Corann didna want to share much, but he allowed us . . . me to stay." Phelan left out the Fairy Pool. That was private. Something only for him. And Aisley.

Reagan reached for the bottle of wine to refill her glass. "Tell us about the Druids."

"Nay," Lucan corrected. "Tell us what they know of the selmyr."

Phelan accepted a plate of food from Dani with a nod of thanks and remained standing as he put a bite of shepherd's pie in his mouth. "I'll tell you both. First, the selmyr. Corann said they couldna help. The last time they contained the selmyr it took every Druid on Skye, and they lost hundreds in the process."

"Damn," Fallon murmured from his chair at the head of the table.

Phelan finished chewing his bite before he said, "That's no' all. Corann said there was only one bloodline who has the ability to wield the spell. The family was long gone from Skye, but he gave me the surname Hunter to begin with. After some searching, we . . . I," he said with a frustrated sigh, "found the surname had branched off in several directions. The one we need to look at is Bennett."

"How do you know?" Ronnie asked from her spot beside Arran in the small grouping of chairs at the hearth.

Phelan refused to tell them about his Fae encounter.

That was also private. "It was a strong lead. I forgot about it until now."

Hayden set down his mug of ale on the table. "So all we have to do is find this family?"

"No' exactly. Corann said the Druids of the bloodline would know the spell. It's somehow inherent in them. We have to find this Druid in order to even think about containing the selmyr again."

Marcail stood at the kitchen door drying her hands from washing dishes. "Will the Druids from Skye help?"

"Nay," Phelan admitted softly.

It was Saffron who stood up with little Emma in her arms. "We're strong Druids. We've brought down two *droughs*. We can end the selmyr."

"I agree," Isla said.

Gwynn was still pounding away on her laptop when she looked up and said, "Tell us of the Druids. What were they like?"

Phelan finished off his meal. "I only saw the two. Corann was old, but Ravyn was verra young. I think she was in her late teens or early twenties. I wasna permitted to see more of them."

"Did you talk to them?" Camdyn asked.

"Aye." Phelan handed his empty plate to Marcail and grabbed a mug of ale from the table. He drank down half of it and pinned Gwynn with his gaze. "Ravyn called herself a Windtalker."

Gwynn's fingers halted on the keyboard as she stared at him in shock. "She can hear the wind?"

"She can. Ravyn mentioned a Healer, Treewhisperer, Waterdancer, Firewalker, and others. I suspect there is a lot about the Skye Druids we doona know."

Sonya had her hand on her chest. "There's one who hears the trees?"

"What trees are on Skye," Phelan said with a shrug.

Lucan tugged on one of the small braids at his temple. "They'd be good allies."

"No' sure that's going to happen," Phelan said and drained the rest of his ale. "They were no' too happy with me being there. It's the prophecy that they're concerned with."

The hall grew instantly quiet as Phelan had known it would. This was something he wished he could discard, but Corann had been worried enough to share the information with him. The least Phelan could do was pass it on.

"What prophecy?" Laura asked.

Phelan propped one foot on the bench next to Charon. "The one that claims a Warrior will pass his seed on to a *drough*. The child that union produces will hold all the evil of the world."

Marcail gasped. "That was the prophecy Deirdre tried to fulfill with Quinn."

"And failed miserably," Quinn added.

Phelan rubbed his chin. "Unfortunately, when I mentioned that to Corann, he said it didna matter. That prophecy wasna for Deirdre. It never states who the *drough* or the Warrior will be."

"Aisley is *drough*," Dani stated in a soft voice that seemed to echo loudly in the hall.

Phelan turned his eyes to Ian's wife. "Aye, she is. She's also unable to have children."

"He's right," Charon added. "Aisley was pregnant once before. She fell on some stairs, which made the delivery complicated. The doctors had to perform a C-section, and her daughter died hours later. I saw the medical records. Aisley can no' have children."

Fallon snorted. "As if a *drough* wouldna use magic to change that."

A retort was on the tip of Phelan's tongue. He only

managed to hold it in at the last second. Fallon had his reasons to hate Aisley.

"Was she *drough* before she had the baby?" Larena asked.

Phelan looked into Larena's smoky blue eyes and shook his head. "Nay. It was after that Wallace found her."

"Does she have the magic to change it so she could have another child?"

"I mentioned it. She said it wasna possible."

Larena looked away without saying more.

Logan rested his arm over Gwynn's shoulders. "Did you explain to Corann that most of us are married to Druids?"

"I did. He wasna impressed," Phelan said. "As far as we know, we're the only Warriors left."

Isla set her elbow on the table and propped her head against her hand. "That is if Wallace doesn't find more as before."

"That's right," Laura said. "I know the Warrior he had with him, Dale, wanted Aisley. If it happened once, it could happen again. Jason has the ability to find *droughs* and Warriors. It's not a good combination."

"Which is why we need to find him," Lucan said.

Broc visibly jerked as if someone had hit him in the stomach. "That's no' going to be a problem. Wallace is at his mansion."

"How do you know that?" Phelan asked. "Did you look for him?"

"Didna need to. He sent out a signal announcing his presence."

Hayden slammed his hand on the table. "It's time he dies. He wants us to know where he is, then I say we take the fight to him."

* * *

Jason could only imagine the chaos at MacLeod Castle right about now after he broadcasted his whereabouts. There would be no more games of hiding and trying to gain the advantage.

He already had the advantage. And he was going to make full use of that fact.

Jason walked up the stairs onto the main floor of the house. His last session with Aisley had been productive. She was a strong woman, but no one could stand up to the torture he knew how to dole out.

While he'd been hitting her with physical torment, he'd been delving into her mind while she tried to keep from screaming.

How simple it had been to find the sadness that still gripped her over the loss of her daughter. Jason had used that grief to lure her to the dark side.

She'd been so strung out on drugs and malnourished that Aisley would have done anything for anyone. Lucky for him he made her believe her magic was weak but would be strong once she was *drough*.

He'd tempted her with whispered words of bringing back her daughter and getting revenge on her parents. It was the latter that Jason thought she'd carry through with. When she hadn't, he'd taken matters into his own hands to prove a point.

His steps slowed when he felt something touch the shield he had around the mansion. It wasn't magic to keep people out, but rather to call Druids to him. Only *droughs*, or those Druids who had evil festering inside them, would be able to pass through the defense.

Jason opened the front door and stepped out onto the entry. Six Druids stood at his gate looking confused and uncertain. The first walked through the barrier without hesitation. Two more followed.

He didn't need *droughs*. In fact, the ones coming to

him would only be a diversion to the Warriors. He'd take all Druids that came to him if he didn't worry about an attack of conscience as Aisley developed. He had to be sure everyone with him wouldn't betray him again.

"Welcome," Jason said to the three *droughs*. "I've been waiting for you."

The youngest of the group, a skinny teenage boy, had dyed black hair and skin powdered white, with black eyeliner and lipstick. "You do know what I am, right?"

"Do you know what I am?" Jason asked. "I'm your leader, lad. Keep that chip on your shoulder around everyone but me. I plan on ruling the world in a matter of days. That's after I kill some Warriors and Druids."

"Count me in," Emo boy said and came to stand beside him.

The girl had on a waitress outfit and bright red hair that stuck out in short spikes all over her head. "Can I use magic?"

"Of course," Jason answered.

"Fine. I'm in. As long as you don't tell me what I can and can't do with my magic I'll follow you."

Jason motioned for her to stand on his other side. That left the remaining female who looked to be in her mid-forties. She wore baggy, frumpy clothes and had dark circles under her eyes.

"And you?" he asked her.

"I've a family."

He shrugged. "It's your choice. Me or your family. Though, I'm no' sure why a *drough* would have any choice at all."

She shoved her frizzy, graying hair behind her ear and came to stand in front of Jason. "I'm Matilda."

"And I'm Jason Wallace. Your new master," he said as he looked at his three *droughs*.

CHAPTER
FORTY-SIX

Phelan looked out the castle window at the dawning of a new day. They had been up all night discussing how to attack Wallace. Tempers were short and everyone was exhausted. They were also divided.

The only ones not present were Aiden and Britt who were still working on finishing the serum to combat the *drough* blood.

Despite the urgings of Cara, Phelan had no interest in getting some rest. Every time he closed his eyes he saw Aisley, felt her in his arms, tasted her on his tongue.

"He's taunting us," Ronnie said. "Our answer shouldn't be an attack."

Arran brought his wife's hand to his lips to kiss it. "Sweetheart, you're no' used to our ways yet."

She rolled her eyes. "I may be an American and still new to the castle, but it's obvious to me. Jason is setting a trap for us. We'd be fools to walk into it."

"Wallace, Declan, Deirdre," Fallon said. "They've all set traps, and we've gotten away."

Sonya's lips flatted as her amber eyes caught Fallon's gaze. "Yes. We lost friends in the process. We all remember how powerful Deirdre was when she regained her body. I've a feeling Jason is going to be worse. I agree with Ronnie."

"And I agree with my wife," Broc said.

Ian nodded from his position straddling the bench. "As much as I'd like to find this wanker and end his miserable life, I doona think going to the mansion is the right call."

"We willna be able to lure Wallace back to Dreagan," Charon said.

Ramsey shook his head of black hair. "That was a one-time thing, I agree. Will the Dragon Kings be willing to help if we need them?"

"I can talk to them, but we'd be better off thinking it's just us."

Galen walked out of the kitchen with his fourth plate of food in an hour. "Agreed. I doubt Wallace will come here either."

"Then where?" Tara asked with a mug of coffee held between her hands as she snuggled beside Ramsey. "We can't exactly have a battle in the middle of town."

Phelan smiled and looked at Charon. "There is one place we can."

"Ferness," Charon said.

Fallon gave a reluctant nod. "How long do your people need to evacuate, Charon?"

"No' long. I'll make the call now," he said and got to his feet.

Talk would then turn to strategy. Phelan didn't need to hear it. It was always the same. The Druids would be protected by a few Warriors while the rest of them attacked. It had worked countless times in the past.

The problem was, Phelan wasn't sure it would work this time.

For the next hour, he listened as the Druids argued with the men about how they would benefit from being closer to the action and the Warriors answering with a resounding no.

Phelan knew how strong Aisley's magic was. He'd felt it, seen her use it. Days ago he would've been happy to have her by his side in battle.

He looked around at the couples as they sat together smiling, sharing whispered words and silent looks. He'd never been jealous of any of them until now. Until Aisley.

She'd opened up his heart and shown him something new and wonderful. To know she had done it only to betray him stung his pride like nothing else could.

As a Warrior, he should have seen through her beauty and words. He should have felt her black magic. It didn't matter how much he wanted her. He should've known.

He didn't know how long he was lost in thought until he felt a hand on his shoulder. Phelan looked up to find Laura beside him.

"We're all going to rest for a few hours," she said. "I know you Warriors don't need sleep, but we do."

Phelan nodded and rose from his seat. "I think I'll . . . go do something."

"You know we're here for you, Charon and I."

"Of course," he said hastily and looked around at the empty hall.

Laura patted his arm. "Of course. Get some rest, Phelan."

He waited until she was up the stairs and out of sight before he sank back onto the chair and dropped his head in his hands. He had to stop thinking of Aisley.

"I'd ask if you want a drink, but I can see you need it," Charon said as he held out a glass of whisky in front of him. "Laura is worried about you. Truth be told, so am I."

Phelan accepted the glass and downed the whisky. "I'm fine."

"Keep telling the lie, and it'll eventually become truth?" Charon asked. "I tried it. It doesna work."

"You didna crave the touch of a *drough*."

"Nay. I craved the touch of Laura who I thought had no magic at all. Which is almost the same."

Phelan took the bottle of Dreagan scotch from Charon's hand and poured more into his glass. "I want to forget her."

"Marcail can take away your emotions if that'll help."

It would, but somehow Phelan wasn't ready to relinquish them. Not to mention he didn't want to face Quinn's wrath when Marcail got sick from helping him. "Nay."

"I knew you'd say that."

They sat in silence for several minutes drinking.

"You need to talk to her."

Phelan drew in a deep breath. He wasn't going to pretend he didn't know Charon referred to Aisley. "Impossible."

"It's no'. I hate to admit it, my friend, but I believe she cared for you."

"It was an act."

"How do you know? Let Reaghan go with you. She can look in Aisley's eyes and determine if she's telling the truth."

Phelan chuckled. "I can't imagine Galen would be happy to put his beloved wife in the same room as a *drough*."

"There are Druids here who can help. Let them, dammit."

The frustration lacing Charon's words was impossible to miss. He knew his friend was just trying to help, but Charon didn't realize there wasn't anything anyone could do.

"I can no'."

Charon leaned forward and shook his head. "Damn, but you're a stubborn bugger."

"It's why you appreciate my friendship."

Charon didn't return his smile. Instead, his dark eyes

pinned him. "She changed you. For the good, I might add."

"There's no use buttering me up," Phelan said with a forced laugh. "I may be a prince, but I doona have a throne."

"Joke all you want," Charon said as he rose and set aside his glass. "You know I speak the truth."

Phelan watched his friend walk away. The one thing he and Charon always promised each other was the truth, no matter how hard it was to hear.

He knew all too clearly how Aisley had changed him. The armor he'd always worn was stripped from him, leaving him bare and exposed. He felt defenseless.

"Fucking wonderful," he murmured.

Phelan stood and slowly made his way up the stairs to his room. There wouldn't be any rest for him, but at least he could wallow in his self-pity without others seeing him.

Maybe then he could face them again with some measure of his armor back in place.

A moan fell from Aisley's lips as she came awake. She'd been having the most delicious dream involving Phelan, the Fairy Pool, and the waterfall.

The tingling of her skin from the dream faded abruptly as the discomfort from her numerous injuries brought her fully awake.

She wanted to rub an itch on her nose, but she couldn't lift her arms, not after Jason had placed dozens of shallow cuts all over her arms, neck, and face.

Blood pooled beneath her cheek from lying on her side. As disgusting as that was, she couldn't roll over. Even if she could endure the pain from the rest of her body, the welts on her back from the caning would stop her.

How much time had passed? Days or weeks? Being

locked in the dark dungeon took away all track of time. Aisley wondered what Phelan was doing at the same time she hoped he would find a way to kill Jason.

"Please, God," she whispered, then waited to be struck dead for praying. When God didn't take His wrath out on her, she sent a silent, heartfelt plea to Him for Phelan.

She wasn't sure He would even listen, but it was worth a shot.

"Why don't you pray to me?" came a deep, eerie voice from inside her cell.

Aisley's heart skipped a beat and fear slithered down her spine. "Who are you?"

"Look."

"If you haven't noticed, I can't. My sight was taken."

The sound of cloth moving reached her. A second later, thick, black-soled biker boots came into view. The man squatted next to her.

The shadows clung to him, but she could tell he was young. He wore dark jeans, a dark shirt, and a black leather jacket. She was able to see his hair was dark and cut short yet she couldn't see the exact shade. His eyes, however, were easy to see. They were black.

"Does this form please you, Aisley?"

Something about the voice made her blood freeze in her veins. "Why do you care?"

"It's one of many forms I can take. Tell me what pleases you, and I'll look the part."

An image of Phelan entered her mind. Almost instantly the man transformed into Phelan.

She closed her eyes, her chest heaving from the sight of him. "Stop it. You aren't really him."

"It's what you wanted."

"No. Just . . . go away."

There was a pause. "I no longer look like Phelan. Open your eyes."

Aisley peeked through one eye. When she saw the image of Phelan was gone, she opened her eyes. "Who are you?"

"You already know the answer to that. Wouldn't you rather ask what I'm doing here?"

"I suppose you've come to hurt me like Jason has."

The man's chuckle was the most evil sound she'd ever heard. "I've come to help you. All you have to do is ask."

"Jason pledged himself to you. You helped him come back."

"Actually, I didn't." The man ran a finger down her cheek, and as he did, he took the pain with him. "Jason delved into places I didn't think he had the courage to go. He's helped himself to magic."

Aisley took in a deep breath and slowly released it. Without the pain wracking her body she was able to think clearly. She knew the man before her wasn't a man at all but actually the Devil.

She also knew exactly what he was asking.

"I can restore you, Aisley. I can triple the magic within you. I can help you kill Jason."

"Why don't you just take away his power?"

The Devil smiled. "That would be too easy. I have more . . . finesse than that, my dear."

"Why me?"

"Because you have that passion inside you just as Deirdre did. The difference between you and her is that you're smarter. Deirdre grew reckless in her long years of power. She forgot who was really in charge."

"And I won't forget?"

"I won't let you." He scratched the tip of her nose that itched. "So, Aisley. What's your answer? Shall I take away all your pain, grant you more magic than you can imagine, and help you kill your cousin?"

CHAPTER
FORTY-SEVEN

Aisley couldn't look away from Satan's black eyes. He was trying to woo her to use as his own. And she didn't like it.

"I could make Phelan yours again. You could have him by your side for eternity," the Devil enticed.

"He would be evil."

"Of course." The Devil tugged her arm until she was sitting up. "Those damn *droughs* had no idea how long it took me to lock those gods away in Hell. They were kept in check because they hadn't been unbound. But Deirdre used them to her advantage.

"Just think, Aisley. You could command the Warriors. They're such powerful beings. With Phelan by your side, you could be happy."

She knew that was true, but her soul cried out at the thought of Phelan as evil. Yes he had evil inside him, but he wasn't evil. There was a difference.

The Devil's head cocked to the side as he studied her. "Power doesn't appeal to you, does it?"

"No."

He placed his hand on her stomach. "I could change

what nature did to you. I could heal your scarred womb so that another child could grow there."

She could imagine the child without difficulty. It would have Phelan's blue-gray eyes, his determination, and his loyalty.

Her hands clenched as she yearned to hold such a baby in her arms again, to share the love of a child with Phelan. But it would never be. It could never be.

She was *drough*, and though she didn't believe in prophecies, the Druids on Skye did. Their fear was enough to make her think twice.

As much as she wanted another child to call her own, she couldn't have that baby hold all the evil of the world.

"No," she said and moved the Devil's hand from her stomach.

His gaze narrowed as flames burned in his eyes for a split second. "It's what you want."

"No," she repeated, her voice stronger. "It can never be."

"You've no idea what you're turning away, Aisley."

"I do. More than you realize."

He unfurled his body to tower above her. "But you'll take my offer to kill Jason. If you ever change your mind about the babe, just let me know."

"You misunderstand me. I mean no to everything." She couldn't believe how steady her voice sounded, especially when she was shaking so hard inside.

"No one refuses me."

A shiver raced down her spine at the malice in his voice. "Actually they do. And often. I'm not the one for you."

His smile was slow and cold. "You may want to change your mind. At the rate Jason is torturing you, you'll be mine in a matter of days. Shall I show you what could be in store for you?"

She shook her head, but it was already too late. An image about three feet tall erupted out of the ground. It was of a woman of stunning beauty whose white hair was shorn close to her head.

Surrounding her were creatures that were half-human and half-animal. Demons, most likely. Their skin was a muted red and only semicovered their skeletal bodies, and they had elongated jaws with rows of long, sharp teeth that ripped the flesh from the woman's body.

The demons used their six-inch claws to slice her as well. Her screams were filled with terror and pain. And just when Aisley thought it was over, the woman's flesh returned and the demons started again.

"Do you know who that is?" the Devil asked.

Aisley shook her head, unable to look away from the image.

"Deirdre. I warned her to listen to my instructions, but she chose to go her own way. There was an instant when her plan could've worked and she took over the world. But the Warriors won. Deirdre then became mine. She'll be tortured like that forever."

Aisley shivered. He was threatening her with the same treatment once she died if she didn't take his offer. The idea of suffering that way made her want to agree to anything.

Yet she'd already made so many wrong choices in her life. She was destined for Hell anyway. She wouldn't make things worse.

"Find someone else."

He slowly shook his head. "You'll be praying to me soon, Aisley. I know what Jason has in store for you. You won't survive it. The pain will be unbearable. That's when you'll change your mind and pray for me. I'll be waiting."

Without so much as a sound, he and the image of Deirdre disappeared. Almost at once the injuries he'd taken from her returned.

Aisley closed her eyes and concentrated on taking

deep breaths so as not to pass out. She wanted to be awake when Jason came for her.

Phelan smiled as his hand cupped her ass before he caressed up her back. He loved the feel of her skin and the way she responded to his touch.

"More," she whispered as he kissed her neck.

He rolled her onto her back and covered her body with his. Her legs parted easily. He looked into her fawn-colored eyes and knew life would never get better than it was with her.

With her hands at his side, she urged him to her. His cock jumped, eager to be inside her and feel her wet heat. He angled his hips, and with one hard thrust, filled her.

She cried out, her nails sinking into his skin. Her back arched, which shifted her hips. He began to drive within her with long, slow movements.

Her moans filled the room. They urged him on just as her body did. He began to thrust hard and deep, pounding into her as his own desires surged.

"Phelan now!" she screamed.

He came awake instantly, his body on fire with need and tangled in the sheets. Phelan jerked the sheets away from his sweat-soaked body with a curse.

He could still feel the touch of her skin beneath his palms; the dream had been so real. Every time he closed his eyes it was the same. He knew better than to fall asleep.

Phelan swung his legs over the side of the bed and braced his hands on the mattress. When that didn't calm him, he rose and walked to the window. He threw it open and took in a deep breath of the sea air.

He waited until his body cooled before he dressed. A glance at the clock told him he'd only slept for an hour, but it had been an hour too long.

The memory of the dream would stay with him all day. No matter what he did, he couldn't shake Aisley from his thoughts. Even knowing what she was, who she was related to didn't help.

He stalked from his room and made his way down to the great hall. The only one there was Galen who was eating again.

"You look like hell."

Phelan flipped him off. "Nice to see you, too."

Undaunted, Galen asked, "Want to talk about it?"

"When I'm dead."

"Charon told us about you being a prince."

Phelan stopped on his way to the kitchen. He turned and walked back to the table and stared at Galen, who sat across from him. "What do you want to know?"

"Nothing. I know you've never been comfortable here or around us, but I hope you know you're always welcome. We're your friends, Phelan."

He looked away and blew out a harsh breath. "Aye, I'm a prince. I'm some rarity in my family. It makes no difference."

"Really?" Galen said and pushed away his empty plate. "Why do I get the feeling it makes you feel even more alienated from others than before?"

Phelan made sure Galen wasn't touching him and using his power to read people's thoughts. This was one of the reasons Phelan didn't like to come to the castle. Everyone was always in his business. The fact they were usually spot-on only irritated him further.

"What of it?" he asked as he looked at the Warrior.

"We're all different. It's what makes us individuals. You can no' take the blame for what your family did for you. It's what families do."

Phelan rubbed the back of his neck, uncomfortable

hearing Galen, but even more awkward because he wanted to talk about it. "I didna know what they sacrificed."

"Children rarely do of their parents. They're no' supposed to. You were no' supposed to. It's the way of things."

"Is it? How do I know? What family have I been around to learn these things?"

Galen stood and walked around the table. "This family. You've seen and experienced it without even knowing it. You've seen us sacrifice, but more importantly, you've sacrificed."

Phelan was about to argue that point when Galen held up a hand.

"It's true," he went on. "How many times have you willingly helped one of us heal with your blood? How many times have we called for you to aid us in battle? How many times have you protected the Druids?"

Phelan swallowed, unable to answer.

"Exactly," Galen said with a small smile. "You've been a part of us since the first time you fought by our side. We're an unconventional family, but a family just the same."

"I've been an arse."

Galen chuckled, his blue eyes twinkling. "That's true, but it makes you you. Better grab what food is left over before the others come down. If they ask, I wasna here. Reaghan says I'm eating the others' share." Galen snorted and backed away.

Phelan couldn't believe he was smiling as he watched Galen hurry up the stairs. He walked into the kitchen to find Charon leaning against the counter drinking a tall glass of milk.

He met his friend's gaze and nodded. "I suppose you heard all of that?"

Charon finished his milk and set the glass in the sink.

"Aye. Galen was right about all of it. It took awhile for me to see my place here as well. There are times I still feel like an outsider, but that's my doing and nothing to do with the others."

"Things have changed," Phelan said. "Wallace is more powerful than ever before."

Charon frowned and pushed away from the counter. "How do you know?"

"I felt his magic, but . . . I was told."

"By?"

Phelan hesitated. The Fae hadn't told him he couldn't tell others about her, but he wasn't sure if he should. He walked farther into the kitchen until only a few steps separated him and Charon.

"Phelan?" Charon urged worriedly.

"When I was on Skye, I found the Fairy Pool."

Charon shrugged. "Every tourist sees the Fairy Pools."

"Nay. *The* Fairy Pool."

"Are you telling me that you . . ." Charon trailed off and raked a hand through his hair. "Shite."

Phelan crossed his arms over his chest. "I know. Aisley saw it, too. Corann wasna happy the Fae allowed us to find it. But there's more."

"More?" Charon asked in surprise.

"Aye. A Fae came to see me yesterday."

Charon stared at him as if he'd just declared passionate love to a fruit basket. "A Fae? You mean . . . a real Fae?"

"I didna stutter," Phelan answered testily. "She said Wallace came back with more magic than Deirdre ever had."

Charon braced both hands on the large table that served as an island in the kitchen. "Fuck. This is bad."

"I know. I doona want the others to know of the Fae. No' yet at least. No' until I know what they want with me."

Charon turned his head to look at him. "You have my word. I'm glad you told me about Wallace. We'll need to take precautions for the battle."

"You know no' all of us will survive the upcoming battle. Wallace will see to that."

Charon's lips compressed into a tight line. "Aye. You've the right of it."

Phelan watched his friend leave the kitchen. He didn't have a wife being put in danger. He didn't have someone who counted on him.

If someone was to lose their life, he would be the one to do it. They were his family, after all. It would be up to him to look after all of them.

CHAPTER
FORTY-EIGHT

Malcolm glanced at his phone to see he'd missed four calls from Fallon. None from Larena. Which was strange. If those at the castle really wanted to get in touch with him, Larena was the one to call.

He then saw a text from Phelan telling him they were setting a trap for Wallace in Ferness. Malcolm looked out over the mountains.

Did he go and help the others again? Or did he stay away? Larena would never forgive him, but it was becoming harder and harder to be around her or the others.

If there were no more Druids there wouldn't be a reason for Warriors. It wasn't that he wanted his friends to die, just that he realized things would be better off without Druids or Warriors.

As cold and empty as his soul was, did he remove the last drop—and that's all it was—of feeling from himself and not go to Ferness?

Malcolm took a deep breath and remained where he was.

* * *

It was hours later that Phelan stood on the roof of Charon's building and stared over the deserted streets. Signs had been put up blocking the road in and out of Ferness saying there was a gas leak.

It wasn't yet noon, but Phelan already felt as if the day had lasted an eternity. He and the other Warriors had their places throughout the town and surrounding area, waiting for Wallace to arrive.

If he arrived.

Phelan wasn't sure the plan the Druids had come up with would work.

He wished that was their only worry. News had broken a half hour before about a grayish mist that floated upon the air. There were two witnesses to that mist killing an elderly woman in Elgin.

It was the selmyr. They all knew it, but nothing could be done about it. At least not now. Gwynn's research had yielded several other surnames that branched off the one the Fae had given him.

They weren't any closer to finding someone who could contain the selmyr than they had been before. It frustrated him, but more than that, it worried him.

With as much magic as Wallace was broadcasting, and the magic the Druids were answering with from Ferness, Phelan had little doubt the selmyr were going to pay them a visit.

Unlike last time, the dragons wouldn't be there to help.

What unsettled him more than the upcoming battle or the selmyr was the thought of seeing Aisley again. He wasn't sure how he was going to react when he spotted her standing with Wallace, because he knew that's where she was.

A woman he shared his body with, a woman who had given more to him than anyone wouldn't stand with Wallace. Why did she have to betray him? Why couldn't what they had be real?

"How are you holding up?"

Phelan turned around, surprised to find Larena beside him. "I might ask you the same question."

The normally vibrant female Warrior looked frail and weary. Dark circles marred her pale skin and said what she couldn't. Whatever was inside her was slowly eating away at her.

Larena shrugged. "Fallon hovers. He means well, but I was about to scream if I didn't get away for a moment. He only let me go when I told him I was coming up here with you."

"He loves you. He just wants to see you well."

"I know." Her sigh said it all. "Believe me, I know."

Phelan licked his lips. "You've spent four centuries with Fallon. Was there ever a time you regretted it?"

"Never. I knew as soon as I saw him that he was different, and not just that he was a Warrior. When I'm with him, I've found my other half."

"I normally only spend a few hours in the company of any one woman."

"Until Aisley."

Phelan glanced at her, noting there was no anger in her voice. "Aye."

"Were you happy with her?"

He thought of Aisley's smile, her penchant for burning anything she cooked, and the way she left a trail of her stuff all over his house. "I was. Until I learned she was *drough*."

"Forget that for a moment," Larena said as she faced him. "You're over five centuries old, Phelan. In all that time, can you tell me another instance you were as happy?"

He couldn't answer her, because he couldn't fathom having a *drough* give him the peace and contentment that Aisley did.

"I take that as a no," Larena said. She laughed softly. "Why is it men always fight what's in front of them?"

"I'm no' fighting anything. She's a damned *drough*."

"She's a Druid," Larena corrected, her voice edged with anger. "You admitted yourself she went through a lot before Jason found her. You don't know what led her to make the decision to become *drough* or if Jason forced her."

Phelan shook his head and looked back over the town, refusing to listen anymore. "Nothing excuses becoming *drough*. Nothing."

"This coming from a man who thinks sleeping with a different woman every night is all right."

"As if I have no' heard that before. The women I leave are satisfied."

"Perhaps. Are you there when they wake? Do you know what happens to them after you're gone?"

"It's no' my problem."

Larena's mouth twisted in a grimace. "No, I don't guess it is."

"What are you getting at?"

"I always took you for a smart man, Phelan."

He threw up his hands in defeat. "Enlighten me then."

"Only you know why you do the things you do. You're the only one who knows what happened in your past to make you the man you are."

"So," he said with a nonchalant shrug.

One perfectly arched blond brow lifted. "So, we might guess why you are the way you are, but only you know the truth."

"Why are you taking up for Aisley? She shot you, Larena. She killed you."

Larena's face went into a cool mask of indifference as she turned her face away. "Dale was going to behead me.

There wouldn't have been anything to bring me back from that. Maybe Aisley did me a favor."

Phelan had heard enough. He shook his head and wished Fallon would come retrieve his wife. "Now you're defending her. You wouldna be struggling with what you are if she hadna shot you."

"And you wouldn't be alive today if Deirdre hadn't unbound your god." Larena's head swiveled back to him. "Life is what it is. We're the lucky ones, because we survive it all and live to see the world change around us. We have chances to change things in our lives that mortals can't. I can't claim to know what drove Aisley to become *drough*, but I know the yearning for a child.

"She held her daughter in her arms. Aisley watched her take her last breath. I want to feel life grow within me. Aisley had that opportunity. I can only imagine the anguish she felt as a mother to not be able to save her child. That would tear anyone up inside."

Phelan didn't want to hear it. He didn't want to think of Aisley in any kind of compassionate way. If he felt pity for her, then he opened himself up to other feelings he couldn't allow.

Ever.

He knew it was time to change the subject. "Can you handle the battle?"

"I doubt it."

Phelan wasn't surprised she didn't try to lie. Larena had always faced whatever life threw at her with bravery and courage. "Does Fallon know?"

"You mean does Fallon know that by releasing my goddess and killing I could give away enough control that she takes over?"

"Aye."

Larena swallowed and gave one shake of her head.

"He has enough to worry over. It'll be up to me to keep my goddess in check."

"Have you told anyone else?"

"Cara and Marcail know. They, like you, suspected."

Phelan wanted to bellow his frustration to the sky. *Droughs* were the cause of all their problems. If they had never existed he would've never been taken from his family, and Larena wouldn't be suffering as she is now.

And Aisley's soul wouldn't belong to Satan.

"What about Malcolm?"

Larena smiled sadly. "My dear cousin has done so much for me already. I don't want him to know what's happening to me."

"He'd want to know."

"I don't care," she said with a shrug. "He barely responds to me anymore. I fear if something does happen, he'll be lost to everyone."

Phelan had long assumed that. "You could help him. Together you two could help the other."

"Phelan, I—"

Larena's words halted as both of them felt a pulse of black magic in the air at the same instant Gwynn let out a loud cry when wind rushed through the streets.

"The wind told Gwynn something," Larena said.

"Aye."

"Is he here?" she asked, looking around. "I can't tell."

"No' yet. Though I'm eager to begin this fight. The bastard needs to die."

Larena pulled her golden locks into one hand at the back of her head and quickly secured them into a ponytail. "That he does. I just wish we could've waited another day to give Britt time to finish the serum."

"That's what I'm here for. My blood, remember?"

She paced from one side of the roof to the other. "Jason isn't going to come. I told Fallon this wouldn't work."

"Oh, it'll work," Phelan said. "Wallace wants to end us. This is the perfect place since we're all gathered in one spot."

"It should work, but it isn't going to. Jason wants this on his terms."

Phelan tried to suppress the anxiety that was building at a rapid rate inside him. He wanted to disregard what Larena said, but he knew she was right.

"He's not coming," Gwynn shouted as she ran out of the bar and into the streets.

"Shite," Phelan said.

He and Larena looked at each other and at the same time said, "The castle."

Larena raced back into the building while Phelan jumped from rooftop to rooftop on his way to Charon. He landed to find Charon scowling at him.

"What the hell does Gwynn mean he isna coming?" Charon demanded.

Phelan felt his gut clench. "Wallace isna coming *here*."

"Where could he . . ." Charon let out a string of curses. "The only ones no' with us are Britt and Aiden. He's going to the castle."

"Aye. I just want to know how."

"Aisley?"

Phelan shook his head. "No' possible. She had no idea of what Britt and Aiden were doing."

"Really? How do we know that? If she's one of Wallace's *droughs* then she was in Edinburgh when Aiden and Britt were attacked. She knows."

"How would she know they didna come with us?"

Charon raked a hand through his hair. "I doona know. If you're right and Wallace is more powerful than before maybe he found out on his own."

Before Phelan could answer, there was a commotion in the middle of town as Fallon appeared with Britt in his arms. He must have teleported to the castle as soon as Gwynn told him about Wallace. Phelan and Charon leaped from the roof, landing with their legs bent before they took off running to the others.

"Britt!" Marcail shouted as she rushed to Fallon.

Phelan saw Fallon release a pent-up breath when Britt's eyes fluttered open.

"Aiden?" Britt mumbled.

"He wasna at the castle," Fallon told her. "What happened, lass?"

She squeezed her eyes closed. "Jason and his *droughs*."

"Impossible. He shouldn't have gotten through my shield," Isla said.

Phelan felt Charon's gaze on him. The time for keeping things to himself was at an end.

"That's my fault."

Everyone turned to him.

Phelan let out a deep breath. "I learned yesterday that Wallace returned with more magic than Deirdre ever had."

"And you didna tell us?" Quinn shouted as he shoved Phelan backward. "You put my son and Britt at risk? Holy hell. What is wrong with you that you would keep this to yourself?"

Charon put himself between Quinn and Phelan. "Easy, Quinn. Phelan would never put your son or anyone at the castle in danger intentionally."

"But I did," Phelan said. "I didna want anyone to know where I got the information."

Britt squirmed until Fallon set her on her feet. It was Marcail and Reaghan who steadied her. "Who did you get it from?" Britt demanded.

"A Fae."

Tara covered her hand with her mouth and stared at

him with wide eyes for several moments. Her hands dropped to her sides. "You saw one? A real Fae?"

"Aye. She came to see me yesterday and warned me that Wallace had gained much magic."

Fallon took a step toward him. "And you didna think this important enough to share with us?"

"Nay. I thought this plan would work, and we could draw Wallace out. Isla said her shield would keep Britt and Aiden safe."

Hayden growled low and deep. "Doona dare to put the blame on my wife. Your hatred of her blinds you to everything. Had you bothered to share that bit of news the Fae gave you, Isla could've strengthened the shield."

"No," Isla said into the silence that followed.

Phelan shifted his gaze to her. Isla turned her ice-blue eyes from Hayden to him.

"If what the Fae told Phelan is correct, there is nothing any magic could do to keep Jason out," Isla said.

Marcail wiped at a lone tear that streaked down her face. "Perhaps not, Isla, but I wouldn't have left my son and Britt behind for that monster to find. God only knows what he's doing to Aiden."

Britt wrapped her arms around Marcail. "Aiden is still alive. Jason is using him to ensure that we come where he wants."

Phelan started to walk away when Britt said, "Wait."

He turned around to see her pull a dropper bottle out of her pocket.

Britt held it up for everyone to see. "Each Warrior needs this."

Phelan was about to ask what it was when he felt a tingle of magic he thought he'd never feel again. His cock responded instantly. It was everything he could do not to rush to Aisley's side.

"It's the serum," Britt said. "Everyone take a drink. It's not as much as I wanted each of you to have, but it's all I could grab when Wallace came."

Phelan barely heard her. He turned to where he felt Aisley's magic. Her magic called to him, lured him. And saints help him, he wanted to go to her.

He felt something touch his arm. Phelan looked down to find Britt holding out the small vial. There was only a tiny bit left. Everyone else had already taken their turns.

Phelan took the vial and drained what was left. Whether Britt's serum worked or not, he was about to put it to the test.

"Now. Where is Wallace?" Lucan asked.

Phelan pointed to the left, to the forest. "There. Wallace is there. And so is Aisley."

CHAPTER
FORTY-NINE

Aisley drew in a ragged, painful breath and looked at the thick forest of trees around her. One of her ribs was broken and pushing against her lungs. Every finger was pulled out of joint and the bones smashed into pieces. Her shirt was stuck to her back by the blood that dripped from the dozens of cuts.

But none of the hundreds of injuries inflicted upon her by Jason was visible. He'd seen to that.

"How are you faring, cousin?" he asked with a malicious smile. "You are no' in any pain, are you?"

"Sod off, you ugly shit."

"Finally found that spine of yours, eh? You do know you're going to die today."

She knew. She knew all too well. And she also knew who would be the one to end her life.

Phelan.

She couldn't wait to see him again. Aisley missed looking into his blue-gray eyes and hearing his seductive voice that always gave her chills. He could read the dictionary and he would still sound sexy as hell.

"You can save yourself," Jason said. "Tell me what I need to know about the Warriors."

Aisley looked to the man Jason had captured. She recognized him as Quinn's son. Aiden was on his knees, his head hanging forward, and his arms held by two of Jason's new *droughs*.

"You didna share that Warrior's bed and come away with nothing!" Jason shouted. "Tell me what I need to know."

Aisley bit back a cry of pain as she turned her head to look at him. "You're the all-powerful one. Find out for yourself."

Out of the corner of her eye, she saw Aiden's head lift to look at her. She wanted to reassure him that there was nothing Jason could do to get her to tell him anything about Phelan or any of the Warriors. But she couldn't show any kind of response to Aiden for fear of what Jason would do to him.

"After all I've made you endure." Jason's voice was low, calm as he walked around her. "Even after I've ensured that I'm the only one who can heal your wounds. I thought you'd have broken by now. I guess I was wrong."

Aisley remained silent. Let Jason say whatever he wanted, let him continue to torture her. She wouldn't be swayed.

"Mummy?"

The child's voice went through Aisley like a knife. She looked down to find a little girl of about two who had long black hair with a pink ribbon tied around her head and fawn-colored eyes.

Aisley couldn't breathe, couldn't move as she stared down at the image she'd always pictured of her daughter.

"Mummy, up," the child said as she lifted her arms to Aisley.

Jason walked behind her and whispered, "What kind of mum would ignore her child, cousin?"

Aisley's vision swam as tears poured unheeded down her face. Her heart rejoiced at the same time her mind cautioned her. But the last image of Gillian in her arms was easy to let go of when she stood before Aisley now.

Nothing, not a single broken bone, cut, or ache could stop Aisley from kneeling before the adorable child. She opened her arms, and Gillian ran into them, her chubby arms wrapping tightly around Aisley's neck.

Aisley sobbed as she held her daughter. Her little body seemed so frail and sturdy all at the same time. And she smelled of innocence and wildflowers.

"I can give her back to you," Jason said.

Aisley leaned back and tried to touch Gillian's cheeks. Her fingers wouldn't bend, so she was only able to lightly run her palm along the cherubic cheeks as her daughter smiled up at her.

"I could make it so that you forgot she died hours after her birth. I'll give you memories of the first time she sat up, the first time she crawled, the first time she ate baby food, and her first steps. Think about all the firsts, Aisley. Her first birthday, her first Christmas."

Aisley kissed Gillian's forehead. Her eyes clashed with Aiden's as he watched her with blood dripping from a cut at the corner of his mouth.

She couldn't forget how Quinn had fought so hard to save his son from Jason in Edinburgh. Aiden was someone's son. If she told Jason anything, Aiden would die after his usefulness was over.

Aisley held Gillian against her and closed her eyes. Ferness was near, and the Warriors would know Jason already had Aiden. The battle Jason craved would happen soon.

"Want ta go home, Mummy," Gillian said as she wiggled against her.

All Aisley had to do was tell Jason she would take his offer. She would have Gillian again. But at what cost? How could she think to raise a child when her soul was going to Hell?

She didn't want Gillian around black magic. Then there was Jason. She knew he had ulterior motives. He would use Gillian for his own and possibly turn her against Aisley.

"All your wounds can be healed in your next breath," Jason said. "You can take Gillian back to the mansion and await me there."

Aisley got to her feet and swallowed past the lump of emotion in her throat when Gillian tucked her small hand into hers.

Jason smiled at Gillian as he ran his hand down her head. "She's such a beautiful lass. But I need your answer. Will you let your daughter die a second time?"

Aisley looked once more into Aiden's dark green gaze. How could she let Gillian go a second time? She'd barely survived the first time. She wouldn't survive a second.

But how could she side with evil once more?

Jason wasn't her only choice. She could always pray to the Devil as he had told her she would. If she did, however, she would lose Gillian.

It all came down to her daughter.

"I'll not fail Gillian again," she whispered.

Aiden's chin fell back to his chest.

Jason smiled widely and clapped his hands together. "I knew the child would get you. You always let it rule you. A word of advice, cousin. Doona ever allow yourself to have such a weakness."

"You said you would heal me."

"In a moment," Jason said and looked around him.

"We're going to have visitors soon. I wonder how angry Quinn is that I took his son. He'll be the first to attack. And the first to die."

Aiden let out a bellow and tried to get to his feet, but the two female *droughs* held him down with their magic.

"Tell me what those at the castle have been working on," Jason demanded of Aisley.

She licked her lips. She had no idea, and she wasn't sure if Jason did either. He could use magic to make her tell the truth. Or torture her more. She wanted neither. If she was going to play this, she had to do it right. "I don't know."

"Liar!" Jason took a deep breath and forced a smile. "You were with Phelan for days. I know you got him to talk. Tell me everything."

There was no way Aisley would tell Jason anything about Phelan. The Fairy Pool and Phelan's royal heritage were meant only for Phelan.

Aisley looked down at Gillian as her heart broke for Phelan and their time together. She hesitated a bit too long in answering, because in the next second, she felt more blood pour down her back.

"Doona think to play me," Jason said through clenched teeth. "I broke you once. I'll break you again."

"All right," Aisley said quickly, and then in a softer voice, "all right. They're working on a way to use their blood against you."

"Interesting."

She let out the breath she'd been holding. As soon as Jason accepted her lie, she knew she had a chance of keeping Gillian.

"What else?" Jason asked.

Aisley shrugged and ignored the hate-filled glare from Aiden. "They're looking for a way to contain the selmyr as they once were."

"Those beasts that killed me? And?"

"That's it."

Jason snorted. "How far have they come to killing the selmyr?"

"The last I knew, not very. They were looking for a certain bloodline that would know what to do."

"And that's all you know?"

"That's all I know," she said.

Jason rubbed his hands together. "My enemies are close. Do your part, and I'll keep my promise to you."

"My part?"

He spared her an irritated look. "Kill Phelan."

Aisley could no more kill him than she could Gillian. She loved Phelan, the kind of love a person could only dream about. She didn't know why love had come to her, only that it had.

Her past choices kept her and Phelan apart, but it didn't stop her love. Nothing, not even her death, would end her love for him.

Fortunately, Jason walked away to talk to a young lad. Aisley had a tough choice before her. She could kill Phelan and keep her beloved daughter by her side and face whatever consequences came from that.

Or she could turn against Jason and try to kill him. She'd lose Gillian and most certainly her own life. But Phelan would be saved.

It came down to Gillian or Phelan.

How could she make a choice?

Gillian wanted her while Phelan despised her. If given the chance, Phelan would kill her.

Fresh tears fell as Aisley inwardly screamed at the unfairness of it all. Either choice ended with her losing someone she loved. It was a no-win situation, and Jason knew it. The Jason that had come back from the dead had a hard edge to him, a ruthlessness he'd previously lacked.

It was clear he would do anything—and stop at nothing—to have what he wanted.

As if sensing Aisley was wavering, Jason turned to her. "Gillian, come stand beside me, lass. I'll keep you safe."

Aisley didn't have the hand strength to keep ahold of her daughter. A look from Jason silenced any argument Aisley was about to make.

Gillian ran to Jason's side, her laughter filling the forest. The battle about to begin was going to be a deadly one. And her precious, beautiful daughter was standing next to the man who had instigated it all.

Why couldn't Jason have stayed dead?

Why couldn't the Devil stop playing games and end Jason now?

Why couldn't Phelan have killed her as she asked?

Aisley sniffled through her tears. Somehow she was going to have to keep both Gillian and Phelan alive. It didn't matter what happened to her so long as she didn't have to watch one of the two people she loved die.

The choice Corann had warned her about was here. She just prayed she had the magic to get through it.

CHAPTER
FIFTY

Phelan's skin tingled from the feel of Aisley's magic. There was great sadness in her magic, but it didn't stop him from vowing to kill her as she'd asked him to do in Inverness.

Mixed with Aisley's magic was the cloying, sickening feel of *drough* magic. Phelan recognized Wallace's magic from the rest of the *droughs* he sensed.

It was Wallace he'd felt on Skye. Whether or not the bastard attacked Aisley or it was some elaborate setup didn't matter.

"Come out, come out, wherever you are!" Wallace's voice shouted through the trees.

Phelan nodded to Charon and walked the path his friend had told him about. It would take Phelan around to flank Wallace. Malcolm was supposed to take the other side, but they hadn't heard from him. Whether he showed up or not was anyone's guess.

There was time for one more try. Phelan moved silently through the trees as he sent a quick text to Malcolm. Almost instantly Malcolm responded to let him know he was already there and watching Wallace.

Phelan smiled. It was going to be up to him and Malcolm. The other Warriors would do their part, but they also had to keep the Druids safe. He and Malcolm didn't have that problem.

Wallace was set up atop a small rise that was protected by huge oaks, alders, pines, and chestnuts. There was a steep slope leading up to Wallace's back. The ground on the remaining three sides were gentle rolling hills.

Phelan clenched his jaw when he felt the magic behind Wallace preventing anyone from attacking there. Wallace had set up the battlefield distinctly to his advantage.

Much as they had done at Dreagan. Wallace hadn't known what he was walking into then, but Phelan and the others certainly did.

No one knew this woodland as Charon did. As soon as they'd discovered that's where Wallace was, Charon had drawn a quick map of the forest.

Once Broc discovered exactly where Wallace was, it was simply a matter of Charon showing where everyone needed to go to be most effective.

Phelan unleashed his god and watched the gold claws extend from his fingers as he braced a hand against the trunk of a tree. Fighting *droughs* was what he was meant to do.

To his left the other ten Warriors had taken their places while the three MacLeod brothers would be visible to Wallace.

Phelan peered through the foliage and spotted Quinn with Fallon and Lucan on either side of him. Quinn's rage was palpable. The brothers removed their shirts so Wallace could see the black skin and claws of their shared god.

As many battles as he'd been in, Phelan knew this one could change everything. With Aiden being held captive, it was up to Fallon and Lucan to control Quinn if something should happen to his son.

Phelan continued through the trees until he found the protruding rock formation Charon had told him about. He lay outstretched on his stomach and peered down at Wallace. Though he wasn't as close as he wanted to be, there was a distinct advantage to him taking the higher ground on the next hill.

He let his gaze slowly sweep the area until he spotted a young lad, Wallace, and a black-haired little girl. The toddler gave him pause, especially when she turned her head and he saw fawn-colored eyes.

Phelan continued his search until he found Aiden being held by two female *droughs* using magic to keep him submissive. Though Aiden was fighting it.

A smile pulled at Phelan's lips. It was just like a MacLeod to be stubborn enough to think he could get out of a situation like that alone.

But no matter how much of Aiden's magic Phelan felt, it wasn't enough for Aiden to overcome his captors.

Then Phelan saw Aisley.

His breath left him in a whoosh, as if someone had kicked him in the gut. Her midnight locks were in disarray and tangled. Her clothes were dirty, and he could almost swear he smelled blood on her. Fresh blood.

She was standing a ways behind Wallace and in front of Aiden. Yet she didn't move. Not a twitch of her fingers or quirk of her lips. Only the breeze rustling the leaves dared to sweep through her hair.

A strand tangled in her eyelashes. He waited to see her move it out of the way, but nothing happened. Her gaze was riveted on the little girl Wallace had ahold of.

Phelan made himself look away from Aisley. If he continued, he was likely to think the expression on her face was one of dejection and pain.

He knew better.

After how easily she'd lied to him, Phelan didn't trust

what his eyes saw or what his ears heard. He'd already anticipated that if he came in contact with her he would believe the opposite of whatever she said.

"Are you going to wait forever?" Wallace shouted to the forest.

Phelan peeled back his lips when he saw Wallace exchange a smile with the lad next to him. The bastard thought it was funny. By the time Phelan got done with him, Wallace wouldn't have anything to smile about.

The MacLeods walked out of the shadow of the trees and halted. Fallon had his arms crossed over his chest while Lucan's hung by his side in anything but a casual stance. Quinn, however, had his hands fisted and his lips peeled back as he growled.

"Put a leash on it," Wallace told Fallon of Quinn.

Fallon quirked a brow. "Release his son, and I willna have to."

Wallace opened his mouth in a dramatic *O* and glanced over his shoulder at Aiden. "You mean him? I'm afraid that's no' going to happen."

"Then prepare to die, *drough*," Quinn said menacingly.

In response, Wallace laughed. "You dim-witted thugs think you can walk up and kill me? After all I survived? I came back from the dead and gained more power in the process."

"You're no' the first," Lucan said. "Deirdre did it before you. Better, I think, too."

Fallon nodded. "Deirdre did do it better."

"I doona give a shite how many people have done it," Wallace ground out, his vanity showing by the thickening of his accent. "I'm back, and you willna be getting rid of me so easily."

Quinn took a step toward him before Lucan and Fallon grabbed his arms. "Keep thinking that. We've no' killed two powerful *droughs* for nothing. You're next on the list, Wallace."

"And I'm shaking in my shoes," Jason said with a chuckle. "What none of you yet realize is that I have the advantage."

Lucan gave a derisive smirk. "With three *droughs*?"

"With three *droughs*."

It was Wallace's cool demeanor that got Phelan's attention. The bastard might be a sociopath, but he had a plan. And one they weren't prepared for.

There was no time to warn the others. Phelan called up his power and altered the forest so Wallace thought the MacLeods were gone. It was done seconds before Wallace let loose a blast of magic along with three knives that rose from the ground and aimed right at the MacLeods.

Phelan spotted blood on the knives and knew it was *drough* blood. The brothers got out of the way of the knives and magic and scrambled back into the forest. Only then did Phelan drop the imagery. Wallace let loose several more blasts of magic in the trees that came too close to hitting the Warriors.

If Phelan didn't do something, Wallace would get lucky and manage to hit one of his friends. Phelan got to his feet. Before he could jump in front of Wallace, lightning zapped through the forest and zinged one of the women holding Aiden.

Aisley waited for the lightning to strike her. Instead, it was only one of Jason's newest recruits that fell to the ground, her lifeless body smoking from the zap.

Her knees were locked, which was the only thing keeping Aisley upright and still instead of running to Gillian. Out of the corner of her eye, Aisley saw Aiden elbow the other woman. She was older, and he was able to gain an advantage, even with the *drough*'s magic.

She wanted to see if Aiden got loose, but Aisley's attention couldn't be diverted from Gillian who was still beside Jason as he continued to blast his magic in the trees.

Aisley screamed Gillian's name when the lightning came again and struck steps from her. When Gillian started to run to her, Jason grabbed Gillian's arm to keep her with him.

"No," Aisley said. She wouldn't stand by and watch her daughter be put in danger.

Balls of fire, more lightning, and even water shaped like a spear hurdled into the small clearing coming closer and closer to Jason.

The teenager was taken out by a water spear to his chest. Jason paid him no heed. It was as if the *droughs* Jason had recruited meant nothing to him.

Her magic welled within her. She could use it against Phelan and the others. If she did, it would prove to Jason she was allied with him.

It would give her Gillian. She could rock her daughter to sleep at night, teach her about magic, life, and boys.

The world spun as Aisley's ears rang and she found herself on her stomach on the ground, pine needles sticking into her cheek. By the smell of burnt earth, it seemed she had almost been struck by lightning.

It was the sound of Gillian screaming for her that had Aisley moving. She bit her lip and tasted blood when she moved her hands beneath her to push herself up.

The wounds on her back gushed blood. She had already been weak from lack of food and the torture. The more blood she lost, the weaker she became. How could she help Gillian then?

Aisley grew dizzy when she put pressure on her injured hands to steady her. Slowly she moved her legs so that her knees were underneath her.

She blinked and focused on her fingers. That's when

she saw the dark trail of blood that ran down her arm and over her hand to pool on the ground.

"Mummy!"

Aisley tried to send magic to Gillian to bring her, but Jason was too powerful. Even with his concentration on the Warriors, Aisley couldn't get to him.

Phelan saw the blood running down Aisley's arm. But what sent a shock through him was the child screaming for her. It couldn't be possible though. Aisley's daughter had died when she was just hours old.

"That's the other magic I feel," Phelan said as it all began to make sense.

He expected Aisley to run to her daughter, but it was taking her an obscene amount of time just to climb to her feet. Had Malcolm's hit hurt her more than he realized?

Phelan started to go to her when he remembered who she was—what she was. Instead, he turned his attention to helping Aiden get free of the *drough* holding him.

It was almost too easy. Aiden had already caught her off guard, and it took little effort on Phelan's part by altering the *drough*'s perception of the world for Aiden to get away.

Instead of disappearing into the forest as Phelan expected him to do, Aiden went to Aisley.

Phelan turned away from the scene and focused once more on Wallace. His fellow Warriors weren't putting the full force of their powers into the attack because Wallace held the toddler.

If they were going to get anywhere, Phelan would have to remove the child from Wallace. Maybe then he could get off a clear shot at Wallace, ending it all.

Or would it end it?

There would still be Aisley.

CHAPTER
FIFTY-ONE

Aisley yelped in pain when a large hand gripped her upper arm painfully and yanked her to her feet. The blood ran quicker down her arm. She lifted her head to find Aiden's angry green gaze directed at her. "If you're going to kill me, do it."

His forehead creased in a frown. "Kill you?"

"I begged Phelan to do it. Did he send you?"

"I want to know why you lied to Wallace."

She weakly tried to pull away. Now that she was standing she could get to Gillian. "I didn't know anything. He wouldn't have believed that, however. I had to tell him something."

"You knew what we were working on. You were part of the attack on Britt in Edinburgh."

Aisley's shallow breathing still didn't combat the pain of her ribs. "Jason knew she was helping you. That's all the incentive he needed to want her dead. Now, if you aren't going to kill me, then let me get to my daughter."

"She's no' real."

Aisley shook her head, not caring how it pulled the torn muscles in her back. "She is. He brought her back."

"I can see her, but she's no' real. He's using it to get to you. Help us, Aisley."

"You don't understand."

He gave her arm a squeeze. "Tell me you doona love Phelan."

"I . . . I can't."

"Then help us. Get your daughter so we can fight Wallace."

Aisley pulled her arm out of his grasp. "Get to your family before Wallace sees you."

"If he finds out you let me go, he'll kill you."

"I'm dead anyway. I've known it for months now."

A muscle twitched in Aiden's jaw. "Does the surname Murray mean anything to you in regards to the selmyr?"

Aisley blinked, not able to hide her surprise. It was only thanks to her mother's obsessive hobby of learning their family tree that Aisley knew her great-great grandmother's maiden name had been Murray.

"You do," Aiden said.

Aisley gave him a push. "Get away while you can."

"The selmyr have been spotted close. They'll be coming," he said before he faded into the dark of the forest.

She turned back to Jason when Gillian screamed. Part of her daughter's hair was burned from a fireball. As long as he kept Gillian with him, the Warriors wouldn't attack as they should.

Damn Jason for putting her child at risk.

Aisley closed her eyes and called to every last bit of magic she had within her. It pulsed and grew until she could feel it swirl around her.

Then she opened her eyes and held out her arms to Gillian. "Come," she said at the same instant she directed magic at Jason's back.

It propelled him to the side, giving Gillian enough

time to get free and run to her. Aisley smiled as her daughter's little legs ran as fast as they could toward her.

"Nay!" Jason bellowed.

Aisley once more found herself on her back from Jason's magic. She turned her head to look for Gillian, but she was gone. Only the pink ribbon that fluttered slowly to the ground remained.

All around her magic, fire, water, and lightning flew. The ground shook and cracked at Jason's feet. Somehow his magic was being thrown back at him. Mixed in was the magic of the Druids who hurled their own volleys at him.

But Aisley felt none of it. The grief that tore through her was just as raw, just as visceral as it had been the day Gillian died in her arms.

She'd held it all in then. She wouldn't now.

The scream welled in her chest until she had no choice but to let it out.

Phelan used his power to constantly shift Wallace's perception of the trees so he wouldn't know where the attacks were coming from.

The scream that tore from Aisley reached all the way to Phelan's soul. He felt her grief and anger. He heard the anguish and heartrending sorrow.

Her hand was still outstretched where the toddler had been running to her. Jason had killed the lass.

Phelan shut his mind and heart off to Aisley's pain and concentrated on helping his friends. Wallace was so confident no one would attack at his back that when the opportunity came, Phelan jumped from his spot to land in the clearing.

Off to his right was Aisley. She was struggling to get to her feet again. To his left was Wallace, a smile of victory on his face.

"No' for long," Phelan murmured.

Without turning around, Wallace broadsided him with a burst of magic that pinned him against a tree. Phelan bellowed and struggled against the hold, but he couldn't shake loose.

Then a knife near Wallace's feet rose in the air. Its blood-coated blade was pointed right at his heart. Phelan barely had time to prepare himself before the blade flew at him.

Aisley's magic swarmed around him. The blade swerved. Instead of hitting his heart, it sank into his arm.

"No."

The word was spoken calmly, quietly by Aisley in the chaos of battle. She was on her feet but swaying. Blood dripped from both hands, and it looked as if her black shirt was wet on the back.

Jason glanced over his shoulder at her. "I'll get to you in a moment, you treacherous bitch."

"No."

Phelan sucked in a breath as Aisley's magic, beautiful and erotic, brushed against him again. He couldn't believe she was going to attack Jason.

With one hand held out toward his attackers, Wallace used some kind of defense to ricochet anything directed at him as he faced Aisley. Phelan understood then that Wallace had been playing with them. He could take them out at any time.

"Were the past couple of days no' enough for you?" Wallace demanded of Aisley. "Shall I do more?"

"You've done all you can." Aisley visibly swallowed and blinked as if to clear her vision. "You took her away."

Jason smirked. "As if I'd have let your darling daughter remain. I used her to have you fight for me."

A lone tear stole down Aisley's face. Phelan could see the tracks of earlier tears in the smudges of dirt, but that one tear touched him as nothing else could.

"I had a visitor yesterday. Satan," Aisley said.

Wallace laughed. "I doona believe you."

Phelan felt the *drough* blood rushing through his body, but it wasn't as debilitating as before. Britt's serum seemed to be working.

"He wants you dead, Jason. It seems you came back from the dead, along with more magic, without any aid from him. He's not happy. He wanted me to take your place. He offered to give me the magic to kill you."

Phelan was proud of the way Aisley stood so bravely and composed in front of Wallace. But a niggle of worry wouldn't let go while he listened to her speak of Satan as if she always traded conversations with him.

Had Wallace pushed Aisley past the breaking point by killing her daughter?

"You lie," Wallace said, though his voice lacked the conviction of his words.

Aisley shook her head. "I'm not. Satan said all I had to do was pray to him."

"I didna come back from that awful void for this! It was only because of my need for retribution against you that I'm here at all. You were family, Aisley. I was never supposed to doubt you."

She shrugged, the lines bracketing her mouth telling Phelan how much that small movement pained her. "In the words of Justin Timberlake, cry me a river."

Joy spread through Aisley as she watched Jason's cool façade crumble. His angry bellow only made her smile. She welcomed the magic he directed at her. It would end her life and her suffering.

The smile died when Jason didn't direct the blast at her, but instead lobed it at Phelan.

Aisley watched as Phelan's face contorted in pain. He was already pinned to the tree by Jason's magic.

"I've already taken away your daughter," Jason said with a malicious grin. "Shall I kill Phelan as well?"

She saw him lift his hand, saw the magic swirling in an orb that grew by the second. Aisley didn't think, just reacted. The pain of her injuries was forgotten as she raced toward Phelan.

Jason reared back his hand and let loose the magic. Aisley dove in front of Phelan and took the impact of the blast. Her breath was knocked from her as she slammed into the ground.

"Selmyr!" someone shouted.

She could feel the life draining from her. Aisley wanted to look at Phelan, but she couldn't turn her head. She suspected her back was broken along with all the bones barely mended.

Jason forgot about the MacLeods and turned all his magic onto the approaching gray mist that moved so quickly across the sky that Aisley could barely keep up with it.

Aiden had been right. All the magic they used had done nothing but call out to the selmyr.

"Murray," she whispered.

Corann had told them only the Druids of the bloodline would know the spell. She wasn't sure she could because she was *drough*, but she was their only chance.

It wasn't her life she was trying to save, but Phelan's and the people he considered family. If she wasn't from the bloodline nothing would be lost. If she was, she could end the selmyr.

Aisley concentrated on her magic. It took her three tries because of the agony of her body before she thought she imagined the sound of drums. She needed them now, needed someone to help her.

The mist filled the clearing before it faded away, leaving the frightening, lanky, white-skinned monsters she knew she would never forget.

Jason didn't use a bubble of magic like last time. He ran away like the coward he was.

Aisley would've laughed had she been able to. Thankfully, Warriors poured out of the forest and began attacking the selmyr, ripping their spines from their bodies.

But they weren't coming away unscathed. The selmyr were quick and there were too many of them. For every one a Warrior killed, ten more were biting him.

She had to somehow find the spell in her subconscious. Unless Corann lied and there was nothing that could stop the selmyr.

But that couldn't be. He had given them a surname. Phelan found where it had changed, and then Aiden discovered her great-great grandmother's maiden name. It couldn't be a coincidence.

Aisley saw a flash of gold and caught sight of Phelan as he delved into the fray. There was so much she wanted to say to him. He wouldn't listen, and she didn't expect him to. Not after keeping who she was a secret.

She took a few seconds and watched him move with speed and efficiency, his beautiful gold skin shining in the sunlight. His bellow would make any Highlander proud, as would the way he rushed into the battle with his gold claws swinging and his fangs bared.

He glanced at her, and she stared into the gold eyes of his god. The metallic color went from corner to corner, but she knew he was looking at her. Then he turned away.

All she could do for him now was protect him and his family. Aisley pushed aside the pain wracking her body and listened for the drums.

When Wallace ran away, Phelan was free of his magic. He pulled out the knife and let it drop to the ground as he stood beside Aisley, looking down at her broken body, unsure of what to do.

It was the selmyr coming toward her that propelled him into action. He leaped over her and rushed by the creature, reaching around to grab its spine as he did.

The feel of his claws sinking into the selmyr's skin and the feel of its spine ripping out of its body made Phelan smile. Until six more selmyr started toward Aisley.

He stood between her and them. There was no way he was going to allow them to touch a single hair on her head.

Phelan bellowed as a selmyr sank its fangs into his shoulder. He elbowed the creature off while he kicked another in the head. Phelan spun and thrust his hands into the backs of two selmyr before he jerked his arms back, their spines in his hands.

He looked down to see Aisley's eyes closed, but her magic was still there. That's the only thing that kept him going.

CHAPTER
FIFTY-TWO

There was a huge explosion of magic that made Aisley's eyes fly open. The selmyr hovered over the clearing in their gray mist, as if waiting to begin their smorgasbord.

"Aisley."

Her skin tingled at the sound of Phelan's voice so close. She bit back a cry as agony swallowed her when he rolled her onto her back, supporting her in his arms as he sat on the ground.

"I'm so sorry," she said, noting he tamped down his god and all that glorious gold skin was gone. "For everything."

His blue-gray eyes held no emotion. "You saved me."

"I couldn't watch you die."

"The child?"

She glanced away. "My daughter."

"Created with Wallace's magic," Aiden said as he knelt near Aisley's feet. "I heard everything."

"I need to speak to your Druids."

Phelan shook his head. "In a moment. You're injured. Tell me where so I can heal you."

He didn't let her answer before a gold claw cut open

his wrist and his blood dripped into what she suspected was a rather nasty wound in her gut. The pain was ebbing away. It cleared her mind, but she knew it had nothing to do with Phelan's blood and everything to do with the fact she was dying.

"We don't have long," said a female from out of Aisley's line of sight, her voice clipped with anxiety.

Aisley swallowed. "I need to talk to them, Phelan."

He gave a nod and several more faces came into view. She knew who they were from the red book Declan had created and Jason had used. Yet, she'd never met any of them except for Laura.

"It will take the magic of every Druid here. Do you have anything to contain the selmyr?" she asked.

Phelan's gaze jerked to her face. "You know who can perform the spell?"

"Yes."

A moment later Fallon stood behind Phelan holding a wooden box. "This is what they were in originally."

"Perfect," she said. It still held magic from the first time, so it would do wonderfully to trap the selmyr.

Phelan's grip on her tightened. "Why is your wound no' healing?" he asked angrily.

Aisley placed her hand over his arm and the cut that had already healed. "I wanted to tell you who I was from the beginning. But being with you made me happier than I've ever been. I was selfish to take that time and lie to you."

"Nay," he said with a shake of his head, his dark hair falling on either side of his face. He jerked his head around. "Sonya! I need Sonya!"

Aisley knew her time was short. Unimaginable torture awaited her in Hell but being in Phelan's arms made it easier to bear.

"Who can contain the selmyr?" Charon asked.

Aisley swallowed as tears gathered. She couldn't look away from Phelan. He was all that was handsome and good and brave. She hated to leave him, but by doing so she would save him and the others.

It was Aiden who answered for her. "She's the one."

Phelan brushed her hair away from her face. "That can no' be. Corann said the spell would likely claim the Druid's life."

"I'm already dead," she told him.

"I can save you."

"No. It's what I tried to tell you. Jason made sure of that. No amount of magic, or even your amazing blood, can help me."

Phelan felt as if the weight of the world rested on his chest. He couldn't draw breath, couldn't wrap his head around what Aisley was telling him.

"What did he do?"

Her smile was sad. "A spell to prevent anyone but him from healing me."

"It's just one wound," Sonya said as she hurried up. "We should be able to combine our magic and get past Jason's."

Phelan knew by the way Aisley wouldn't meet his gaze that it was more than one wound. "What did he do to you?"

"Tortured her," Aiden said. "Bringing her to the brink of death. Repeatedly. He said he'd do the same to me once he won this battle."

Phelan couldn't wait to get his hands on Wallace. He was going to flay the skin from his body an inch at a time.

"I'm running out of time," Aisley said.

He looked around helplessly. "There has to be a way."

"The selmyr are breaking through my shield," Isla said tightly. "We need to do something now."

Aisley's fingers, stuck at different angles, touched his face. "You know what I have to do."

"It willna kill you. Do you hear me? Doona let it. Stay alive so we can get around Wallace's spell."

She smiled, her fawn-colored eyes swimming in tears. "Put the box on the ground and keep everyone away from it."

"Aisley," he urged.

"I'll do my best."

It was all he was going to get from her, but Phelan knew it wasn't enough. Isla's shield began to crack. The selmyr would once more descend upon them. Everything hinged on Aisley.

Something dripped from his arm that was holding her. He looked down to see it was blood. The idea of someone as beautiful and wonderful as Aisley tortured made his soul and his god bellow in fury.

He looked up as the mist began to pour through the crack in the shield.

"I know you won't believe this," Aisley said. "But I love you."

Phelan looked down at her, unsure of what to say. He'd have time to think of it after she was healed. Then he would know how to respond.

Everyone moved away as the spell tumbled from her lips. Everyone but him, that is. He couldn't make himself release her. There was no magic inside him to aid her, but he would give her whatever she needed.

The ground began to vibrate rapidly, the leaves raining down from the trees. Phelan looked at Camdyn, but the Warrior shook his head to let him know he'd had nothing to do with it.

Aisley's magic grew and expanded with each word of the spell. It was then he understood she was causing the disturbance.

Phelan watched the mist pause as if unsure what was

going on. When they tried to retreat, Aisley sealed the crack in Isla's shield trapping the selmyr inside.

The Druids formed a circle and linked hands, offering their magic alongside Aisley's. The tremors were so violent, it felt as if the world was about to break in two.

Phelan held Aisley close. The spell fell faster from her lips, coinciding with the vibrations.

Several Warriors surrounded the Druids while the MacLeods kept watch over Britt. But everyone had their eyes on the mist. The selmyr were desperate to get out of the shield. The mist rammed the shield again and again, but it held.

The sheer amount of magic coming from Aisley made Phelan's skin tingle and need course through him. How he missed holding her, seeing her. Touching her.

"Phelan."

He looked at her, sure he'd heard her whisper his name. But her eyes were closed and the spell still underway. There was a shout as the mist dove at the Druids on its way to Aisley.

Suddenly her eyes flew open, her body tensed as she finished the spell.

The screams of thousands of selmyr filled the air as the mist was forced into the box. Ronnie hurried over to it and slammed the lid closed when the last of the mist was inside.

"It's over," Phelan said and looked at Aisley with a smile. That smile fell when he felt the magic draining from her as fast as her blood. "Fight, Aisley."

She tried to smile as her eyes closed. And she took her last breath.

"Aisley," he said and shook her. "Fight, dammit. Fight!"

"She's gone."

Phelan looked up to find the Fae woman standing

before him. She didn't wear a sassy smile this time. The sadness in her swirling silver eyes said it all.

He swallowed and pleaded, "Please help her."

"I can't. I'm sorry." The Fae knelt next to Aisley and rested her hand atop hers before she also touched Phelan. "She saved you. She saved all of you."

"And there's nothing you can do?"

She shook her head of long blue-black hair. "Aisley knew by doing the spell it would take the last of her life."

"So she's in Hell now?" Phelan asked, hating to even think about it.

The Fae rose in one graceful motion. "There is much left for you to do, prince. I'm going to ensure Wallace can't bother any of you for a few days so you can bury Aisley. It's all I can do. I'm sorry."

Phelan didn't watch her disappear. His gaze was on Aisley. Bury her? He wouldn't bury her. The thought of her locked underground as she had been at Wallace's turned his stomach. Her spirit needed to soar.

He gathered her limp body in his arms and stood. Then he turned and started toward Ferness.

"How is he?" Hayden asked Charon.

Charon shook his head as he stared at his whisky. Phelan had been locked in the storeroom with Aisley's body for hours, refusing to come out or allow anyone in.

"Is the pyre ready?"

Hayden poured himself a glass of whisky and sank onto the couch. "Aye. Just."

"I should go tell him."

"No need. Isla is taking care of that."

Charon frowned at Hayden. "Was that a good idea?"

"My wife is stubborn. She also yearns for Phelan's forgiveness." He scratched his chin. "Isla was never fully *drough.* Aisley was. How does a *drough* fight against everything they are?"

"I wish I knew. Maybe it would help Phelan heal from this."

"Will he ever heal from this?"

Charon drained his glass. "Doubtful."

Phelan sat staring at Aisley's body. He cleaned the blood and dirt from her, changed her into a long black gauzy dress he'd gotten from Laura, and combed her midnight locks.

Never again would he look into her fawn-colored eyes or run his fingers through the silky strands of her hair. Never again would he feel her satiny skin or hear her scream in pleasure. Never again would the sound of her laughter brighten his day, nor would he trip over her discarded shoes.

Never again would he feel her magic or know the taste of her kiss.

"I should've listened to your explanation," he told her. "You tried to tell me, but I couldna get past the idea that you were *drough*. You were running from Wallace. I knew you feared whoever it was, and I wish I'd have known then. I would've never let him get to you."

He blinked and felt something drop onto his cheek. Phelan swiped at it and found a tear. The last time he'd cried was after he'd been chained in Deirdre's prison as a young lad.

Phelan squeezed his eyes closed as he recalled the wounds and injuries he'd found on Aisley's body as he washed her. How she had been able to even stand, much less stay alive, he would never know.

"I was too afraid to admit how much I cared for you. What a fool I've been. I never got to tell you that I lo . . . I love you, Aisley. And now you're gone."

He waited for her to sit up and tell him what an idiot he

was. Phelan was prepared to grovel at her feet, anything, if only she'd come back to him.

There was a soft knock on the door. A touch of magic could be felt. He knew of only one Druid who would dare approach him at that moment.

"Come in, Isla."

The door creaked open and she stepped inside before closing it softly behind her. "Is there anything I can do?"

"Nay."

"I'm sorry, Phelan. I truly am."

Emotion he'd been holding back choked him. He nodded, but didn't try and speak.

Isla stood beside him and rested her hand on his shoulder. "Aisley looks beautiful."

Phelan rose and walked to Aisley. "The pyre is ready, is it no'?"

"Yes. It doesn't have to be done now. We can wait."

"She deserves to be set free."

Phelan was surprised when Isla laid a small handful of wildflowers beneath Aisley's hands, which were clasped over her stomach. He lifted his eyes to Isla and found her crying silent tears.

"I forgive you for your part in what happened to me," he said. At her surprised expression he jerked his chin to Aisley. "She told me to let go of the past. She was right. I should've done it long ago."

Phelan carefully lifted Aisley one last time. He was tempted to do as Isla suggested and wait, but he knew it was wrong. He would be staring at a body, not the soul that had once been housed within it.

Phelan followed Isla through the forest to a spot near a small stream. On either side of the path were Warriors and Druids from the castle. And to his surprise, he spotted Rhys, Constantine, Banan and Jane, and Guy and Elena.

The pyre was built up over the ground so that Phelan

had to take two steps so he could place Aisley's body on top. He smoothed out her gown and hair and placed one last kiss on her lips.

"Be free," he whispered.

When Phelan turned around, Charon was waiting at the bottom of the steps with a torch. Phelan took it as he walked down. Before he changed his mind, Phelan thrust the torch into the bottom of the pyre and walked back to the group.

The hardest thing he ever did was watch the fire grow, the flames getting closer and closer to his beloved Aisley.

CHAPTER
FIFTY-THREE

Aisley felt the warm sun on her face, the light flickering even behind her closed eyelids. She opened her eyes expecting to find herself in Hell with Satan waiting with a smile to begin her torture.

Instead, she was in a forest.

She looked down to a dress of gauzy black and bare feet, but the pine needles weren't hurting her. Aisley was growing more confused by the second.

Off to her right, a stag came bounding through the trees before he slowed to a trot and then stopped. He lifted his head and sniffed the air. The animal proceeded hesitantly before he halted again and lowered his head. When he lifted it, water dripped from his muzzle.

Aisley started toward the stag, amazed when the animal looked at her but didn't run away. He seemed not to mind her presence.

The loch came into view with the sunlight glinting off the water that was smooth as glass. She smiled and stopped beside the stag.

"It's so beautiful."

The animal went back to drinking. Aisley grew bold

and skimmed her hand along the stag's back. His dark red fur was soft and bristly. With one jerk of his head he could gorge her with his antlers. Yet, she wasn't scared.

Not about the animal, the fact she was somewhere she didn't know, or that she was shoeless. Why was she shoeless? And why had she expected to be in Hell?

Then she remembered.

"I died."

Her contentment burst as she thought of Phelan. All her memories of the battle returned. She recalled how gently he'd held her, how wonderful it had been to see his amazing blue-gray eyes looking at her.

It was a memory she would never let go of. Whether she was in Hell or Purgatory, she would hold onto that last memory of Phelan with all she had.

Aisley lifted her gaze and looked across the loch. Her body jerked as she caught sight of the cabin. Phelan's cabin.

"It can't be."

The stag blew out a breath before he turned and walked away. Aisley didn't follow. She stayed rooted to the spot looking at the cabin and the splash of color from the flowers Phelan had planted.

After awhile she sat, her knees huddled against her chest with her arms wrapped around her legs. She couldn't figure out why she was there.

It had been the last place she had been happy. Maybe that's why. Or it could be some trick of the Devil's. She wanted to swim across the loch, but what awaited her in the dark depths of the water?

For two days she sat there staring, the sun rising and setting without anything bothering her. She didn't get thirsty or need any kind of nourishment.

When the sky burned a brilliant red and orange from the setting sun on the second day, Aisley stood and walked into the water. Whatever happened to her, she had to try and make it to the cabin.

She dove beneath the water and swam as fast as she could across the expanse. Not once did her muscles tire. All the while she waited for something to grab her feet and yank her down. But nothing did.

Her feet touched ground on the opposite side of the loch and she walked out of the water. Aisley reached back to wring out her hair only to find it dry. Her clothes were dry as well.

"Well, I am dead," she said to herself.

Her gaze came to rest on the cabin, and she forgot all about her dry clothes and hair. Flashes of her time while at the cottage assaulted her.

The first time Phelan had brought her to his home, the first time she saw him gardening, the first time they'd made love. The first time she realized she loved him.

She didn't try and stop the tears. She cried for what had been, and what she had lost. She cried for her mistakes, and the one thing she'd done right, which was Phelan.

But most of all she cried because she would never know his touch again.

"Is this my torture?" she screamed.

If it was, Satan couldn't have gotten anything that would hurt her more.

Aisley angrily wiped away her tears and stalked to the cabin. She took the stairs and threw open the door. But she couldn't make herself go inside.

It was hard enough standing in front of the cabin. By going inside, she would relive those few glorious days she and Phelan had had as if they'd been the only two people on the face of the earth.

Darkness grew with the last light of the sun falling

behind the mountains. Aisley sniffed and lifted one foot. After a deep breath, she stepped over the threshold.

She closed the door behind her and made her way to Phelan's bedroom. Everything was as neat and tidy as the first time she saw the cabin. She smiled wryly at the times she'd seen him pick up her stuff to pile it together.

Neatness had never been something Aisley managed to obtain. Usually people got angry with her. But not Phelan. He never said a word no matter how many times he tripped over her shoes.

She walked into his bedroom and crawled onto the bed. Aisley lay on her side looking out the large window that faced the loch.

Her time might have been short at the cabin, but the memories had been the best. The mornings waking up to see the magnificent view of the loch and mountains with Phelan's arms around her.

The evenings when they had made love and fell asleep listening to the sounds of the forest.

Aisley closed her eyes and knew nothing could make her leave the cabin now.

The flames were licking at Aisley's feet. Phelan wasn't sure he could stay and see her body burn. But he couldn't leave her either.

He couldn't shake the feeling that she was going to need him. Which was absurd because she was dead. Lifeless.

Gone.

Phelan wanted to bellow his anger at the unfairness of it all. Scream at himself for not giving her a chance. How was he going to get through eternity after losing her?

More than that, how could he live with himself for what he'd done to her? He'd turned his back on her and given Wallace the chance to hurt her. After Phelan had sworn to keep her safe.

"This isna your fault," Charon said.

Phelan fisted his hands that hung limply at his sides. "Ah, but it is. I gave her my word, and then broke it."

"She didna tell you who she was."

"I knew her, Charon. I had spent days with her. I should've at least given her the courtesy of listening to what she had to say. It was my blind hatred of *droughs* and being betrayed that prevented it."

Charon sighed and shook his head. "It's always easy to look back at something and think what you could've done or said differently. But that isna how life works. We are faced with something, and we react."

"As much as I hate *droughs*, why is it I'd do anything to have her back?"

"Because you love her."

Phelan clenched his jaw as emotion swelled through him. "Aye. I love her. And I've lost her."

"Take your vengeance on Wallace," Charon said. "Make him pay."

"I intend to," Phelan promised, fury dripping from his words.

His chest ached and it grew difficult to breathe as the flames reached Aisley. He could barely see her now. Soon the only thing that would be left were her ashes.

Aisley woke to the sounds of whispering, of a multitude of voices, but she couldn't make out what they were saying since they were talking over each other.

They began to fade, and she quickly rose from the bed and rushed out the back of the cabin to follow them. They led her into the woods.

Then they began to move faster until Aisley was running to try to keep up with them. She effortlessly jumped over fallen trees and gullies.

With the sunlight filtering through the trees, the birds singing, and the trees swaying in the wind, it felt as if Aisley was in a magical forest.

With her long gown gathered in her hands to help her move easily, Aisley found herself smiling the deeper into the forest she went.

She began to hum as she ran after the voices. It took her awhile to notice her humming matched that of a distant sound of drums. She stopped in her tracks, her heart pounding, because she knew those drums. They were from the ancients who had spoken to her the last time she was in the forest.

The same ancients that had helped her find the spell to contain the selmyr.

"Aisley!"

She jumped at the sound of her name from the voices. Suddenly, they surrounded her. They began to all talk at once again, growing louder and louder until she had to cover her ears.

A hand softly touched her shoulder. Aisley jerked her head around to find a woman of incandescent beauty standing before her. She had thick black hair and fawn-colored eyes. Aisley would've sworn she was looking in a mirror if it wasn't for the fact the woman's skin was several shades lighter than her own.

"Hello, Aisley," the woman said.

Aisley's hands dropped from her ears. "Who are you?"

"A very distant relative. I'm the one who trapped the selmyr the first time. You were amazingly brave to face them."

"You." Aisley paused and swallowed as she tried to

wrap her head around what she was seeing and hearing. "How do you know what I did?"

The woman smiled. "We've been watching you. We always watch the Druids, *mie* and *drough* alike."

"Where am I?"

The woman frowned. "I thought you knew. This is the place you brought us."

"I brought you?" Aisley asked incredulously. "I thought I was brought here."

"Nay, sweetling. But wherever this place is must mean a great deal for you to be here now."

Aisley looked around and thought of Phelan. "It means everything."

"You made a noble sacrifice in taking the magic meant to kill Phelan."

"I'd do anything for him. I just wish I'd have met him earlier in my life. Maybe then I wouldn't have made the wrong choices."

"It's those choices that led you to him. Just as his choices led him to you. To change the past would change the outcome of the future. Is that what you really want?"

Aisley shook her head. "Never. I don't want to forget a single moment of my time with him."

"And what of Jason?"

"He needs to die," she said calmly. "He has an agenda that doesn't help Druids, but hurts them. He may not be killing Druids for their magic as Deirdre did, but he's using them just the same."

The woman nodded sadly. "Aye, child, he is. Without Druids, the magic of the land could fade."

"Could?"

"There are still magical beings out there. You've already seen one and learned of another."

"Dragons and Fae."

"Aye. They help to keep the magic alive. But Druids play an important factor in all of it."

"Are those the only magical beings?" The woman merely smiled, which was all the answer Aisley would get. So she tried another question. "Why are you here?"

"You're my descendant. It's my right to be able to talk to you."

"How long can I remain here before I must go to Hell?"

The woman's face crumpled into a mask of pity. "Oh, sweetling, I thought you realized. Satan lost his hold over you."

"What?" Aisley asked and took a step back, her words too crucial not to need to hear them again.

"You might have undergone the *drough* ceremony, but the moment you forfeited your own life to save another, the Devil lost his claim to your soul."

Aisley took in a deep breath and looked around. "So I'm in—"

"Heaven," the woman finished. "You can stay here if you wish."

That made Aisley frown. "What do you mean I can stay here?"

The woman smiled, making her face glow. "As my descendant, you also inherited a very special gift I had, Aisley. Have you ever heard of the phoenix?"

Aisley numbly nodded her head.

"You can rise from your ashes, sweetling. It's your choice. Remain here, away from Wallace, or return to Phelan's side and continue fighting."

"What if Phelan doesn't want me?"

"Will that stop you from fighting against Wallace?"

"No."

She gave a nod of approval. "I didn't think so. So what will it be?"

Aisley looked around the forest before her gaze returned to her ancestor. "Will I be able to talk to you again?"

"I've spoken to you many times. I'm part of the ancients, and I'll always watch over you."

"Then I want to go back."

"Good choice, sweetling."

She closed the space between them and hugged her. Aisley didn't have any family left. The one before her, an ancient, was all she had, but she wasn't going to let the opportunity pass her by without feeling a part of something.

"Thank you," Aisley whispered.

The woman returned her hug and squeezed her. "Follow your heart. It won't lead you wrong. Oh, and one more thing, time moves differently here. It's only been eight hours since you died."

"Yet two full days have passed here."

"I know," she said. "Now, close your eyes and think of regenerating."

Aisley did as she asked, and within seconds she could taste the fire in her mouth, feel the ash swirling around her. Pure, unadulterated, beautiful magic flowed through her.

The magic swirled around her mixed with fire and ash. She'd never felt so powerful or so strong. And it was just the beginning.

CHAPTER
FIFTY-FOUR

Phelan's breath grew shallow as he watched the flames engulf Aisley. His soul cried out from the loss of the only woman who was his match in every way.

How was he going to go through the rest of his days with eternity stretching endlessly before him without her by his side?

"What the hell?" someone behind him said.

Phelan pulled out of his musings to find the flames wrapped around Aisley's body like a cocoon. No longer could he see any trace of her body. The flames were too bright to see through them.

"I feel magic," Arran said.

Phelan took a step back as magic slammed into him. It was magic he knew, magic he thought he'd never feel again. "Aisley," he whispered as he stared at the pyre.

He tried to go to it, but Charon and Rhys held him back.

"She needs me!" he yelled at them.

It was Rhys who got in front of him and shoved his hands into Phelan's chest. "Wait. Just . . . wait."

"Why?"

Constantine moved to stand beside him, his surprised gaze on the pyre. "It can no' be."

"What?" Phelan bellowed.

Con turned his head to look at him. "Watch."

Phelan wanted to demand to know what Con was keeping from him, but he found himself turning back at the fire. It had begun to move around Aisley, twisting and turning in a beautiful display of light and heat.

There was a burst of sparks that floated up into the sky before the flames died back. And there, standing atop the pyre was Aisley in all her naked glory as if she were born of fire.

Her midnight hair billowed around her from the wind while the ends danced with flames. Fire licked at her bare skin harmlessly, as if it gave her life.

Her fawn-colored gaze was fastened on him. He walked slowly toward her, hardly able to believe his eyes.

"A phoenix rising from the ashes," Rhys said behind him.

Phelan watched as Aisley twirled her hands through the flames as if moving through water. "Aisley."

She showed him her wrists. It took him a minute to comprehend that the scars from the *drough* ceremony were gone. The scars from her C-section and the cut on her left side from Jason were still visible.

"Aisley," Phelan repeated.

The image of someone appeared in the flames beside Aisley. The woman glanced at Phelan before she leaned over and whispered something in Aisley's ear and then disappeared.

Aisley stepped off the pyre and down the steps, the ends of her hair still blazing, but as she left the fire behind, the flames at the ends of her hair died away.

He reached out a hand and touched her cheek to find it warm. "How?"

"Apparently one of my ancestors had this gift. I inherited it. I'm no longer *drough*, Phelan."

"It wouldna matter if you were. As long as you've returned to me," he said and pulled her into his arms.

There was a loud cheer behind him, but he didn't hear them. The center of his everything was back in his arms.

Something was thrust into his hand, and he realized it was a blanket. Phelan quickly wrapped it around Aisley, who smiled at him.

They were surrounded by people, but he only cared to talk to one. "So you died?"

Aisley nodded. "I went to Heaven. It seems that when I took the magic Jason meant for you and sacrificed myself to save everyone that the Devil lost his hold on my soul."

"I'm so glad to hear it," Laura said with a bright smile.

Rhys clamped him on the shoulder. "You've got a phoenix, Phelan. You doona know how lucky you are."

"Aye, I do," he whispered and claimed Aisley's mouth for a kiss.

He tried to deepen it, but she ended it before he could. She pulled back and smoothed her hands over his chest. "I had a choice. I could've stayed in Heaven, or return . . . to you."

"I love you," Phelan said. "I was too afraid to realize what it was until it was too late."

"And I love you, my handsome Warrior."

It was too bad they weren't alone. Phelan wanted inside her right then. But they weren't alone. They were surrounded by Dragon Kings and his extended family.

"Who was the woman?" Con asked.

Aisley glanced at him before she looked at Phelan. "My ancestor and an ancient. She was the first to contain the selmyr. She also passed on her rare ability to me."

"What did she whisper?" Phelan asked.

Aisley's smile grew. "She said a phoenix doesn't get

reborn just once. I can use it as many times as I need to in order to remain with you through the centuries."

Phelan jerked her against him and buried his head in her neck. "I doona deserve you."

"You do," she whispered. "We've both suffered. I don't want to live in this world without you."

"You doona have to. I want you with me always."

"I like the sound of that."

Phelan lifted his head and smoothed back her hair. "I was such a fool."

She placed a finger over his lips. "Shh. The past is the past. We've got a chance to start anew."

"Will you spend it with me, Aisley Wallace? As my wife?"

"As if you even have to ask."

This time when the others cheered, Phelan lifted his woman high and shouted with them.

He didn't know what he'd done to be blessed so, but he wasn't going to question it. As everyone began to return to Ferness, Phelan took Aisley's hand and started to follow when he caught sight of the Fae standing off to the side.

She gave him a wink and a thumbs-up. "Good going, stud."

Aisley looked from the Fae to Phelan. "Is that . . . ?"

"Aye," he answered as the Fae disappeared. "I've got so much to tell you."

"Talking can wait," Aisley said as she let the blanket fall and turned to him.

Phelan smiled at his soon-to-be wife. He quickly discarded his clothes and pulled Aisley against him, kissing her with all the love, passion, and need coursing through him.

Their future was just beginning, and it shone brightly before them.

EPILOGUE

Three days later . . .

Rhi stood off to the side tapping a finger on the bar. She glanced at her silver-and-black-painted nails as Phelan and Aisley celebrated with their guests after their wedding. Music blared, drinks flowed, and laughter filled the building.

"What are you doing here?"

Rhi curled her lip in annoyance as Constantine walked up. "Go away."

"I've every right to be here. Now answer me."

She rolled her eyes and cocked her head to the side as she raised her brows. "Sod off, Dragon."

"I didna believe it at first when I heard a Fae had approached Phelan. What do you think your queen would think if she learned what you've done?"

Rhi lost her attitude and faced the king of Dragon Kings. "What do you want, Con?"

"I want to know what you want with Phelan."

"He's a prince."

Con grunted. "I know this. Tell me something I doona already know."

Rhi looked down at the little box sitting on the bar. "That is for Phelan to tell you if he chooses."

"What's for me to tell him?" Phelan asked as he walked up with Aisley, their hands linked and bright smiles on their faces.

"Hey, stud. So you got hitched, huh?" Rhi asked with a wink at Aisley.

Aisley surprised her with a hug. For a moment Rhi didn't move, then she awkwardly patted her on the back.

Rhi cleared her throat as she stepped away and pushed the two-inch box toward Phelan. "This is for you. From my queen."

Phelan glanced at the box with a frown before he reached for it. "Your queen?"

Rhi didn't respond as he pulled at the ends of the gold ribbon and then lifted the hinged lid. She didn't need to look in the box to know it held a gold ring with a coat of arms etched on top.

Phelan ran his thumb over the stripes and line of crowns going from the top left corner to the bottom right. "I've seen this before."

"On your father's hand," Rhi said. "He gave it to my queen before he died. It was to be given to you."

Phelan shook his head. "I doona understand."

Rhi glared at Con who was still there. She shifted so that her back was to him and she stood between him and Phelan. "You are a prince, Phelan, but not just of Saxony."

"He's your prince as well," Aisley said with awe.

Rhi winked at Phelan. "Didn't see that one coming, did you, stud?"

"If I'm your prince, why did you leave me in Deirdre's prison?"

She looked away and fidgeted. "Once, a very, very

long time ago, one of your ancestors had a rollicking good time with a Fae. She became pregnant, but never told her Fae lover. We aren't supposed to mate with humans. For any reason."

"Why?" Aisley asked.

Rhi shrugged. "It doesn't matter. Your ancestor bore a boy child who later ascended the throne in Saxony. Every hundred years or so someone of that line would be able to heal anything with their blood."

"All because a Fae bedded one of my ancestors?" Phelan asked, his brows knitted.

"Yep. Mortals are attracted to the Fae. Why do you think women always flocked to you?"

Phelan grinned and pulled Aisley close. "My charm."

"You've got that in spades, stud. The simple truth is, we didn't know of you, not until you were taken by Deirdre. It was years later when your father lay dying that he called to the Fae. He told his story, and we confirmed the truth of it."

"So my brother's line who survived, do any of them have my blood?"

Rhi shook her head. "It ended with you. The brother you speak of was taken into your family's home ten years after you'd disappeared."

"How does that explain how he's your prince?" Con asked from behind her.

Rhi gritted her teeth. How she hated the Dragons. They thought they were the end all be all. "He's our prince because the male Fae happened to be the queen's brother."

"And the surprises keep coming," Aisley said and grabbed one of the shot glasses full of vodka from the bar. She drank down the shot and looked up at Phelan. "Are you all right?"

He shook his head. "Why didn't you get me out of Deirdre's mountain?"

"We couldn't. Just as the Dragon Kings didn't interfere, neither did we," Rhi explained.

"So what now?"

Rhi pushed away from the bar. "I expect you'll be getting a visit from the queen soon. She's anxious to meet you. She was going to introduce herself while you two were at the Fairy Pool, but you were otherwise occupied."

Phelan watched her give a little wave with her fingers before she sauntered out of the bar. He glanced down at the ring.

"A prince of Saxony and the Fae. What have I gotten myself into?" Aisley asked.

He kissed her hard and fast. "I've got women around the block waiting in line for me. You doona want me, one of them will."

"Oh, no. I don't think so. I came back from the dead for you. You're all mine, prince or not."

Phelan forgot they weren't alone when Con laughed. He looked up at the Dragon King. "I got the feeling that we Fae didna like you."

"We've a history," Con said with a shrug. "The Fae wanted this realm. We were no' going to give it up. So, they carry a grudge."

"But they're here," Aisley said.

"They can visit," Con explained. "Some can remain for months or years, but always they must return to their realm."

Phelan pulled the ring from the box and slid it on his right ring finger. It fit perfectly. He let out a long breath at having his father's ring on his hand.

Aisley leaned her head against his shoulder with a smile. "We've more presents to open."

Phelan looked up to find Con gone. He set aside the box and pulled Aisley along with him to the table weighted down with gifts from everyone.

Neither he nor Aisley were prepared for so much, but it's what family did. At least that's what he was learning. Tomorrow was a new day with an old enemy. But for one more night, Wallace would be pushed to the back of his mind.

Phelan had Aisley, his friends, and family. Life was good.

Jason sat in his office and seethed. He'd had the Warriors and Druids in his reach. Then the selmyr had arrived. They were the only thing he truly feared because his magic only strengthened them.

How could he fight something without his magic? It didn't seem fair.

But if he'd gotten those from MacLeod Castle once, he could do it again. At least Aisley was dead. His vengeance was complete.

"Oh, she's not dead," came a deep voice from his left.

Jason turned his head to find the Devil sitting in the chair that had been vacant a moment ago. "Come to kill me?"

The Devil smiled and smoothed his hand over his slicked-back black hair. He sat up and adjusted his tie. "No."

"Then why are you here?"

He rose, his tailored suit fitting his tall, muscular form elegantly as he walked to look out the windows. "You've never been known for your good looks have you, Jason? Matter of fact, everyone used to tease you because you had such a hawkish face. No amount of expensive suits can make yours fit you as mine do."

"You tried to use Aisley against me."

"Your problem is that you want what everyone else has and you don't even know it."

Jason stood and shoved his hands into the pockets of

his slacks. "I've all I need. Now what did you mean that she's no' dead?"

"Aisley," he said and looked over his shoulder at Jason.

"Impossible. I made sure no magic or anything could heal her."

"She's a phoenix."

"A what?"

The Devil sighed dramatically and faced him. "A phoenix, you shit. She's able to come back from the dead. She and Phelan were married just a few minutes ago."

"Is that all you came to tell me?

"I know that revenge burns in your gut," he said. "That hate brought me here. The question is, Jason, what are you going to do with it?"

Jason laughed. "I'm going to kill them all."

"Of course. But first, you must have the prophecy fulfilled, the one where a *drough* has the child of a Warrior. That child will house all the evil of the world."

"I had a difficult enough time finding the last Warriors. I doona have the time to let them gain control over their gods."

"There is, however, one Warrior of the MacLeods whose soul is dead. Malcolm could be yours with little effort. And I've just the Druid to help you."

Jason rubbed his hands together and smiled. He liked this plan very much.